REVENANT

GINA & ANNE MARIE DICARLO

Dear Joanne,
Thank you for supporting us!
We hope you love the
read.

Anne Marie &
Gina

Black Rose Writing | Texas

ISBN: 978-1-68433-866-5
PUBLISHED BY BLACK ROSE WRITING
www.blackrosewriting.com

Printed in the United States of America
Suggested Retail Price (SRP) $21.95

Revenant is printed in Calluna

*As a planet-friendly publisher, Black Rose Writing does its best to eliminate unnecessary waste to reduce paper usage and energy costs, while never compromising the reading experience. As a result, the final word count vs. page count may not meet common expectations.

For Oscar and Beebz

REVENANT

PROLOGUE

The late spring morning was warm and the bright sun welcoming as Andrei Korzha stepped at last from the woods and into the outskirts of Copaci. He had been hunting for the better part of four days, trekking high into the Carpathian Mountains that surrounded his small hometown village. It was his favorite pastime, and with most of his days filled up with blacksmithing, a trade handed down to him by his father, he didn't have as much time as he would have liked to explore the woods and hunt.

Andrei couldn't really pinpoint a source to the allure the woods held for him; he figured it was most likely a combination of things. The feeling of walking in shadowy places with only trees for company, the thrill of tracking the herds that lived in the mountains, the pulsing adrenaline rush he got when he finally made contact with his prey... All of it thrilled Andrei and made him wish for the days when he could slip away from his duties and go home to the mountains. To Andrei, the mountains were his Eden, his escape from life's troubles, the source of his true self. People and places might change, but his mountains never would.

People like my wife. The nagging thought entered his mind before he could stop it, interrupting his tranquility and making him frown. Before his mood could sour he pushed the thought away, focusing again on the peace his journey had brought him. It had been a fruitful hunt and it was going to be a beautiful day; he wouldn't spoil it by letting his mind wander down dark roads.

A bird flew by overhead, catching his eye. Its black wings were spread fully, embracing the sunlight that touched its feathers and warmed its body. Steady and confident, it rode the gentle breeze lazily, enjoying the simple pleasure of flying.

For some inexplicable reason, the soaring bird reminded Andrei of his first wife, Daciana. Perhaps it was the sense of freedom that emanated from the small creature- its lack of ties to the world below- that made him think of his nymph-like wife. Or perhaps it was the bird's beauty- subtle yet overpowering at the same time- that conjured up her image: long hair, slender limbs, bewitching smile. Perhaps it was neither. Still, he watched the bird until it was a mere speck in an otherwise spotless sky, squinting to keep it in his sight as long as possible.

He sighed. Deep down, he knew that his love for the woods in part stemmed from a wish to be close to Daciana, to remember her and the time they had spent together alone in the mountains. It was his way of coping with the grief that would never truly leave him.

Still, he had found solace in Elena- Elena and their daughters, Madalina and Ana.

Daughters that now seem wary of their own mother.

Once again Andrei pushed the thought away. Elena was suffering from a few mood swings, nothing more. He was sure that once she worked the bad blood out of her system, she'd be back to normal like nothing at all had happened. He loved her, and that was what mattered, wasn't it?

Wasn't it? Try as he might, he could not quite dispel the persistent doubt that hung over him like a suffocating shroud.

Andrei shifted the weight of his kill on his back, relieving one shoulder temporarily of the burdensome weight. Trying to banish any lingering worries, he began whistling a childhood tune, one that always cheered him. As he intoned the familiar melody, his thoughts turned to his daughters. He smiled. As wonderful as it was to be in the mountains, he loved nothing more than coming home to his family. The thought of them made him stride even more quickly homewards.

Copaci was small, inhabited by almost as many dogs as people, so it wasn't long before Andrei reached the road that led to his house. Walking up the weathered dirt path, he gazed at his two-story cottage, pride written in his eyes. He had taken care over the years to preserve it just as he had when Daciana was alive, and that care was still evident down to every eave and shutter.

He laid his kill down in the backyard, his muscles at last relaxing. He took a moment to admire the buck; it was a prize that he would be proud to share with the old butcher who lived down the road. Andrei was sure to get a good price for it. He let loose a hearty, audible sigh and went inside, the door swinging shut behind him.

"Elena? I'm home, love."

Silence answered him, thick and ominous. He frowned, a worry line creasing his brow. It was nearly noon and strange that his family wouldn't be at home. "Elena? Are you here? Madalina? Ana?" Once again there was no answer.

Moving through the house, he scoped the rooms but found no one. "Girls?" He paused at the landing as he went up the stairs, cursing softly. A strange feeling had come over him, one he couldn't explain yet one that made the hairs on the back of his neck stand on end.

It was the feeling that something was terribly wrong.

His mind returned to the thoughts of Elena that had preoccupied him earlier, the nagging doubts that had refused to abate despite his own self-assurances to the contrary. Unease turned to dread as he made his way down the silent hall towards the bedroom his daughters shared. His footfalls echoed like thunder in his ears and with each step, his panic grew. Shaking, he unconsciously held his breath as he turned the knob.

As the door opened and Andrei saw the room, he stumbled back, nearly falling. It was a scene straight out of the darkest nightmare imaginable, and the sight made him choke on the air in his lungs. He wheezed violently, the color draining from his face. "*No...*" The sound was more like a strangled sob than a word, uttered with more pain than even a dying animal could muster.

His girls, his *precious* girls, lay in their beds, pale and lifeless. *Bloodless.* Their blood was drenching the sheets and pooling on the floor; macabre flecks dotted their pillowcases like crimson sparkles. He stumbled blindly over to the bed and fell down beside it, crushing fistfuls of his daughters' bloody sheets in his hands.

Sheets soaked with the life of his children.

A scream, gut-wrenching and mangled beyond recognition, burst from his lips, adding fury and anguish to the room's death-filled haze.

"Madalina...Ana..." He sobbed, his daughters' names choked out in painful gasps. The girls' throats and wrists had been slit, the wounds jagged and amateur. Judging by their hacked appearance, the murder weapon had been too dull to make clean cuts.

Andrei hugged one, then both, of his dead daughters to his chest, sobbing and groaning. He pressed his hand against the jagged gashes that now marred the skin on the girls' tender necks, pleading with God to undo what had been done to his children. Andrei moaned, rocking back and forth on his knees. His shirt turned a splotchy and vibrant red as he wept, his tears making the red patches on it run as though the shirt itself were bleeding.

As he held them, memories raced across his vision. Memories of Madalina learning how to cook, laughing as she spilled sauce all over her apron. Memories of Ana wearing his clothes and pretending to be a hunter, all but engulfed by the huge garments as she snuck around the yard. Memories of both girls smiling with innocent joy as they showed him the flowers they'd picked for their mother's birthday...

Suddenly he jerked up, his eyes going wide.

Where was his wife? Was she dead too?

Laying his daughters down as gently and quickly as he could, he ran on wobbly legs into his own bedroom.

He forced himself to twist the doorknob and push the door open despite his agonizing fear, preparing himself for the worst.

The room was empty.

Andrei stood still, his mind blank. Where was his wife?

A noise woke him from his momentary stupor, the sound of a door creaking open. It took him only a moment to recognize the familiar squeak of the back door. Walking to his bedroom window, he peered out.

And saw his wife, Elena.

She was walking away from the house, her back to him. He felt relief for a moment before the reality of her appearance struck him. Her feet were bare, and her long skirt was blood-soaked at the hem, soiling the ground as she walked. As his eyes traveled up her figure, Andrei saw more blood. In her left hand was a small object, its surface lined with bloody streaks. *The mirror.* As if she could feel his stare, Elena turned her head around for a moment and caught his gaze.

Her eyes- her warm, brown eyes- were flat, and the expression on her face told Andrei everything he needed to know.

She had killed his daughters. Their daughters. And the expression on her face wasn't one of remorse; it was one of feral elation.

Andrei heard a strange sound, a bizarre keening that filled his ears. It took him a moment to realize that the pitiful sound was coming from his own throat. He forced himself to swallow. He breathed in and out, regaining some control over his body.

Then his grief and anguish turned to a blind rage and he had only one desire: to go after his wife.

He ran down the stairs and out the front door. In a matter of seconds, he'd grabbed a butcher knife from his shed and circled back around the house on the side where Elena had been standing moments earlier.

He breathed heavily and scanned the path. He was beginning to think he'd lost her when he spotted a blur of movement off to his right. His hunter's instincts taking over instantly, he ran after her, knife in his hand, murder in his heart.

He would hunt her, catch her. And then...

Andrei didn't allow himself to think past that.

As his legs carried him closer and closer to his prey, a small part of Andrei was thinking about the Elena he had known, about the woman she'd been before her eyes had begun to glitter with an unknown darkness. And then she'd begun to change, ever since he'd brought her the gift from the woods and she had first held it in her hands...

"Andrei, it's so beautiful! Where did you find it?"

Elena looked up at him, eyes aglow with gratefulness. In her hands she held the small vanity mirror, her fingers moving over the intricate detail work on its frame.

Andrei smiled. "It must have been meant for you, sweetheart. I found it in the woods, literally half-buried in the ground. I wouldn't have seen it at all, but a bit of sun landed on it and it caught my eye. It's pretty, isn't it?"

"Very. And it seems old. I wonder who it belonged to."

Andrei leaned down and kissed his wife on the forehead. "Well, it's yours now."

If only he could blot out that fateful day from their lives! He'd been a fool to think that Elena's personality changes had meant nothing. His once patient and gentle wife had become terse and cold-hearted. Initially, her displeasure had been directed only at him; she had begun to find fault in all that he did and to avoid his attempts to show affection. Within a few short months, however, his warm and passionate wife had become cold, not only to him, but to their children as well.

And I pretended nothing was wrong. He had ignored all of it, even after his girls had tried to warn him...

"Madalina? Ana?" Both girls looked up at their father, tired looks on their young faces.

"Where's Mama? Hasn't she told you both to get to bed yet?" Andrei frowned.

Madalina spoke in a quiet voice, barely above a whisper. "No Papa. Mama's been in her room for hours and..." She broke off and cast a nervous glance at her little sister.

"And what?"

"She's...she's been talking to herself." Madalina walked over to her father and put her arms around him. "Papa, I'm scared."

Andrei felt blame suffocating him as he ran. How could he not have known? Elena had changed! His little girls had seen it but he had turned a blind eye, afraid to admit that his wife might be losing her mind. If only he had done something, his daughters might still be alive.

If only.

He was responsible for their deaths as much as Elena was.

Tears of reproach coursed down his weathered cheeks. Wiping them away, he increased his pace.

Elena had run faster when she'd noticed him following her and now she was off the road and running into the woods. Woods that led to a different patch of forest than where Andrei had been hunting. Woods that he'd avoided for years.

Andrei knew where she was going but couldn't explain her reasons for heading there. As he reached the tree line, he pushed aside his fears and ran ahead, concern for his own safety evaporating. He no longer had a reason to live. His existence had only one purpose left: to make Elena pay for what she had done. Determined not to lose her in the dense wood, he clawed the low branches and brambles away from the narrow pathway with his bare hands like a man possessed. By the time he reached the clearing that housed the castle, his hands, arms and face were covered with lacerations, his own blood mixing with that of his girls. His breath was ragged and shallow, his body tired, but his eyes held a preternatural strength as he looked for his wife.

And there she was.

Standing over by the castle's entrance, Elena didn't see Andrei as he approached, didn't hear him until he stepped on a twig not five inches from her.

She spun around and faced her husband, the movement disconcertingly quick. Propelled by adrenaline-laced fury, Andrei slapped her hard across the face, drawing blood. Stunned, she fell to the ground, the wind knocked from her lungs.

She gasped in pain and looked up at him, her face contorted into a mask of rage and hatred.

Andrei sucked in a breath. The person looking up at him didn't resemble his Elena at all. Her features were the same, but the person who wore them was not his wife. And the most striking contrast was the eyes. Elena's beautiful brown eyes were gone, and in their place, Andrei was certain he saw icy blues ones staring back at him.

Without a second thought, Andrei screamed and fell on his wife, the blade of the knife sinking deep into her chest.

The blue eyes bulged, and the mouth contorted in a silent scream. Moments later, the eyes that stared up at him were brown and lifeless.

Shaking, Andrei climbed off of his dead wife, his gaze fixed on her inert form.

Once more, she looked like Elena, his wonderful, devoted Elena, the woman who had rescued him from the brink of madness and anchored him solidly into the world of the living after everyone else had long since given up on him.

The horrible malice in her eyes was gone.

Had he imagined it? Had she really killed their children? Was it possible that Elena hadn't been responsible... for any of it?

He'd never even given her a chance to explain.

What have I done?

Howling in pain and desperation, Andrei got up and ran into the castle, a plan already forming in his head.

Dragos Ozera, the lone policeman in Copaci, was swatting at a fly in his office when he heard the woman calling for help. The fly forgotten, he quickly ran outside, drawn by the urgency in her voice.

He blanched at seeing Mihaela Bochinsky, the oldest daughter of Andrei Korzha, stumbling down the main road. What on earth was going on?

"Mihaela? Mihaela! It's Dragos. What's wrong?" He ran over to her.

Her roving, tear-filled eyes found his and she fell into his arms. "My..." She choked on her words, then tried again. "My...*sisters*." Her violent sobs drowned out everything else she tried to say.

Dragos held her close, a sick feeling filling his stomach. Mihaela wasn't the histrionic type. If she was sobbing over her half-sisters, there was a reason.

Something must be very, very wrong.

As he listened to her tell of her gruesome discovery at her father's home, Dragos thought of his own young daughter and Mihaela's grief became his own.

He'd left Mihaela with her husband, telling him that he was going to find out what had happened.

The atrocities he'd found in the Korzha's home had made his head spin, as did the chain of events he'd pieced together at the crime scene.

Andrei had finally snapped.

Even after all the years of peace, he'd finally gone mad. He must have killed his little girls and run off, possibly after Elena, who was missing.

Acting quickly, Dragos had followed the trail of blood into the woods and from there, the trail that Andrei must have followed, judging by the mess of torn underbrush that marred the path. He reached the castle grounds within the hour.

His eyes still adjusting to the light of the clearing, he squinted at the remains of the abandoned estate, looking for some sign of life but finding none.

Elena lay dead at the mouth of the ruined castle, a knife buried in her chest up to its hilt. Knowing that there was nothing he could do for her, Dragos left her where she lay and circled around the castle looking for Andrei, his gun drawn.

He had almost made a full circle when he saw him, hanging from a parapet on a withered piece of rope. His eyes were open and staring, full of despair even in death.

It was a long time before Dragos found the energy to move away.

CHAPTER 1

"Can you see anything?" Renee Bryant scrunched her eyebrows, squinting out the window of the train.

Lou put a hand on the back of her sister's shirt, tugging gently. "Nope," she said. "Nothing. But if you lean out any further, you're going to fall."

Renee clambered back in, dropping down to the floor with a thud. She sighed, running a hand through her cropped brown hair. "I wasn't going to fall, not with you holding onto me." She shook her head in exasperation. "But maybe I *should* climb out the window. I think by this point it would be quicker to walk the tracks to Cluj rather than waiting for this damn train to sort out its business. I mean, what kind of maintenance are they doing?"

Lou could sense her sister's frustration, and she shared it. The eight-hour train ride from Budapest to Cluj-Napoca, Romania was long enough without an unscheduled delay. And they were supposed to start their assignment tomorrow; if they didn't get a good night's sleep... Lou squirmed at the thought of having to work on a shoot with a tired Renee.

"C'mon," she told her sister. "Let's go get some drinks from the dining cart." She held out her arm.

Renee gave her a small smile, looping her arm through Lou's. "Are you afraid I'm going to get cranky?" She laughed at Lou's expression. "Good cause for concern, I guess. All right, let's go get some coffee or something."

They began winding their way to the dining cart, weaving through people and luggage, listening to the other disgruntled passengers lamenting the hold-up. One passenger in particular, a pregnant woman who looked about ready to burst, was clearly irate at the situation, one hand around her tumescent belly, the other gesturing rudely at her husband, as if blaming him for her discomfort. Lou gave them a pitying smile as she passed, glad that they were not in the same car as she and Renee.

The coffee was weak, but it served its purpose. Renee bounced back a little, her frame relaxing slightly. "Good suggestion, Sis. A little caffeine makes everything better." She sat down in one of the dining tables, looking out the window at the stagnant scenery.

Grassy fields, mountains in the distance...not too bad, Lou thought. She took the seat across from Renee. "Well, if we were going to be stuck anywhere, this is a pretty nice spot. That view is gorgeous."

Renee nodded in agreement. "True." She set her cheap cup of coffee down in front of her. "Despite this, I'm really glad we came over early and went to Budapest. Seeing where we came from was incredible."

Lou smiled. "I know! It felt like coming home a little bit, you know? Like...the city, the food, the people...it was familiar, in a way. Besides," she added, "it's about time we took a little side trip while on assignment. What's the use of traveling everywhere if we're always on a ridiculously tight schedule? We should carve out a few more days for ourselves while we're out and about for *Itinera.*"

Renee gulped down the rest of her coffee. "Definitely. I can't wait to tell Ian about our weekend." She stood up abruptly, glancing down at her watch. "Shoot! I told Ian I'd meet him for dinner at eight. We're barely going to get into the city by then at this rate." She dropped her disposable cup in the trash. "I'm going to go try and email him. Hopefully the wifi is working..."

Lou watched her walk away. She raised her own coffee to her lips, thought better of it, and dumped the rest of it in the trash. She began slowly walking back towards their cabin, enjoying the sight of the world outside of the windows. Maybe she should go grab her camera, take advantage of the delay…

"Oh…" She tripped, catching herself from falling on the nearest seat. Glancing back, she saw the elderly woman, her feet stretched out in the aisle. Lou felt herself reddening. "I'm so sorry," she stammered. "I should have been looking where I was going."

The grey-haired woman waved a dismissive hand, moving her feet back under her seat. "And I shouldn't have been cluttering the aisle. It's just that my legs get so stiff…" She grimaced, massaging her thighs. She looked up at Lou. "A word of advice, my dear: never get old." She winked, the crow's feet around her eyes deepening.

Lou gave her a smile. "I'll do my best."

"I'm Bella, by the way."

"Lou."

Bella gestured at the seat across from her. "Well, Lou, why don't you sit and keep an old woman company for a while? You can distract me from my aches and pains."

Lou sat down, happy to oblige. Some good conversation would be a great way to pass the time. "Are you from Romania?" She asked.

"Hungary. A little place called Apátistvánfalva. I'm visiting my son in Cluj."

"My sister and I were just visiting Budapest. Our grandparents were from the city. It's a lovely place."

Bella's eyes brightened. "Ah, you're Magyar? How wonderful."

"Yes. Well, half, anyway. My mom was Hungarian. My dad's American." She tucked a strand of hair behind her ear. "My sister and I work for this travel magazine in Philadelphia called *Itinera*. We're starting an assignment in Romania tomorrow, but we wanted to take a weekend for ourselves first and see where our family is from."

Bella nodded sagely. "Knowing where you come from is very important." She quirked an eyebrow. "You said you work for a travel magazine? What are you doing in Romania?"

"We're photographing eight castles around the country, starting with Banffy outside of Cluj. Three of us are photographers, and we're working with a journalist who will write a piece to go along with our spread."

Bella leaned back in her seat, her legs seemingly forgotten. "That sounds like a big endeavor."

Lou nodded. "It will be a lot of work, but it'll be fun." She leaned forward, resting her elbows on the small table between them. "You know," she added, playfully dropping her voice to a conspiratorial whisper, "one of the castles we're photographing is Bran Castle—home to the notorious Count Dracula."

Bella laughed, a hearty chuckle. "I take it you like the darker tales, then?"

Lou gave her a mischievous smile. "The darker the better. I love a good spooky story, and I've always found the supernatural ones intriguing."

"Indeed." Bella gave her a sideways glance. She opened her mouth and closed it again, stopping herself before she said anything more.

Lou shrugged apologetically. "Sorry, I didn't mean to sound morbid. I'm just fascinated by things I don't quite understand, like the supernatural."

"So you believe there is truth in superstitions?" Bella asked.

"I'm certainly open to the possibilities," Lou replied, feeling suddenly uncomfortable. She wished she hadn't said anything. Bella probably thought she was ridiculous—some naïve American who believed in eastern European mysticism. She looked back out the window. "I wish I had my paints," she said after a moment, both to change the course of the conversation and because it was true.

"I used to paint," Bella said, a bittersweet note lacing her voice.

"Really?" Lou looked back at her. "I went to college for classical art. Photography I like, but painting I love."

Bella smiled fondly. "I understand your passion. There is such joy in creating art with your own hands." She sighed. "If not for my arthritis, I would still be painting."

Lou felt a wave of compassion for the Hungarian woman. "I'm sorry. I don't know what I'd do if I couldn't paint anymore."

Bella shook her head. "Such is life. But I am a woman of many interests, and I've found other things to occupy my time in recent years." She paused, and when she spoke again, her voice had dropped in decibel. "You said earlier that you are open-minded, and so am I. I've dabbled in the art of divination and found my niche with Tarot cards." She pierced Lou a penetrating stare. "Would you like me to read for you?"

"You have your cards with you?"

Bella didn't break eye contact with her. "I always have them with me." Her voice became even softer. "So, would you like a reading?" She asked again.

Lou felt a trickle of unease shoot down her spine. Renee would have laughed at her reaction, but then again, Renee didn't believe in anything outside of the realm of the ordinary. *But I do*, Lou thought. She could see the excitement in Bella's eyes, and she felt her own fear diminishing, curiosity taking its place.

What harm can a simple reading do? It'll probably be fun.

"Okay," she said at last. "You can read for me."

"Excellent!" Bella rummaged around in her carry-on until she found what she was looking for. "Ah," she said, withdrawing her hands. "Here we are."

She laid a weathered stack of cards on the table, reverently putting them down. Their backs were black with a small silver star in the center. Bella leaned over the deck, then drew three cards from the top and placed them side by side. "This is a simple three-card spread. One represents past, one present, one future."

Lou looked down at the three cards, wary once again. The blackness of their color was dark and rich, and she felt that beneath their surfaces were hidden secrets and mysteries.

Bella pointed to the one on Lou's left. "This is the card for your past." She turned it over slowly, and Lou held her breath, waiting.

The card revealed a man standing with his head bent in a somber fashion. There were two gold cups behind him on the ground, and three at his feet. The three in front of him were on their sides, spilling their blue contents onto the earth. Dark grey clouds hung low in the sky, adding an aura of sadness to the whole picture.

"The Five of Cups." Bella looked up at her. "It signifies loss," she said. Her eyes softened. "Did you lose something or someone when you were growing up?"

Lou felt an old sadness settle in her bones. "I lost my mom when I was twelve," she said quietly. "She died of cancer two weeks after she was diagnosed." She blinked back sudden tears. "Stage four brain cancer. There wasn't much that could be done."

Bella gasped. "Oh, you poor child. I am so sorry. I can't imagine how terrible that must have been for you."

Lou looked down at her fingers. "It was hard for me, but at least I had my older sister Renee for support. Renee had no one."

"Not even your father?"

Lou uttered a humorless chuckle. "Our dad was too busy drowning his own sorrows to take care of two teenage girls." Lou met Bella's gaze. "But we pulled through together."

Bella exhaled, watching Lou curiously. "It's good that you had each other. But I'm sorry about your father; he should have been there for you."

Lou shrugged, letting the comment roll off her shoulders. She'd heard it a thousand times before. "Renee and I are all the family we need." She softened her tone. "Really. Please don't think I'm some kind of martyr. There were a lot of happy moments in my childhood."

And awful ones, too, an inner voice added, the thought coming on the heels of her spoken words like a reflex. *Don't forget about what you did, and about what you put your sister through...*

"I'm sure there were, dear." A minute of silence passed before Bella spoke again. "Maybe we should continue? I think it's time to leave the past behind."

Lou had almost forgotten about the Tarot cards. She glanced down at them again, staring at the two that still remained face down on the table. She nodded for Bella to reveal the next card.

With a flourish, she flipped the card over, and Lou leaned closer to the table, studying it. On its surface was a robed woman sitting in an impressive throne, a slender rod in one hand. Its tip blazed with orange fire, illuminating the darker space around it. Sunflowers decorated the throne, and a black cat was perched below her, its green eyes vivid. It was a beautiful card.

"The Queen of Wands." Bella sounded impressed.

"What does it mean?"

"The Queen of Wands symbolizes a very strong woman, one who has charisma and creativity. She is a doer, a nurturer, a traveler. It is a very positive card."

Lou smiled, shaking her head. "And clearly meant for Renee. Do the cards always refer to the person you're reading for?"

Bella shook her head, bemused. "No, but what makes you think this card has nothing to do with you?"

"My sister is all of those things, not me." She gave a self-deprecating laugh. "Is there a things-never-go-to-plan card? I feel like that would be more representative of me."

Bella gave a disapproving *tut.* "You sell yourself short, Lou. I can tell just from the few minutes I've known you that you are a very interesting individual." She pointed to the card. "I think this card does refer to you. Do you see the cat? He represents an interest in magic, in the supernatural. Does your sister believe as you do?"

"No," Lou admitted. She searched for an explanation that fit with her negative self-view. "Maybe the card refers to both of us."

"Perhaps." She gestured towards the one still facedown card. "And now for your future."

Lou looked down at the last card. *Future.* She felt her muscles tensing, felt her heartbeat increase. The other two cards had held a certain allure, yes, but there was something so much more tantalizing – and forbidden – about the final card. Looking into the past and into the present was like walking down a familiar path with a blindfold on. You might not be able to see, but you've been there before and know what to expect. But the future...that was like jumping into a dark pit of unknown depth. It was dangerous and uncertain, yet you couldn't resist the urge to give in, the urge to fall...

Bella turned over the last card.

Lou let out the breath she had been unconsciously holding as she peered down at her third card.

It was subdued in color. A snowy stretch of open land filled its space, with a few snow-covered trees. In the night sky shone a full moon, a visible face etched in one side. All in all, it seemed like a very peaceful card. The only strange thing was that it was upside down. Lou looked up at Bella, realizing that the older woman hadn't yet offered an explanation.

The expression on the other woman's face made Lou blanch, the blood draining from her own. "Is...is something wrong?" She stammered.

"I've never drawn this card before." Her voice was barely audible, and Lou had to strain to hear her. She swallowed hard, fear creeping once more over her. "Is it a bad card?"

"It is a Reversed Moon. A Moon is one of the major arcana, the most powerful type of cards. And this one is reversed."

Lou didn't understand. "Does the position hold some kind of importance?" She glanced back down at the card that had so affected her elderly companion.

"Usually, reversed cards hold an opposite kind of truth."

Lou cocked her head, assessing the card. "Well, the opposite of the moon is the sun. Isn't that a good sign?"

She hoped Bella would concur with her, but Bella shook her head. "The Sun has its own card. So in this case, the opposite of the Moon is not the Sun. It is the Dark of the Moon."

Lou felt goosebumps rise on her arms. "What does it mean?" She asked, her voice hushed.

"The Moon usually refers to wildness, magic, psychic abilities. Dreams and hallucinations and other things associated with night. In its face-up position, the light of the Moon can guide you, but in this position, there is no light. Only darkness. There is nothing to show you what is lurking there with you or who might be coming for you. The darkness hides the truth." Bella paused, then continued. "It is also possible that the reversed position indicates a power shift, that the things which once were dominated by light – dark forces, malevolent entities – now hold the power." Bella sat back slowly in her chair, eyeing Lou with wariness. "If I were you, dear, I would be very careful. This omen is bad."

Lou felt her mouth go dry. She looked down at her last card again, no longer comforted by its mild color palette. Now the ground seemed too stark, the trees' shadows sinister, the moon's face cruel. She wished the card were still face down.

This omen is bad...

"Lou! There you are. Jeez, I've been looking everywhere for you!"

Her sister's voice startled her so badly she almost fell out of her seat. She and Bella had been conversing so quietly that Renee's speaking tone was unnervingly jarring.

"Oh...hey." Lou cleared her throat. "This is Bella. She's from Hungary."

"Nice to meet you," Renee said, giving Bella a warm smile. Then she frowned as she took in her expression and the cards on the table. She gave Lou a disparaging look that spoke volumes. "Well, we'll be arriving in Cluj in less than fifteen minutes. I just wanted to find you before we got there."

Lou frowned in confusion, then looked out the window. The countryside was flying by, blurs of green rushing past. "I...I hadn't even realized the train was moving again."

Renee's frown deepened. "Lou, the train's been moving for almost an hour. There was a pretty loud announcement when we got up and running. You didn't hear it?" "No, I didn't." She stood up. "I guess I got distracted." She forced a smile, trying to hide her unease. "Bella's been great company."

"I'm the lucky one," Bella interjected. "I was happy to have someone to pass the time with."

Renee gestured back towards their train car. "I'm going to start collecting our things. Come help me after you've said goodbye, okay?" She gave Lou a pointed look and then waved to Bella as she turned away. "Have a nice trip to Cluj," she said by way of parting.

Lou's gaze flickered again to the Reversed Moon card. Forcing herself to look away, she took a calming breath. She finally looked at Bella and tried to lighten the mood. "I guess I should thank you; I was so engrossed that the time literally flew by." She reached out and gently clasped the woman's wrinkled hands. "Truly, though, I had a lovely time talking with you. I'm glad I met you."

"And I you," Bella said, the wariness never quite leaving her eyes.

Lou straightened and gave her a final smile. "I hope you have a wonderful time in Cluj with your son."

"And I hope your magazine assignment is a success. Take care."

Lou began to walk away when Bella called out to her. She glanced over her shoulder and instantly regretted it. Even from a few feet away, the look of fear in Bella's eyes was unmistakable.

"Please be careful," the old woman warned. "Do not let your guard down. Be safe."

"I will," Lou promised. She needed to leave before her fear got the better of her. Nearly shaking, she grasped the door handle of the car and slid the door open. When it closed, she leaned back against it, happy for the temporary isolation. Bella's words echoed in her head. *Be safe.* "I will," Lou whispered to herself.

As she moved forward into the next car, though, a small part of her wondered if it was a promise she would be able to keep.

CHAPTER 2

Have you decided what you would like?" The young waitress asked in heavily accented English, her impatience with the young man seated solo at the table visibly evident despite her polite smile.

Ian McAlester looked up from the menu in his hands and offered an apologetic smile in return. "Not yet, no. Sorry to keep you waiting; I'm sure my girlfriend will be here soon." He laid the menu down on the table. "Tell you what, though: if she's still not here in fifteen minutes, I'll put in my order anyway. I promise not to keep you here all night," he added with an apologetic smile.

The girl nodded, mollified by the handsome Irishman's gregarious charm, and promised to return in a little while. As she walked away, Ian let his gaze briefly travel around the small but pleasant room that doubled as the restaurant/pub for One Chocolat Pension, the hotel that the *Itinera* team had booked for the duration of their stay in Cluj.

Showered and shaved, he felt almost human again as we waited for Renee's slim, athletic figure to appear in the doorway. He had arrived in the city a few hours ahead of schedule, only to find that Renee and Lou were a few hours *behind* schedule. Something about a train delay. He sighed. *Even the best laid plans...* He took a sip of water, enjoying the cool burst of refreshment it offered.

Ian hadn't seen his girlfriend of three years in over a month, as their assignments with the magazine had taken them to opposite sides of the globe.

He missed her like crazy.

Reflexively, his hand traveled to the pocket of his jacket. Ian closed his fingers over the petite box that he had been carrying with him for months, his mind drifting to the one pending promise that waited within.

He had bought the ring in St. Petersburg at the beginning of the summer. It was an antique, a beautiful square-cut canary diamond surrounded with smaller clear stones. It was a gorgeous piece, but its beauty was not the sole reason Ian had settled on it. The ring had a history, and Ian knew that Renee, with her love of the past, would appreciate the story behind it, that it would matter to her. He wanted more than anything to see the look on her face when he gave it to her.

Ian looked towards the empty doorway, then back down at his hands, his thoughts on his girlfriend. He had known for so long that Renee was the only woman for him and that he wanted to spend the rest of his life with her. Deciding on Renee had been easy, but popping the question? Asking had proven more difficult than he had anticipated.

I just need the right moment...

Ian had fallen in love with Renee for a lot of reasons, one being her fierce independence. Another reason was her devotion to family—specifically to her sister Lou. But that same devotion was part of the reason the ring was still in his pocket and not on her finger. Ian wanted Renee to feel as ready as he was to start a life together, and it seemed like she would never get there unless Lou felt secure too. Every time he had hinted around about tying the knot, there always seemed to be some obstacle or reason why the timing wasn't right.

As he ran his thumb lightly over the velvet of the box, familiar doubts began to gnaw at him. What if Renee was using Lou as an excuse? What if she didn't see their relationship going anywhere? What if she didn't *want* it to? He tried to push the thoughts away, but as he sat alone at his table, staring at the empty place setting across from him, the doubts seemed more justified than ever.

Renee Bryant took the stairs down two at a time, almost knocking over an elderly man on his way up in her haste. She muttered an apology and fast-walked the rest of the way until she arrived at the restaurant door in the lobby.

As she caught sight of Ian, she flashed him a wide smile and made for the table. Her boyfriend met her halfway, gathering her into his arms as she approached. Renee sighed, leaning into him. Then she stood on her tiptoes and placed a kiss on his lips, smiling.

"I've missed you," she said simply, but the expression on her face betrayed far more than the simple statement of truth.

"Me too, *mon cheri*," Ian murmured as he cupped her chin affectionately. "More than you know. I couldn't wait to steal some time together tonight. This last assignment was almost unbearable; I can't stand not seeing your beautiful face for that long."

Renee blushed as they made their way back to the table, surprising herself with the sudden rush of emotion at Ian's declaration. Their recent separation had deepened her longing for his company and Renee had to admit that her favorite preoccupation of late was reminiscing about their time together, both in and out of bed.

"So did you personally get the train up and running again today?" Ian teased, yanking her back into the present moment.

She rolled her eyes. "No, but if they had taken any longer to repair it, I might have tried to."

Ian shrugged, picking up his menu. "At least you had Lou for company."

Renee murmured her agreement, but the truth was somewhat different. The memory of her sister's anxiety after her conversation with the woman on the train dampened her present happiness, causing a fleeting frown that her observant boyfriend immediately noticed.

Ian lowered his menu, cocking an eyebrow at her. "What? Did the dynamic duo have an argument?"

Not wanting to spoil the moment, Renee shook her head emphatically. "No, not at all. We're as thick as thieves, trust me...it's just..."

Renee let the words trail off as she searched for a way to communicate her concerns without sounding like an overbearing parent. Deciding that the incident with Lou could wait, she finished her thought with a dismissive wave of her hand. "Really, it's nothing."

Before their conversation could take another turn, Ian reminded, "We'd better choose something to eat before the kitchen closes and our waitress throws us out." Scanning the menu, they decided to share a platter and a carafe of wine. Even before Renee had set the menu aside, the waitress reappeared to take their order as if on cue.

Renee watched her hurry away. When she turned back, Ian was studying her, his deep blue eyes twinkling. She gave him a bemused smile. "What?" She asked.

"Renee, I know I've mentioned it before, but know that I have spent a lot of time this last month thinking about us and the future. I really want to make us permanent when we get back to Philadelphia."

Old butterflies stirred in her stomach. "I want that too, Ian, but I feel like the timing's not right yet. I still feel responsible for Lou; I can't leave her on her own." Renee shook her head, frown lines forming on her forehead. She thought of her sister, who had been sleeping soundly in their hotel room as she'd tiptoed out to meet Ian, her small form curled on the bed, one sock on, one sock off. *Vulnerable*, she thought. *Lou is still so vulnerable...*

Renee felt compelled to make her case to Ian despite her earlier decision to let the matter pass. "Take today for example: I left her to her own devices after the train stalled and she ends up sitting with a local woman for a Tarot card reading. Can you imagine?" Renee shook her head and continued without waiting for Ian's reaction. "She was in a funk for the rest of the day, all because of some psychic quack. God only knows what that woman told her." She looked for understanding in her boyfriend's eyes. "I have to worry about her; she is so easily manipulated sometimes."

Ian sighed, and Renee sensed a bevy of emotions reflected in his handsome features. "Lou is not a child, Renee—she's twenty-five years old. At some point, you're going to have to stop being her mother and be content with just being her sister."

"I know that," Renee conceded, "but now might not be that moment. Jeremy broke up with her last month."

Ian's mouth curved down in a frown. "I never liked that asshole."

"I know. I wasn't a big fan of his, either."

"But hon, still; Lou's an adult. Break-ups are going to happen. You have to trust her to handle the ups and downs of her own life."

"You mean like she did six years ago?"

The question was sharp, pointed, and Renee watched as her boyfriend visibly flinched. "That's not at all what I'm implying, and you know it," he replied, his tone sober.

"But Ian, you *know* what happens when I back off, when I give my sister space. I can't...I can't go through that again. And neither can she. And since Jeremy broke up with her, I'm worried now more than I've been in a long while that she'll spiral and we'll have a repeat of what happened six years ago."

Ian leaned back, sighing. "I get that. I do."

Renee took the bait. "But?"

"It's just... you always seem to bring Lou up when I talk about commitment. Are you sure Lou is the issue here? I'm starting to feel like what you really mean is that you don't want *us* to go anywhere." He gave her a wry smile. "Are you trying to let me down easy? Because frankly, Renee, I'd prefer it if you'd just say so."

Even though he'd spoken kindly enough, his words hit her like a slap to the face, and she felt instant panic hum through her. She reached out to grab his hands, shaking her head emphatically. "No, that's not it at all," she said. "I love you, I'm just..."

"Not ready," Ian finished for her, making her blush in embarrassment.

Is he going to break up with me? The thought brought another wave of panic, but she forced herself to suppress it. Pushing her doubts away, she focused on the one thing she could acknowledge at present: she couldn't be Lou's parent forever.

"I'm sorry. You're right. I'm holding on too tight. I guess I just can't stop worrying about her, you know? Lou was only twelve when mom died, and I've told you that Dad was completely clueless about raising girls." She scowled, reflecting on her failings. "Not that I did a stellar job. If Lou had gotten the guidance she needed from Dad or me maybe...well, maybe there wouldn't have been any...*incidents*."

"Hey," Ian interjected softly. "You did the best you could."

Renee could see love and understanding in the look he was giving her, though his earlier exasperation was not completely gone.

Their silent communication was again interrupted by the return of the waitress with their food and the check, a hint that they had overstayed their welcome in the now empty restaurant. Renee glanced down at her cell phone resting on the table and realized that it was past 10:00pm local time.

As they ate, their conversation turned to the assignment at hand, and Renee was grateful for the levity it brought. Discussing their relationship was tricky, but discussing their assignment was safe, neutral territory.

Simon Brody, their historian, was due to arrive that evening, according to the schedule he had sent via email. The team's guide and interpreter, Christer Malin, had already been in Cluj for two days, but had not yet put in an appearance at the hotel. Ian had rented the car the team would use for the duration of the assignment at the airport, a time-saving strategy given that they were planning to drive out to Banffy Castle first thing in the morning.

"Eight castles in four weeks," Ian chuckled. "Cody Buckley is a slave-driver."

The image of Cody, the *Itinera* team's editor in Philadelphia, with a whip in hand was not hard to conjure. Renee had battled with the seasoned editor on more than once occasion about the timeline for the current project.

"We can do it; Lou and I worked out the details ahead of time—it's tight but doable."

"This is why Cody loves you so much, babe," Ian teased. "You never, ever say that something can't be done. You are the most determined woman I have ever met. And by the way, Cody is not the only guy who loves you for that reason." He winked at her and rose from the table in search of the men's room. "Be back in a flash."

As Ian walked away, Renee's thoughts turned back to their earlier conversation, her mood souring. *Am I using Lou as an excuse? As a reason not to commit to something more with Ian?* She pondered the possibility. Though he had tried to hide it, Renee knew how crestfallen he'd been over her reaction to his suggestion of marriage, and rightfully so; every time he mentioned it, she gave him some lame excuse as to why it wasn't the right time. *I'm an idiot. He's not going to wait forever. He may not have broken up with me tonight, but that doesn't mean he won't do it.* A thorn of anxiety wormed its way in. *Have I stalled him one too many times? Is my devotion to Lou so overbearing that it's damaging my relationship?*

Then again, Lou didn't have the best track record with being left to her own devices...

Renee took a generous sip of wine and then let her gaze wander around the room, hoping that a little distraction would help her relax. The restaurant seemed to be much older than other parts of the hotel. The wooden floor was inlaid parquet, the pattern washed out by years of wear from the footfalls of patrons. The interior was dimly lit, and while the furnishings were quality pieces- tables and chairs made of cherry-wood- there were visible nicks on almost every surface. Dusty, framed antique maps decorated the walls, and although modern lighting had been installed, the lights were kept on low in favor of candles resting in wall sconces about the room. The weathered atmosphere sent Renee's imagination back in time, and it was while she was spacing out that she spied a familiar figure searching the room at the entrance to the restaurant.

"Brody!" Renee called, rising to her feet. "Gosh, I'm so tired I didn't even see you!" She waved her hands in greeting, flashing him a warm smile.

Simon Brody made his way over to her, an answering smile lighting up his intelligent, unpretentious face. He reached her with a few strides of his long legs and Renee threw her arms around him in a bear hug.

The journalist chuckled as he pulled away. "It's good to see you too, Renee," he said. Despite the fact that Simon had flown from Heathrow to Cluj and endured a long taxi ride to the hotel, his customary baseball cap was still in place, disheveled brown hair evident beneath. The sight of it warmed her heart. It had been a year since they had last been on assignment together and she had missed working with the even-tempered, brilliant historian. She was thrilled that he had agreed to join their team for the Romanian castle shoot.

"The year has agreed with you, Renee. You are as beautiful as ever," he said, his unguarded exuberance bringing a deep flush to his cheeks. Trying to recover his dignity, he added quickly, "I mean, you look well, very well." He tugged his cap down. "I know there will be time to catch up, so I'll skip to business: has the rest of the team arrived?"

Before Renee could answer, Ian's voice boomed out a greeting. "Simon!"

Simon spun around to face him, hand extended. Ian shook the proffered hand and clapped him heartily on the back, giving him a welcoming smile. After a brief exchange of pleasantries, Simon pulled a chair up at their table, vowing to stay only a few moments.

The three briefly touched on the events of the last week and the preparations to date. Simon related that since he had received Renee's invitation to participate in the assignment a month ago, he had been busily researching the histories behind each of the castles they would visit. The fascinating folklore of the area had inspired some unique and innovative ideas for the prose that would accompany the photos in the magazine spread. Renee listened as Simon animatedly shared his thoughts, liking what she heard. His ideas were sure to attract readers.

Finally, Simon took a breath. "Banffy Castle is first, I remember you saying. When are we setting out tomorrow?"

"In the morning, the earlier the better," Renee said. "All we're waiting on is one Christer Malin."

Glancing again at the time on her cellphone, Renee noted that there were still no messages from the Swede. Excusing herself, she dialed his number again, only to be shuttled directly to voicemail, just as she had been all night long.

She chewed on her lip, fighting a surge of anxiety. If he didn't show up... She forced the thought away. *He'll be here. He's just...* But her mind couldn't come up with any good reason as to why he hadn't returned any of her calls. Despite their former guide Zach Thompson's assurances that his friend was reliable, Renee was starting to wish she'd chosen one of Cody's contacts instead.

She glanced at her phone again, willing it to ring. *Where could he be?*

CHAPTER 3

The early September night was hot, and the streets of Cluj-Napoca, Romania were filled with people enjoying the weekend. In the center of the vibrant downtown, a very awake, very drunk Christer Malin was sitting on a red leather stool in a local's-only bar nursing his fifth drink, his gray eyes bloodshot, his feet tapping to an old rock tune blasting from a pair of prehistoric speakers, his small black duffel resting against one of the stool's chipped legs.

He was alone, companionless for the nth night in a row and unaware of the cell phone with six missed calls beeping in his back pocket.

As the bartender – a buxom blonde with raccoon eyes – walked by, Christer pointed to his empty glass. "Another, thanks."

The raccoon eyes stared uncomprehendingly at him.

Realizing his mistake, Christer switched from Swedish to Romanian.

The raccoon eyes blinked in understanding.

A minute later he was downing the fresh drink. When he finished it, he set money down on the bar and rose, gripping the stool to avoid falling.

Come on, Christer, you can't be smoked right now.

He managed to make it to the door despite the spinning in his head and the shaking in his legs.

As he stepped outside and filled his lungs with fresh air, he bumped into a girl on her way in, knocking her back a step. The guy she was with steadied her, then got in Christer's face.

"Hey pal, try watching where the fuck you're walking."

Christer's eyes were still on the girl he'd barreled into. She reminded him of one of the American women that had been on his last hiking trip. Having to deal with her was nine days of endless torture. He could still hear the echo of her shrill, strident voice in his head.

"Whiny bitch," he mumbled aloud.

Her companion's eyes narrowed. "What's wrong with you? Don't you *dare* talk to my girlfriend like that. Drunk asshole."

Christer saw the fist a second before it made contact with his face. He ducked – not quickly enough – and stumbled back a step, his face stinging. Angry, Christer lunged forward and countered with a brutal sucker-punch, knocking the wind out of his would-be opponent.

"Stop it!"

Holy hell, she even sounds *like the American.*

Stepping around the pair, Christer walked away, his pace irregular. To a passerby, it might appear as if he were dancing a drunk tango.

Can't be that smoked, he thought. *My instincts are still pretty good; certainly good enough to deal with assholes.*

You're the only one acting like an asshole, came the follow-up thought, but Christer brushed it aside.

He collapsed two blocks away, puking violently into a trashcan. Then, too feeble to keep going, he slumped down against it. He felt something hard against his backside as he reached the ground. Reaching back, he retrieved his phone from the pocket, staring at the screen and trying to make sense of the words on it.

Six missed calls? What the hell?

It wasn't like he had any friends in Cluj who would call him; he'd only been in Romania for ten months, working at Carpathian Tours, trying to make a new start in a new place. Friends weren't high on his priority list.

Trying to regain his equilibrium, he rested his head back against the trashcan's grimy metal surface, closing his eyes and focusing on breathing evenly. *I must be a sad sight, sitting here like a squatter,* he thought gloomily. *How far I have fallen...*

He wasn't a drunk by nature; truthfully, he had never been one to party excessively in the past. But that was before...

He gave a ragged sigh, his mouth dry.

She wouldn't be very proud of him, he knew. In fact, there was a good chance she wouldn't even recognize him. But still, what could he do? No one coached you for what happened after the shock wore off, for how to deal with all the grief and pain and emptiness that came in the weeks and months after you lost someone. No one told you who you were supposed to rely on for support when the one person who'd always had your back was the same person buried six feet under. At least alcohol numbed the feelings and provided a respite from his woes. He might hate himself for it – and he knew *she* certainly would – but Christer wasn't ready to sober up and face the reality that the life he had planned would never be.

Shaking his head, Christer snapped open his phone and listened to the two voicemails left by a woman named Renee Bryant, asking him why he hadn't met their party...

Shit. Nice big apeshit. The photographers from *Itinera*! He was supposed to meet them...he looked at the time on his phone...six, no—seven, hours ago.

Great. What a wonderful first impression I'm making.

Forcing himself to stand, Christer Malin walked in the direction of the Chocolat Pension, praying that he'd have a chance to take a shower and get his act together before he met them in the morning.

He was a street away when he realized he'd left his duffel at the bar.

The bar crowd had shifted dramatically from when he'd first been there. Most of the couples were gone, the college kids mostly dispersed. Only a few of the earlier patrons were still there, the regulars, men trying to drown themselves in the bliss of alcoholic stupor, if only for a time.

The rest of the bar was empty save for a table in the back. A group of girls were huddled together, whispering among themselves.

Christer eyed them warily, his senses sobering after the walk back in the cold air. He knew from their appearance - dark skin, dark hair, long skirts - that they were Roma. Gypsies. Many of them kept to themselves, wanting to distinguish themselves from *gajikane* society. Some groups, though, were less traditional in their thinking.

Turning his back on them, Christer walked to the bar, over to the stool he'd occupied earlier. His black bag wasn't on the floor.

"Shit.*"A lost bag. Just what I need.* On top of it all, he could feel his eye beginning to swell. He was going to look like hell in the morning.

He checked underneath all of the other stools and was just about to ask the bartender if she'd seen anyone walk out with a black duffel when he heard a voice behind him.

"Sir?"

Christer spun around and found himself face to face with one of the Roma girls, her dark eyes full of mirth. A smile played at the corner of her lips. "Is this yours?"

She held up his duffel, tapping a finger on its side. Snickers and whispers came from the table behind her. Her smile broadened mischievously.

Christer found it hard to peel his eyes off of her. She was a looker, no doubt about it. Despite his better judgment, he felt himself respond to her, the alcohol and basic male instinct winning out.

He returned her smile, taking a step towards her. "It is, yes."

She handed it to him, her fingers brushing his. The fingers of her free hand trailed down his arm as she stepped closer to him. "Don't you think I deserve something in return for watching your bag?"

Christer pretended to think about it. "Perhaps I could find *some* way to repay you," he teased, obvious nuance in his voice.

The Roma opened her mouth to reply, then froze. Her eyes grew larger, looking almost cartoonish in her small face. Her hands came up and gripped the front of his shirt tightly, her knuckles whitening.

"*Narkree...narkree.*" Her words came out in a hoarse whisper.

Christer dropped his bag, startled and slightly frightened. "Excuse me?" All the playfulness was gone from his voice.

"*Narkree!*"

Her table of friends stopped whispering and the drunkards at the bar turned their heads. A blanket of silence descended in the room, and Christer suddenly found it hard to breathe.

"Let go of me," he said, trying to pry her hands from his shirt.

Her grip only tightened, her hands latching onto him like inextricable chains. "Don't..." She breathed out in a wheeze, then snaked her hands up to his collar, forcing his head down with surprising strength. "Don't listen. It's not...It's not..." Her voice trailed off, her eyes going dim for a moment, almost as if she were searching for a word just out of reach.

All at once her eyes lit up again, blazing with intensity. She put her lips to his ear, so close that Christer could feel her warm breath on his neck. He shivered, feeling goosebumps rising.

"It's not *Annika*," she breathed.

The words released him from his temporary paralysis, and he shoved her roughly away from him, his shirt wrinkled from where she'd held him.

She stumbled, then caught herself. When she looked up at him, her expression was icy, the look of intensity replaced with one of ire. "What's your problem?" She spat at his feet. "*Didlo moosh.*"

Giving Christer a final, withering stare, she turned and walked out of the bar, her friends rushing after her.

Christer remained where he was, his mind racing.

How could she have known about Annika? How?

Inside, he felt a deep, familiar yearning fill his heart, a yearning that tore at him like starving piranhas.

Annika...

Feeling more sober than he had in a long time, Christer picked up his small duffel and walked out of the bar and into the night, wanting to put as much distance between himself and the Roma girl as possible.

He was running by the time he reached the end of the block.

CHAPTER 4

Romania, Present Day

A dusky half-light was stealing over the mountains, one that cloaked the high ridges in the fabric of evening. There was no breeze, only the constant humming and chirping of the insects that filled the forests and valleys. As usual, the lonely stretch of Carpathian peaks was nearly deserted.

High up on a large, jutting rock that overlooked an immense valley, mostly covered in the shadows cast by the branches of the ancient trees that surrounded it, were two young people sitting hand in hand, surveying the world below them.

It was a place they frequented whenever they could, as much for the view as for the intimate privacy of the mountains; no one ever bothered them there, and they had not once happened upon any other living creature. It was their own peaceful slice of paradise.

"So, you *are* leaving." Irina Lazar rested her head on Fane Adamescu's shoulder, trying to keep the disappointment out of her voice.

Her boyfriend sighed. "Irina, you know how much it means to me, to have this opportunity. I'll be the first member of my family to get a college education."

Irina looked at their intertwined hands, at their fingers laced together, trying to imagine her hand without his. "I am happy for you, Fane. I just wish..." She squirmed. "I don't know. I wish you weren't going so far away."

Fane met her eyes, his own full of conviction. "I will come back for you, I swear. I'll come back with a degree and a job, and we can move to the city.

Together. I just have to do this first." His voice went low and husky. "My father would have wanted me to make something of myself, Irina; you know that better than anyone. This would have been important to him too."

Her brown eyes were full of sympathy. She squeezed his hand, a tender gesture. "I know." Her voice was small and thin. Looking into his eyes, into the handsome face she knew so well, she still felt vulnerable. She'd loved Fane for so long. He was her rock, her best friend, and she was scared at the thought of being without him by her side every day.

Fane sensed her turmoil and hugged her close. "I love you," he whispered into her hair. "It'll all be okay. You'll see."

Somewhat comforted by his embrace, Irina leaned into him, pressing her face against his chest. He smelled like fresh pine and sunlight. It was a smell she would miss.

She felt his muscles stiffen beneath her cheek and looked up at him, moving back slightly. "What is it?"

Fane was scanning the woods behind them, his dark brows drawn together, a line of consternation creasing his otherwise smooth forehead. "I don't know. Probably nothing."

Irina kept her eyes on his face, waiting for him to say something else.

Suddenly, he stood up, his entire body tensing.

Nervous, Irina copied him, clutching at his arm. "Fane, you're scaring me. What is it?"

He shook his head and put a finger to his lips. "I saw something." He moved his finger from his lips, pointing towards the woods. "Back there."

It was then that Irina noticed how quiet it was. The usual cacophony of nighttime noises was gone, replaced by a silence that made her shiver. "Fane?"

He looked at her, gently holding her by the arms. "I'm going to go take a look."

Irina bit her lip, saying nothing.

He saw the look of panic in her eyes and cupped her face. "Just a quick look, okay? And I have my knife, if I need it. Just stay here and wait; I'll be back before you can miss me."

"Fane, wait!" Irina put as much force into the whisper as possible, but it made no difference. He was already walking into the trees, the hunting knife in his hands.

Irina hugged her arms around herself. She felt cold, though she couldn't be sure if it was because of the dropping temperature or her fear. A minute passed, then two, as she stared after Fane into the shadows, the seconds ticking by as she waited for him to reappear.

Please, Fane, come back. She felt tears of worry prick her eyes. *Where are you, Fane?*

"Irina." The voice called out to her from the shadows.

"Fane?" She took a hesitant step forward, then stopped. Something about his voice sounded wrong. She swallowed. "Fane?" She repeated.

"It was just a deer, Irina. There's nothing to be afraid of."

Wanting to believe that everything was fine, that Fane was fine, she left the rock and walked into the trees.

She blinked a few times, giving her eyes a moment to adjust to the darker space. She looked right and left, a fresh wave of panic coursing through her. She didn't see Fane anywhere, and without him, the trees felt as if they were pressing down upon her.

"Fane, where are you?" Her voice was shaking.

"Walk to your right, Irina. I am close."

She did as he asked, even though a small part of her wanted to run as fast as she could in the other direction.

Then she saw him. "Oh, Fane..." she breathed, hurrying towards him.

He was leaning against a tree, eyes closed, head bent.

Irina gave him a smile of relief, reaching out to hug him close. "Why didn't you come back? I was scared to death."

The words were barely out of her mouth when she saw it.

Blood, dark and glistening, everywhere. It was all over his shirt, soaking it, still warm. And Fane wasn't moving. "Oh, *please* no," she choked, her voice catching. *"No."*

She shook his shoulders, holding her breath. "Fane?" As she looked up at his face, she saw the wicked laceration, the terrible slash that took all her hope away. She screamed, falling back on the ground at his feet, unable to tear her eyes away from the awful sight.

Fane's neck had been ripped open, violently, and although Irina wasn't a doctor, she knew he was dead.

She hugged her knees to her chest, rocking herself back and forth as she cried, lost in sorrow. "Oh Fane," she sobbed, "Fane..."

A twig snapped somewhere nearby, making her jump, and a second later she saw something move in her periphery.

Terrified, she shot up, her heart pounding. She took a step back and fell, her legs failing her.

Hardly breathing, she picked herself up again, scanning the woods around her. Whatever had killed Fane was out there, watching her, *playing* with her. The thought made her sick.

Clutching at the locket around her neck, the one that Fane had given her, she took a calming breath. She was not going to die here; she would survive. She would survive for Fane.

Without another thought, she ran, speeding away from the rock, away from Fane's body. She raced down the mountain, quickly navigating her way in the dark, intuitively knowing where to go after so many years of hiking up to their rock.

Once, she thought she heard something running behind her, its footfalls growing louder and closer with each passing moment. But then it was gone, and she was drawing close to the edge of the woods.

She saw the break in the trees and gave a hiccupping sob, overcome by a wave of relief.

Safe. A few more steps and she would...

She saw the figure detach itself from a tree in front of her, blocking her way. It faced her, silent and dark.

Instinctively, Irina knew it was the creature that had killed Fane, the one that had been chasing her. She also knew that it had only pretended to let her get away. And she knew, without a doubt, that it was going to kill her.

Despite it all, she made a dash for the tree line, running diagonally to avoid the killer, unwilling to give up.

Faster than she could have imagined, it was upon her, slashing at her with its massive claws.

She fell hard and hit her head, dazed. She pulled herself to her hands and knees, looking for her attacker, just as she felt another deep slash tear across her back. She fell forward again, aware of the warm wetness spreading all over her, the fight leaving her body.

Other figures had materialized, more and more of them, all closing in on her.

She would have thought that they were wolves, or bears even, but animals couldn't talk, and she was certain that one of them had impersonated Fane.

They were all around her, staring down at her. She couldn't see what they looked like; she couldn't even raise her head from the ground.

As if from miles away, she heard a hideous laugh, one that wormed its way into her ears and scratched at her insides with its mockery. *Trapped*, it was laughing. *You are trapped and you are going to die.*

Irina screamed then, filling the mountains with her cries as the creatures descended upon her.

And after a time, a far too long time, silence reigned again.

Romania, 1426 A.D.

The woman stood very still in the corridor, her hands clenched into fists at her sides. The corridor was long and dark, lighted only by two torches burning at either end, their ornate sconces barely visible in the flickering half-light. Elongated shadows obscured the rest, including the woman.

A muffled gasp of pain sounded from behind a closed door, near to where the woman was standing. The gasp was followed by a thud and a strangled cry, barely discernible as human.

Moving closer to the door, she could discern two voices from inside the chamber, one voice brusque and raised in anger, the other soft and pleading. A malevolent look flashed in her eyes. She knew what would happen next; it was not the first time she had served as a silent witness to such an episode. Behind the door, the woman's pleas for mercy would stir the man's anger and lust, and then her pleas would become screams that echoed through the castle long into the night. The tenants and servants would pretend not to hear. There was nothing they could do and they would never interfere. They would not dare.

She, however, was not like the others.

Filled with determination, she grasped the handle, then paused, her resolve wavering. Her hand hovered in space and a muscle clenched spasmodically in her jaw. Conflicting emotions played on the dark lines of her face.

Not now. She must be patient.

Silently, she backed away a pace, turned abruptly, and walked swiftly towards one end of the corridor. As she passed by the torch mounted on the wall, the fire illuminated her face, setting her green eyes ablaze with an evil light that was akin to the gaze of Medusa before she turned an enemy to stone.

She continued to walk, winding this way and that through the labyrinth of passageways until she came to her own quarters. She passed her bedchamber without lighting a candle, for her eyes did not require light to see in the darkness, and walked out onto her balcony, finally stopping. Her hands gripped the rail and she exhaled.

Monster.

The word pulsed inside her like a mantra and radiated from her being in waves of dark emotion. She forced herself to breathe evenly, willing her body to be calm.

Monster.

She drummed her fingers on the stone railing in no particular rhythm. Her mind was elsewhere.

Indeed, Istvan was a monster. Like so many other men in positions of power, his ego and arrogance had become bloated, and cruelty and corruption had replaced a once-benign manner. No doubt his Székely blood was to blame, at least in part. His love, like that of all men, was sadistic, his passion twisted. His soul yearned to inflict pain on others; pain- the diversion he most liked to indulge in. The suffering he caused on the battlefield had found its way into his own castle. To Istvan, there was no longer a distinction between the two. He hurt his enemies, his servants, and...*her.*

The woman's knuckles whitened on the rail as her hands tensed.

Sabina. Sweet, beautiful, docile Sabina.

How could he harm her? *His own wife!*

The woman gasped suddenly in surprise and glanced down at the railing. Blood oozed from beneath her palms, staining the stone railing a dusky brown in the dim light. Realizing its source, she unclenched her hands and observed the bloody nail marks imbedded in her palms.

"Xenia, calm yourself. Restraint is key."

The woman spoke the words aloud, her voice betraying none of the raging turmoil within her.

Deal with Istvan she would. But not now. Her plans were like the pieces of an intricate puzzle that required methodical patience to complete; each piece was the foundation for the next.

The devil would come soon enough for Istvan Solovastru. She would see to that. And then Sabina would be free... free to follow the path that Xenia would lay out for her.

But not tonight.

Xenia closed her eyes and held her breath. A gentle breeze rustled her long skirt, but she remained as immobile as a statue, her mind reaching into the future.

Minutes passed.

Finally, content, she exhaled deeply and opened her eyes.

Soon, Istvan. Soon. Your torment of Sabina is coming to an end, as are you.

"Hold on a little longer, Sabina. All will be well..."

Xenia's voice trailed off into the night, joining the peaceful susurrus of the surrounding forest.

Soon...

CHAPTER 5

I finally got him."

Hearing her sister's voice, Lou turned, her long ponytail swinging. "Christer?"

Renee sighed. "Yup," she said. "But I'm pretty sure I woke him up; he sounded groggy. He promised to join us in the lobby in a half hour. I can't wait to hear his explanation for this."

Lou was relieved. Renee had started repeatedly dialing Christer's cell phone at seven in the morning, without success. They had originally planned to be on the road by now, but the missing guide had derailed their departure. With every passing moment, Renee's anxiety and irritation levels had increased exponentially. Lou could only recall a few occasions in the past when her normally calm and collected sister had come close to unraveling. Lou knew that Renee didn't like working with people unless she was sure they were reliable.

Which Malin, it seemed, was not.

Lou covered a yawn with her sleeve, fighting back her exhaustion. Renee's fitful sleeping had kept her awake for almost the entire night, and the day had begun earlier than she would have preferred.

"Can I interest either of you ladies in a cup of coffee?" Simon asked, walking over to meet the sisters where they stood in the lobby. Unlike Lou, Simon was well-rested, looking awake and happy. His hair was sticking out of his baseball cap in its usual messy fashion.

"Brody, that sounds wonderful," Renee crooned, momentarily distracted from her anger. Unlike Lou, Renee loved her morning coffee, a habit that Simon had picked up on when he'd worked with her before. Lou sometimes imagined that if Renee didn't get her morning stimulant (one packet of Splenda and hold the milk) she might go into withdrawal.

Simon smiled when Renee used her old nickname for him. Flushing slightly, he quickly lowered his head to hide the color spreading on his cheeks. "Would you like coffee?" He asked Lou.

"I'll pass, thanks." Lou gave the Brit a smile and pretended she didn't see the blush beneath his cap. *Poor sap.* She sighed. *Renee, if you only knew how many guys had a thing for you...*

"Okay, just one coffee then. And Renee," he turned towards her, "did I overhear correctly that you got in touch with Malin?"

"Yes. Finally. He's in his room getting ready. He said he'd be down soon."

When Christer Malin finally did appear almost an hour later, Renee had finished two cups of coffee and Ian had returned from gassing up their car. The foursome was seated on chairs in the lobby, looking irritable.

Renee was the first to notice him. She stood up, setting aside a map she'd been studying. "Christer Malin, I presume?"

"Yes. I'm so sorry to have kept you all waiting."

Lou looked up at the tardiest member of their group, then stared.

Christer Malin was tall, muscular, and blond, with a crooked smile that brightened his face. If it hadn't been for the ugly shiner beneath his left eye, he would have resembled a Swedish Apollo. Lou felt her anger at him evaporating.

Renee extended her hand to Malin, followed by Ian.

"We were beginning to doubt that you'd put in an appearance." Ian smiled. "And from the looks of that eye, I'm surprised you *did* show up. That's quite the shiner."

Before Christer could supply an explanation, Simon interrupted. "If it's okay with all of you, I'd like to continue this little get-to-know-you session in the car. We have a bit of a drive to get to Banffy Castle, and our planned departure time was much earlier than this."

Everyone agreed. The cameras and equipment were packed in the trunk already, so it took almost no time to get on the road. Ian had loaded their gear while they'd been waiting for Christer; only a few of the smallest D-SLR cameras were in the backseat. He'd managed to make everything else fit nicely in the trunk.

Ian drove and Christer rode shotgun; he had the longest legs, and no one had even suggested that he try and squeeze in the backseat.

As they drove through the city, Christer explained that he had had to track down his suitcase the previous night. He said he'd forgotten where he'd left it and that his phone had been inside the front pocket. By the time he got the messages after finding his bag, it had been too late to call Renee back, he said.

Lou wasn't sure that was the whole truth, or *any* of the truth, judging by the shiner he was sporting, but she decided not to dig for details. Renee and Ian apparently felt the same; only Simon scowled at the back of Christer's seat, his expression dark.

After a few minutes of silence, Simon commented, "Since we are traveling through a very historical city that some of us have never been to before, I feel obliged to give a little history and background on the place."

Lou focused on Simon for a few minutes as he began detailing the city's history before her attention strayed back to Christer Malin. She found herself making up ridiculous scenarios about what might have happened the previous night: Christer had been frequenting a strip club, participating in a drug deal, running from the police, doing secret government work…

She caught herself as the stories became even more outlandish. *God, it's like my imagination's doped up on Ritalin or something,* she thought. *And why should I care about what Christer was doing last night? I don't even know him.*

As Simon continued on to talk of Cluj's industries and economy, Lou looked out the window, forcing her mind to dwell on something other than the man in the front seat. They were out of the city now, on their way to Bontida, the small village north of Cluj and the location of Banffy Castle, their first shoot.

She tuned back in as Simon's discourse turned to the castle.

"...was completed in 1543. Baron Banffy had ordered its construction in 1437, more than a hundred years prior. It's a mixture of Renaissance and Baroque styles, a reflection of its architects, Agostino Serena and Joseph Emmanuel Fischer von Erlach, respectively. Its last addition was completed in 1850."

"It's pretty impressive; its nickname is the 'Versailles of Transylvania'," Christer interjected.

"Yes, that's right." Simon said, a hint of irritated surprise in his voice. He continued, "Of course, it has served capacities quite different from that of a traditional castle in more recent times. In World War II it served as a German army hospital and during that time it was burnt dramatically; its structure sustained great damage. During the Communist era, no effort was given to repair Banffy and it remained a shell of what it once was. Now, however, it is being extensively renovated."

Renee smiled next to Simon and gave his knee a pat. "Thanks for the information, Brody. As always, you've managed to fill me in on more than what I would have learned in a month's time in high school."

Simon seemed mollified by her praise. Renee looked knowingly at her sister. Both of them knew that Simon loathed being interrupted during one of his speeches, a fact that Christer was ignorant of. Simon's first impression of Christer was easy enough to make out as a bad one, and followed by Christer's disruption now, it was clear that the two weren't going to be thick as thieves anytime soon.

The group was quiet for the rest of the trip, only Ian and Christer exchanging a few words back and forth in the front seat.

The scenery in the communes of Bontida, Coasta, Rascruci, and Tauseni – the four that made up the town – was rustic in the most idyllic sense of the word. Small clusters of thatched-roof houses dotted the landscape. Here and there, steeples punctuated the sky, each church surrounded by cemeteries that held the remains of countless generations of villagers whose descendants no doubt still populated the small hamlets. There were people dressed both in modern clothing and ethnic garb of vibrant colors. Most of the main roads in the town were dirt, and for as many cars that drove by on the road there was at least an equal number of horse-drawn carts loaded with hay, produce, and other farm-related cargo. Ignoring the cars and power lines, the team from *Itinera* could have easily believed they'd stepped back in time.

"Hey guys, there it is," Ian said.

Sure enough, Banffy Castle lay in front of them at the edge of the town, looking like a giant in comparison to the homes that surrounded it. Still, it paled next to the real Versailles. Maybe at one point in history, before German soldiers had ravaged it during World War II, Banffy too had been magnificent.

Despite the sections being renovated, the castle was still impressive. It was easy to imagine the beauty that once was, despite the still-charred facades and roofless towers; it held a sad kind of charm. Its main body was in the shape of a great U with one side slightly shorter than the other and two extended sections in the middle. A smaller outbuilding was located not far from the openings of the U.

After Ian parked the car, the group located and met briefly with the person in charge of the current renovation team from Transylvania Trust, a stout man whose English was flawless.

Yes, the photographers had been expected and yes, arrangements had been made for them to have access to Banffy both this afternoon and the next day, if necessary.

They thanked him for accommodating them, Simon lingering for a while to inquire on the progress of the renovations, everyone else dispersing.

The sky grew progressively more overcast as the day wore on and its clouds had taken on an ominous tint by mid-afternoon. Then, all at once, the sky opened up and it began to rain.

"Shit! Lou, grab the cameras!" Renee yelled. Lou was already running with her gear inside the castle, hastily packing her lenses away. It took Renee a moment longer to do the same, so when she joined Lou beneath the archway she had taken cover in, she was dripping, her short hair plastered to her face.

"That's a great look, Renee," Lou said.

Renee laughed. "Well, it saved me the trouble of having to get a shower, so yeah, I'd agree." She looked up at the arch, then back behind where they stood. "I guess now would be a good time to try and do some work inside?" The inflection at the end made her statement a question.

Lou nodded. "Not a bad idea. How 'bout we split up? Divide and conquer?"

Renee ran her hands through her wet hair, squeezing out drops of water. "I'll go..." She looked right and left, then pointed to the right. "That way. Later, Sis."

Lou watched her sister walk away and then gazed back out at the rain. The drops were big and fat, making muddy splotches on the cleared ground. She sighed, her eyes half-closing. She loved watching rain; the monotonous sound and look of the drops was soothing and entrancing.

Feeling experimental, she unzipped her E-620. Photographing rain wasn't really easy and usually the results weren't worth the effort, but she wanted to try anyway.

She angled the camera so that the foreground – part of the archway – was in the shot, and began to play with her f-stops and shutter speed until she found a combination that she was happy with. The rain was falling at an angle, bending towards the arch, and the drops were large enough that they splashed a little when they made contact with the stone floor.

Lou took a few shots, making some minor adjustments as she tried to freeze the drops in frame. She was so focused on what she was doing that she jumped a little at the sound of someone's voice.

"I like the rain too," Christer Malin said from behind her.

Lou whipped around to face him, startled, and almost barreled into him. "Sorry," she said. "I didn't mean to jump. You just...I didn't know anyone was here."

Christer gave her a crooked smile. "No worries; I didn't mean to scare you. Or interrupt you. Please, continue."

Lou turned her camera off. "That's okay. I was pretty much done anyway. These shots were just for fun."

"It suits the castle, don't you think?" Christer posed.

Lou frowned. "What?"

"The rain—it's sad and somber, but beautiful too. Kind of like Banffy."

Lou stared at him, nonplussed. She hadn't expected an opinion like that to come out of the Swede's mouth.

Pretty faces don't always hide a shallow heart, Lou, she chided herself, feeling guilty. *Come on. Not everyone is a Jeremy Paxton.*

"You okay...?"

It was only then that she realized she was standing there gaping at Christer. *God, Lou, how rude can you be?* Mortified, she felt color creep into her cheeks.

She cleared her throat. "Do you want to see them? The pictures, I mean." Her blush deepened. What was she doing? *She* hadn't even bothered to look at her pictures yet. She certainly shouldn't be showing them to anyone else.

He leaned in, ignoring her embarrassment. "I'd love to."

She turned her camera back on and brought up the pictures. The first two were dreadful and she skipped over them as fast as she could. The third wasn't too bad; the fourth was even better, the burnt-out archway looking – as Christer had said – somber, haloed by the rain.

"Wow. That's really good. Truly. You've captured something unique...you should definitely use this one."

"You think? Hopefully Renee won't think it's too melodramatic. I tend to go overboard sometimes."

"Why would she think that? This is good, not overdone."

Lou was all too aware of Christer's closeness. She could see the muscles of his chest beneath his shirt, and when she looked up to meet his eyes she was taken aback by their intensity. His grey eyes were the color of the sky: stormy.

She backed away a step, turning off her camera and busying herself with putting it away. She needed space from Christer; that was a fact. She was acting like a bumbling idiot, like the geeky high school girl with a crush on Mr. Popular. Still, she couldn't deny the intensity of the physical attraction she felt to this handsome stranger.

She forced herself to face him again. "So, what were you up to today? Besides stalking me." She raised her eyebrows, feigning reproach.

Christer's face grew serious. "Nothing. Stalking you is my sole occupation." Lou blinked at him and he laughed, his humorless expression melting. "Okay, not really. I went with Ian into Bontida, helped him talk to a few of the locals. They were friendly enough, pretty interested in him. One little girl sorely wanted to have his camera. Ian was a good sport; he let her hold it."

Lou shifted her weight from foot to foot. "That's Ian. He's just a happy, friendly person. He'll make a great dad some day," she added.

"Yeah, I agree with you there." He paused. "Pardon my asking, but he and Renee are...together, right?"

Unbidden, Lou felt a twinge of disappointment, then instantly squelched it. Was it at all surprising that Christer would be interested in Renee, even after only a few hours? The answer was a resounding no; men in general always seemed to be interested in her sister. *And Renee deserves the attention*, she thought. Her sister was a wonderful person; any man would be lucky to have her.

When Lou didn't answer, Christer thought he'd overstepped his bounds in asking. "Forgive me, that was rude. I've only just met you. I shouldn't be prying."

Lou looked up at him, feeling foolish. "No, don't be sorry. God, it's not like they're some secret. Yes, they're together. They've been together for just over three years."

Christer nodded, saying nothing.

The rain slowed and stopped, leaving only puddles and beads of dew on the grass as signs of its presence.

Bending down, Christer picked up the tripod Lou had been carrying earlier. "Here, I'll get this. What do you say you and I go find some trouble to get into?" He gave Lou a playful nudge on the arm and she relaxed. He exuded an easy nonchalance that was infectious. Despite the less than cordial feelings Simon clearly felt for him, Lou found herself warming to Christer.

She smiled. "Sounds like a plan."

Târgoviste Evening Post
Monday, September 9th

Reports of another child abduction in Târgoviste have caused renewed anxiety within the local community. In the early morning hours of Saturday, September 8th, authorities were called to the home of Janos and Eva Razvan to investigate the disappearance of the couple's five-year-old daughter, Zsuzsanna, who appears to have been abducted from her bedroom earlier that evening. Zsuzsanna Razvan is the third in a string of child disappearances reported in the river provinces surrounding the Leaota Mountains since May of this year and authorities now suspect that a serial kidnapper may be at large in the area. According to statements made by investigators on the scene, the police were unable to gather any recoverable prints or forensic evidence to pinpoint a potential suspect. No visible signs of forced entry were noted, nor were the child's parents alerted to the presence of an intruder in their home at the time of the suspected abduction. The Razvans' dog was found dead in the front yard of the family home. Deputy Serban Kozar, lead investigator on the case, described the scene:

"The discovery of the dog is puzzling. The mangled condition of the corpse would lead one to believe that a wild animal had attacked it, although we strongly believe that the kidnapper killed the dog to prevent a confrontation with an awakened family member. The Moroeni family, whose child disappeared in June from neighboring Dumbrava, also owned a dog that vanished on the night of the abduction. Despite this, however, we remain encouraged as no blood was found in Zsuzsanna's bedroom, leading us to believe that the child is still alive..."

Currently, none of the families of the missing children have received any demands for ransom and despite large-scale volunteer search efforts organized by several local community groups, none of the missing children have been located to date.

CHAPTER 6

I t was almost five o'clock when they left Râsnov and headed back to the city of Brasov. In the week that had elapsed since their first shoot at Banffy Castle, the team had found little time to relax, driving from one locale to the next with little downtime. Everyone was looking forward to an evening off.

They stopped for dinner at a tourist hotspot, foregoing the local establishments in an attempt to blend. Their fellow Americans were easy to spot among the various patrons, dressed in khakis and unfashionable walking sneakers, a few even touting fanny packs, no doubt bulging with cameras and day-trip paraphernalia. Despite the relative coolness of the early evening, the American tourists looked sweaty and fatigued. Their voices carried over the din of the restaurant, complaining of the slow service and non-functional air-conditioning. Next to the Americans sat a buxom redhead who was unsuccessfully trying to quiet her wailing baby. Her older toddler boys were gleefully engaged in a food tossing competition aimed at the neighboring table, smug in the knowledge that their actions would go unpunished.

Renee breathed a sigh of relief when the hostess guided them to the far end of the room, away from the other Americans and the impish toddlers. Observing that particular vignette of life with children made her glad that her career was her life's sole occupation at the moment. *Well, maybe not my sole occupation,* she mused as she slipped her hand into

Ian's. Her boyfriend, in his usual good humor, flashed her one of his killer smiles.

As the waitress passed out the one-page menus, the din of the noisy patrons and rowdy kids grew decidedly louder, competing with the Romanian music playing in the background, a ridiculous medley of Frankenstein-inspired violin riffs that served as the *pièce de résistance* in the comical cacophony.

The group exchanged glances, and, sharing the same thought, they simultaneously burst into laughter. Renee elbowed Ian and assumed a mock tone of annoyance. "Ian, this is the last time you get to pick the place for dinner," she scolded.

"Come on, this place is fantastic!"

Ian's facetious humor made Renee shake her head.

Christer joined in, feigning seriousness. "Actually, Ian, you picked a *very* local place. It's full of Romanian mystery. For instance, it's said that after midnight, any tourists still here are served on the menu the following day." He looked solemnly at each one of them. "You could be next."

Everyone laughed at that. Even Simon chuckled slightly.

"Funny as it is, we used to play a game like that when we were little," Renee said, adding to the light-hearted atmosphere. "Lou, do you remember? Most kids pretend to be princesses and heroes, but we always wanted to be witches and sorcerers. Hansel and Gretel was a favorite of ours—we used to pretend we were trapping all the kids we didn't like at school in our enchanted house and baking them in our cauldron."

"Are you sure you still don't do that? Some of the things you've cooked have tasted a little peculiar..."

"Hey!" Renee gave her a boyfriend a shove, eliciting a broad smile.

"Just kidding," he said, hands raised in guilty surrender.

Continuing in mock defense, Renee elaborated, "Lou was always the more deviant one, by the way. Stories about séances, Ouija boards, horror movies—she got ideas from everything, and so our attention to detail was painstakingly accurate—spells and incantations taken straight out of the Encyclopedia of Witchcraft." She laughed. "Both of us had wild imaginations back then."

"Yes, and if I remember correctly, yours was actually more gruesome," Lou said. She turned to the others. "Renee played her role quite well. If I didn't procure other children for her evil designs, I was the one who ended up in the cauldron for dinner or baked in a pie."

"Sisterly love at its best," Renee chimed in. But even as she said the words, the merriment died in her eyes. She looked at her sister. Had Lou really changed since they were kids? She was still intrigued by the supernatural, still tantalized by unexplained phenomena. *She got a Tarot card reading from some stranger on a train, for God's sake...a reading that she still won't talk to me about.* Just how much did Lou actually believe? The idea scared her.

Ian roused her from her thoughts as he reached an arm around her shoulders. "See?" He teased. "It's that same sweet nature that drew me to you." Winking at the others, he added, "She hasn't changed at all; you should see what she does to me when I don't toe the line."

Christer watched the couple tease each other. It was obvious that they were in love; the way they moved and interacted made that clear. It was nice to know that some people were still finding happiness in the world, despite his own lack of it.

Lou refreshed the conversation, noticing that Simon had become very interested in the restaurant's decor, careful to look at anything except Renee and Ian. "So Simon, you've worked in Romania before, right?"

Simon stopped eyeing the light fixtures. "Yes, I have. Twice, in fact. Though I have to say, the company is much more enjoyable this time."

Lou smiled and Renee said, "Thanks, Brody. It does feel kind of like a reunion of our old group, doesn't it?" She looked at Christer. "Almost a reunion. If Zach Thompson were here, it would be a party." She raised her wine glass. "But here's to new friends," she said, her words directed at Christer with the intent of putting their rocky introduction a week ago in Cluj behind them. "I hope we can have our own happy reunion in a few years and reminisce on many good times."

The others raised their glasses and Christer finished, "Let's make it so."

Despite the weak flavor of the restaurant's house red, they all took hearty sips, happier drinking to friendship than actually enjoying the cheap wine.

"So how long have you known Zach?" Christer asked.

Renee turned to Lou. "How long has it been? Two years?"

"Two and a half," Lou answered. "But if feels like longer. Zach's the kind of guy that you spend a day with and feel like you've known him forever."

There were nods of assent all around. Ian started laughing, recalling a particularly memorable incident with the gregarious Aussie. "Zach. What a guy. Do you remember the time he decided to enter that camel race when we were on assignment in the Gobi desert? I've never seen- and I hope I never again see- a camel run like that."

The sisters laughed. "I wish you two could've been there." Renee gestured at Simon and Christer. "It was a riot. And he won that race, God only knows how."

"I can only imagine," Christer said. "When I worked with Zach, he was always the life of the party. He's a real ace."

Renee leaned forward and put her elbows on the table. "So, Christer, I've got to ask: how did you end up in Romania? Zach said you'd only been here a year or so. What's the story?"

"Well, I grew up in Stockholm, traveled a bit, but never moved out of Sweden. I love Sweden; I never planned on leaving." He paused.

"I literally grew up on skis, exploring the mountains and climbing during my teen years. I was never much for the books, so I went to school for sports, focusing on climbing and mountaineering. By the time I was twenty-eight, I had my dream job with the Swedish Arctic Alpine Search & Rescue. The pay was adequate, but the scenery was fabulous, and hey: who doesn't want to be a hero, right? During my time with the team, I met my wife, Annika. She was a member of the team too— one hell of a climber— gutsy and beautiful."

Startled at the disclosure, Lou shot her sister a glance, her face betraying a look of disappointment. Christer, oblivious to the interchange, continued his soliloquy, a look of immeasurable sorrow in his eyes.

"We had two wonderful years together, a lifetime in fast forward." He paused, idly pushing the food around on his plate. "Then there was an accident. *The* accident. A group of tourists one weekend, college kids on holiday – cocky dicks – decided to go climbing even though the forecast warned of blizzard conditions. Things went wrong and Annika and I were on the team that went to help them. I went first and helped the first guy back. When Annika rappelled down, though, the kid she harnessed panicked- severely. The carabiner anchoring their rope gave way and they... they fell." Christer's face convulsed in an awful grimace, his eyes miles away.

The group fell silent, everyone staring at their plates. A shocked silence permeated the air. Christer leaned back, his face now devoid of emotion. "After Annika died, I spent a few months backpacking solo through Europe; I just needed to escape. When I was passing through Romania, I heard about a position that had opened up with Carpathian Tours, so I took the job. It just felt good to start over."

Renee looked at Christer across the table, empathy written on her face. Now she wished she hadn't asked. She blinked back tears, noticing that Lou was doing the same.

God, life is so unfair. Poor Christer.

She sucked in a breath when she heard Simon speak. She knew- better than anyone- that Simon understood what Christer was going through, but she'd never expected him to bring up his own demons; he was normally very reserved.

"Christer, I'm...I'm so terribly sorry. I know what it's like to lose someone, to see it happen. Believe me." He met the Swede's eyes. "At least you were not to blame." Simon's voice had become fainter and fainter with emotion as he spoke, his last words barely audible.

All eyes were fixed on Simon, the confusion palpable, yet no one dared delve further into the meaning behind his strange declaration. Only Renee knew the nature of the pain Simon carried with him. She was one of the only people in the entire world that he'd opened up to about the darkness in his past, one of the only people he'd confided in. She could only imagine how much empathy he felt towards Christer in that moment.

An awkward silence had descended upon the group, spurring Renee to shift the topic of conversation to the itinerary for the next day's shoot.

"I think we need to lighten the mood around here with a little shop talk," she announced, offering a wan smile to her companions. Successfully drawing everyone's attention away from Simon, Renee shot him a momentary glance, acknowledging her friend's relief and gratitude with a barely perceptible nod. "We are two shoots down and three days ahead of schedule."

"True enough. We planned to spend equal time at both Miko and Fagaras, but the two castles only took a week combined," Ian concurred, but he was quick to remind the others that unexpected delays were also just as common, and time saved on one shoot could be easily squandered on another.

"Ian, don't be so pessimistic. I think this just proves how amazing we are as a team." Lou gave her sister's boyfriend a teasing smile. "The glass doesn't always have to be half empty, you know. Maybe all our shoots will go as smoothly. Besides, if we finish early, I for one expect Cody to ante-up with a bonus." Lou's suggestion brought a round of 'here, here' and clinking glasses raised in toast.

Renee smiled at her younger sister's optimism, but experience in the field taught her that Ian was right. The shoot at Râsnov was proving more extensive than originally predicted. Located south of Brasov, the fortress was immense, situated on top of a mountain hill that overlooked the town that shared its name, and although it had fallen prey to tourist trends- big Hollywood letters spelled its title on one side of the hill- it was still a mighty work of architecture with a great deal of historical significance.

The discussion moved to particulars and Simon rejoined the conversation, his previous recalcitrance forgotten. Renee knew that Simon was particularly excited about the shoot at Râsnov, as the shy historian would have the chance to shine given his extensive knowledge of medieval history and considerable talent as a writer. As Simon continued to elaborate on his ideas for items of special interest that might add depth and historical context to the photo layout, Renee reached out and intertwined her fingers with Ian's. Feeling his warm squeeze of reciprocation, she tuned out, turning her thoughts inward. *How lucky are we...doing what we love with the people we love most beside us.*

Life was good indeed.

As she enjoyed the comfort of the moment, Renee failed to notice her sister's anxiety. Eyes wide with unease, Lou was staring out the window of the restaurant, her gaze fixed unwaveringly on the light of the full moon.

Romania, 1428 A.D.

Sabina Solovastru sat bolt upright in her bed, the sheets tangling about her. She was drenched in sweat and her heart was pounding feverishly.

I can't take this anymore. I can't.

Sabina hugged herself tightly, willing the panic – and the dream that had caused it – away.

The wretched, awful dream. It was recurring, a horrible nightmare that had plagued her for months, ever since Istvan had died.

Since Istvan was *killed*, she corrected herself. He had presumably been poisoned by a disgruntled chambermaid, a young girl about her own age. It had seemed strange at the time; the girl was simple-minded and had gone about her duties in quiet solitude, never seeming the type that could plot murder—especially not Istvan's. Yet she had. Irrefutable proof had been found on her person in the form of a vile of poison, and a most impressively deadly one at that. Despite the girl's pleas of innocence, she'd been executed for her crime.

Crime. Sabina gave a small laugh. *I'll be forever in the poor girl's debt.*

Shaking off the remaining tremors, she forced herself to stand and get out of bed.

She needed to focus on facts—not on a dead girl and a dream. Istvan's murder had saved her life. *That* was undeniable. Her brute of a husband had become increasingly cruel and abusive in the time leading up to his death, and Sabina hadn't forgotten the days she'd spent in bed unable to move after one of his attacks. It had been like living in prison with only a malicious jailer for company. Day after day and month after month she'd endured his abuse, unable to attend social events or travel to town or even write a letter to her mother. Yes, everything was better with Istvan dead.

Except the dreams.

The setting of her dream changed frequently, but the progress was always the same. Although they had now healed completely, the scars on her back, remnants of the wounds inflicted by Istvan during his many rages, would begin to itch and tingle. Like the vines on the outer walls of the castle, the scars would pulsate with new life, growing, inching down her back and around her torso, enveloping her body in a hideous cocoon. The creeping tendrils would spread upwards towards her face. Growing thick and red, the pulsing veins would crisscross her once beautiful features, twisting and distorting them beyond recognition. She became a nightmarish hag, a caricature of the monsters conjured up to scare wayward children. She would begin to scream, mindlessly. Then she would wake.

At first the dream had been intermittent, tormenting her only when she was troubled or worried. Now the dream came every night, and with each repetition it became more vivid and she more hideous. The skin on her face, now obliterated by whip-like scars, sagged and withered. Her eyes shrank into hollowed sockets. Tiny tendrils extended from the corners of her eyes, folding over her pupils until she could see nothing but darkness.

Sabina shuddered anew, the horrors of sleep reawakened in her memory. She whimpered. If only Xenia were there to comfort her.

She felt a little of the darkness recede as she thought about her friend, the mysterious Roma who had become her companion and confidante over the past year. Xenia emanated raw power, a heady kind of tonic that Sabina craved. She was a magnetic person physically too, a tall dark beauty with mesmerizing green eyes, and Sabina had been drawn to her like a moth to flame. She had turned to her for help after some of Istvan's most brutal beatings and Xenia had never failed to comfort her. Without Xenia, Sabina wasn't sure that she would have survived.

As if by magic, Sabina looked up and saw the dark woman standing by the door, a concerned look in her eyes.

"Sabina my dear, is it the dream again?" The woman's voice was deep and mellifluous.

Sabina nodded, reaching out her hands to her friend. "Oh Xenia, what am I to do? I cannot bear to wake another night with these images in my mind."

Xenia grasped Sabina's hands tightly in her own and led her to a chair, gently forcing her to sit down. Then, still holding her hands, Xenia knelt in front of her. "Then don't. Your suffering should have ended with Istvan, not continued like this." She tucked a long blonde strand of hair behind Sabina's ear. "Have you been taking the sleeping potion I brewed for you? I've known it to work wonders."

Sabina trembled, her face paler than usual in its sorrow. "It isn't helping. And sometimes when I wake up and look in the mirror, I see myself as I am in the dream- a hideous crone is the reflection staring back at me!" She swallowed convulsively. "Xenia, I know you have power. Please, I am beseeching you- please help me."

The dark woman hesitated, then released Sabina's hands. She looked down at the floor. "There is something we may try, something much more effective. Not only could this potion banish your dreams, but...Well, it could enhance your beauty indefinitely."

Sabina's expression was one of confusion and hope, a strange mixture of emotion that made her look oddly child-like. "What?"

Xenia met her gaze and held it. "You heard me. This potion has the ability to keep time at bay; it has the power to keep you young. Youthful. But..." Her voice trailed off.

Sabina was breathing rapidly, a flush appearing on her cheeks. "Make it for me. Please, Xenia. I don't care the cost, just brew it."

"My sweet Sabina, you are so naive...you must at least *know* of the cost. Shall I tell you what it is?"

Sabina only stared at her, lost in the possibilities Xenia had presented her with.

Xenia continued, "The cost is a crime. This potion requires blood. Human blood. Virgin blood." Her expression clouded over, concealing her emotions. "What do you think of that?"

Sabina paled anew. "Human blood? You mean we have to...to *kill* someone to make this potion?"

Xenia cocked an eyebrow and appraised her friend with an unfathomable expression. "That is a blunt way of putting it, but yes. We must *kill* someone." Suddenly full of terrible intensity, she leaned forward and gripped Sabina's shoulders. "Tell me though: would it not be worth it? Would it not be a small price to pay for eternal youth and happiness? Not every life is important, it's true. But yours, Sabina, yours is. Fate has presented you with this opportunity, just as fate brought me to you. Do you not trust me, Sabina? I implore you to do so. I can give you everything you've ever wanted and take away all of your pain." Relaxing slightly, she let go of Sabina's shoulders and tipped her chin up. "Now that you know the cost, what do you think?"

Sabina was silent for a long time, held fast by Xenia's direct stare. For a moment it seemed as though time itself stood still, as if nothing besides the two of them existed.

Somewhere in the back of her mind, Sabina heard a small voice shouting at her, willing her not to listen to Xenia's dark reason. But it was too small a voice to make a difference. Xenia's logic made sense. *What is one life worth? Aren't some worth more than others? Aren't I worth more?*

I am. The words filled her mind and she believed them. Xenia said she was important, and so she was. After all, she had suffered so much at the hands of her husband. She was entitled to happiness.

"I cannot put a cost on my life," she said, surprised at how strong her own voice sounded. Suddenly, the dream seemed as far away as Istvan and his abuse.

Xenia smiled and stood up. Slowly and gently, she bent down and kissed Sabina's forehead. "And so we begin," she whispered.

Then she turned and walked out of Sabina's room, her footsteps silent as she went. Sabina watched her friend's back as she left, unaware of the expression that Xenia now wore.

It was one of triumph.

CHAPTER 7

The dream always began the same: the field of planted corn whispering songs on the warm breeze, the smell of earth and the lingering fragrance of fertilizer that was strangely inoffensive and almost comforting—the smell of home.

As he breathed in the memory, the scene unfolded in his mind. He could see the length of the long dirt road bordered by the weather-beaten fence that he had been assigned to paint to 'develop his work ethic', as his father had been prone to say. Beyond that lay the seemingly endless field of crops and pastures that bordered his family home from their nearest neighbor. It was late afternoon and the sun hung in the sky like an orange ball.

Perhaps the strangest part of the dream was the sense that he was different, physically. His body felt small—compact and younger. His limbs felt gangly and awkward as they had before maturity had turned him into a man. He felt good and whole. Happy.

As always, he was lying in the tall grass, looking at a brilliant azure sky punctuated by an assortment of cumulous clouds. As he pondered the impossibility of it all, a laugh like a musical note ringing in his ear told him that she was with him once more...

The young girl was sprawled next to him in the grass. Her blonde curls shone like a halo around her head, radiating like the light of the sun itself.

"Simon! See...that one there...it's an elephant! Can you see the giant trunk?"

"That's not an elephant, silly; it's too thin to be one. It's clearly a giraffe. Haven't you ever seen a picture of an elephant?"

"Yes, I have! Anyway, if I say it's an elephant, then it's an elephant. For all you know, Simon, he's on a diet." She stood, brushing the loose grass off her jeans and jacket. She closed her eyes and turned her face upwards to the sun, basking in the warmth of the Indian summer. "Mother said we had to be back at the house an hour before supper to help set table. That leaves us an hour or two to explore the old pasture beyond Mr. Neville's shack, so let's go already!"

"Wait...!" Simon pleaded, but she was already gone, the trail of her long hair just visible through the tall stalks of corn.

The scene shifted.

The sun was dropping from the sky. The red streaks and glorious hues of the sunset had lost their usual appeal and were now more like grasping fingers, rending light from the encroaching shadows. The wind was whipping at his back and the air was cold.

He was standing on top of a hill and could see the far edge of the property, which sloped slightly downhill to a line of trees. The little girl was beckoning to him as she started toward the tree line and the dilapidated shack.

A sharp, splintering sound rent the air, and, in the span of a heartbeat, the girl vanished. Heart pounding, he raced over the distance between his location and hers. With each step, his breath grew shallower, but he never slowed. He couldn't. He had to—

Stumbling over a collection of loose stones, he came to a sudden halt, teetering over empty space, his knees buckling as he came to understand what had happened.

The black pit yawned before him, beckoning.

Jump, *it tempted him.* Do something.

But he was paralyzed.

Then, from deep, deep down, her voice:

"Help me, Simon! Please! I'm so scared! The water's so cold. Simon, help me! So scared… Pleeeeease."

He promised her he would. He vowed it. Then he ran.

This time he'd get help, this time would be different, this time…

He toppled over the tree limb like he always did, the fall as inevitable as the rest of it. There was a sharp pain that filled his head, the sound of rushing water, and the feeling of falling as his hands clawed at empty air.

His eyes opened to the night sky.

He could hear the voices of the farmhands as they shouted to one another.

The girl, the girl, the girl…

He dragged himself up and lurched toward the light of the lanterns. As he neared, he saw her: wrapped in a blanket, her beautiful long hair hanging wet and dark from under its hem, dirt and debris caught in the blonde tangles. Her arms dangled lifelessly, and her skin was grey.

Tears burned his cheeks as he began to sob. "It should have been me," he chanted, pleaded. "It should have been me. It should have been me…"

The dead girl lifted the blanket and turned her head to him. Her eyes were open, cloudy in death, soulless. Her face twisted, her features flooding with condemnation from beyond the grave.

"Yes, Simon," her corpse spat in hatred. "It should have been you! You promised you would help me. You promised it would be okay. You promised! You promised! YOU PROMISED!"

"No!"

Simon woke up gasping, tangled in damp sheets. His eyes were blurry with tears and sweat. Wiping his face with his shirt, Simon no longer felt as young as he did in the dream. He felt every bit his age—weathered, old, and very tired.

The dream that had haunted his teenage years and countless nights after that had reentered his life in a vengeful way, bringing with it all of the memories that were seared forever into the fabric of his mind. Its recurrence had happened on and off over the years, sometimes for a particular reason, sometimes for seemingly no reason at all.

Of course, he had a good guess as to why it had returned this time.

Râsnov.

He'd known about the castle's famed ancient well – it was his job to know the history on all the castles they were featuring – but he had naively thought that he was past being affected by such things. Besides, the story had little in common with his own: according to legend, Turkish prisoners had dug the well after being promised freedom upon its completion. They worked on digging it for seventeen years, but contrary to the promise, they were executed when it was done, cursed forever to haunt the castle.

It was a different tragedy entirely than the one that had befallen his sister.

Apparently, though, there was enough similarity between the two to dredge up Simon's guilt. He shouldn't have been surprised; the guilt was always there, always present, and apparently, even the weakest catalyst had the power to trigger a response in him.

With a weary sigh, Simon stood and walked out of his room, taking a seat at the kitchen counter in their rented apartment. He had no idea how long he'd been sitting there, staring into space, when a voice broke the silence.

"Brody? You're up early. Everything okay?"

Simon turned to see Renee walking over to the counter, fully dressed.

He glanced at the clock. "I should ask you the same; it's only five o'clock. How long have you been up?"

She sat down on the stool next to his. "I couldn't sleep. Somebody was arguing outside my window, and while Lou can sleep through anything, I can't. I just decided to start my day a little early, you know, get some editing done so I can send an update to Cody." She eyed him closely. "But I don't think that's why you're up. Is this because of yesterday?"

Simon grimaced. The previous day he had forced himself to document the legend of the well and translate the crude inscriptions on its surface, fighting hard to keep his past out of his work. But to no avail. He had become increasingly agitated during the afternoon, finally snapping at

Renee and Christer. Renee, knowing the source of Simon's angst, casually brushed the incident off. Christer Malin had been less understanding.

Determined to establish a positive working relationship with the Swede after the revelations of the previous evening, Simon had sought him out at the end of the day and offered an apology and invite to a pub. Over a few well-nursed beers, Simon ended up telling Christer his sad tale and admitted to the heavy burden of guilt that he had carried for so many years. Christer had been quiet as Simon related his childhood experience, but when Simon was finished, the big man had simply patted him on the back and told him that there were no hard feelings. It had felt strangely good to tell Christer about his sister, maybe because Christer too knew what it was to lose someone.

Still, opening up to Christer hadn't made the dreams go away.

"I've been dreaming about Gretchen again," he admitted.

Renee's eyes filled with compassion, but she stayed silent, sensing that he needed to tell her more.

Simon exhaled like a man who had been holding his breath for far too long. "It was my fault, you know," he went on quietly. "That's why it haunts me."

"Simon." Renee's voice was gentle. "You were just a kid."

"Age isn't an excuse," he said. He met her gaze, suddenly filled with the need to tell her the rest. "I was an awkward, clumsy boy," he continued, "not all that different from the current version you see now. The day it happened...it was perhaps the one time in my life that I needed to be capable, needed to act, and I failed miserably. And Gretchen paid the price for my ineptitude. All I had to do was run and get help, and I couldn't even do that. My sister died, alone and cold, suffocating slowly in a watery, dark well." His voice cracked, betraying the weight of the guilt he'd carried for so many years. "How can I ever forgive myself, Renee? How could anyone?"

"Oh, Simon." Her expression was pained. "I can't even imagine how awful it must have been to go through that. And then to relive it in your dreams..." She shuddered. "No one deserves to endure that. But Simon— you are not to blame for Gretchen's death; it wasn't your fault."

Simon shook his head. I don't know if I will ever stop blaming myself." He gave a mirthless laugh. "I don't know if I ever should stop blaming myself."

Without answering, Renee reached over and wrapped her arms around him, drawing him close in a fierce hug. She held him like that for a time before releasing him.

It took Simon some time to meet her gaze, but when he did, he saw the saddest smile on her face—full of grief and empathy.

"I think I understand the guilt that plagues you," she said. "At least a little. After our mom died, Lou had a hell of a time coming to terms with her death. And I was so wrapped up in my own grief that I didn't notice just how dark a place she was in. And then later, when I knew exactly how bad it could get, I still didn't pay enough attention, and she nearly died because of it." She paused. "I'm lucky, so lucky, because I got a second chance with Lou, a chance to make sure I don't fail as a sister. You never had that opportunity, and it's not fair." Her eyes softened. "But what happened to your sister – no matter how guilty you might feel – was not a result of your neglect or indifference. You tried, Simon, and sometimes that's all we can do."

The lump in Simon's throat was so large by this time that he could not articulate words. He merely nodded and managed a thin smile.

Renee kissed him on the cheek before rising. "You okay if I go back to my room and do some editing? Because I'm happy to stay if you need me to. I could make us some coffee, see if there's enough in the cupboards to whip up some carb-filled comfort food..."

Simon shook his head. "I'll be fine. Thank you, though, Renee. For everything."

"Okay." Her lips tilted up. "By the way, Brody, I don't think you're awkward. You're one of the most sensitive, caring men I know. I'm glad to call you my friend."

Simon watched her walk back to her room, his heart thudding like a drum in his chest, his emotions running unchecked. His eyes were moist, not from the guilt of his sister's death, but now from a sense of loss and longing for something that could never be. Renee was beautiful—inside and out. She didn't think that she was as empathetic as her sister, but she was wrong. She was a true and good friend, and if there were anything she ever needed, Simon vowed that he would be there for her.

He sighed. Ian was a lucky man.

Refusing to dwell on such thoughts any longer, Simon booted up his laptop. As he waited for it to load, he gazed out the window and the steady drizzle falling in the fog of the early morning. Renee, Ian, and Lou had wanted to return to Râsnov later that day to take some wide-angle shots from the town looking up at the fortress, not wanting to omit the impressive hillside panorama from their pictures. Judging from the rainy weather, though, they weren't going to get that opportunity today.

Regaining a modicum of composure and calm, he decided to turn his attention to a few local legends he had stumbled across involving a documented seventeenth century vampire case in a small nearby hamlet. There was no better distraction on a rainy morning than getting lost in a few scary folktales.

Or a better way to banish Renee from his thoughts.

CHAPTER 8

Romania, Present Day

The old cemetery was almost entirely empty. The worn, makeshift headstones were moldy and the names they bore faded, the memories of the people at rest below them all but gone too.

The only visitor who broke the silence of the place was a lone woman, her long curly hair wrapped in a black scarf. She was kneeling beside one of two fresh graves with a bouquet of wildflowers in her hands. She had picked them herself and tied them with twine, and now she laid them gently on the newly turned plot at the base of the headstone. Her tears wet the stone as she leaned forward to kiss it, as she pressed her lips against the name engraved on its surface. Her eyes were glassy when she pulled back. "Hello, Irina," she whispered, her voice breaking. She gave in to her grief then, letting herself feel all of the pain she had bottled up ever since she'd gotten the news of her sister's death two weeks earlier. Sobs shook her body, raw and painful, and she sank into the grass beside the grave. She had never known sorrow like this; nothing had ever even come close. This weighed her down in spirit *and* body, and for a long span of minutes, she couldn't free herself from its immensity. All she could do was bear it, endure it.

Some time later, she at last found her voice. "You would have been nineteen today," she said, sitting back on her heels. It didn't matter that they had been ten years apart in age; she and her younger sister had been as close as any two siblings could be. She ran a finger over the flowers. "I brought these for you. Do you remember when we used to pick them together? You always told me these purple ones were your favorite, that someday you would have them in the bouquet at your wedding." She squeezed her eyes shut against another wave of tears, but they fell down her cheeks anyway. She took a moment to compose herself and then continued on in the same thin, quiet voice. "I miss you, little sister," she murmured. "And I am so sorry that I wasn't there to protect you from them."

She rose then, picking herself up shakily. There was grass and dirt on her long skirt, but she did nothing to clear it away. A look of steely determination crossed her face as she stared down at her dead sister's resting place. "I am sorry that I couldn't protect you," she repeated. "But I will avenge you. I promise." Her eyes hardened as she looked off into the distant mountains. "I promise."

Ferka looked up from where he was sitting as Chalea burst into his tent, sighing wearily at her confrontational posture. "Chalea, do come in," he greeted her unnecessarily. As if he could keep her out.

"We need to talk, Ferka." Her tone was imperious. She threw a newspaper clipping down in front of him, the paper crumpled from where she had been clutching it. She gestured at the article on the bottom of the page. "There are more reports, as I suspected there would be. My sister and Fane were only the first. An elderly gentleman went missing last week, and another child has disappeared." Her lips tightened. "Do you still believe it was an accident? That these are all coincidences?" She crossed her arms over her chest, daring him to deny it. "You are our leader, Ferka. You have to do something!"

He stood. "Don't raise your voice; others might hear."

"Let them." Her green eyes blazed at him.

"They will hear when I want them to hear." His tone was authoritative. He didn't like using his position to subdue others, but Chalea sometimes needed to be reminded of who was in command. She was invaluable and often right about things, but she still had to answer to him, whether she wanted to or not.

He waited to speak until she had calmed down. "The disappearances and murders are not coincidences; I would never insinuate that they were. It would be a disservice to Irina's memory to even suggest it."

Chalea flinched when he said her sister's name. "I'm glad you feel that way," she said. "I..." She leaned in closer, lowering her voice. "I sense them, Ferka. I have been reaching out for weeks now. It is hazy and unclear, but I know it to be true. They are here, in Romania. I would stake my life on it."

The older man nodded. "I believe you. But their location...?" He trailed off, hoping that she would be able to give him more to go on.

Her shoulders hunched forward in defeat. "I do not know; it is all too vague. I'm sorry." She looked up, her green eyes piercing him. "But we cannot sit idly by because of my failings, Ferka. More will die."

"We will begin searching. I will organize two small scouting parties. Before they leave, give them any insight you have, no matter how trivial. Sometimes one detail is all we need." He gripped her shoulders, squeezing them reassuringly. "If they are back, we will find them. They cannot hide forever."

CHAPTER 9

The weather's supposed to be nice tomorrow, so with any luck we should be able to wrap up at Râsnov." Renee fought to be heard over the other late-night patrons, mostly working men sharing drinks and jokes.

They were in the historical district of Brasov, stopping for drinks before heading back to their apartment. Seated at a table in the back of a crowded bar, the five were happy to rest their sore feet for a while.

The persistent rain had cut short their productivity for the day. After a morning spent discussing the truth and myth behind various chilling supernatural cases, the group had toured around Brasov well into the evening, visiting Council Hall, the Black Church, and a myriad of other historical and note-worthy places. They even visited Rope Street, a curious cut-through only four feet wide that was intended for use by firefighters and was now marked as Europe's narrowest street.

And Lou had been glad for the diversion. When they'd been cooped up in the apartment that morning, she had grown weary of listening to Ian, Renee, and Simon arguing about the science behind a dead man's fingernails growing and the legitimacy of a few vampire sightings. She had taken her paints out to the balcony to get away, only to have her peace of mind broken by Christer.

"Sorry to interrupt, but I thought you might want a jacket. The weather's not exactly warm and you've been out here a long time."

"Honestly? I didn't even realize how cold it was."

"I know the feeling. When you're completely absorbed in something, it's easy to ignore all of the peripheral things."

"Yeah. Thanks for the jacket."

"That's going to be an amazing watercolor when you're done; I'm already taken in by it. Your blending of colors really brings it to life."

"Thanks, but it's not finished. And it's not that good."

"It's better than mine would have been."

"You paint?"

"I'm not sure other people would describe what I do as 'painting', but yeah, a little. Just when inspiration strikes, which it hasn't anytime recently. But this...you've got the bones of something great here, Lou."

"You're just being nice."

"As much as I like to flatter pretty women, I'm being genuine here. I didn't mean to embarrass you, but you shouldn't hide your talents. It's okay to believe in your own merits."

"You know, Christer, if being a tour guide doesn't work out for you, you have the potential to be a great life coach."

"Lou, I'm not patronizing you. I'm just being honest. I think you are quite something..."

Lou stretched in her seat, forcing herself to return to the present. Renee caught her eye, obviously having noticed her daydreaming, but Lou just shook her head. *Forget about it, Sis.*

She was probably just imagining the little flirtations with Christer, looking for a distraction to keep her mind from returning to Jeremy Shit-for-Brains Paxton. Christer was attractive and kind of mysterious, and she was vulnerable after last month's break-up. There was nothing else to it.

"...Yup, and then we can move on to Bran Castle," Ian was saying when she tuned back in. "Or 'Mr. Fang's Castle', as you put it, Lou."

Lou smiled. "Indeed."

"Bran Castle is going to be one of the highlights of our spread; the stories associated with it, as well as its gothic appearance, all draw interest to its infamy. It's going to be really fun to bring that out; we'll get to

capture a place that has served as a muse to literary minds for decades."
Renee gestured with her hands emphatically, her enthusiasm spreading to
the others.

"Yeah, Bran's the one I've really been wanting to shoot," Ian agreed.

Simon turned to Christer, who was sitting on his left. "Have you been
to Bran Castle before?"

The blond man didn't appear to hear the question. His attention was
riveted to the table beside theirs, where a group of burly men were
conversing animatedly. The members of the red-nosed, bearded party
were focused on one particularly large man. Their stout beers all rested on
the table, momentarily forgotten as they listened with rapt attention to the
speaker's voice.

Christer seemed to be doing the same.

"Christer?" Lou asked.

"Sorry?" He answered without turning his head from the neighboring
table. Then, he forced himself to rejoin his own group, turning back slowly,
his eyes trailing behind, lingering on the burly man. "What did you say?"

Simon tried again. "I was just wondering if you'd ever been to Bran
Castle. Have you?"

Again, Christer's attention shifted away. "No." Then, unabashedly, he
added, "Hold on a minute. I want to hear the rest of this story." He nodded
towards the speaking man.

The others exchanged confused glances, wondering at the reason for
Christer's blatant eavesdropping.

A minute later he turned back to them, a glimmer of excitement in his
eyes. "That man over there has been sharing quite the story with his
companions. Listen to this: he was on a hunting trip last week and he'd
tailed a big buck. He had it in his sights when it bolted. He pursued, not
wanting to lose his prize. At the edge of a clearing, it stopped and faced
him. He was going to shoot it until he realized where he was: 'The Castle',"
Christer quoted with his fingers. "Apparently he was so terrified that he
backed away and went home without any catch at all."

He looked around the table. "I don't think he's referring to Râsnov or
Bran; his description of the woods doesn't match either of their

surroundings. Which means, I'm assuming, that there is another castle somewhere nearby."

Simon frowned, his eyebrows knitting together beneath his cap. "That's quite impossible. I've done extensive research of the Romanian castles and fortresses and I am positive that there are only two here in Brasov."

Christer nodded quickly. "That's what I've always thought too. But what if there is something here that's undocumented?" He turned to the photographers. "Want me to ask?"

They all concurred, their curiosity aroused.

Christer stood up and moved to the men's table, holding out his hand to the man who had been speaking. He exchanged a few words with him, motioning to the group from *Itinera* a few times. A moment later Christer nodded in response to something the man had said and flashed a smile, leading him back to their table and ushering him into a seat.

The man looked ridiculously large in comparison to Simon, who was sitting next to him. He was the epitome of the rustic man: his sleeves were rolled up to expose knotted, thick veins and his skin was weathered and lined from years of outside labor. His eyes were small and black, their color matching that of his tangled beard.

He spoke to them in Romanian, Christer translating.

"I explained that you were Americans – sorry Simon – working for a travel magazine and currently in Romania on assignment photographing castles. I said that I overheard him make mention of a castle and asked if he could share some information about it. His name's Karl."

Karl gave them a smile, his beard curving up with his lips.

They introduced themselves and shook hands with him. Then he began speaking.

Christer let him go on for a time, then translated. "The castle he happened upon in the woods is called Solovastru Castle. It's off the main roads, set back and secluded; most locals don't venture there, and most travelers don't even know about it."

Karl's voice rose in a pitch as he continued, his beady eyes growing larger.

Christer continued, "Solovastru, he says, is a cursed place. The ghosts of the original family are said to keep watch over their property still. No one who has any sense goes there—the omens are too bad." He paused, trying to catch up with Karl. "Apparently, there have been deaths associated with the castle over the centuries. A lot of deaths. The most recent occurred just over fifty years ago. A man went mad and killed his wife, then hanged himself from the castle walls."

The listeners flinched a little at this revelation, their imaginations conjuring up an unwanted mental picture.

Karl put his beefy forearms on the table and looked at each of them. Clearly, the man was a consummate storyteller, gifted with the ability to infuse drama into his tales. Despite the language barrier, the group could easily see that. They would have been unsurprised to learn that Karl's reputation as the local raconteur preceded him.

Christer translated, "He says that ghosts aren't the only ones that haunt Solovastru. There have been witness accounts of strange creatures wandering the woods at night, creatures that lurk in the shadows. Almost every person that has seen one of these creatures has disappeared without a trace. A few of the lucky ones survived to tell the tale, but fate came for them in time too."

Karl lifted a finger in warning. "You must not to go there," he said in English. "Must not."

Christer asked him a question in Romanian, waited for a reply and then turned to the others. "He said that we should stay away—that going there will be the death of us."

Renee whispered, "Christer, this is such an amazing opportunity. We're not superstitious. Just...see if you can find out how to get there."

Christer turned back to Karl, exchanged a few words with him. Karl shook his head, his beard shaking. His meaty hands clenched into fists on the table.

"He says that we're foolish to try, that we should respect the dead and leave them in peace."

Renee looked at Ian, a silent thought passing between them.

"Renee's right," Ian said. "This mystery castle would be an amazing wildcard in our shoot. We've got to get directions from him."

Christer tried again. This time, Karl sighed. He ran a hand through his tangled beard and shook his head sadly. Turning to Christer, he began speaking, gesturing occasionally with his hands.

Christer clapped the big man on the back and thanked him, then went up to the bartender and ordered him a beer. Karl walked back to his own table and sat down, giving the group only a terse nod as he left.

When Christer returned, he clasped his hands in front of him on the table. "Well, I got us directions. They're pretty vague, probably because he doesn't want us to find it. But I've worked in these woods and mountains for a fairly long time; from his description, I have a good idea of the castle's location. We should be able to find it without trouble."

"I'll try and look for some background tonight when we get back to the apartment," Simon said. "See if I am able to shed any light on our enigmatic castle."

"This is going to be amazing." Renee spoke the words in a fast blur. "Just think: we're going to have footage of a never-before documented castle, rumored to be cursed and haunted. It's like the Kobe beef of castle folklore."

Ian and Lou shared her enthusiasm.

"So, are we postponing our wrap-up at Râsnov?" Ian asked.

The others nodded.

"Let's go tomorrow," Renee said. "We'll find this castle, shoot it, and be back on schedule the next day. It's going to be one worthwhile detour."

Flagging down a waiter, Christer ordered them all another round of drinks. "I'll sketch a rough map tonight so that we don't have any trouble tomorrow." He laughed. "Talk about picking the right bar to sit down in."

Simon raised his mug. "To spontaneity: may it yield us a successful discovery."

Smiling all around, they clanged their mugs together, happy at the thrill of an adventure.

From the neighboring table, Karl watched the group surreptitiously, ignoring the drunkards at his own table. Frowning, he downed the rest of his free drink and tried to ignore the voice inside his head yelling at him for speaking to the Americans.

He wished that he hadn't given them directions.

Some things were better left lost.

Romania, 1428 A.D.

The woods surrounding Solovastru castle were quiet, the air still and warm on the summer night. Only the occasional hoot of an owl and tread of a deer broke the silence. All seemed peaceful.

In the lower regions of the castle, however, all was not peaceful. The dungeons were damp and dank, the air thick with a cloying mustiness that overran the senses. A few rats scurried along the walls, grotesque creatures with raised haunches and yellow teeth. They belonged to the night and it served them well.

As quickly as they had appeared, the overlarge rodents scampered away, hiding themselves in holes and dark corners. Approaching footsteps were always a warning alarm for them, and by the time the two women walked by and the light from their torches illuminated the stone walls, all of the rats were gone.

"I don't like it down here, Xenia. It reeks of death."

Her companion gave a mirthless laugh. "So it does. Come now, Sabina, keep up with me."

The taller woman stopped suddenly, holding Sabina back with her arm. "Here we are," she said. "Go fasten your torch to the wall. I'll be back in a moment."

Sabina did as she was bid, her hands shaking slightly. When Xenia had suggested that she participate more fully in their project, she'd thought it was a good idea. But now, standing in the dungeon at night, the idea had lost some of its appeal.

She was entertaining the thought of running back up the stairs and out of the dungeons when she heard the whimpering. She stopped breathing instantly, her whole body frozen. Something coiled in her stomach- fear perhaps- and sweat broke out on her forehead.

Xenia reentered the large room, leading three young, malnourished girls in her wake, each chained to each other by the waists and hands. All three were blindfolded and gagged, their dresses soiled. Sabina didn't know how long they'd been in the dungeons, but judging by their gaunt appearance, it must have been some time.

Xenia turned to them briefly and whispered something too low for Sabina to hear. As she straightened and walked towards the wall to fasten her torch, the three girls remained where she'd left them, still whimpering but standing still.

The torch hitched securely, Xenia at last turned towards Sabina. Walking purposely towards her, Xenia reached out her hand.

At first, Sabina didn't think her friend was holding anything, but when she looked more closely, she saw the knife, its sharpened blade gleaming with wicked intent. She shied away instinctually from the weapon.

Xenia held it out to her. "You have nothing to fear from this; I promise. I think you will feel something quite different from fear when it's in your possession."

Not wanting to disappoint the dark woman, Sabina took the proffered blade and held it up in front of her. Gingerly, she ran a finger down its edge. Startled suddenly by the sound of a rat, she jumped and pricked her finger. Blood instantly budded to the surface.

As Sabina eyed the ruby liquid, her pupils dilated with sudden desire. Her blood was beautiful, a deep yet vivid red that brought tears to her eyes.

"Beautiful, isn't it? Blood is a living substance, Sabina, the essence of human beings. Tell me: have you ever seen a more perfect crimson?" Xenia's voice was deep and silky, and Sabina was entranced by her words. "I'm sure you haven't. Only blood- *human* blood- has this quality of perfection." She gestured to the chained girls. "These girls are merely packages, merely shells that need to be broken to get at the perfection within. Their blood is what lives; they are simply breathing husks."

She touched Sabina's face tenderly. "With this weapon, you have the power to unleash their beauty and set free their blood. Don't you feel the warmth radiating from it? It's calling to you like a lover... a lover that desires to feel flesh, to *cut* flesh. Deeply. Don't deny its lust. *Listen*. Listen and act."

Xenia gently pushed her forward and Sabina walked towards the girls, her eyes fixed on them. Xenia withdrew a key from an unseen pocket of her clothes and unchained the girl closest to Sabina. Then she stepped back and waited. "Make her bleed," she whispered.

A crazed squeal erupted from Sabina's throat and she lunged forward, slashing with her knife. The blade was so sharp that for a second it seemed as though she'd missed the girl completely. Sabina breathed raggedly and waited, her eyes wide, the knife clutched tightly in her right hand, blood dripping from its tip.

Then the girl sank to her knees, a choker of red encircling her neck. She tried to scream, but her air had been cut off and the gag was still in place. She jerked back and forth, asphyxiating in silent agony as her own blood washed over her, painting her dress with red streaks. A few moments later she collapsed and lay still, blood still running from the wound.

Slowly, Sabina turned towards Xenia. Her friend and mentor was staring back at her, her expression enigmatic. When she spoke, her voice was cautious, guarded. "Sabina..."

"Look what I've done, Xenia. *Look*. I did this." She twirled around once, laughing gaily, blood from the knife spattering the ground as she turned. "Me! A murderess! Oh Xenia, imagine what we can do!" Her laughter filled the cavernous dungeon with an otherworldly eeriness, and when it ceased echoing, not even the distant sounds of the rats were detectable.

Xenia's lips twisted upwards into a smile, her eyes fierce. She had wanted- hoped- that Sabina would enjoy the act of killing, but never had she dreamed that the primal act would infuse her with such vitality.

Sabina was radiant.

She had come to the dungeons the widowed wife of an abusive husband, but that skin was now shed. The woman who turned towards the two remaining girls, helpless and cowering in fear, the woman who raised the already gore-stained weapon another time, the woman that Xenia was staring at with a look of adoration- she was no longer that girl. She was the mistress of Solovastru castle.

Not even the rats would dare cross her path.

CHAPTER 10

You're sure those directions are right? I feel like we've been driving off road for a while." Lou leaned forward, poking her head into the front seat.

Christer shook his head. "I know it feels that way, but I'm positive this is right. I mean, if this castle were on any of the frequented trails, more people would know about it. It makes sense that it would be a ways back into the forest."

Lou leaned back and looked out at the window, gripping the seat in front of her as the car drove on the uneven terrain.

They'd left the main trail road about four miles back, turning onto one of the lengthier, less traveled trail routes in the area that wove its way up into the Carpathian Mountains. From there, Christer had navigated them still deeper into the woods, branching off from that trail onto their present road, a narrow, overgrown trail that clearly wasn't meant for automobile traffic. The car was working hard, crunching over leaves, rocks, and branches, jostling the passengers.

Christer cut the engine. "I don't think we can go much farther by car; we don't want to risk getting stuck or breaking down out here. We need to walk the rest of the way, which-" he looked down at his hand-drawn map, "- shouldn't be more than a few miles."

Renee already had her door open. "All right. I could use some air anyway. I was feeling a little nauseated; bumpy rides aren't my thing."

Ian clambered out behind her, stretching his arms. He went to the trunk and fished around for his smallest SLR camera, fastening it to a neck strap and putting it on. He swung a small drawstring bag over his shoulder, loaded with extra zoom lenses.

He smiled at his girlfriend. "You look pale...did you see a spider or something?"

Renee walked over and punched him hard in the arm, grimacing. "Jackass. You know I get carsick."

They packed a small amount of gear, leaving all of the unmanageable larger equipment in the trunk. Christer locked the doors, more of a reflex action than anything else. The chances of someone else happening upon their car this deep in the woods were slim.

Christer led the way, weaving a path through the dense trees. The light overhead was faint, the leafy ceiling blocking most of the sun from reaching the forest floor. They walked for the better part of an hour, the scenery remaining unchanged. All around them was omnipresent green, a mix of tall tree trunks and leafy branches. Roots, tangled and intertwined, made the woody obstacle course difficult to navigate, causing them to stumble more than once. As they continued to hike, the only discernible difference was the wildness of the undergrowth; far from the frequented hiking trails, nature had reclaimed the ground with a vengeance.

Suddenly Christer stopped. Simon, following closest, nearly ran into him. "What is it?" His breathing was labored, evidence of his fatigue from the trek.

Christer spoke in a low voice as the others reached him. "Look. About twenty or so feet away, up in that tree," he said, gesturing. "Do you see them?" He started to move closer, the others doing the same.

When they stood only a few paces away from where Christer had first gestured, they all knew immediately to what he had been referring.

Something was hanging from the lower branches of a large tree.

"Are they crosses?" Lou asked.

Simon nodded. "I believe so. Handmade."

A row of them was strung from the branches, suspended in the air. They were wooden and imperfect, with rough edges and gnarled surfaces.

They varied in shade and size, clearly the work of different hands. Still, their basic shapes were the same.

Lou felt goosebumps rising, a coldness filling her limbs. There was no breeze this deep in the woods, so the makeshift crosses hung still in the air, unmoving. The stagnancy of the sight made her uneasy. *The omen is bad...* Is this what the Hungarian woman on the train had read in her cards? As she looked at the crosses hanging there like morbid marionettes, Lou couldn't convince herself that they were harbingers of anything good. Maybe the old woman had been right to warn her...

"It looks as if Karl wasn't the only one afraid of this area," Christer commented.

Renee turned towards Simon. "What do you think, Brody? Why are these crosses here?"

"Crosses are common talismans to ward off evil; they were a very prevalent symbol of protection in Eastern Europe, especially in the Middle Ages. If I had to venture a guess, I'd say that our castle had a very infamous reputation in its day."

"So it's close then, right?" Ian asked, his eyes scanning the vicinity for a break in the trees.

"It should be. These talismans wouldn't have been placed randomly in the woods— it's why they've been strung up on such a prominent tree. I'm sure the castle is very nearby."

The group fell quiet, spreading out and searching the woods, their depleting energy levels boosted by Simon's prediction.

"And here we are," Ian said, his voice carrying to the others. "I think I found a clearing." He stood at the edge of a cluster of trees, facing away towards a break in the woods.

Beyond the break was sun and grass, appearing like an oasis in a desert.

Their excitement outweighing their tiredness, the group made their way to the break, Renee half-running out in front, eager to see what lay beyond.

They all stopped when they reached the tree line, stepping out into the clearing with wide eyes.

In the midst of the grassy clearing stood the remains of a once-grand gothic castle, the edifice noticeably scarred by the work of time.

Its walls were stone, dark and molding in places. Pointed gothic arches held both the intact and decaying parts of the castle aloft, supporting the entire framework. Its towers rose steeply above the roof, and its flying buttresses cast long shadows on the ground, causing the facade to look harsh even in the pleasant afternoon light. A few molding gargoyles decorated the roof, protecting their masters of old from their immobile perches.

As Simon took in the castle and clearing, something caught his eye. He turned to look, and his heart nearly stopped.

For a second, a mere passing moment, he thought he saw a girl out of the corner of his eye, shimmering just at the edges of his periphery.

A blonde little girl.

Simon blinked, stumbling back a step.

What on earth...?

Ian gave him a questioning look, but Simon shook his head.

When he looked again, no one was there.

Hold it together, Simon.

"It looks like we've found the mysterious Solovastru Castle," Christer said, bringing him back into the moment.

No one was there, Simon. It was just a subconscious hiccup, he rationalized.

"Wow..." Renee mouthed the word. "This is amazing." She started moving forward, the others following her, Simon forcing himself to walk forward and forget about what he'd seen, or *thought* he'd seen.

Lou was the last to move, her feet seemingly rooted to the spot. She'd felt something as soon as she'd stepped into the clearing, a feeling she couldn't explain. It rose from deep inside her belly, almost like the sensation of butterflies. But not quite. The feeling tasted of uncertainty, of confusion.

For some reason, a small inner voice was urging her to turn around— turn around and walk away, back to the car, back to civilization, back to Philadelphia. The voice was urging her to leave.

Though she couldn't shake the feeling, she forced her feet to move, managing to walk after the others. There was no earthly basis for her uncertainty, and she wasn't about to let the others think that some scary stories and crude warnings had gotten the better of her.

"Well, what do you guys think? Was it worth the excursion?" Renee's hands were akimbo, her smile radiant. Nothing excited her more than a novel discovery.

"Well worth it," Ian said, his smile mirroring hers. One of the cameras was already in his hands, the lens cap having been shoved hastily into his jeans pocket. "I'm going to take some shots of the outside. I'll shoot as much as I can: the parts that stood the test of time and the parts that didn't. This castle's magnificent."

"So it is," Simon murmured, his eyes roaming over the arches, studying details.

He began walking around the castle, Christer accompanying him. Christer gave Lou a smile as he passed her.

Renee turned to her sister, her eyes alight. "Well, shall we take a look at the inside? See what we find?"

Lou nodded, squelching the wariness bubbling inside of her. "That is what we came here to do."

"Okay. I'm all for taking time to inspect something, but you've been staring at that same section of wall for almost five minutes. What's up?" Christer raised an eyebrow at Simon.

The Brit adjusted his baseball cap, revealing frown lines of perplexity beneath its brim. "I am...well, *confused*, I suppose," he said. He pointed to the right side of the tower he was studying, indicating a section about two-thirds of the way up its face. "See for yourself."

Christer scrutinized the spot, trying to determine what had so fixated his companion. Suddenly he stopped squinting, no longer ignorant.

In the area that Simon had pointed to there was a spattering of bricks. There was one larger section fully encased with them, and a few others located sporadically around them. They did not serve any apparent purpose, and they certainly weren't used as a kind of decoration. On top of their seemingly random location, the brick-laying job seemed botched at best; some of the bricks weren't even set properly, their sides jutting out from the wall with no effort made to conceal the mistakes.

"You've noticed the bricks, I see. Have you figured out the purpose yet?" Simon glanced at Christer before continuing. "The bricks that form the larger conglomerate have been placed inside what was once a window. In gothic archetypes such as this, large windows were very common. Stylistically, it is a very recognizable shape."

"Obviously the owners decided that it let in too much light," Christer scoffed. "It's a shame blinds didn't exist back when these were popular."

Simon rolled his eyes, gazing back up at the bricks. "Perhaps. But what do you think would possess someone of nobility – for only someone of importance would abide in such a place – to brick up a window that probably contained some beautiful stained glass work? And to do so in this poor manner?" Simon shook his head. "It is so strange."

As he looked once more up at the bricks, Christer found himself agreeing with Simon. What had been the motivation behind filling in the window?

It was very strange indeed.

"Renee! Come take a look at this."

Renee turned around and walked back down the long corridor towards her sister. Most of the outer wall had collapsed inward, and light was streaming in from the holes, illuminating the rubble-strewn floor.

"What's up?"

Lou laid a hand on the wall to her left and pushed. Almost immediately, a few of the bricks crumbled away, revealing an older surface beneath.

"I accidentally knocked one of these bricks in when I was walking by, and then I realized that they had no business being here at all. Why would there be a random layer of bricks in the middle of a corridor?" She continued to knock bricks in as she spoke. "Why cover up a wall with another wall?"

Lou stepped back and let Renee see what she had been standing in front of.

Renee gasped. Where Lou had been standing a moment earlier, behind the layer of bricks, was a rusty hasp. Though there was no longer a latch, its purpose was obvious.

It was a door.

"Oh my God," Renee breathed. She hastily worked to knock down the remainder of the bricks, Lou helping. When the sisters were done and all of the bricks lay strewn on the floor with the rest of the rubble, they stepped back and stared at the hidden door, their faces twin images of amazement.

"It's a door." Renee stated the obvious. She looked at her sister, then back at the door. "Why do you think it was covered up?"

Lou shook her head. "I don't know. Maybe the owners stored something of value inside and wanted to make sure no one could steal it."

"But then they wouldn't have been able to access it either," Renee rebutted.

"Maybe there was another entrance...like a trapdoor or something," Lou offered.

"Maybe." Renee shrugged. Her eyes filled with familiar excitement. "Want to find out?"

Grasping the hasp gingerly, as if the door itself would crumble away as the bricks had, Renee pushed, exerting as little pressure as she dared.

It creaked with disuse but moved inward, protesting every inch.

Eagerly, Renee pushed it in the rest of the way, squinting into the darkness.

When their eyes had adjusted, the sisters stepped over the bricks on the floor and across the threshold, stopping just inside.

It was as if they had stepped back in time. They were in a large chamber, and judging by the wooden bed in the center, its ancient curtains still hanging in dingy remnants from its tall four-poster frame, the chamber had served as a bedroom.

A few pieces of matching wooden furniture filled the room, a small writing desk and storage chest among them. A few holes – some large enough to accommodate a full-size person, some small enough for only mice to fit through – had broken up various walls, letting in little streams of light.

The sisters walked around the chamber, their steps small and cautious as they took everything in.

Suddenly Lou gasped, the sound startlingly loud in the silent chamber.

Renee's head whipped around. "What is it?"

Lou pointed to the floor on the far side of the bed, her hand shaking. "I think...I think these are human remains," she whispered.

Renee was beside her in a flash, all caution forgotten.

On the floor lay a pile of almost fully decomposed clothing, barely recognizable yet unmistakable nonetheless. And peeking out from the sleeves and neck of the decayed garment were bone fragments and teeth, still somewhat attached to a jawbone.

Renee stepped back as though burned. Lou managed to tear her eyes away from the sight on the floor, directing her gaze at her sister. "Are you okay?"

Renee breathed in deeply, then out through her mouth. "Yeah, just taken aback. Of all the things we could've stumbled upon, I never would have guessed that we'd find someone's bones." She stood still for a moment, then grabbed Lou's arm. "Let's go get the guys and bring them in; they won't want to miss this."

Lou shook her arm out of her sister's grasp. "I think I'll wait here, see if I find any other—" she searched for an appropriate word, "—skeletons."

"Are you sure you want to stay here by yourself?"

Truthfully, Lou still felt the urge to run away; her instincts were on overdrive, her whole body poised for fight or flight. Instead of admitting this to Renee, however, she managed a nonchalant smile. "I'll be fine; it's not as if I believe in ghosts. The only thing I have to worry about is the ceiling collapsing in on me, and I don't think that's going to happen anytime soon."

"Okay then. I'll be back soon." Renee hurried from the chamber.

Lou looked down once more at the remains, trying to imagine the person that had once filled the clothing, the person that had once smiled with the teeth.

She knew that after she died, it would only be a matter of time before she looked likewise, her remains all but disappearing back into the earth, one with the soil as though she'd never been there at all. It was a disconcerting idea. In an effort to distract her morbid train of thought, she walked away from the bed, surveying the rest of the room.

She'd made two full circuits around the room when she noticed something odd resting near one of the holes in the wall.

Curiosity aroused, she bent down and blew the dust off of its surface, coughing as a wealth of specks flew in her face.

She waved her hands in front of herself, clearing the air. When the dust had settled down, she picked up the object, grasping it by its slender handle.

It looked almost like...

She turned it over. *A mirror.* Small and ornately decorated, it was beautiful, no doubt worth a fortune at one time.

Lou held it out in front of her with reverent care. She used the hem of her shirt to wipe off its surface, cleaning it until she was able to see her reflection.

The weight of it felt good in her hand, and she found herself smiling at her reflection. For some reason the mirror seemed to soften her features and warm her complexion. She felt prettier, as though the mirror were presenting her best features in the most optimal way, as if she were looking at herself through a lover's eyes. She knew the idea was silly; mirrors couldn't improve anyone's looks, but she felt a happiness settle over her regardless.

The crunch of footsteps caught her attention, and she hastily tucked the mirror into her carry-on bag, zipping it closed just as Renee stepped once again into the room, the others following behind her.

"You okay?"

Lou nodded. "Fine. I didn't find any more skeletons." She hoped the others couldn't hear her heartbeat racing; it sounded like a drumbeat in her ears.

There was no reason as to why she'd hidden the mirror. It was a find the others would probably love to see, and she should have shared it with them. But an almost involuntary impulse had made her conceal it, her alarm bells ringing.

She would show it to them later.

"This is incredible!" Simon exclaimed. He turned to Christer. "It wasn't just the window that was sealed up: it was the whole chamber. It's been bricked up inside and out."

Lou joined the foursome huddled by the door. "What do you mean?"

Simon turned towards her. "When we were outside, I noticed that a section of this tower had been bricked up, presumably where a window had been." He began to walk around the chamber, his eyes searching the walls. He stopped by the bed, looking not down at the skeletal remains, but up. "Here it is- or was, I should say."

Both Renee and Lou had neglected to notice the bricked-up window before when they'd been by the bed; they'd been too distracted by the bones.

"Jeez," Renee said. "An entire chamber walled up, sealed off entirely from the rest of the castle." Her gaze drifted towards the far side of the bed. "With someone inside." She shivered involuntarily.

Ian put an arm around her shoulders. "Just because someone's bones are in here doesn't mean that they were walled in; maybe when this person died, their family wanted them to remain in the castle."

Simon pursed his lips. "Perhaps. But then why not lay the person on the bed? I find it hard to believe that anyone would leave a deceased loved one sprawled on the floor. That's hardly a gesture of respect."

"Maybe the bones were placed here later; we don't know when the person died in relation to when the room was bricked up," Christer reasoned. "They might have even climbed in through one of the larger holes to take shelter from the elements; they could have been a thief or a vagabond or a gypsy." His expression clouded over.

Without thinking, Lou blurted out, "I think she lived here. I think this was her room."

All four spun around to face her. Renee frowned. "Why would you say that?"

Lou felt herself blushing. *Why* did *I say that?* "I don't know. It's just...well, it looks like a girl's room and I'm pretty sure that the bits of clothing were a dress. I was just guessing." She grimaced at her own asinine response.

Renee's frown grew deeper.

Ian stepped between the sisters and raised his camera. "I have an idea. Why don't we take a few shots of this room from the outside and inside and include it as an aside in the spread? It's definitely going to draw readers in."

The others nodded in agreement, their tension easing somewhat.

Ian squeezed Renee's arm. "Come on. We can speculate about what happened here in the car. Right now, we only have a few good working hours left, so let's just focus on what we do best, okay?"

Renee sighed and reached for her camera case.

As she unzipped her bag and fished for her own camera, Lou's fingers brushed the handle of the mirror. Glancing around at the others, she pushed it deeper into her bag.

There would be plenty of opportunities to show it to them later.

CHAPTER 11

By late afternoon the team had wrapped up the shoot of the castle's interior and the mysterious room that had sent everyone's imaginations running wild. While the girls had decided to concentrate their efforts around the castle for the remainder of the day, the men had agreed to venture a little further into the woods beyond. Heading in the direction opposite that of their arrival, they made their way from the clearing.

They had walked for only a few minutes when Christer again spotted a structure obscured by the trees and foliage.

"Ian! Simon! Take a look at this!" He shouted. "I think I see a small steeple just poking out above the trees, maybe a hundred meters or so off."

Both men jogged over, eager to spot yet another novel discovery.

"You don't miss anything Christer," Ian said, shaking his head in bemused admiration. "Seriously. You have the eyes of a hawk."

Christer smiled sarcastically. "Eyes of a trained tour guide, more like. Believe it or not, I do spend a good deal of time in the mountains and woods; it's kind of in the job description."

Simon reined them in. "Let's get a closer look," he suggested. "If your initial guess of a steeple is correct, Christer, I think we may have happened upon the family chapel." He cleared his throat. "Private chapels were common in the medieval period; wealthy nobles often commissioned the building of one to afford their families the luxury of private church services, such as the celebration of mass, vespers, and sacraments."

When they reached it, it was obvious that Christer's assumption *had* been correct: there was no mistaking the structure for anything but that of a chapel.

The badly decayed exterior was of gothic design, similar to that of the castle. Its gabled roof was a patchwork of missing sections. While the stone exterior walls were largely intact, the arched entryway was only partially covered by the remnants of the heavy oak door that had once filled the threshold. A large, circular, stained-glass window depicting the design of a cross still decorated the space above the entryway.

To the right of the small church stood a bell tower with a pointed steeple, the very one that Christer had espied from afar.

After clearing bits and debris and brush out of the way, the three made their way into the church, speechless. It was if they had walked onto the set of a movie: the walls of the small chapel were covered in beautifully painted frescos depicting the passion of Christ, and the ground's mosaic floor was undamaged. The rest of the structure, however, was in disarray. The wooden pews had long ago rotted and decayed, and the once-vivid carvings on the altar were now unrecognizable. The arched stain glass windows on either side of the main aisle were broken and covered with tangled vines that extended up the walls, reaching tendrils working to draw the entire structure into the ground. They were many and thick, and they blocked much of the afternoon light from entering.

"Well, I say," Simon exclaimed. "Imagine if this were to be restored; it would be a gem!"

Christer eyed the remnants of the stained-glass work. "It may not have been the Transylvanian Sainte-Chapelle, but it was probably quite something when it was intact."

"It makes you wonder what really happened here," Ian mused, kicking up the thick layer of dust and debris that rested on the floor. When everything settled, the three were able to see the family crest formed by the mosaic floor design at the rear of the church, a two-headed dragon encircled by a wreath of laurel leaves, holding a cross in one talon and a sword in the other. Around the dragon's chest hung an amulet gilded with a giant letter S.

"The Solovastru crest, I suppose," Simon murmured.

Still staring at the floor, Ian shook his head. "None of this makes any sense at all; some of the townspeople – like our friend Karl for instance – know that this is all out here, and yet no one has made any move to preserve or restore it."

Nodding his agreement, Simon made his way to the altar. "It does make one wonder." Taking stock of the inscriptions around the altar, his eyes traveled to the sacristy. Behind it he noticed a door, its ancient latch still in place. Surmising that this might lead to a crypt, he gestured for the other two men to join him.

"Well, gentlemen, perhaps we can shed some light on the mysteries we've discovered today. Look here." Giving the door a stout push, the badly aged and weathered barrier gave way easily, revealing a spiral stairway, its steps encased in the dust of centuries, undisturbed.

"Swedes first?" Ian joked, giving Christer a slap on the back.

Christer responded with a wide grin.

Peering down into the darkness that swallowed up the stairs as they wound downward, each of the three suppressed their momentary trepidation and reached for their flashlights.

By the time the sun was nearing the treetops in its evening descent, everyone had rendezvoused back at the castle. Spirits were high as the group excitedly shared the results of their exploratory efforts with one another. Fearing the loss of daylight, the five continued their discussions as they trekked back to the car. The walk, which had felt endless earlier, now seemed to take no time at all, mostly due to the animated discussion concerning all that they'd uncovered – and all that they *hadn't* uncovered – about Solovastru Castle.

Simon, Ian, and Christer exhaustedly recapped the finding of the chapel and its crypt, excluding nothing. Simon even made mention of the family genealogy deduced from the inscriptions within the crypt, while Ian embellished his story with chills and thrills, garnering multiple eye rolls from everyone.

Ever the planner, Simon was already strategizing their next move.

"I want to visit a colleague of mine at the Transylvania University of Brasov; he might be able to recommend someone we can talk with to sketch a history of the castle and the family for which it was named. From what we were able to see in the crypt, the earliest Solovastru burials date back to the 1200s. The last interment in the crypt – the most recent that we were able to find, that is – was that of Istvan Solovastru, born 1386, died 1427."

"You know, I'm sure that we can locate period maps and land deeds in the official county records. That might shed additional light on the castle's owners, inhabitants, history, etc.," Christer speculated.

"I really hope that's the case," Ian added. "I find it inconceivable that this beautiful castle and its contents were simply left to decay; it's as if all of the castle's residents just walked out, never to return again." He gave a brusque laugh. "God. If not for the decay, our castle could've been the Romanian Herculaneum; it's a place where you can literally just step back in time. There wasn't even any evidence of theft." His face bespoke the puzzlement shared by all.

"Ian, it's like we've stumbled onto a real true-blue mystery—one that just might make our shoot an incredible success," Renee said, linking her arm through his. "And to think I wasn't all that jazzed about going to Romania." She smiled. "This trip just keeps getting better and better."

While everyone continued to speculate and theorize about the demise of Solovastru, Lou walked quietly behind the group on the trail, lost in thought.

She and Renee had wandered through the rest of the castle's rooms after leaving the walled bedchamber, marveling at the extent of valuables that had simply been abandoned to the ravages of time. One particular item of interest was one that they'd found in the castle's great banquet hall: a portrait of a young woman, still hanging in its place of prominence above the ornately carved mantle of the main fireplace—no doubt a mistress of the castle and perhaps the very woman whose bones lay in the interior room. It had been a striking image. On canvas, the artist had captured the woman's ethereal beauty, as well as the fire in the eyes. Those eyes had captivated Lou, their blue depths hinting at another side to the beautiful woman—a darker, more devious side that Lou was distinctly aware of in a way she couldn't explain. Her sister had offhandedly commented that she thought there was a resemblance between Lou and the long-dead woman, but she'd simply laughed and shook her head, hiding from Renee the growing sense of unease she felt as she lingered in the room. Images had flashed through her mind— a blazing fire in the hearth, the swinging pendulum of the grand clock, the ornately carved chairs and silk tapestries that had hung on the walls— images of what the room had once looked like. Convincing herself that she was suffering from an overactive imagination, she had swallowed her uneasiness, saying nothing to Renee as they walked through the rest of the castle.

Lou had been only too glad to leave. It was only now, back in the woods and headed for civilization, that she felt as if she could once again breathe freely.

By the time they threaded their way through the dense forest and arrived back at their car, the sun had slipped beneath the treetops, leaving the woods aglow with the faint hues of twilight. Both Renee and Lou were tempted to take the time to capture the moment on film.

As if she could read her sister's mind, Lou leaned towards Renee. "Remember when we used to make Halloween scrapbooks as kids? Tell me that this moment wouldn't have made the best cover page."

"It would have been our best ever. I wish we could stay and snap a few photos…" Renee let out a breath. "But we have another hour back to Brasov and I want to spend some time tonight engrossed in today's photos of Solovastru." She beamed. "I'm itching to give Cody a call, but I really want to work on the layout and the story and surprise him. Can you imagine the look on his face when he sees this?" Her rhetorical question was met with smiles and nods all around.

The rest of the trip back to their hotel was uneventful, as was the meager meal that passed for dinner at a small inn near their rented apartment.

They spent the evening figuring out how they could best keep to their original timeline for the Brasov shoots, finally deciding to divide and conquer. Ian, Renee, and Lou would return to Râsnov to complete their earlier shoot, while Simon and Christer would pursue any external sources that could shed light on the history of Solovastru. Satisfied that the plan was set, the men retired first, leaving the two women alone in the kitchen.

Renee, sensing heaviness in the air, gently took her sister's hand into hers. "Lou, is everything okay with you? You've barely said a word all night. Everyone else – including me – is busting at the seams with excitement, but you seem…" Renee shrugged. "I don't know. Are you down again about Jeremy?"

"No. It's been days since I've thought about him, actually." *Mostly because I've been thinking about Christer instead.* Lou sighed. "Don't worry, Renee. I'm fine. Really. I think I'm just a bit spooked, is all. I can't shake the thought that…well, if a place was so bad in the minds of the people that they just up and left one day without ever looking back…I don't know. Just…maybe it'd be better if it was never revisited, you know?" All her words came out in a rush and for a moment, she wanted desperately to tell her sister about the haunting sense of déjà-vu she'd felt at the castle and the unexplained foreboding that was growing ever stronger within her.

"I think people are conditioned to think that way because of legend, lore, and superstition. In reality, though, places don't carry the imprint of things that happened in the past." Renee squeezed Lou's hand, meeting her gaze. "There are no such things as curses." She squeezed her hand again to emphasize her point before relaxing her grip. "Get some shut eye, Sis; you look exhausted."

Lou simply nodded and gave her sister a peck on the cheek before heading to their bedroom. Once alone in the room, Lou sat on the bed and tried to sort out her emotions. She was usually a very settled person, comfortable in her own shoes, but today she just felt… She frowned, her eyebrows knitting together. The fact was, she wasn't sure how she felt.

Maybe I just need to chill out for a while, she mused.

Pulling off her dirty clothes, she reached into her bag to retrieve her favorite sweatshirt, but instead her hand closed around the handle of the mirror she had taken from the room with the bones.

The mirror.

She had completely forgotten about it and her intention to tell Renee and the others about it. Taking it out of the bag, she turned on the bedside lamp and studied it more closely, noticing for the first time the small symbols etched into the handle.

She frowned as her fingers moved over its surface. *How strange. It's in brand new condition; I could say that it was made last week, and no one would doubt it.* The ivory handle was uniform in color, creamy and even, and the glass looked newly polished. *Then again, it's possible that it* was *made last week. It's not like I can say how long it was lying in that chamber before I found it.*

Lou stared at her reflection in the glass, again aware that she felt more attractive than usual. Her brown eyes even seemed to have a nice blue tint to them. She yawned, the day's exertions catching up with her.

"What's that?"

Lou felt the blood drain from her face. Panicking, she instinctively shoved the mirror back in her bag before turning to face her sister. "Oh, nothing really. Just something I found." She tried to smile, but all she could focus on was the pounding of her pulse in her ears.

Renee eyed her with concern, her mouth opening and closing as if she were searching for the right thing to say. "Lou, are you sure you're okay? You look...well, just a little *off,* is all."

"I'm fine. Just tired."

"Lou." Her sister looked pained. "You'd tell me if something was up, right?"

The sliver of panic in Renee's voice made Lou internally flinch. "Renee, I'm fine," she insisted. Then, knowing where her sister's mind was going, she added, "I'm just a little tired and a little overwhelmed about today. Not everything is life or death."

"It was six years ago."

"Yeah. Six *years* ago. Are you ever going to let that go, Renee, or are you going to hold that over my head forever?"

"That's not what I'm—"

"I'm not some porcelain doll that's about to shatter, okay? I'm fine. Please just let me get some rest."

Renee said nothing, but the hurt on her face was almost enough to make Lou stammer out an apology.

Instead, she kept quiet, and Renee finally shook her head and left the room without another word.

Calm again, Lou quickly took the mirror out of her bag and put it into her nightstand drawer. *Renee just startled me; that's why I didn't show it to her.*

She would show it to her in the morning, when tensions had lessened and after she had gotten some needed rest.

Yawning again, she stretched her arms over her head, laying there for a moment before she propped herself up on her elbows. She'd been planning on grabbing a shower, but she felt so overcome by the sudden need to sleep that she decided to forgo it. Instead, she slipped on a pair of pajamas and laid her head on her pillow. Within minutes, she was sound asleep.

She pulled the coverlet tight around her body as she stared at the walls of the chamber, unable to sleep. Moonlight flooded the room and from somewhere in the dark forest beyond, an owl posed its questioning hoot to the night sky. Mercifully, the stone walls of her bedchamber blotted out most of the noises of revelry coming from the great hall. Her husband and a few of his soldiers had just returned from a successful three- day hunt; there was much celebration. When all went well, their spirits were high. Drinking and boasting of their exploits and prowess, the men would entertain themselves for hours, often falling into a drunken stupor at the tables. Better that way. At other times, the local serving wenches would end up fanning the men's lusts, hoping to satisfy their own appetites as well.

How she hoped that he *would satisfy his desires somewhere else.*

Almost as soon as the thought echoed in her mind, she heard the heavy footfall of boots approaching her door.

No!

He was coming. He was close...

With a crash, the door opened. She sprang up on the bed, breathing heavily, her eyes wide with fear as she watched him stagger into the room. He was barely able to hold himself upright in his drunken state. As he berated her with his evil words, he stripped off his weapons and clothes. His intent was clearly evident as he approached her, naked.

"Come here and satisfy me as a good wife should." He grabbed her by her hair and pulled her face towards his grossly erect member. She nearly gagged at the stench of sweat and beer that emanated from him. Not again! As he forced her to pleasure him, she swore that she would have her revenge. How she hated this man! Not content with her performance, he stripped away her nightdress and roughly fondled her breasts, pinching and squeezing until tears of pain rolled down her face.

Animal! Without thinking, she bit him, hard, drawing blood. For a moment, he was so startled that he failed to react. Bellowing in pain, he backhanded her, knocking her to the floor, and leaving her so dazed that she could not move. She knew what would follow. It was worth it though. She had hurt him this time and it felt good. Very good. She ran her tongue over the blood on her lips. As he continued to abuse her, she retreated within herself and, despite the pain she was forced to endure, she smiled.

Renee awoke to the sound of her sister's faint moans. Listening in the dark, she debated whether or not to turn on the light and check on her. She watched Lou's dark form twist and turn and then fall still again. Moments passed in silence. Deciding that everything was all right for the moment at least, Renee shut her eyes and willed herself to sleep again, trying not to let her worry run rampant.

Unlike her sister, no dreams disturbed her sleep.

Romania, 1429 A.D.

The woman's approach was silent. Her footsteps were lithe and catlike and the black robes that billowed around her helped her to blend in with the night. No one noticed her, not even the people she passed by closely enough to touch. To them she was nothing more than a shadow, a diaphanous wraith that the eye wasn't fast enough to catch in its sights.

She made her way, silent and sure, through the passageways of Solovastru Castle, towards the place where she knew the mistress of the castle resided. She was a master of disguise, but her talents weren't needed to help her reach her destination. There were not many servants living at Solovastru Castle; in the past few months, a rumor had circulated that there were less than ten servants left in the mistress's employment.

The intruder was almost certain that this was the truth; she could all but taste the emptiness within the stone walls. She could taste something else, too: the faint presence of decay...

"Csilla," a voice whispered, so close that she could feel breath on her neck.

She spun around- still making no sound- and dropped into a crouch, her hands forming lethal claws. Then she recognized the person that materialized in front of her, the person that she hadn't seen in the shadows behind her.

Xenia stepped into the light and looked down at the woman in front of her, a hint of mirth twinkling in her eyes. She cocked her head to one side. "It is customary of guests to request an invitation, should they wish to visit," she said.

Csilla straightened up and bowed slightly. She was a fool for not expecting Xenia to sense her presence. As impressive as her own skills were in the arts of stealth and secrecy, she couldn't compare to Xenia. Xenia was as cunning as a fox and infinitely more dangerous; both physically and mentally, she was uncannily shrewd and dexterous. It would be a fatal mistake to cross her.

"Xenia, forgive me. I am disgraced."

"You are not. Now, what business have you here? I assume this was not a social call. Did Miksa send you?"

Csilla shook her head. She wasn't surprised that Xenia had asked about Miksa; he was the only one in their group that ever dared to question Xenia about her motives and agendas. This time, however, she was not a messenger. "No. I came on my own. To see if the situation is as rumored and to warn you." She took a step closer to the taller woman. "Xenia, you must know that the disappearances are drawing attention to Sabina Solovastru, as well as the company she keeps. Soon there will be investigations."

"I'm unconcerned with rumors and even less concerned about the people spreading them. Sabina and I are in no danger."

"Yes, but even so..." Csilla paused, not wanting to argue. But then she willed herself to continue. They couldn't afford to lose Xenia. "I know you and Sabina are..." She searched for an appropriate word. "Intimate. Xenia, you are the best of us, but I only hope that your judgment has not been clouded due to your love for this girl."

Xenia's eyes flashed for a second and Csilla feared that she'd stepped too far in speaking her mind. Fighting the instincts screaming at her to run, she held her ground.

Xenia calmed herself, tucking her emotions away. "Csilla. Yes, I love Sabina, but I am not vulnerable because of it. The girls we kill will not be missed by anyone. Countless people disappear every day and the mass of humanity carries on. So let me reiterate: we are not in danger."

Realizing that she would get nowhere with her argument, she changed tactics. "Xenia, we've been talking. Talking about leaving, relocating. Miksa believes- and most of us agree with him- that it is time for us to move on.

We've lived in these woods too long. Most people don't know of us, but old tales tend to root deeply in superstitious cultures like this one. We should leave, Xenia. But we need you. Please, give us permission to go and please-join us. Do not abandon us after all this time."

Her voice had taken on a pleading quality that she knew sounded pathetic, but she didn't care. She had to make Xenia see reason.

Xenia's green eyes became hooded, her expression stony. Despite her best intentions, Csilla knew she hadn't persuaded Xenia of anything.

"Csilla, tell the others that we will go. But not yet. We are in no real danger and I refuse to run away from a place I've become attached to simply because of *rumors*." She paused, then added, "And when we do go, Sabina will be coming with us."

Csilla tried to hide her surprise, careful to keep her face impassive. She knew that Xenia desired Sabina, but she hadn't suspected that the dark woman felt *that* deeply about her. What would the others think?

Before she could betray any of her thoughts, she bowed deeply. "I will go and pass along your message. As always, I pledge you my loyalty."

Xenia inclined her head. "See yourself out, Csilla."

Xenia watched Csilla steal into the forest from her old chambers, the ones she'd occupied before she'd moved into the rooms adjacent to Sabina's own.

She knew that Csilla was right; it was only a matter of time before fingers started pointing at Solovastru Castle and Sabina. Then there would be an investigation. By then, however, she and Sabina would be long gone. The authorities would find nothing but bodies and an empty castle.

Sabina. So much planning, so much effort, but so very worth it.

Xenia frowned. She'd noticed the look on Csilla's face when she'd revealed her plans for Sabina. Csilla was astonished, and if she were being honest with herself, Xenia felt similarly. Never had she expected to become so attached to Sabina Solovastru. She'd wanted her from the first, but never had it crossed her mind that she would ever love her.

And now she did. Deeply. Sabina had become the center of her life in a very real way. It had been so, so long since she'd felt so alive, and now Sabina had awakened her to a higher kind of living, one rich in lust and blood and power. She and Sabina were a good match, greater together than apart. Like oxygen and fire, each fanned the other into brilliant flame.

After all this time, Xenia had found her soulmate.

No one would take Sabina from her, now or ever.

She intended to keep Sabina safe for the rest of her life. She'd suffered extensively at Istvan's hands, and – unbeknownst to Sabina – Xenia's hands as well.

Xenia had never physically harmed Sabina, no, but she had caused her mental distress. The dreams, those awful nightmares that had plagued Sabina for months, had been the work of Xenia's black magic. It had clawed at her heart to subject Sabina to them, but without the dreams, Sabina would not have traveled down the path of murder that Xenia had set for her. She would not crave the blood as she now did. She may not have entrusted herself to Xenia.

Sabina was the pawn, she the queen. It was her duty to keep Sabina safe and move her as she willed. And so far, her game of chess had been successful.

We're almost ready now. So, so close.

The hoot of an owl roused her from her reverie, and she retreated from her old chambers, walking more quietly than Csilla had through the castle.

When she reached their bedchamber, Xenia sat down in a chair close to where Sabina lay and watched her sleep, her green eyes never moving from her lover's face.

Sabina dreamed peacefully as her dark guardian kept watch over her.

CHAPTER 12

Simon laid on the horn of the rental car, his fingers drumming impatiently on the steering wheel.

Where the hell are you, Christer?

Before turning in for the night, they had agreed to meet at 8:00am sharp to make the drive to the Transylvania University of Brasov. Simon had managed to reach his old friend, Professor Anton Huber, late in the night via email and the professor had graciously agreed to meet them before classes the following day. It would be extremely rude to keep him waiting.

Simon honked again. A curtain on the window of the second floor opened and the vague form of Christer gestured rudely in his direction. *Too bad, my dear chap, if I interrupted your beauty sleep.* Patience was definitely not one of his virtues at the moment.

After what seemed like an eternity, the big Swede finally appeared at the front door. He lumbered out to the car, muttering apologies. "Sorry...had to grab a cup of coffee to clear my head; didn't sleep well last night, couldn't get my shit together this morning." He seemed to notice his surroundings for the first time. "Nice wheels, by the way; didn't think a 'bloke' like you'd go for a jeep." He gave Simon a sarcastic smile.

"Yes, I suppose it is rather out of character," Simon replied. "I take it you don't have me pegged as the manly type?" He gave Christer a good-natured smile. "Well, *some* of us have to choose brains over brawn, my friend. At least I am punctual and have my- to borrow from your vernacular- 'shit' together."

"Touché." Christer chuckled in defeat, handing his indignant friend his second cup of coffee as a peace offering.

"Thanks," Simon replied, mollified. "I was just about to suggest than you run behind the car, but given your penitent attitude, you may ride instead."

Glancing at his watch, Simon started up the rented Jeep and sped away from the curb. They'd have to make good time, despite the morning traffic.

He filled Christer in on his previous experiences with Huber as they made their way into greater Brasov.

Simon had collaborated with Huber on other research projects in Romania and Hungary and found him to be an excellent source of historical information. He had given Huber a brief recount of their onsite exploration of Solovastru, the surrounding woods, and the talismans. Discretion prompted Simon to hold back any mention of the bricked-up chamber and its skeletal occupant for the moment.

Meeting Simon's expectations, Huber had said that he could further elaborate on the castle's ancient occupants and its condition. As far as Simon could tell, Huber was intrigued by their interest in the site and their plans to highlight it in the magazine; he had even suggested to Simon that they include a third party in their discussion that morning- a local historian and ethnic expert who was familiar not only with Solovastru but the nomadic Roma as well, people that Huber had mentioned in his email as having an interesting connection to the castle.

As luck would have it, they managed to bypass morning traffic and arrived at the campus with a few minutes to spare. Taking the first available parking spot, they quickly located a campus map and followed the route to the liberal arts building.

After several wrong turns in the maze-like, antiquated building, the two men finally found themselves shaking hands with Anton Huber, Professor Emeritus of European Studies. The diminutive gray-haired man greeted them warmly in Romanian, clapping a hand on Simon's back as he ushered them into his office. Switching to English, he offered them a seat at a small round table where an attractive, middle-aged woman was already sitting. She rose to greet them, offering a charming smile. Anton introduced her as Marta Bartikovich, Assistant Professor of Ethnic Studies and long-time friend and colleague. She grasped Simon's and Christer's hands in a masculine shake that belied her small stature, assuring them that it was no trouble at all to take time from her day to meet with them.

"Truthfully," she began, "I am much intrigued by your reason for being here. Anton shared some details with me and has told me that your group from America stumbled upon Solovastru Castle."

"Yes, that is correct," Simon answered. "Hearing about it at all was a stroke of luck- we just happened to be in the right place at the right time." He leaned forward. "As I mentioned in my email, we want to include Solovastru Castle as our wildcard in the shoot. I was hoping you could shed some more light on its history for us."

"Perhaps it would be good to recap what you have learned so far, Simon," the professor proposed. "Then Marta and I can fill in your gaps."

Simon nodded. "Of course." Clearing his throat, he began to summarize. "By researching available sources, we were able to determine that the castle was constructed between 1207 and 1218 with some later renovations and additions over the next half-century. The original owner of the castle was Lajos Solovastru, the great-great grandfather of Istvan Solovastru, the last family member interred on site. According to historical documents, the Solovastru family was one of nobility, Székelys employed as an Eastern defense by the King of Hungary. I spent time researching the most recent generation and found that Istvan was married at the time of his death but had no offspring or heirs. Curiously, we were not able to locate his wife's coffin in the family vault below the chapel." He leaned back in his chair. "Aside from these limited facts, I was unable to uncover anything more substantive in my research, and nothing at all about why the castle to this day lies in abandoned disrepair."

"It is amazing that you were able to discover as much as you did," Marta said. "Almost all knowledge of the Castle and the Solovastru family is out of public circulation. Most of what we do know comes to us in lore and legend, passed down orally for generations." Smiling, she leaned forward so that her elbows rested on the table. "And what stories they are, especially those dealing with the last generation. For instance, legend has it that Istvan's death was no accident. Apparently, his young lover, a maid who worked in the castle, was responsible for his untimely demise."

Simon and Christer exchanged glances.

The Professor picked up where Marta had left off. "His wife Sabina fared no better, I'm afraid. Popular belief is that she was driven to madness after losing Istvan, eventually turning homicidal. She was accused and found guilty of the murders of several young women from the neighboring villages. For her crimes she was executed—walled up in her own bedchamber. That is why you did not find her body in the crypt beside that of her husband."

"In the crypt, no, but we *did* find her remains—or believe we did," Simon interjected, revealing the information he'd previously withheld.

With encouragement from Anton and Marta, he and Christer proceeded to recap the discovery of the bones inside the castle, beginning with the odd layer of bricks they'd seen on the outer tower wall.

Silence hovered like a fog over the group when they finished speaking, all four of them lost in thought.

Christer was the first to speak.

"So why leave the castle and its history in obscurity?"

Marta answered him with a string of rhetorical questions. "Why indeed. Why are there so few formal documents, so few known facts? Why have there been no attempts to restore Solovastru Castle to its former grandeur like many of the others here in Romania? Why does the castle still look like its residents simply walked out of it yesterday, yet over five centuries have passed?"

She paused for effect, looking at the three men in turn. "The answer is attributable to the superstitions of the local people. The people living at the time of Sabina Solovastru's execution considered the castle to be cursed as a result of the evil acts committed there. It was rumored that Sabina was a witch and practiced the dark arts; some even believed she had sold her soul to the devil. The castle was abandoned almost immediately after her condemnation. The people felt that to do differently would have been to cross God.

"Some years later, when the memory of the killings had dimmed, the locals began to loot the castle. A series of unfortunate events followed, and people ascribed the misfortunes to the cursed items taken from the castle. The stolen goods were collected and burned in the village square. At that time, the closest village to the castle- where most of the people resided- was Copaci, which was completely abandoned in the 1950s. Remind me to comment further about that later. After that, no one ventured into the castle. The woods surrounding it even came to be looked upon as *bantuit*, or haunted, as stories of disappearances and strange happenings grew. Not all the stories were true, but enough of them were to spread fear. Between those and the band of Roma that lived in the surrounding woods, the people grew more and more afraid to venture out from the town."

Anton, seeing the look of amazement on the faces of the men, queried, "Are you and Christer familiar with the Roma people and their history in Romania?"

Both men nodded, but Simon indicated that his knowledge was somewhat superficial and asked the professor to elaborate further.

Standing up, Anton ambled over and plucked a book from an overcrowded shelf on the wall. Tabbing to the appropriate spot, he adjusted his reading glasses and paraphrased for the group.

"The gypsy peoples originated from a region of Pakistan, as evidenced by the fact that the Rom language is close to the older forms of Indian languages. Three tribes – Rom, Sinti, and Kale – left India, migrating through Armenia and Persia and finally the Byzantine Empire. Within the Byzantine Empire, they dispersed into the Balkans, reaching Wallachia and Moldavia, where such populations are still found today. When they entered Western Europe, the tribes were granted letters of protection from the King of Hungary, but the privileged situation did not last long as their way of life fostered hostility with the indigenous people."

Anton closed the book with a slap, replacing it on the shelf. "By that I mean the gypsy penchant for community property. You see, for the Europeans, private property was sacrosanct, whereas the Roma regarded all things as common property. There is actually no word that means 'to possess' in their language. Ignorant of this, the Europeans looked upon them as thieves and ostracized them. It is one of the reasons they are often referred to as Gypsies."

He joined them at the table again, continuing with his history lesson. "In each host nation, the gypsies commonly take on the name and language of their hosts, but within the Rom, they maintain their own language, names, customs, music and Indian accouterments. Even after six hundred years in Romania, many of the Roma communities here are still very separate and have not assimilated."

"Can you tell us something of their religious beliefs?" Simon asked.

The professor deferred to Marta, who had studied the Roma for years.

"As far as their religion, it has been suggested that the Roma were originally Hindu; there are various connections, even down to the language. For example, the Romany word for cross is *trushul*, the same word used to describe Shiva's trident. Their other beliefs are varied. The Roma have always believed in psychic powers, and the use of Tarot cards is prevalent. They also believe that there are certain Roma among them who possess great power through the ability to perform magic. We would refer to them as witches, but within Roma society they are known as *chovihanis*. While most Roma people do adopt the prevalent religion of the area they live in, they tend to retain their other beliefs as well, creating an interesting blend of Christian mysticism.

"I have come across several tribes of Roma over the years, though, who have not assimilated Christianity into their belief system. These tribes hold devotion to Kali, the Hindu goddess of destruction and consort to Shiva. In my estimation and from my observations, I believe this religion to be the darkest, most cult-like among the Roma. I do my best to avoid them, as I would recommend to anyone who asked my opinion."

Throughout Marta's dissertation, Simon had been taking notes on his laptop, his fingers feverishly trying to keep up with the overload of information.

"Anton, Marta, this information is invaluable. Thanks to your knowledge and expertise, I'll be able to write quite a colorful piece for

Solovastru," Simon said, genuinely grateful for their assistance. "One further thing: Marta, you mentioned earlier that the presence of the Roma and various mysterious happenings led to the abandonment of Copaci. Can you provide any more detail?"

"Yes," Marta replied, "and this will sound incredible to your ears, I am sure. Over the course of the town's history, an unusually high number of children disappeared and were never found. Additionally, several bodies were found in the woods, drained of blood. This led to talk of the undead, or *strigoi,* prowling the woods. And while there were only rumors, a growing number of people began to suspect and blame the local Roma. Many of the families that lived in Copaci left; a few stayed, determined to ignore the fear that had driven the majority away. Even they, though, could only ignore so much.

"About fifty years ago, the worst of the worst happened. The deaths of the Korzha family. Andrei Korzha was a blacksmith who owned land outside of Copaci. He had a wife and two young daughters – good kids – from what people have told me. The little girls were found brutally butchered to death in their beds, and their mother was found outside of Solovastru Castle, stabbed to death. Andrei's body was found hanging from the parapet of a tower. People assumed that Andrei had snapped- he'd had a history of erratic behavior ever since the death of his first wife. Of course, when it became known that both Andrei's and his wife's bodies were found at the castle, the remaining people in Copaci decided that it would be best to move away as the others had done. Copaci became a ghost village almost overnight. Since then, efforts to explore the castle or restore it have been vehemently resisted by the locals, and the government considers it not worth the effort given its remote location and inaccessibility by road to accommodate tourism."

"Wow." Christer exhaled the word. "That is some story."

"Some story indeed," Simon echoed. "If only there were more details available." He looked at Christer. "Perhaps we can track down any living relatives of the Korzhas to see if there is more to that story than is generally known. I can't speak for you, but *I* am very much curious to know more."

The two men rose to their feet, Anton and Marta doing likewise.

"Thank you both for everything, and for taking time out of your day to meet us," Simon said.

"I'm always happy to see an old friend, even if the reason is business rather than pleasure." Anton smiled. "Be sure to send us a copy of your magazine when it is published; I am looking forward to seeing the finished product."

Exchanging promises to stay in touch, the men departed, deciding to head to Brasov's records building to look for anything regarding Copaci and the Korzha family.

CHAPTER 13

Romania, Present Day

D id you hear that?" Gavril whispered, glancing behind him. Sweat ran down his brow, making a muddy track as it traveled through the dirt caked on his face.

His friend Costin shook his head slowly, putting a finger to his lips. *Quiet.*

Gavril swallowed and turned away, gazing into the dark woods in front of him. He couldn't see anything, but he kept his gun trained on the shadows. Every once in a while, he thought he heard something, but he wasn't sure if it was real or if his ears were deceiving him. The deep forest had ways of playing tricks on the senses. The unsettling silence hovered around him.

Snap.

That was definitely something, though. No denying it.

Snap.

"Costin, it's coming this way!" He hissed. His friend came up beside him, his own gun loaded and at the ready. Gavril felt a cold bead of sweat trickle down his spine, raising goosebumps. He shivered.

A figure burst out of the trees to their left, bloody and running. Costin and Gavril lowered their weapons. He was one of theirs.

"Ivan!" Gavril called out, but if the other man heard him, he didn't acknowledge it. He kept on running, stumbling as he went until he collapsed over an obtrusive root, falling headlong onto the ground. Gavril raced over to him, Costin at his heels. When they reached him, they knelt down beside him, shocked by what they saw. Ivan's abdomen was sliced open, his guts literally spilling out, and he was holding onto himself as if trying to keep his body together.

The dying man looked up at his friends, his eyes glazed with fear. "*Run,*" he rasped. "Get out of here. We are...outmatched." He coughed, wheezing blood.

Gavril cradled his head, looking to Costin for advice.

But Costin shook his head. Nothing could be done.

Ayeeeeei!

They whipped around as they heard the scream, eyes scanning the woods for signs of movement. Costin placed a hand on his shoulder. "We need to leave. Right now."

"But what about Ivan? What about the others?"

"Ivan's dead. Look."

Gavril looked. Ivan was staring up at the sky, his eyes dim and lifeless. The color was already draining from his face, the paleness of his skin highlighting the look of fear still etched on his features even in death.

Gavril rose shakily and Costin grabbed at his tunic, yanking him hard. "I said we have to go, Gavril. *Now.*"

Gavril nodded, but just as his equilibrium returned, he stumbled back in terror, pointing over Costin's shoulder. His companion spun around.

It was simply standing there, its flat eyes appraising them.

Costin fired his gun, his adrenaline-fueled reflexes reacting before Gavril's. His aim was precise, perfect, and yet the bullet sailed through the air and landed with splintering impact in a tree, missing its target.

It was gone.

"Run!" Costin shouted.

They did just that, their legs pounding through the forest, their arms pumping at their sides as they sprinted.

Suddenly there were footsteps behind them. Gavril raised his gun, still running, and fired behind them.

"It's us! Don't shoot!" The panicked voice was familiar.

Gavril watched in relief as he saw Andrei and Peter appear behind them, bloody but breathing.

"The others?" Costin asked as he ran.

"Dead...all dead. They attacked before we even had a chance to think, Costin. They're brutal."

"They? How many?" He slowed a little, turning to face the other men.

Peter shook his head. "I don't know; it was impossible to tell."

In tacit agreement, they all picked up their pace, desperate to break free of the woods. Gavril thought he heard a whisper to his right, a laugh to his left... *They are playing with us*, he thought. *Toying with us! God help us.*

He ran faster. The monotonous woodland flew by, a blur of brown and green as they pressed on. For a time, the only thing Gavril was acutely aware of was the sound of their labored breathing, the crunch of twigs underfoot, and the frantic beating of his own heart.

"*No!*" Peter's scream was cut off abruptly. Gavril turned around, only to see Peter's head fall forward onto the ground, rolling around at his feet. His body jerked and spasmed before it too fell. It landed in an unnatural position on the forest floor, blood pouring out in pulsing gushes from where the head used to be. Blinking in disbelief, Gavril took a step towards Peter's body.

"Gavril! Run, damn you! He's DEAD!"

Costin's voice cut through his shock and somehow his legs moved, taking him away from the horror. He pushed himself far past his physical limits as they ran for their lives, until his lungs were burning from exertion and he couldn't run any longer.

Wheezing, he reached out to steady himself against a tree. He gulped in a ragged breath and was about to take a second when he looked up and froze.

It was back.

Though he knew it was impossible, he would have sworn he saw its lipless mouth curl up in a smile.

And then it lunged forward, covering the distance between them with blinding speed.

Gavril raised his gun.

Chalea heard them before she saw them. Raised voices, shouts. She stood up and moved aside the flap of her tent to see what was going on.

She was met with chaos. Costin was supporting a very bloody Gavril by the waist, leading him towards her. Ferka was behind them, looking at his wounded son and talking heatedly with Andrei. When he noticed Chalea, he jogged over towards her, reaching her before the others.

"Chalea, the scouting parties were attacked. Three of ours are dead. Only Costin, Andrei, and Gavril made it back alive." He gripped her shoulders, his voice of command forgotten, overshadowed by the worry of a father. "Please heal Gavril. I don't care what you have to do. I can't lose him; he is my only son, Chalea."

Rarely did she see him so affected, and his vulnerability moved her with compassion. "I will do all that I can, Ferka." She couldn't promise him any more than that. The heavy weight of guilt settled about her like a cloak. *This is my fault.* After all, it had been at her insistence that the party had been sent out.

She turned to Costin and helped him get Gavril into her tent, steeling herself against the bloody man's delirious moans. Then she nodded to Ferka and shut out the rest of the world, praying that she would be able to save her leader's son.

Hours later, she stepped outside, taking a refreshing breath of the cool nighttime air. It had been a long, tiring day, and even though her body craved sleep, she needed to be outside in the open for a little while. She saw Ferka by the communal fire, his back rigid as he stared into the flames. Chalea walked over to him. "He will live," she said.

The older man visibly relaxed. He sighed, turning to face her. "Thank you," he said sincerely. "And not just for Gavril." He gave her a small smile. "We would be lost without you- truly."

Chalea felt a rush of pride at his words, her eyes moistening. She had always looked up to Ferka, and to hear him say that meant more to her than anyone's praise had in a long time.

She composed herself before she spoke again. "I tended to Andrei as well. His head wound was severe, but there will be no permanent damage." She swallowed hard. "This was a crushing blow, and all for nothing."

"No, not for nothing. We know now that they are indeed back, and more active than they have been for many years. This break in pattern...it means that something has changed." He looked off into the mountains. "We will have to confront them again, and in fuller force. We cannot afford for them to kill anyone else, and we cannot afford for them to take our woods. We have a duty here."

"Yes, but as I have said before, I cannot see clearly..." Chalea trailed off, cursing softly. "We need to attack with the upper hand. If we search them out blindly, this disaster will be repeated. If Costin had not taken one of the orbs with him, no one would have returned."

Ferka fixed her with a determined stare. "What do you need? What can help you find them?"

Chalea shook her head, discouraged. "I don't know," she admitted. "But if we don't think of something, they will win." She looked up, watching the smoke from the fire curl into the sky and disappear. "And if they win," she whispered, "there will be no survivors, here or anywhere."

CHAPTER 14

Sick of tossing and turning, Christer sat up, throwing the sheets off and swinging his legs over the side of the bed.

He knew why he couldn't sleep; conflict always seemed to keep him up, even when he wasn't directly involved.

Ian, Renee, and Lou had returned around dinner, as silent and somber as mourners at a funeral. He and Simon had tried to find out what was wrong, but the photographers had shut them down, Renee most of all.

Despite the tense atmosphere, they'd spent the evening filling the disconsolate threesome in on their meeting with Anton and Marta. The stories, especially the details about the Roma and Copaci, seemed to distract them a little from whatever was plaguing them, but when Lou said she was turning in for the night, the tension had erupted.

Renee had snapped at Lou, her expression full of hurt indignation. Cringing, Lou had left the room, and a few minutes later Renee had stormed out of the apartment. Ian had left shortly after, saying nothing.

It had been a strange night, and for the first time since he'd met them in Cluj, Christer wished he were alone in his apartment back in Bucharest.

No, not really. I just wish I knew what the hell was the matter. He rubbed at his eyes. *Well, I'm up now. May as well mix myself a drink or two, enjoy a buzz.*

Standing up, he walked quietly out of the room, not wanting to wake Simon. Although he hadn't been rooming with him very long, Christer knew Simon well enough to realize that he tended to be a grouch if he was woken up unexpectedly.

He shut the bedroom door carefully, then turned into the kitchen and almost jumped in surprise.

Lou was seated at the counter, head down, face covered by the crook of her arms. For a second, he thought she was sleeping, but then he noticed the slight shake in her shoulders.

She was crying.

So much for my drink.

He walked towards her softly, not wanting to startle her. "Lou?"

Her head came up quickly, revealing tear-stained cheeks. She wiped her face with the sleeve of her sweater, hastily trying to brush away all evidence of her crying.

She sniffled. "Hey."

He frowned. She looked so forlorn sitting there, her small frame bent in a defeated posture, her face so full of sadness—the sight of her tugged on his heartstrings.

He took the seat next to her, then turned himself so that he faced her, taking both of her hands in his. They were cold. "What's wrong?"

She looked down, saying nothing.

Christer squeezed her hands gently. "You know you can talk to me if you want; I'm here anytime you want an ear." He paused, then added, "If you just want me to sit here with you, that's fine too."

That brought her head up, her eyes finally meeting his. "Thank you." Her voice broke a little and she blinked back more tears. "I just...I had the worst day today. I upset Ian and Renee, I upset myself, I..." She retracted her hands and stood, facing away from him. Then she took a few steps into the living room and sat down on the couch.

After a few moments, Christer joined her. He put enough distance between them so that she could have her space.

Lou looked at him, her eyes still brimming with tears. "I said some things today that I should never had said." She grimaced. "You could see the pain and anger in my sister's eyes when she looked at me tonight: it was written all over her face. Talk about staring daggers. But it's not like I don't deserve it." She bowed her head, giving in to her tears.

Christer almost put his arms around her, wanting to comfort her, but he wasn't sure that that was what she wanted. So instead, he tried to infuse his voice with as much gentleness as possible. "We all do stupid things sometimes, Lou. It doesn't mean that you're a bad person; you're just human. Your sister loves you, no matter what. You may have upset her today, but in the end, you two are family. Forgiveness is part of that. It'll be okay."

"Christer, you don't understand." Lou sighed. "My sister and Ian have been dating for three years now and they are really in love with each other. Ian would marry my sister tomorrow if she'd agree, but Renee is still worried about…" She trailed off for a moment, a guilty look flitting across her face. "She's worried to leave me on my own."

Christer didn't understand, and the confusion must have showed on his face, because Lou barreled ahead when he made no comment.

"After high school, my sister rented an apartment in downtown Philly and I moved in with her. I didn't want to stay with my dad—we weren't close. Renee and I were, and she was always the one I turned to when I needed help." She paused. "When I was in my second year of college, Renee got her first big job and while she was away on assignment, I…something happened. Something bad. And it was my fault, my problem, but Renee has never let it go, never moved on. And it doesn't matter that I've grown up, that years have passed, doesn't matter that I've tried to convince her I'm okay and can handle myself now—she doesn't buy it. *That's* why she keeps putting Ian off." She straightened up, running her hands through her hair, and then she fixed him with a look that was all guilt and shame. "I know all this, but for some insane reason, today I told Ian that Renee had no intention of ever marrying him. I told him that she was just stringing him along while she looked for someone better."

Christer was taken aback. "Why…why would you say that?" He asked finally. He and Lou had begun to spend an increasing amount of time together, and in that time, he'd never once heard her utter something unkind about anyone, let alone something so ugly and untrue.

Lou shook her head. "I don't know! It was like I wanted to see her suffer and I don't even know why." She made a pained sound. "God, what is wrong with me?"

Tipping her chin up, Christer answered her with a sincerity that he rarely showed anyone. "Nothing's wrong with you. Lou, listen to me: there is nothing that cannot be undone. Go and talk to your sister. Tell her how sorry you are for what you did. She will believe you. I do."

She looked at him for a time without saying anything, her gaze filled with a deepness he couldn't define. Then, still quiet, she moved closer to him and laid her head against his shoulder.

The breath he hadn't been aware of holding came out when she leaned into him, and, inexplicably relieved, he put his arm around her.

He felt a few tears wet his shirt as she spoke again. "Renee has always been there for me, has always put my happiness before her own. I think she feels she has to." Lou sighed. "She thinks I don't notice, but I do. She raised me because she thought it was her responsibility, and I let her because it helped her deal with the pain of losing Mom. We both need each other, just in different ways. If I thought I'd done something to permanently ruin our relationship, or my sister's future..." She let the thought hang unfinished.

Christer felt a sudden pang go through him, an old ache. *She's sensitive like Annika*, he thought. *Able to see what people are hiding, able to see their true feelings.* It was a bittersweet moment of recall, but one that made Christer glad that Lou's presence had kept him from mixing a drink. And it dawned on him in that moment that since he had met her, his dependency on alcohol had waned dramatically. He'd started seeking out her company more often than seeking out a bottle.

Almost unconsciously, he began to stroke Lou's hair as she cried, instinctively trying to soothe her. In a small way, it seemed Lou's quiet intuition and warm heart were helping him on the road to reclaiming himself, so seeing her so hurt – even if it was pain she'd brought on herself – made him ache.

Wrapped in Christer's arms, Lou could almost pretend that everything was going to be okay. Almost. In telling Christer about the events earlier in the day, she had held back the fact that after she had sabotaged her sister's relationship with Ian, she had made a blatant pass at him. Ian had looked at her as if she had stuck a knife in his back. He had literally fled from her presence and had not spoken a word to her since. Wondering how she was going to fix the mess she had created, she gave in to a fresh wave of tears.

Christer drew her closer.

"The scariest thing about the way I acted was *why*," she whispered when the tears stopped. "I just felt this sudden urge to lash out at Renee, to say something I knew would hurt her. And there was a part of me that felt satisfied when I succeeded." The last few words stuck in her throat. "Why would I do that? I'm not the kind of person that likes to inflict pain on *anyone*—least of all my sister. What the hell got into me?" She choked out a long, tired exhale. "I just wish I could take it back."

The right words eluding him, Christer simply held her tighter.

Romania, 1429 A.D.

Sabina Solovastru tightened her robe around herself, tying and retying the knot at her waist, desperate to give her antsy fingers something to do.

Finished fidgeting, she eyed herself in the long mirror that hung on the wall by her armoire, appreciative of the reflection staring back at her. Her slim figure was delicately feminine, her facial features noble and symmetrical. Her blonde hair fell down around her elbows, its lightness a fine contrast to her dark robe. Most striking of all, however, was not her physical appearance but the aura she projected. It was one of power, albeit power laced with a hint of madness.

She smiled and turned away from her reflection to look at the two girls who lay – tied, gagged, and blindfolded – on the floor. They were twins: small, brunette, and ethnic-looking like Xenia. Identical little pearls ripe for harvesting.

A large washbasin stood in the middle of the room, close to the doomed girls. Sabina ran one finger over its rim, imagining its white surface covered with blood, as soon it would be.

Over the past few months, she and Xenia had killed an increasing number of young girls, their appetites growing harder and harder to sate. It was more than just the brews that Xenia made with the murdered girls' blood. It was the *kill*, the act of taking a life, that had become the insatiable game between the two.

Sabina gasped as she realized that Xenia had entered the chamber and was watching her. The way the dark woman could move around so silently never failed to elicit her surprise; if it weren't for Xenia's feet planted firmly on the floor, Sabina would have sworn that she'd floated into the room.

"You look ravishing, my dear," Xenia said.

Sabina blushed, proud at being praised. "I *feel* ravishing, too. Xenia, I am so impatient to begin. Just look at these girls. Perfect little mirrors of each other."

Xenia nodded. "They are quite a pair." She moved over to where they were laying and roused them, making them stand on their feet. Both girls were trembling. They were holding hands, despite the chains around their wrists, their knuckles white with exertion. A trickle of blood ran down the seam of their hands, evidence of the chafing done by their shackles.

Slowly, Xenia took the blindfold off one of the girls. She was about to undo the second when Sabina stopped her. "Xenia, leave it on. It'll be more interesting this way," she said.

Xenia glanced at her, then shrugged. "This is your play, as it were. Do what you wish."

Sabina smiled, a malicious sneer that looked grotesque on her pretty features. The girl without the blindfold on cringed.

"Don't cringe yet, little one. The real fun has not even begun," she chortled. Walking with deliberately slow steps, she made her way to the desk in the corner of the room where her collection of weaponry lay. She held up various instruments of torture for the girl to see, ones with hooks and serrated blades. Finally, she decided on a straightedge razor, a small one that fit nicely in the palm of her hand.

Carrying it back to her victim, she waved it in front of the girl's face, then pointed it at her twin. "This is for her. Watch what I can do with this little blade."

While Sabina played her sadistic game, Xenia was careful to collect the blood she spilled, not wanting to waste a single drop.

Ten agonizing, horror-filled minutes later, the first girl lay dead upon the floor, her face and body a bloody jigsaw puzzle. All of her major veins lay open, and her skin had lost all of its color, her body drained of blood.

Her twin was weeping silently on her knees, crumpled beside her dead sister.

When Sabina roughly pushed the sobbing girl into the washbasin where Xenia had already deposited much of the dead twin's blood, she didn't even struggle. Her fear of dying had fled, replaced with a desire to erase the recent horror from her memory. Now death was a release.

Satisfied that the living twin had suffered enough watching her sister die, Sabina slit the girl's wrists deeply and vertically, ensuring that she died quickly.

Xenia removed the girl's body from the tub and placed her next to her mangled sister. Then she turned back to Sabina, her eyes like smoke. Seconds passed. "Take off your robe, Sabina," she whispered.

Sabina started. "Shouldn't we prepare this blood before it coagulates? We can't afford to waste it. Our continued entertainment can wait."

Xenia shook her head even as Sabina finished speaking. "We're not going to use this blood in any brew or potion. We are going to use it in its purest form, fresh from the source. Have you so little faith in me still that you think I would lead you astray? My dear Sabina, do not disappoint me so. I promise you will not regret this turn of events."

Still curious, Sabina unknotted her robe and let it fall to the floor where it pooled around her feet. She shivered as she felt the chill night air on her bare skin.

She watched as Xenia dipped her hand in the washbasin. When she brought it out, it resembled a dripping scarlet glove.

Xenia extended her blood-covered hand towards Sabina. Then, holding her gaze, she smeared the blood over Sabina's face, painting her with red.

Sabina gasped involuntarily. The blood was still *warm*. She shivered again, but this time it wasn't due to the cold.

Moving with intimate grace, Xenia coated Sabina's body in blood, saving her hands for last. When she reached them, Xenia painted them finger by finger, massaging each digit before she moved to the next. Then, finally finished, she stepped back and looked at her creation with admiration.

"And one more thing." She moved back again to the tub and dipped one index finger into the blood. "Come here, Sabina."

Sabina complied.

"Now for the real power, the truest use of blood." She held out her finger, gently brushing Sabina's lips with it.

Sabina, her eyes locked with Xenia's, opened her mouth and sucked the blood off of the proffered finger, her face euphoric in a lusty kind of ecstasy.

A devilish glint appeared in her eyes and she put her own hand in the washbasin, imitating Xenia. Then she held out her finger in like fashion, allowing Xenia to taste the blood too.

At Sabina's enthusiasm, Xenia felt something stir deep within her. "Oh, Sabina. My sweet, dear Sabina," she breathed, her tone reverent.

The dark woman's passion burst forth in a torrent and she clutched Sabina to her, crushing her lover's lips with her own. Sabina melted against her.

When she broke the kiss, she kept her forehead pressed to Sabina's so that their lips were lightly touching.

Without warning, Sabina drew Xenia's bottom lip between her own and bit down hard, drawing blood.

Startled, Xenia's eyes flashed. She pushed Sabina an arm's length away, one eyebrow cocked.

Sabina laughed. A raucous, throaty laugh that exposed a mouthful of bloodstained teeth.

As if it were contagious, Xenia began to laugh too, her own cackles filling the chamber.

Their laughter grew and grew in volume until it reverberated throughout the castle, filling the halls and chambers with their mad symphony.

As they laughed together, the dead twins kept watch, the one without the blindfold staring sightlessly at the lovers, a silent witness to their depravity.

The twins' hands, which had clasped each other so tightly through their chains, now rested inches apart, never to touch again.

CHAPTER 15

Renee adjusted the EF 50mm lens on her EOS, setting it to its maximum aperture of f/1.2. Exhaling, she looked through the lens, every muscle still as she took her shot.

She took a series of them, making minor adjustments to the aperture size until she was pleased with the result.

The forefront of Bran Castle was crisp and clear, offset by a blur of woods around it. The effect was creepy, exactly the mood she'd been aiming to capture. It was a perfect portrayal of the medieval castle, showing off its stark angles and imposing facade.

In spite of the prior day's nightmare, she smiled. There was no better cure for an aching heart than work.

The moment wasn't meant to last, however, and Renee frowned as she saw her sister approaching from the corner of her eye.

She was tempted to run away, her legs already preparing for motion, but she sighed. She wasn't about to act childish. Lou should be the one keeping her distance.

"Renee?" Lou stopped a few feet away, so that she was below Renee on the incline. She worked to make eye contact with her sister, forcing herself not to look at her feet. "I need to talk to you."

Renee kept her eyes fixed on the viewpoint of her camera, refusing at first to acknowledge Lou. After a prolonged pause, however, she turned off her camera. She steeled herself against the desire to immediately forgive her sister, not wanting to excuse Lou's behavior so easily. *Why is it that I can never stay angry at her? Even when she does something like this?* Stalling, she began packing her lenses away, working in silence until everything was zipped up in her bag. Only then did she look at her sister.

"What is it, Lou?" She spoke the words with a purposeful edge.

"I need to apologize."

Renee's posture became defensive, so her sister hurried on. "Please, just hear me out."

Renee crossed her arms and stared her sister down. Finally, she nodded.

Lou took a deep breath and began. "What I did was inexcusable; awful. You're my sister and I love you more than anyone else in the whole world. To hurt you like that…I just—I don't know what my problem is. I am so, so sorry." Lou walked the few steps separating them so that they stood at eye level. "I know it doesn't make up for anything, and I know it doesn't make the pain go away, but I needed to say it anyway. Whatever you want me to do, I'll do it. If you want me to leave you alone, if you want me to go home, just say the word and I'll go. I just want to try and make things right. Somehow."

Renee looked at her for a long time without saying anything. A mix of emotions played across her face, mostly ones that made Lou crumple inside.

Just when Lou didn't think she could stand the silence anymore, Renee spoke.

"I don't want you to leave, Lou. But I do want you to leave me alone today. I need time alone with Ian to try and work things out." Her eyes narrowed. "And I'd prefer it if you weren't anywhere nearby when I talk to him."

Lou nodded, keeping her eyes averted. "Why don't I go shoot some of the surrounding forest? You and Ian can work on Bran."

"I think that's a good idea." Renee leaned over and hoisted her duffel bag onto her shoulder, then started walking towards the castle, eager to get away from her sister.

She didn't look back.

Lou watched her go, forcing herself not to run after her and beg forgiveness. At least Renee had stayed long enough to hear her out. They may not have reconciled, but at least it was a step in the right direction.

Oh Christer, I wish you were here. You always seem to have the right words to say.

The off-handed thought of the handsome Swede brought a wistful smile to her lips. There was no denying the growing attraction she was feeling for the man. He was genuinely nice to her, and the other night he had comforted her even though he could have just as easily left her alone to deal with her problems. And he hadn't expected anything in return. It was hard to find people like that. *Renee is like that too...*

Sighing, she looked at Bran, needing a distraction from her worries.

It was impressive and a little frightening, though that might have something to do with the notorious vampire associated with it.

Looking at the castle, the story seemed believable. The walls were tall and littered with towers, and their white color was dingy rather than pure, aged by time. Set alone on the incline, it dominated the entire area, a jagged extension of nature itself, and the perfect place for a bloodthirsty killer to call home.

Lou wished she could photograph it herself; she'd been waiting all along to work on Bran, even when she'd joked about it before they'd come to Romania.

But that wasn't going to happen. Renee wanted space from her, and space was what she would get.

There was really nothing of interest in the surrounding woods—Lou knew that. They were thick, the trees dense and tall. Their appeal was that they spread out far enough from Bran that Lou could pass a few hours while Renee talked to Ian.

Her thoughts were disturbed by a male voice, echoing up to her from the castle.

Listening more closely, she could just make out the voice of a tour guide, talking about the legend of Dracula, his voice animated.

She smiled. No doubt Dracula's connection to the castle was what brought the crowds. Everyone wanted to hear about 'The Impaler' and his vampiric escapades- his infamy was what sold the tourists, not the fortress nestled in the countryside.

It was ironic, in a way. Places never seemed to get any attention without the allure of the dark or supernatural; castles like Bran were always more famous because of legends than because of their architectural significance.

Shaking her head, Lou turned away and made her way to the edge of the woods.

Once she passed into the shade of the trees, she paused, her right foot hovering in the air. Gently, she lowered her foot and stood motionless.

There was no breeze, and the woods were still. Not quiet, though: she could hear the crunching of leaves and the chatter of birds overhead.

She frowned. For a second, she had felt... *different.* Like her limbs were all wrong, her facial muscles foreign as they changed expressions. Even her mind had felt strange, though she couldn't define how.

The feeling passed just as quickly as it had come, only to be replaced with a sudden sense of heaviness, as if a great weight had settled on her shoulders. She felt overwhelmingly tired as she struggled to perform the simple task of walking, each step a monumental effort.

Soon the heaviness became oppressive, clinging to her like thick mud. Even her eyelids seemed to grow heavy, and she felt a dark shadow descend upon her, obscuring her vision. The shadow became a cocoon that grew ever tighter around her, swallowing her up. Breathing was now an effort and dizziness threatened to overwhelm her. Claustrophobia transformed into panic and tears of frustration welled up; she tried to push back against the force that was now penetrating her very self but failed, her resolve too weak to overcome the darkness.

She opened her mouth to scream, but it was as if the mud had reached her throat and choked her vocal cords: no sound came out.

Before she could formulate another thought, everything went black.

CHAPTER 16

How long have you worked here?" Ian asked between bites of his salad.

"Almost five years, giving four tours a day, three days a week, in four languages." Chalea smiled, tucking a strand of dark hair behind her ear. "Long enough to learn everything there is to know about this place."

Ian nodded. He was grateful for Chalea's company, a nice distraction from his own. She was a Roma, and Ian had never met anyone quite like her before. She was charismatic and intriguing, and he sensed that she held secrets. He wasn't sure why exactly, but there was a depth to her gaze, a knowing timbre to her voice that belied simplicity. He felt that there were deeper mysteries there. Her green eyes were direct and piercing, but despite their intimidating quality Ian found himself completely lost in his conversation with her. She was full of stories about memorable tourists and castle folklore, and she'd been entertaining him over his late lunch with a slew of her most comical experiences.

Finishing the last bite of his garden salad, he put his fork down. "So, I'm guessing you've met your fair share of believers over the years. Any real fanatics?"

Chalea's green eyes twinkled with amusement. "Oh yes. I've met a handful of characters in my time here. A few of them even believed that Dracula was alive and living here now and that we just wouldn't admit it—like it's a conspiracy or something." She shook her head in disbelief. "I remember one man in particular, an American. He didn't just believe in Dracula and vampires; he wanted to *be* one. He actually pulled me aside after a tour and tried to pry information about turning from me. And he didn't give up, either. He told me that he wasn't going to stop until he'd gotten what he came for." She sighed. "Some people just don't know the difference between fact and fiction."

"Apparently not," Ian said. "I imagine this is fun as far as professions go, though, isn't it?"

Chalea sobered and sat quietly for a moment. "Mostly, yes, but there are times when tourists show little respect. Some have even been afraid of me, of us. The Roma, that is."

Ian was incredulous. "Why? My experiences with the Roma here in Romania have been positive. I have found the people to be gracious and hospitable. You, especially."

She smiled at him. "I appreciate your kind words, but not all are so devoid of prejudice. The Roma have never been truly welcome in this country, or many others, for that matter. Many consider us thieves, lazy and stupid. Others avoid our people out of fear, as many of my kind are knowledgeable in the ways of divination and magic." She paused. "Why, in the time of Dracula, gypsies were believed to be the protectors of *strigoi,* or the undead, fiercely guarding them in their daytime slumber...to the death if necessary." She frowned suddenly, as if regretting her words.

"Come on. Surely modern people have dispensed with this type of nonsensical thinking, right?" Ian countered.

"Why are you so convinced that it is nonsensical?" She studied his face. "You look genuinely surprised. Ian, you must understand- old superstitions and legends that linger a long time are often based in truth. To this day, there are Roma that have evil reputations." Her eyes darkened. "And some of them deserve to be viewed that way. I refer to the ones that haven't assimilated, the ones that keep to themselves. They've been connected to all manner of dark things: black magic, satanic rituals, and vampires among them." Chalea's eyes told Ian that she was deadly serious. Her comments were not the tour guide version of fanciful history.

"There are certain Roma you think are bad?" Ian leaned forward, intrigued.

Chalea nodded. "My father always told me to avoid the small nomadic groups that live in the mountains here in Transylvania, especially the ones who still worship ancient gods. He said that they are not to be trusted, that they are killers."

She looked at Ian, but he had the feeling that she was miles away, somewhere in her memories. "My father brought me up to believe that danger is real and that we have to be prepared to face it. I used to think that I was, but..." Chalea's wall of composure seemed to crack, a dam of emotions threatening to spill forth. "I lost my sister, Ian. I lost her to these Roma." She blinked back tears, successfully plugging the dam. "She and her boyfriend Fane liked to wander off in the woods to be alone; they'd been sneaking off together for years." She uttered a mirthless chuckle. "Foolish, young love. I used to chide them, warning them not to go out alone, but they never listened. And now they are dead, taken before their time."

Ian was horrified. "My God, what happened?"

Chalea seemed to return to the present. "I told you. These nomadic people are not to be trifled with. They murdered my sister and her boyfriend. We found what was left of their bodies, discarded disgracefully in the forest. They had been mutilated, almost beyond recognition."

"Oh God." Ian frowned. "Was there an investigation? Did the police catch the people responsible?"

Chalea shook her head. "For a Roma? There was a perfunctory investigation. A few questions here and there. Not much effort. In the end, the authorities decided that it was a wild animal attack. My people know better, though. No animal would have done that to them." Her shoulders slumped forward. "They will never get the justice they deserve. Not from the police, at least." She muttered the last sentence under her breath, almost too low for Ian to hear.

"That's awful. I'm so terribly sorry." Ian felt a wave of sympathy for the Roma woman.

"Me too," she replied sadly. "Working here has been a nice respite from my troubles, but now... I am not sure how much longer I will be able to divide my time. Everything is becoming more and more complicated." She watched a bird fly by overhead, then stood up, stretching. "And I am sorry to weigh you down with such a story; I know it's not exactly appropriate for mealtime." She looked down at him, regarding him watchfully with her green eyes. "You're very easy to talk to, Ian. And now I must get back to work, as I am sure you must too." She smiled, the gesture not quite reaching her eyes.

He stood too, giving her a warmer reciprocal smile. "Well, the feeling's mutual," he said as he checked the time on his phone. "I can't remember the last time I took an hour-long lunch. I'm glad I met you." He stuffed his cell back into his jeans' pocket. "Maybe if there's time when my group's done our work I'll come back and take one of your tours."

Chalea chuckled warmly. "Only if I can count on you to not be one of the crazy tourists. I will not arrange a meeting with the master of the castle for you."

Ian grinned. "I promise to be on good behavior."

As Chalea was saying goodbye, Ian caught sight of Renee on her way over.

His good mood instantly dimmed, all of his current problems pressing back into the forefront of his mind. The hurt and anger began to worm their way in again, and he didn't want to deal with them. He wanted nothing more than to walk away with Chalea and stay distracted as long as possible from all of it.

But he and Renee needed to talk. He loved her, and despite the awful secret that he'd learned of yesterday, that love still counted for something. He'd owed it to both of them to work things out.

The tour and the rest of the afternoon's work would have to wait.

CHAPTER 17

Lou sat up, gasping, her head spinning as if it were about to explode. *What the hell?*

She was sprawled on the forest floor, sore all over, with no idea how long she'd been lying there. Her clothes were disheveled, crusted with dirt and splinters.

Where am I?

The question terrified her, because she had no idea what its answer was. The last thing she remembered was getting out her camera to photograph the forest canopy. Then nothing.

Camera...Where was her camera? She scanned the ground around her but found nothing. *Great. Just great.*

She moved to run a hand through her hair in irritation, but paused, a sick feeling filling her stomach.

Her hand had something on it. She glanced down at her hands, the feeling of sickness spreading.

Blood. Her hands were stained with blood.

Shocked, she bolted up, only to be rewarded by a wave of dizziness. Before she could fall over, she leaned against the nearest tree and closed her eyes, focusing on breathing evenly in and out. She slowed her inhales and exhales until they were counts of eight. Then she opened her eyes, sure that she'd managed to get control of herself.

She was far from okay, however. She had blacked out, something that had never happened to her before. Her camera and gear were missing, she was a mess, and she had blood on her hands. Blood that wasn't hers.

What is happening to me?

She already had enough problems to deal with; she didn't need any more to pile on to the existing ones.

She took a step away from the tree, holding onto the trunk just to make sure that she had regained her balance. Satisfied that she wasn't going to fall over, she began to take notice of her surroundings, looking for any sign of a trail.

It didn't take her long to find one. Her bag, her camera resting carefully on top of it, lay right in the middle of the only path in sight.

She rummaged in her bag for her water bottle and poured all its remaining contents over her hands, cleaning the blood from them as best she could.

Wiping her hands on her stained shirt, she picked up her camera, making sure that it wasn't broken.

It wasn't—it had even been turned off, the lens cap put on.

While a part of her was relieved, another part of her felt uneasy. No one else was out in the woods, so she must have placed her bag and camera on the trail herself at some point during her blackout, which meant that she hadn't just fallen on the ground and hit her head or tripped over a jagged root.

She had been moving around, actively doing things, almost as if she'd been sleepwalking during the day.

But I've never done that before...

Well, technically, that wasn't entirely true. But the last time she'd blacked out, she'd known why. She'd been desperate, reckless, foolish, and since then, she'd vowed to never, ever reach that point again.

Yet here I am.

Frustrated, she shoved the empty water bottle and her camera in her bag. As she was pulling her hand out, it brushed against the handle of the mirror.

For a second, Lou felt surprised, but then she remembered that she'd put it back in her bag that morning, not wanting to leave it in the apartment.

Hastily, she pulled it out and held it up to her face.

Oh my God. She had a nasty cut on her left eyebrow, but it wasn't bleeding. The blood had caked and dried, leaving an angry mark in its place. There was also dried blood around her bottom lip, outlining it like psycho-inspired lip liner. Using the less dirty sleeve, she wiped at her face, managing to get most of the blood off.

At least the state of her face explained the blood on her hands. She must have fallen after all; head injuries were funny. It wasn't that odd that she couldn't remember exactly what had happened.

Feeling a little better, she put the mirror back in her bag and swung it over her shoulder. The weight of it felt okay, and the earlier dizziness hadn't returned. Not wanting to be caught in the woods after dark, she started back down the trail the way she'd come.

In her hurry to get back to the castle, Lou failed to notice the mutilated body of the cat hidden in the leaves just off the path. The gaping wound across the feline's neck still seeped blood onto its downy fur, and its head hung back grotesquely, almost completely severed from its body.

She also failed to notice her own utility knife lying discarded next to its corpse.

CHAPTER 18

Deep-set blue eyes regarded Simon and Christer with unguarded apprehension. The tension in the small kitchen was palpable, and both men struggled to put their interviewee at ease, knowing that their ability to convey positive intentions would have direct bearing on the amount of information they could glean from the elderly woman.

A tedious and painstaking search of courthouse records in Brasov had eventually led them to Mihaela Bochinsky, the daughter of Andrei Korzha and his first wife. Mihaela was Korzha's only surviving heir, and as such, she had inherited his property after his death. Fortunately for the team, Mihaela had not traveled far from her roots, even after she and her family had abandoned Copaci. She had spent the majority of her life within a small radius of the place where she had been born, and her small cottage on the outskirts of greater Brasov was just a short drive from where they were staying.

Now eighty-nine years old, Mihaela was living alone in the small, well-tended house she had shared with her husband until his death a decade ago. Simon and Christer had tracked her down using the most recent address they'd come across, praying that by some miracle she would be at home and willing to talk with them. They could hardly believe their good fortune when Mihaela had opened the door and allowed them inside.

Although she sat erect in the high-backed chair at the kitchen table, Mihaela's demeanor bespoke an age-old fatigue that had settled heavily upon her, working its way even into her soulful blue eyes.

Simon studied her surreptitiously. Her grey hair, still long, was braided and pulled back into an intricate knot at the nape of her neck. Her clothes looked old and worn, but were nicely put together. Frown lines were etched on her face and her full lips were turned downed at the corners. In her eyes he saw a sorrow that he was quite familiar with—the sorrow of loss that never truly heals. Despite her weary appearance, though, Simon imagined that at one point in her life Mihaela had been quite stunning. If not for her grave mien, he felt that she still would be. If only the world weren't so cruel.

He felt an immediate empathy for her and offered her a smile to try and ease the tension. Although Mihaela returned his smile, her eyes did not.

Speaking as clearly and slowly as possible so that she wouldn't have trouble understanding him, Simon gave Mihaela his official credentials and explained the purpose of their visit. He told her that the magazine was interested in documenting the history of Copaci in connection with their photographs of the nearby castles, and he added that any personal information she would be willing to share would be appreciated and handled discreetly.

As he spoke, Mihaela's expression became more and more guarded, her frown lines deepening. Sensing that her family history was a source of pain and humiliation, Simon quickly prefaced any further requests by assuring her that they would most certainly present her point of view without bias.

Mihaela listened to him without comment, thinking. She wasn't naive; she knew the real reason that they wanted to talk to her, what personal information they were hoping she'd divulge. They wanted to know about her father's alleged killing spree, to hear her morbid tale in all its gory glory. To them, her family's story meant little more than intrigue to draw readers in, and she had no great desire to tell them anything.

However, talking to them would also mean a chance to clear her father's name and tell the real story, the one that no one except for her husband had believed at the time of the murders.

As strangers, Mihaela figured that the men would at least be unbiased and willing to listen to her without judgment.

It would be a nice change.

The events of fifty-seven years ago had indeed taken an unparalleled toll on her and her family. Afterwards, people had treated her differently. Friends began to call on her and her children less and less frequently until they didn't call at all. People whispered behind her back. Phrases like madness; passed down the family line; bad blood- all had become common fodder for gossip.

At first, their words had been knives in her heart, but after a time she had learned to shut out both the words and the pain they brought. It didn't solve anything, but it made daily life tolerable.

Unsurprisingly, her children had moved away when they were grown, hoping to start new beginnings where no one would judge them based on their family's history. She supposed she could have done the same, but after so many years, the idea of leaving Brasov- let alone Romania- left her feeling hollow; her home was all she had left.

After seeing that the men did not need a refill on the tea that she had served upon their arrival, Mihaela smoothed her apron and addressed Simon and Christer in English. Although she spoke slowly and her accent was thick, her words were clear and her command of the language was good. Christer settled back in his chair, happy that he wouldn't need to serve as a translator.

"I will share what I can with you. But I am wondering: why would an American magazine have such big interest in my small Copaci?"

Christer and Simon exchanged peripheral glances before looking at their hostess. Simon gestured towards Christer, indicating that he spoke for both of them.

"First, I want to thank you again for graciously allowing us into your home. I confess to being at a loss as to how to begin, but seeing as you've asked us an open, honest question, we must give you an honest answer. As

I explained, our magazine is focusing on eight castles throughout Romania, the closest to you being Râsnov. Or so we thought. Since then, our team has learned of and visited Solovastru Castle. We decided to use Solovastru as an addition for the magazine story, and we want to learn more about it. From others, we learned of its fateful history, and of its owners, and of the effect those events had on Copaci. Our research regarding Copaci led us to the story of the Korzhas and eventually to you."

Simon paused, looking at Mihaela with compassion. "We do not wish to bring up your pain, or to make you relive what I'm sure must have been a nightmare. We only want to know the truth. From our sources, we have been told that your father went mad and murdered his young daughters and wife before taking his own life. That is all we know, yet I suspect that we are missing some of the facts. Please, Ms. Bochinsky, tell us if there is more to this story."

Mihaela's eyes welled with tears. "Yes, young man," she said, falteringly. "There is much more."

Simon and Christer sat silently, patiently waiting for the old woman to regain her composure. Simon struggled to banish the twinge of guilt at making Mihaela relive her painful memories.

She dabbed at her eyes with the corner of her apron before continuing. "My father did not kill himself or his family." She paused, looking purposefully at both men. "Andrei Korzha was a good man, a gentle man. A man with a big heart. He loved my mother greatly and missed her terribly after she died. I never knew her; she died giving birth to me, and my father raised me by himself. He could never quite hide his sadness, but he was still a good father to me.

"I married young and started my own home. It was then that my father met his second wife, Elena. She was very beautiful and much younger than my father, but she seemed to love him, so I was happy for them. Elena gave my father two daughters: Madalina and Ana. My sisters were a joy to me, and I miss them every day, even after all this time. I can still see them laughing and running... and then there are other images too...ones that I wish I did not remember..." Mihaela's words trailed off and for a moment she seemed too stricken to continue.

Finally, she spoke again. "Everything was wonderful for many years. I remember Ana was six when the trouble began. My father found an antique mirror while hunting in the woods near Solovastru and he gave it to Elena as a gift. She was quite taken with it. I only know this as he had told me later—before the awful events of that day. After that, Elena began to change towards all of us, even the girls. Whenever I saw my father, he looked unhappy. He and Elena had always gotten along and made each other happy, but she began to act as if she despised my father. She neglected her housework and did not prepare meals each night as she used to. She would lock herself in her room and ignore everyone for hours. Madalina and Ana became afraid of her and her moods; my sisters spent a lot of time at my house during those last weeks. They began to show a preference for their father's company, even wanting to go on hunting trips when school was finished."

"Did you witness the change in Elena's behavior firsthand?" Christer asked, wondering if Mihaela had simply been eager to believe her father and in his innocence.

"Oh yes," Mihaela responded emphatically. "I can recall very distinctly a visit to the house about a week before their... deaths. My children and I had been gathering wild berries to make jam and I had made many jars. It was one of my father's favorite sweets and I wanted to bring him and my sisters some jars for their breakfast bread. When I arrived, I found that the girls had gone into town with their father. Elena was home alone. She had always been friendly towards me before, but as I stood in her doorway that day, I felt unwelcome. She was cold and haughty- different from the woman I knew. When I asked after my father, she sneered at me and told me that the 'ignorant peasant' had gone to town – those were her words – and that she did not know or care when he would return. She did not invite me to stay or offer me anything. She turned her back to me and sat at the kitchen table gazing at her reflection in that fancy hand-held mirror. She was obsessed with herself, especially in the end.

"I decided to leave my gift for the children and my father and go home. As I was leaving, I saw something, and I swear to you that what I tell you next is God's truth. I caught a glimpse of Elena's reflection in that mirror, and it was not Elena I saw staring back at me- it was someone else. They were still Elena's features, but the spirit wearing them wasn't Elena's. The woman in the mirror had a twisted, evil look upon her face, a look I had never seen before and never want to see again. Everyone in Copaci thought my father was possessed, but they were wrong. It was not him, but her, who was possessed."

"Mihaela, what do you think really happened that day?" Simon reached over and gently squeezed her hand.

Sensing the genuineness of the gesture, she responded, "I believe that my father brought something evil back with him in that mirror from Solovastru, an evil that twisted and destroyed my stepmother. I think she killed her own daughters, and when my father realized what she had done, he killed her and then himself for he could not live with his grief."

"I am assuming that you told the villagers what you've told us. Why didn't anyone believe you? What you told us seems very plausible, and because your father and Elena were both dead when they were found, there was no evidence to determine who really killed the girls. Why simply blame your father?" Simon found himself trying to make sense of it.

"I do not know. Perhaps it was easier for them to believe that a man and not a woman could be capable of such atrocity. Perhaps blaming my father was just an easier answer." Mihaela sighed. "Whatever truth you believe, know this: Solovastru Castle is cursed. Its evil destroyed those that lived in it centuries ago and eventually those around it. Its blackness extended to Copaci and pushed everyone away. Only a few gypsies remain on its outskirts, and even they do not stay long."

Christer whistled through his teeth, his mind reeling. "So, you really believe Solovastru is evil?" His eyes traveled the room, taking note of the crucifixes and icons of the Blessed Virgin. He need not have asked his question; it was obvious that belief in the mysterious was not so far-fetched for Mihaela Bochinsky.

In lieu of an immediate answer, she leaned forward and took both of Christer's hands into hers. "You are young, and it is hard for you to recognize evil when you meet it. But trust me when I tell you that Solovastru is evil, down to its very walls. There were so many bad things that happened there and in the woods around it, things people cannot explain away. No one goes there anymore. You too must promise me that your team will abandon this effort to explore the castle and its history. Nothing good will come of it. Take what you already have, move on, and don't look back."

Both men stopped short of promising the old woman that they would not return to Solovastru, but they assured her that they would be cautious and thanked her profusely for sharing her memories with them.

On his way out the door, Simon promised that he would write about her father as she portrayed him. At this, Mihaela's eyes once again filled with tears.

Reaching into her apron pocket, she withdrew a small pewter crucifix and pressed it into his hands. "For protection. Remember, the evil that was born at Solovastru is an evil that does not die. It is always searching for another way to return and bring misery and destruction. Please, stay away. But, if you choose to return to Solovastru, please seek advice and wisdom from the Roma gypsies. Because they practice the old ways, they have much knowledge in dealing with forces outside modern understanding. Trust me in this; you will not regret it. God keep you both."

Romania, 1430 A.D.

The dusky evening was cold. The wind howled relentlessly through the bare trees, carrying a light snow on its breath. Winter's presence was visible all around.

Xenia was unaffected by the chill. She wore only her usual lightweight robes as she wove a path through the trees. Her hem was wet, soaked by the muddy ground. She did not take notice of it, however, or of the wintry elements that filled the woods around the castle. She was distracted, her thoughts straying this way and that like rats in a maze searching for the way out, not knowing if it was just around the corner or far, far away.

The crack of a twig drew her attention, despite her pondering. Her reflexes were as reliable as ever.

She stood erect as a figure walked towards her from behind a grove of bare trees. When the man drew closer – for it was a man – he stood at least a head taller than Xenia, broad-shouldered and dark. His heavy brow was wet with snow.

Reaching her, he bowed, more an inclination of his head than a bend from the waist. "Xenia," he said.

"Miksa. What a pleasant surprise."

The man straightened fully and smiled, a gesture that looked as innocuous on his features as the fangs of a venomous snake. "I somewhat doubt both parts of that statement," he said. "Still, I am not here to challenge you or wish you ill. I'm here on behalf of the others."

When she made no reply, he continued, "While I am unaware of all the details concerning your stay at Solovastru Castle, I do know enough from

Csilla and from others to draw my own conclusions. Too many girls have been killed for people to ignore. The townspeople are going to come for blood, and soon. Do you know what will happen then?"

Xenia seemed to look through him, her green eyes distant.

"Xenia, she is going to be executed. Your *Sabina*. She is going to die. The authorities will be at the castle possibly as soon as tomorrow."

In a moment of audacity, Miksa reached out and gripped her shoulders in an iron hold, forcing her to look at him. "Do you understand what I am telling you? She will be killed! And you will be found out, if you stay. If that were to happen, we would all be in jeopardy. You – *we* – need to leave. Now."

Xenia shook him off and struck him across the face, her nails cutting into his cheek. "Touch or speak to me again as you just have, and my next cut will be across your throat."

The two faced each other in silence for a few moments, only the wind filling the gap in their conversation.

After a few minutes, Miksa bowed deeply. He had not wiped his cheek from her attack, and a few drops of blood dripped onto the snowy forest floor as he bent over. "Forgive me. I should have restrained myself." He caught her eye as he stood. "However, you must listen to sense. We have been hunting in these woods a long time; at *your* behest, and in order to ensure our secrecy, we have been careful never to kill so great a number of people as to draw attention. We have limited ourselves to a mere pittance of the blood tribute to which we are entitled. You and Sabina have been more...active, however, and now we are all at risk of discovery." He hardened his tone. "There is danger, and it is immediate and insurmountable. We *must* leave."

In a moment of uncharacteristic vulnerability, Xenia withered a little, lines of ancient exhaustion showing on her face. "Miksa, I know." She sighed. "I know." She walked over to a nearby tree and leaned against it, ignoring the water that soaked into her robes from the wet bark. "I have ignored the obvious in an attempt to prolong the present. I shall do so no longer. I am going to go back to the castle for Sabina and we will meet you in two days' time at the old rendezvous point."

Miksa stepped closer to her, an incredulous expression on his face. "Xenia, you intend to...?" He let his question trail off in the wind.

Her strength returning, Xenia stepped away from the tree. "Yes. I intend to turn Sabina." She stared pointedly at the slash on his cheek. "Do you find fault with my decision, Miksa?"

He retreated a step. "Not at all, Xenia. I am simply disconcerted. Csilla did tell us your wishes, but I assumed she was exaggerating." Another venomous smile played on his lips. "However, I am not in opposition to the idea; I think it is time we had a new addition to our group. If you feel Sabina Solovastru will be the right one, then I fully agree and support you."

He bowed again in genuine deference. "As ever, I remain loyal to you. I look forward to our journey in two days' time. I wish you haste, Xenia."

Then he was gone, running silently off into the trees before Xenia could reply.

She frowned after him. Miksa was the only one of her own that she often regretted turning. While he did respect her and heed her command, he had become insolent and strong-willed over the years, eager for a power struggle. At the same time, he was also wise and protective of their clan, an irreplaceable ally. She knew that he would challenge her one day; he sought to lead the group and be a Maker, something he could only achieve when she was out of the way. When that day came, she would end him. Until then, however, things would remain as they were.

Pushing thoughts of Miksa out of her head, she took off through the woods, running faster than humanly possible back to Solovastru Castle.

...the authorities will be at the castle, possibly as soon as tomorrow...

She felt a feeling of dread swell within her, gnawing on her bones. She pushed herself faster and faster, praying that she would make it back before it was too late.

When she reached the clearing that surrounded Solovastru Castle, it was indeed too late. Men from the nearby villages were teeming around the place like ants, armed with weapons and anger, their faces mirroring the lust for revenge that was burning within them.

Keeping back in the trees, trying to hide but poorly concealed beneath the naked branches, she listened.

"...she'll burn in hell for this. Mistress of the devil, whore of a demon. So many murders... I'd like to kill her myself."

"...She's to be brought before the tribunal in the morn. They're wasting no time with her; there's no need. Bodies of so many missing children have been found..."

"...they should torture her first, just to hear her scream. Try to appease all the grieving families..."

"...end of Sabina Solovastru. If only we could have caught that witch, too..."

"...to keep looking. There's a chance we still might find her."

Xenia felt herself shaking, tremors she couldn't control coursing through her body.

No. This could not be so.

Oh, my darling Sabina...

The large branch she had been clutching in her hands snapped, making a noise that echoed loudly into the clearing.

A few pairs of eyes looked over in her direction, but she was already gone, moving as swiftly away from the castle as she had towards it. The day was overcast, but the sun was threatening to break through the clouds, and she couldn't take the risk of being caught in the open if that happened. She had to retreat.

As she ran back into deeper sections of the forest, her shattered composure returned, accompanied by an implacable will to do something, somehow, to save Sabina.

By Kali's blood, she will not *die at the hands of those filthy villagers!*

Her mind working against the impending terror, she began to formulate a plan.

CHAPTER 19

The highway was slick with rain, the road ahead a shiny, wet sea. The five had been on the DN1 for over two hours, on their way to the small town of Sinaia in Prahova County, their silence only broken by the sound of rain hitting the windshield.

In the two days following their shoot at Bran, the group atmosphere had grown strange and tense. While no one had yet said it aloud, all of them knew that Lou was the source of it. Lou hadn't told anyone, not even Renee, about what had happened to her in the woods surrounding Bran Castle, but her silence about the incident hadn't made it go away. The others were frustrated by her constant mood changes and recent lack of enthusiasm for their assignment.

Still, they continued on as best they could. The detour to Solovastru and the additional time spent in unraveling its mysteries had set them back almost two days. Mindful of their schedule constraints, they had hurriedly packed bags and equipment into the rental car early in the morning and programmed directions to Peles Castle into the navigation system they had affectionately named 'Sheila'.

Simon stole a glance back in the rearview mirror. Renee was comfortably nestled on Ian's chest, her eyes half-closed, his chin resting on the top of her head. Looking at the two of them, Simon felt a bittersweet pang go through him; he of course was happy that the couple had reconciled, but at the same time, he couldn't help but be the slightest bit disappointed. Before his mind could start spinning possibilities, he looked away from them and over at Lou. Her body was still as she gazed silently out the rear passenger window, her face emotionless.

Simon wondered if the sisters had reconciled after the incident back in Brasov, but he hadn't had the courage to ask either of them about it. It seemed like a topic to avoid, at least for the present moment.

Christer sneezed in the seat beside him, drawing his attention. The Swede had his trusted map spread out on his lap, its pages well marked from years of use. Despite Simon's assurance that the navigation system could save them a lot of trouble, Christer had insisted that 'Sheila' was not to be trusted and brought the map.

Simon was glad to have Christer in the front seat with him. Without his commentary on passing landmarks, the two-hour trip would've been completely silent, a highly unusual occurrence for a group of associates who had become close friends.

They arrived at Peles Castle in the afternoon, the rain now well behind them.

After a brief check-in with security at Peles and a show of credentials, the group gathered the equipment and divided the tasks for the afternoon. Simon and Lou were paired up to cover the scheduled interior shots, much to Lou's disappointment. She had been hoping to photograph the breathtaking outdoor landscape of its alpine-like setting and had visibly bristled when she hadn't gotten her way. Simon tried in vain to dispel her annoyance and disappointment, despite being almost sure it would be a waste of effort.

"You know, Lou," he said, his tone conciliatory, "Peles Castle is a real gem. Peles, and its sister Pelisor, were both commissioned by King Carol I—Peles in 1873, Pelisor in 1899. Peles served as a royal hunting preserve and summer retreat, and the interior truly does rival the beauty of its exterior. Wait until we get inside; I know you will appreciate it."

His attempt to placate her was met with stony silence.

Simon's goal for the afternoon was to study and notate a segment of the 170 rooms in the grand castle that were decorated in varying cultural themes from around the world. Simon knew that Peles contained one of the finest art collections in all of Eastern and Central Europe, in addition to a four-thousand-piece collection of weapons and armor. To put it mildly, he was anxious to have a look.

From the moment they started working, Simon felt as if he were dragging Lou by her hair. In contrast to her normal exuberance, she was slow and completely unenthused by anything. Try as he might to be patient, her attitude was beginning to grate on his nerves.

Even her shots were suffering. Finally, after letting her sorry work slide for over an hour, he said something.

"Lou, could you please retake these close-ups on the tapestries? I think we need to make some adjustments in order to bring out the beautiful hues." He gestured at the digital shots Lou had taken.

"What are you talking about, Simon?" Lou barked, striding over and ripping the camera from his grasp. "The colors came up fine. I know how to do my job. Stop being so anal, if that's not too much to ask." Her words dripped with ice.

He blinked. "Lou... Take a walk. We can resume when you've cooled off." He responded flatly even though he was both taken aback and hurt by the venom in her words, turning away as he spoke to hide how much the exchange bothered him.

As a habit, Simon avoided conflict like the plague, especially conflicts with people he regarded as friends. It was usually an easy habit to keep. Lately, however, he felt as if he were in the presence of a completely different person whenever he was around Lou. As she stalked out of the room, he resolved to have a word with Renee about her at the next available opportunity. Perhaps she could tell him what was going on with her sister.

Lou returned after a time and the two finished their task in awkward silence, neither mentioning the blow-up. By the time they rejoined the others at the end of the day, it was hard to ignore the elephant in the room. The tension in the air was palpable, and Renee, along with everyone else, was becoming increasingly worried about Lou.

Lou was first in the car for the return trip, taking up her previous position. Her attention was focused on the open laptop on her lap, and she didn't acknowledge the others as they clambered into the car. Not wanting to endure an unpleasant drive, Renee and the men tacitly decided to ignore Lou's odd behavior and carry on a conversation amongst themselves, leaving Lou to stew in her own sullen mood.

Now and again, Renee would surreptitiously glance in her sister's direction, hoping that Lou would shake off whatever was bothering her. Her hopes went unfulfilled. Lou was content to keep her own company.

After checking into the small B&B, the team decided to freshen up and meet by eight for dinner and drinks. Everyone was hoping that a little food and relaxation would set things right again.

Renee tried to help Lou with her bags, but Lou shrugged her sister off and stomped upstairs without so much as a word.

Renee stared after her, puzzled. She thought that they had worked through their differences over the incident with Ian, but apparently, they hadn't.

Ian approached her, his expression mirroring her feelings.

"Don't worry; it's going to be okay. I bet she's just stressed. Heavy schedule, foreign country, and close quarters add up to pressure that makes people behave strangely. Just talk with her later. You two are like bread and butter—I don't know a pair of sisters who love each other more."

Worry lines still etched on her face, Renee leaned over to squeeze his hand. "Yeah," she said simply, before following her sister upstairs.

Simon walked up to Ian as Renee left and put a hand on his shoulder. "Ian, we need to talk about Lou."

"Yes, we do," Christer interjected as he dragged the last of the baggage to where the men stood in the lobby. "Something really odd is going on with her. I know I haven't known her very long, but during our first week here, she and I made a connection, you know? For the first time since Annika died, I..." His voice trailed off. "Now, in these last few days, I feel as if I am in the presence of a stranger." Christer shook his head, his handsome features creased with concern.

Simon nodded his agreement and quickly recounted the events of earlier in the day.

"I've known Lou for about three years now," Ian said. "She has *never* acted like this. She's the type who literally wouldn't hurt a fly, and she's a good friend to everyone. She and Renee are usually thick as thieves. The incident the other day with Renee and me was completely out of character. I still can't get my arms around that one."

"Look, maybe the three of us should talk with Renee about her later tonight," Christer suggested. "Try and figure out what's up."

Agreeing that this was the best course of action, the men started for their rooms, each lost in his own thoughts.

CHAPTER 20

Renee hesitated at the door, her hand suspended in mid-air.

Her sister had been in the bathroom for thirty minutes and Renee was becoming more nervous and apprehensive the longer she waited for her to come out. There were things they needed to work out, and every minute she waited to say something was weakening her resolve.

Tired of waiting, she knocked on the door. "Lou, can I butt-in for a minute? I want to talk. We *need* to talk." Renee exhaled the words in a rush.

Not bothering to respond, Lou simply turned the doorknob and let the door swing open.

Renee stopped short when she saw her sister, doing a double take.

Lou had donned a short, black leather miniskirt, high-heeled ankle boots, and a purple cashmere sweater that clung to her curves like a second skin. Her hair was loose and full around her shoulders, her make-up dark and smoky. Her appearance exuded a raw sensuality in a dark and dangerous way.

Renee tried to hide her surprise but couldn't. Her sister always dressed chicly, yes, but never overtly sexy or revealing. Renee hadn't even known that Lou *owned* clothes like that, let alone that she'd packed them for the trip.

"What the hell, Lou? Where are you planning to go dressed like that?" She sputtered, the look on her face betraying her bewilderment and concern.

Lou appraised her sister from beneath heavy eyelashes. "I am going out. Alone. I need some time away from summer camp. I also need some fun— my idea of fun, not yours." Her red lips curled suggestively.

"Lou, this is crazy. You don't know your way around, and unless you've been carting around 'Rosetta Stone' in your camera bag, here's a newsflash: you can't speak Romanian! Something could happen to you. Please don't go," Renee pleaded.

Lou turned back to the counter and began packing up her make-up, ignoring her sister. Last to be put away was the vanity mirror from Solovastru, its surface gleaming as she stowed it into her bag.

Renee frowned when she noticed it, vaguely remembering having seen it before.

And also remembering that Lou had been all too eager to hide it from her.

"Lou, where did that mirror come from?"

The change in her sister was abrupt. Lou almost snarled at Renee as she zipped up her bag, her expression full of malice. "None of your business," she snapped. "In fact, what I do and where I go is none of your business either."

Instinctively, Renee took a step back. Never before had she sensed such coldness from her sister, and for a moment, she felt real fear. *Something is very, very wrong. Who the hell is this person and what has she done with my sister?*

"Lou, please, why don't you let Christer take you out tonight? You two have been spending a lot of time together anyway, and he clearly cares about you. At least if you go out together, I know you'll be safe," she added, determined to make her sister see reason.

Lou walked the few steps separating them, her heels clacking loudly on the tiled floor.

Taller than Renee with her boots on, she looked down at her through narrowed eyes. "Sister, I can take care of myself. And as for your suggestion, I am not interested in spending any more time than necessary with our pretty-boy Swedish babysitter."

Renee swallowed, her voice refusing to work. Lou's words had sounded like the hiss of a snake, and Renee was afraid that the snake was about to strike. Everything about her sister seemed different at that moment; even her eyes had changed. Their color was cooler than usual, and they shone with...annoyance, arrogance...*hatred?* It was hard to tell which was most prominent in her stare.

"Lou," she said, shaking off her unease and placing a gentle hand on her sister's arm. "Please. The partying...this kind of behavior...it nearly cost you everything before. If something is wrong – no matter what it is – please just talk to me. Lean on me. I'm here this time. You don't have to face your demons alone, and you don't have to act out to get my attention. I'm right here."

With a look that could only be described as disdain, Lou brushed her hand aside. "I'm not 'acting out', Renee. I'm not a child. I just want to go out and enjoy myself. And I don't want company."

Without knowing what else to do, Renee looked down at her feet and stepped to the side, allowing Lou to pass.

As Lou was leaving, Renee thought she heard her snicker, but Lou was already too far away to tell.

What is going on with her?

Overwhelmed by worry for the sister she thought she knew, Renee slumped against the bathroom door, tears welling up in her eyes.

Ian. I should go find Ian, she thought desperately. *He'll know what to do; he always knows what to do.*

She ran a shaking hand through her hair. *What the hell is happening?*

Christer sat in the lobby, nursing a beer as he waited for the others to join him. While there was still a good twenty minutes before their agreed upon dinner time, he had decided to get started early. Ever since the discussion about Lou at check-in, he had been plagued by worry. He could think of nothing else, and it made him realize just how much he had begun to care for the beautiful brunette.

Checking his watch, he looked towards the stairs to the apartments above and was startled to see Lou descending. He squinted, then stared, taking in Lou's appearance with shock. Before she could saunter out of the lobby doors, he jumped to his feet and headed in her direction, determined to intercept her.

"Lou, hold up a minute!" He said, raising his voice to get her attention. "Where are you going?"

Lou turned towards him and eyed him with impatience. "Out. Alone. I don't want or need a babysitter, so you can go right on back to enjoying your beer."

Babysitter? "I didn't realize I was such a burden," Christer replied. The words sounded wounded, but he didn't care. Lou was staring him down like someone about to go into battle—just daring him to make a move so she could cut him down. It baffled him completely, but concern helped him find his voice. "Regardless of what you think of me," he said, "I care about your well-being. You could get into trouble here, especially if you go out dressed like *that.*" He softened his tone as he reached out to take her arm. "Lou, if something happened to you, none of us - especially your sister - could forgive themselves. So don't be stupid."

Lou shrugged his hand off and, with a parting, "*I'll be fine,*" headed for the exit.

Christer stood motionless for a moment as he watched her go, lost in thought.

Lou was self-destructing. That much was obvious—especially to someone like him who was well acquainted in the art. Hell, he could've written the how-to guide on the subject. Annika's death had been the catalyst for him, but what on earth was causing these changes in Lou Bryant?

Indecisiveness tore at him: go after her or stay and talk with the others? Fear for Lou blossomed in him. He was outside his comfort zone and he didn't know what to do.

The only thing he did know, without a doubt, was that he didn't want to lose her.

CHAPTER 21

I t was like she was a completely different person," Christer concluded as the waiter left their table in the back of the small restaurant, voicing the phrase that had been in circulation with everyone all day long.

Renee nodded in agreement. "I know."

Simon leaned back in his chair, then leaned into the table, bringing his hands together in prayer-like fashion. "Friends, I find that I am in agreement with Christer too—Lou is definitely not acting like herself. When we worked together today at Peles, she was disinterested, sloppy, argumentative; all qualities I would have never attributed to her in the past."

"It's worse than that, Brody," Renee said, turning her worry-filled gaze in his direction. "I think Lou is spiraling again."

"Again?" Christer asked.

Renee pursed her lips unhappily, then looked at her boyfriend, who nodded his encouragement. "Lou would kill me for talking about this, but at this point, I think it's only fair that you know." She took a breath, preparing herself to share something she hadn't discussed in a long, long time. "Ever since our mom died, Lou has struggled with bouts of severe depression. It's manifested itself in different ways over the years, but I was always there to help her through it, to bring her back. But when Lou was nineteen, I snagged this incredible opportunity and I left her alone. She wasn't in a great way, but she seemed to be managing okay – or, at least, I selfishly convinced myself that she was managing – because I really didn't want to pass up the job. I knew it would be invaluable to my career, and so I...I put that ahead of my sister.

"While I was gone, Lou's depression deepened with a vengeance. She went back on her medication, started abusing it, and then a friend convinced her she needed a change of pace to pick her spirits up. Three weeks later, I got a call from HUP. The nurse on the line said I was the emergency contact for one Louisa Bryant and asked me to come in immediately.

"When I saw my sister in that hospital bed, hooked up to IVs, head bandaged, thin as paper..." Renee's features crumpled at the memory. "I wasn't sure she was going to pull through. And when she did finally wake up, her memory was like Swiss cheese. She couldn't piece together where she'd been, who she'd been with, or what had happened. The doctor assigned to her filled in some of the blanks—told me about the traces of various drugs in her system, hinted that there was some trauma to her...her body, but Lou couldn't confirm or deny any of it. I spent the next two months by her side, trying to help her recover, forced to watch her go through drug withdrawal—and that wasn't even the worst part. When we were back home, Lou would wake up screaming some nights, some of her lost memories coming back to her." Renee shuddered. "I won't go into the details, but guys, believe me when I tell you that some of what she told me still haunts me. It's a testament to my sister's strength of will that she was able to come back from all of that."

"And a testament to yours," Simon said quietly. "No doubt your sister recovered partially in thanks to you."

"I was the one who abandoned her in the first place, Brody. Helping her recover was the least I could do."

It seemed all three men were about to comment on that, but Renee pressed on. "But this time – if my sister is headed down that destructive road again – I'm here. And I want—I have to help her."

"And we're here for you, hon," Ian said firmly. He took a breath. "Look, we need to take inventory," he suggested. "You know—try and pinpoint exactly when Lou's strange behavior began to manifest and whether it could be connected to anything or anyone in particular."

"The 'when' is easy," Renee replied. "After our visit to Solovastru. I remember that Lou was restless that night, tossing and turning in her sleep, moaning."

"And it was just after our visit there that Lou betrayed your confidence with me and caused the blow-up," Ian added. "Since then, nothing's been normal."

Silence hung over the four. Renee was replaying the scene from the bathroom in her mind when it suddenly occurred to her that she should mention the mirror. She wasn't sure why it had popped into her head, but suddenly she perceived its significance with precognitive certainty.

"Guys, Lou took something from Solovastru Castle, I'm certain of it. Don't ask me why I know it; I just do. When I confronted Lou in our bathroom, she had this mirror resting on the counter. An antique-looking thing. The handle had ornate carvings, I think. Anyway, I asked her where it came from because I knew it wasn't something from home; we generally pack together and share stuff to eliminate excess bulk—I'd have recognized it from when we packed.

Lou flipped when I asked her about it—shoved it in her bag, refused to tell me anything about it. I thought it was odd at the time, but then I forgot about it until now."

Simon exhaled, the air whistling through his teeth. He turned to Christer, his eyes suddenly sparking.

"Christer, do you remember our visit with Mihaela and her story about her stepmother and the murders?" His voice dropped. "And the mirror?"

Before Christer could respond, Renee snapped her head towards Simon and interjected, "What mirror? You didn't mention a mirror before when you told us about the Korzha story!"

"Renee, I...I'm sorry," Simon stammered. "It...when we told you the story it seemed inconsequential, just an elderly woman's way of readjusting blame; I had forgotten about it until now. Mihaela Bochinsky believed that the change in her stepmother's personality and behavior happened because of a gift given to her—an antique mirror her husband had found in the woods while hunting near Solovastru. She believed that the mirror was a conduit for an ancient evil, one that eventually possessed her stepmother."

"Oh God, you're right," Christer breathed.

"Could it be the same mirror? Is that even possible?" Ian asked.

"Hold on a second." Renee held up a hand. "Are the three of you really entertaining the notion that Lou might be *possessed?* By a mirror cursed with some ancient voodoo shit?" She gave a hysterical snort.

"I get that it sounds crazy here and now, but what if...what if the things we write off as crazy superstitions are possible? What if they're *not* just superstitions?" Christer interjected.

"That," Simon replied, "is a dangerous question." He turned to Renee. "I know you might not want to entertain this theory, but you *are* the one who mentioned that your sister took the mirror—unprompted," he commented. "I know you consciously eschew things that fall outside of the scientific realm, as I myself do, most of the time, but do you think that some small part of you might believe the impossible has happened here?"

Everyone sat in silence as they waited for Renee to speak.

Finally, she swallowed. "I don't...I don't know," she admitted. "I was raised Catholic and was taught that there are many things beyond human understanding and that good and evil exist...but a cursed mirror? I don't know. It just sounds like a bad fairytale to me." She searched Ian's eyes. "Do *you* think it's possible—that there is something evil working through that mirror...something inexplicable? Do you think it's really the same mirror anyway?"

He reached for her hand. "Whether or not such a thing is possible is secondary to Lou's safety. I say we have a talk with her in the morning and have a look at her little souvenir from Solovastru, okay? Let's not jump to the scariest, most impossible conclusions right away."

Each of them nodded, no one able to muster a response. Myths and superstitions, the folklore that had been meant to sell copies of *Itinera*, suddenly didn't seem so fictitious anymore. For the first time since they had come to Romania, they were starting to believe that there might be more truth lurking behind the stories than they had ever dreamed possible.

CHAPTER 22

She was beautiful and sexy. And drunk.

Tonight is going to be my lucky night, he thought as the girl leaned in close and brushed her lips over his ear. The teasing little gestures made him shiver involuntarily.

He hoped the number of drinks he'd consumed so far wouldn't impede his performance in bed.

His date had explained to him that she was from a village in the far eastern corner of Romania and that she was just passing through, on her way to visit friends for a short holiday. He had never heard of the village she mentioned, but that wasn't so strange; there were dozens of small villages littered throughout the country, way too many to keep track of. Despite his current alcoholic haze, he did notice that her accent and manner of speech were strange though—almost old fashioned.

Not that it mattered. The chick was a sure thing—*that* was what mattered. Frankly, he wouldn't have cared if she spoke Russian. All that really mattered were her long legs and tight ass.

"Pisti, bring the lady and I another round, okay?" He gestured to his old friend behind the bar who flashed him a familiar '*haven't you had enough already?*'look.

"Oh, come on... last one. Be a friend to a friend in need," the man pleaded, hands clasped in mock prayer.

The bartender relented, rolling his eyes and looking past him at the girl. "Okay, Matthew, one last round for you and your lady friend." As he set the drinks down on the bar he leaned in close. "And pay up this time. You look like you can hardly stand, and I want to see the color of your money—tip too."

"Sure, sure." Matthew threw some bills on the bar and turned back to his date, pulling her to him for a kiss, which she enthusiastically delivered.

"You didn't tell me your name, baby. What should I call you?"

"Call me *sugar*." She ran her tongue over her lips suggestively and lightly ran a finger down his arm, raising goose bumps.

"Okay Sugar," he crooned. "How about we leave here and find somewhere cozier to party?"

"Sounds like fun," she replied, stretching lasciviously over the back of the barstool. "Private parties are my favorite."

It took every ounce of self-control he had not to jump up and down for joy.

Moving slowly enough so that he wouldn't fall over, he got off of his stool and helped the dark beauty off hers, squeezing her ass as she stood.

The pair exited the loud, dimly lit bar and headed for the parking lot where he had left his car. When he finally managed to locate it, he clambered in, drunkenly fumbling with his keys. *She is so hot...and willing too. This never happens to me. Oh lucky, lucky night.*

She, however, hesitated, her hand on the passenger door. "You should go home, Matthew, without me," she said. "Don't let me get in this car." She spoke in a strangled voice, almost as if she were trying to push the words out.

What? Is she really playing hard to get now? Fucking tease. "C'mon Sugar, we'll have fun, just get in the car." He put as much honey into his voice as he could.

His words proved unnecessary, though, as she was already climbing into the car, her momentary hesitation seemingly past. "Don't pay any attention to her," she cooed.

Her? "What did you say?" Matthew blinked in confusion.

"Don't pay any attention to me. I say all sorts of things when I'm drunk." The smile she gave him didn't quite blot out the coldness in her gaze.

He forced himself to chuckle. "Whatever you say, Sugar," he said, shrugging off the shiver of unease he felt.

He drove them to a remote location on the outskirts of town, one frequented by young lovers without the means to put up for a motel room. He'd spent enough time puking there after having too much to drink to know that they would have all the privacy they needed.

He killed the ignition and reached over for a kiss, pulling her hard against him. Her dark blue eyes sparkled in the moonlight and her full lips pouted playfully. He ran his hands under her sweater, cupping her breasts through the lace of her bra.

"I have a place for those luscious lips of yours, baby." He smiled suggestively and began to unzip his jeans, gently pushing her head into his lap. Her long hair covered him like a halo as she bent over him.

Moaning when he felt her hot mouth cover him, he fisted his hands in her hair and leaned his head back. "That's right, Sugar. Hell yes..."

Suddenly, she looked up at him, laughing huskily.

"Men are all the same," she whispered. All of the playfulness in her voice was suddenly gone, and the blue eyes that met his were as sober and cold as the ice of a glacier. "They are concerned only with their own pleasure...simple beasts."

All at once, Matthew was afraid. Something about her manner and her words sent a chill up his spine. Pulse racing, he tried to move, but before he could extricate himself from her, he saw the glint of the sharp blade she held in her right hand.

With lightning speed, she brought the blade across his neck, slashing at him.

Funny, he thought calmly. *I didn't feel a thing. Maybe this is just some sick joke. Maybe she didn't even cut me.*

A second later, Matthew knew this wasn't the case. He felt the wetness of his blood spilling down the front of his chest and an odd pulsing in his veins. His heartbeat was suddenly as loud as a drum in his ears, and he found that he couldn't breathe. Even his voice wasn't working.

In his last conscious moment, Matthew wondered why the crazy bitch was leaning in to taste his blood.

Then his thoughts ceased.

Renee heard the click of the lock and was immediately wide awake. Glancing over at her portable alarm clock, she saw it was well past two in the morning. She had dozed on and off periodically through the night, plagued by worry for her sister. Not wanting Lou to know that she had lain awake most of the night waiting for her to return, she feigned sleep, staying as still as possible, her eyes almost completely closed.

She could almost feel her sister's eyes boring into her from where she stood by the bed. Then, after what seemed like an eternity, Lou finally moved to the bathroom and closed the door behind her. Renee waited patiently, debating whether or not to get up and check on her.

Minutes ticked by. *Did she pass out in the bathroom?*

Just as she was about to check, the door opened and Lou, in nothing but lacy panties and bra, made for her bed. She didn't glance in Renee's direction. She got into bed, pulled the covers around her and lay so still that Renee wondered if she hadn't passed out after all.

She listened to her sister's steady breathing for another quarter hour, then decided it was safe to get up and check the bathroom. A part of her cringed at spying on Lou, but under the circumstances, it seemed a necessary evil. If she looked, she might find some clues as to Lou's whereabouts that evening, or even find the mirror and have a better look at it.

She closed the door and flicked on the light.

The clothes Lou had gone out in were balled up in the corner of the bathroom near the toilet.

And so ends a lifelong neat-streak, she thought, frowning.

She untangled the clothes, which were wrinkled and reeking of smoke and alcohol, and inspected the purple sweater, noticing a cigarette burn mark and several stains, deep-colored smears that ran along the edges of the sleeves.

God, this looks like blood. What the hell did you do tonight, Lou?

Renee quickly scanned the rest of the clothes, looking for more stains, her heart in her throat. Here and there, she noted additional dark smudges.

Please, no, she prayed silently. *Don't let this be happening again. Don't let me lose her.*

Not wanting Lou to know that she had touched her clothes, Renee balled them up again and tossed them back into the spot she had found them. She tiptoed out of the bathroom and crept up to her sister's sleeping form, scanning her face and exposed limbs for signs of injury.

Nothing, thank God. Maybe they weren't bloodstains after all.

Renee scanned the floor, her eyes working overtime in the dark. Lou's handbag lay next to the bed, open. Gingerly, Renee dug through its contents, feeling for the mirror, keeping one eye on Lou while she searched.

It wasn't there.

Damn it! Where could it be? No answers came to her in the darkness, so she stood up and, after a moment of indecision, quietly slipped back into bed, feeling defeated and uneasy.

Maybe she lost it.

Renee wanted to believe it so badly that she almost did. Almost.

But the mirror wasn't lost.

The mirror was so very close, tucked into Lou's curled fingers wedged tightly under her pillow.

CHAPTER 23

Yeah, I'm glad we got to see it before it's closed for the season. And thanks for all the interesting tidbits. You know a ton." Cora Beach tucked a strand of purple hair behind her ear and smiled, then stuffed the small brochure she'd been holding into her backpack.

Her friend Liz Randal, her own multi-colored locks bobbing, nodded. "You really do. I'm pleased as punch that we met you, Lou."

The brunette they were addressing smiled. "Ditto. It's so nice to spend time with friendly people." Her full mouth turned down at the corners. "Unlike my own company."

"I still can't believe your boyfriend left you here," Cora said.

Lou bit her lip. "I didn't think he was serious when he said he was going back to Sinaia, you know? I thought he was just blowing off some steam. I mean, visiting Peles and Pelisor was his idea in the first place."

Liz fished in her backpack for her water bottle, then took two big swigs. "Well, as I said earlier, you're welcome to drive back with us."

"Consider it thanks for giving us an impromptu tour of the sister castles," Cora added.

Lou feigned embarrassment. "It was hardly a tour. I just like sharing what I know. And beautiful places like this are so easy to talk about." She gave them a smile. "So where else are you traveling to after this?"

Cora stuck out her fingers, ticking them off as she spoke. "Well, we drove here from Bucharest, which was our first stop. This is our second day here. We're driving back tomorrow, then flying to Budapest. We'll end our holiday in Prague, and from there, it's back to London."

"Mmm...the land of Hungary is very beautiful," Lou input with a twinge of nostalgia. "I hope you have a lovely time."

Cora smiled tentatively, puzzled at her peculiar phrasing. "Thanks. I'm sure we will."

"We always do," Liz added. "We've been each other's travel companions for six years now; we've been on holiday abroad together four times. We get along so well. I can't imagine going away without you."

Cora lightly punched Liz's arm. "Same for me, Lizzie."

As the friends started to reminisce on past trips, Lou tuned out, her expression blank. Periodically, she would scan the area as if she were looking for something before turning her attention back to the girls.

Liz happened to notice her behavior and at once found herself wishing she hadn't invited Lou to drive back to town with them. Liz was naturally perceptive; having grown up in a particularly rough suburb of London, she had learned to trust her instincts when it came to people. And now those instincts were telling her this: something about Lou's behavior was off, something about the way she held herself, something about the look in her eyes. It wasn't anything overt, just that tip-of-the-tongue, corner-of-your-eye feeling that wouldn't go away.

But it was enough to make her feel the slightest bit uncomfortable.

Still, she forced herself to let it go. Lou had, after all, been left stranded by her boyfriend in a foreign place. Being stuck by herself was probably just making her a little edgy, nothing more. She didn't need to read into it.

Liz inwardly rolled her eyes at herself. Sometimes she felt like her degree in psychology had only succeeded in making her a more paranoid human being than she had been before. She saw motives behind everything, and she never accepted anything at face value.

Cora's hand was suddenly inches from her face, waving back and forth. "Earth to Liz? You in there?"

Liz slapped her hand away. "Yes, yes, you can stop now." She yawned. "Wow, I'm a bit more tired than I thought. Do you ladies want to drive back now and grab some lunch? I think I could use some food."

Cora linked an arm through hers. "Me too." She turned to Lou and extended her free arm. "Will you come to lunch with us?"

Lou smiled and reached over to squeeze Cora's hand. "I would love to," she said.

"Brilliant." Cora beamed. "I'll drive. Toss me the keys, Liz?"

"Sure." Liz rummaged in her pocket, then handed the keys to her friend as they walked over to the rental car.

As Liz was about to open the passenger door, Lou reached over and grabbed the handle. "Would you mind if I sat up front? I often get carsick." Her expression was plaintive.

Again, Liz felt uneasy. It was a simple enough request, but there was something about the way she'd asked...

She let go of the handle. "No problem. I don't mind the back."

"Great." Lou got in and closed the door.

Liz did the same, willing herself not to freak out for no reason and force Lou to get out of the car.

She and Cora would be alone again in another hour, and then she'd probably laugh at how spooked she'd been over nothing.

As Cora pulled out of the space and put the car into drive, Lou looked in her rearview mirror, just in time to see Christer Malin running towards the car, gesturing for them to stop. Lou glanced at her companions, but neither of them had noticed him.

Despite the girls' ignorance, Lou felt herself tense. He was getting closer to the car, and she could just start to make out his voice.

But then Cora pressed the gas pedal, and they were driving away, Christer disappearing from sight as they turned onto the main road.

Relaxing, Lou sat back in her seat and smiled, her face triumphant.

"Shit!" Christer yelled, kicking the ground.

He stood facing the direction the car had gone, his chest heaving. If he'd been just a hair quicker, he would've caught them.

But I wasn't. And now Lou's gone.

Gone. The word rang in his head as his breathing returned to normal. "Shit," he repeated.

Turning on his heels, he began to run back the way he'd come. *Think, Christer, think. The car was heading back to town, that's a fact. Maybe we can still catch up to her...*

He spotted Renee and Ian over by a stone wall, heads bent over one of their cameras.

He picked up his speed and bolted in their direction, startling them as he reached the wall.

"What's wrong—what happened?" Renee asked, her voice breaking. She had a feeling that she knew exactly what the answer was.

"It's Lou," he said. "She's gone."

"Gone?" Renee and Ian both looked at him with incredulous expressions.

"Yeah. She took off with these two punked-out girls." He shook his head. "Simon and I kept an eye on her all day, just like we talked about, but..." He paused. "We figured everything was okay. She met these two women and seemed to get along well with them; it was the happiest I've seen her all week. She hadn't been doing anything productive anyway, so Simon and I didn't see the harm in her spending some time with other people, as long as she was somewhere we could see her.

"But we were wrong. I left for two minutes – two *minutes* – to go use the bathroom, and when I came back, Simon was dealing with this hysterical child and Lou was gone." He looked at Renee. "The kid told me that a pretty lady had given him some money to bother Simon. God only knows how she even talked to him—he only spoke Romanian. Anyway, we split up after that, and I happened to catch sight of one of the girls – purple hair is hard to miss – over by the cars. By the time I got there, though, they were driving away."

Renee almost dropped her camera. "What are we going to do?" She looked between the two men. "We *have* to do something!"

"We will." Ian hugged her to him, trying to calm her. "Christer, where's Simon?"

Christer was already running away. "I'm going to go find him. Just wait here."

It didn't take him long. Simon saw him running and met him halfway, his breathing erratic, his hair sticking out in all directions beneath his baseball cap.

His face fell as he reached the Swede. "Lou's gone." It was a statement, not a question.

"Yes, she's gone. But I know where she's headed." Christer gestured behind him. "Come on. We need to hurry if we want to catch up to her."

Simon didn't need to be told twice. Together they ran back to where Christer had left Ian and Renee, Simon's face red with exertion.

The photographers were hastily packing everything in their bags, Renee shoving items into her bag with more speed than care.

Then they were all running to the car, Christer getting in the driver's seat.

Wordlessly, Simon handed him the keys, sitting shotgun.

As Christer pulled out, he looked back at Renee. "Simon and I know what the girls look like and I know what their car looks like. They're headed back to Sinaia, I'm almost positive, so there's a really good chance that we'll catch up to them and find Lou." Seeing the tears in her eyes, he added, "I promise, Renee. We'll find her."

Then he slammed his foot on the gas pedal and fishtailed onto the main road, leaving two zigzags of rubber in his wake.

CHAPTER 24

It seemed that luck was on their side.

They found the girls' car after only a half-hour of searching, parked on a street corner of Sinaia outside a busy bistro.

The four of them burst through the front doors, their entrance turning heads and receiving a look of disapproval from the girl behind the counter.

Scanning the customers, Christer finally homed in on the two punk girls sitting in the back by a window.

"I see them," he said, gesturing for the others to follow him.

Liz looked up to see them approaching and felt a fresh wave of trepidation come over her as the foursome reached the table. Clearing her throat, she made her voice stay amiable. "Can I help you?"

Cora turned to see what was going on, confused.

"I'm sorry to interrupt your lunch," Christer said, trying not to talk too fast. "We're just looking for our friend Lou. I think you may have given her a ride here from the castles."

A look of understanding passed over Cora's face. "Are you her boyfriend?" She asked.

"What?" Christer was momentarily taken aback.

"Because if you are, I should tell you that there is no excuse for leaving your girlfriend alone in a foreign place." She gave him a withering stare.

Renee stepped forward, shaking Ian off. "Hi, I'm Renee. I'm Lou's sister."

Cora frowned.

"I don't know what my sister told you, but she's not having a spat with her boyfriend; she doesn't even have a boyfriend." She paused, working to keep the panic out of her voice. "My sister is unwell. Like, mentally unwell. She's having a breakdown and I think she's a danger to herself. Please, if you know where she is, tell us. We need to find her."

Cora shook her head, looking from one person to the next. "I'm gobsmacked; Lou seemed so normal, so nice. I never would have guessed..." Her gaze moved to Liz. "Did you think there was anything wrong with her?"

Liz sat still, her mind whirring. *Maybe my degree is worth the paranoia; I should trust my instincts more.*

Her eyes full of sympathy, she looked at Lou's sister. "Yes, there was something strange about your sister, I just couldn't tell what. Now I'm sorry I didn't say anything sooner." She looked at Cora, then up at the four worried faces, knowing that she was about to crush the small glimmers of hope she saw there. "I'm sorry. Lou's gone. She told us that she wasn't very hungry when we got here and said goodbye. We don't know where she went after that."

Seeing their crestfallen expressions, she felt awful. "I'm so sorry. Really, I am."

Only Simon managed to mutter a pathetic 'thanks'. No one else said anything.

The truth was that they had absolutely no idea what to do next.

Lou was gone without a trace.

Romania, 1430 A.D.

"Csilla, I would speak to you."

The voice came from behind her. She frowned, grimacing at its source. "What do you want, Miksa?" Her tone was clipped.

The dark man walked around her slowly until he stood facing her. He leaned in slightly, dark eyes fiery with some hidden intent. "It is not a conversation to be overhead." He gestured grandly with his arm, inviting her to take the lead in a caricature of gentlemanly deference. "After you," he said.

Csilla strode ahead of him, head held high. She refused to let Miksa's condescending nature get the better of her. He was her elder, by centuries, and he lauded it over her and the others constantly. If Csilla thought that she could beat him in combat she would have fought him long ago, but Miksa had years of practice and cunning on her. And if she did manage to best him, Xenia would highly disapprove of the loss. For all his failings, Miksa was irreplaceable.

After a time, he walked beside her. He never spoke a word. Their only companion was the soft tread of their footsteps as they made their way through the deep cave systems. Finally, he stopped, turning into a narrow side cave. It opened up inside, the ceiling rising above them. It was far from anyone else, far from any listening ears.

"What do you want to discuss?" Csilla asked, her voice echoing loudly.

Miksa shook his head. "I did not lead you all the way here to have your echoes carry to eavesdroppers. Please give me the courtesy of a private conversation."

Csilla knew what he was asking for and his request troubled her. Still, she raised her hands anyway, calling forth her magic. She felt the warm spark of energy in her veins, flooding them and rushing out towards her spread fingers. A small burst of light issued from her fingertips and splashed against the walls of the cave. Moving gracefully, she waved her arms, weaving a gossamer cocoon around them that deadened all sound in the alcove where they were standing. Once she was done, she lowered her arms, breathing deeply.

When she spoke again, her voice was small and quiet, and no echoes whispered her words back to them. "Now you may speak freely," she said.

"It is time we rid ourselves of Xenia." There was no preamble, no honeyed lead-in, nothing to lighten the impact of his words.

Csilla shrank back in shock, her pale face whitening further. "What are you saying?" She hissed.

Miksa gave her a calculating stare. "You know exactly what I mean, Csilla." His calm composure only served to frighten her more, but he continued, ignoring her reaction. "Xenia has given in to her whims and in doing so has risked our very existence. For a *human*." There was hatred in the way he spat out the word. "She was a great leader once, there is no doubt, but her base emotions prove that her time of power is past. She needs to end."

"She is our Maker, Miksa!" Csilla couldn't keep the hysterical bite out of her voice. If it hadn't been for the magic around them, her words would have bounced shrilly off the walls of the cave. "How could you even propose such a thing?"

"Because a true leader knows when changes have to be made," he retorted in the same calm voice.

"Are you proposing to fight her yourself? To become the next Maker?" The disbelief in her tone seemed to anger the dark man. He visibly bristled, his stance becoming confrontational.

"You think I would fail?" He chuckled. "Csilla, as Xenia is now, she is no match for me."

"I think I've heard enough," she said. How could he say such things? It was enough to make her sick. She had always known he was power hungry, but this... She turned to leave, but Miksa spun in front of her, blocking her path. He grabbed her by the arms, squeezing her painfully.

"I could snap you in half as easily as I could slice the wings off a butterfly. The least you could do is pay me the respect of hearing what I have to say."

Csilla's eyes shone with defiant loyalty. "Xenia has always been good to us. Always."

"Good to us? You know nothing," he said, shoving her roughly away. There was ice in his words. "You think Xenia is good because she gave you everything you ever wanted. You begged for her to turn you. *Begged.* It was pathetic. And yet Xenia granted your wish. So yes, I suppose Xenia was good." His eyes darkened. "To you."

Csilla felt the first prickle of unease stab her. "What do you mean, Miksa? Speak plainly."

"Do you know how I was turned?" He asked.

Csilla realized that she did not know. Never, in all of the conversations they had shared, across all the years, had Miksa ever shared his story. As she pondered the thought, she realized that no one ever spoke of it. Was it possible that only Xenia and Miksa knew it?

Her curiosity got the better of her. "I do not," she admitted.

"Would you like to?" He laughed at her silence. "Very well, say nothing. I will tell you nonetheless." He paused then, and a slight shift came over him. His entire demeanor seemed to change, subtly, but enough that Csilla knew he was somewhere else.

"Before I was turned, I was a prince, born to greatness, set to inherit my father's kingdom. I was also a warrior, cunning and ambitious. I never once lost a battle. But I had my weaknesses, as all men do.

"The day I first saw Xenia I became obsessed. She was exotic and mysterious and intriguing. I vowed that I would have her. Had I known what she was..." His voice trailed off and he sighed. "The folly of youth, I suppose. Xenia returned my affections and one night she led me out into the forest. I assumed of course that it was for a tryst, but I learned all too soon how mistaken I was."

Csilla went cold inside at the thought of Xenia and Miksa as lovers. She had always thought of Xenia as beyond the realm of the senses, until Sabina. But had there been a time when...? Miksa interrupted her reverie.

"She attacked me when I had my back turned, taking me completely by surprise. She moved like a shadow and knocked me unconscious before I could react. When I awoke, she was watching the sky, looking for sight of the full moon. She had bound me to a tree, but I managed to get my knife. I cut my bonds and faced her just as the first sliver of moonlight landed on me.

"I still remember the look of utter calm on her face as she watched me, looking as I pointed my knife at her. 'You cannot best me, Miksa,' she said. 'And besides, why would you want to? I am about to make you immortal'. Then she showed me her true form. I was appalled! She was a monster! I knew then that I was no match for her physically, yet in that moment I knew how I *could* best her, I realized. I held the knife up to my own neck, my intention made clear. I still remember how cold the steel felt against my hot skin. 'I would rather die,' I told her. But she only smiled at me. I wanted to tear that smug grin off of her face and rip her apart, but I held my knife steady. And this is what she said: 'If you kill yourself, I will hunt down each and every member of your prominent family and kill them, even your baby sister, and then I will bathe in their blood and wipe the excess on your corpse.'"

Miksa seemed to shudder at the memory. He took a moment to steady himself before piercing Csilla with haunted eyes. Somehow, his feral expression scared her more than his usual dangerous façade. She was suddenly aware of their isolation and familiarity gave way to fear. Beads of sweat began to form on her brow as she took a step backward, pondering her next move should he attack. But instead of attacking, Miksa folded his hands around hers, cradling them. The tender gesture was unnerving.

"I would *never* turn someone against their will—ever," he whispered. "Csilla, you know only one side of Xenia. But I have seen the monster in her. She took away not only my glory, but also my ability to die a warrior's death. I cannot forgive that, nor should I." He squeezed her hands. "I believe you are a valuable asset and confidante, which is why I share this with you. I will challenge Xenia and I will win. My question to you is: will you be waiting to embrace or defy your new Maker once the battle is done?" He released her hands and stepped back, regarding her closely, waiting for an answer.

For the first time in years, Csilla found herself unsure about what to do. Usually, she turned to her magic for answers, relying in the feel of its presence to guide her instincts. But this was different. A power play was something she had only ever heard of once and the results had been...devastating. If she were to choose a side outright, what was to say her allegiance would not ultimately result in her own demise? Still, she felt herself identifying with Miksa. If he challenged Xenia and won, she would become his second; there would be more freedom to do as she pleased. And if he didn't, well...Xenia need never know her loyalty had shifted. She was and always had been skilled at protecting herself. Her mind was made up.

She bowed slightly, a deferential gesture that spoke volumes. It was a tacit submission and Miksa understood it as such. He smiled – a small, cat-like curling of his lips – and inclined his head.

Csilla left the cave without either of them saying another word.

CHAPTER 25

S imon, stop."

Christer stretched out an arm to keep him from walking away. "What is it?"

Christer merely shushed him, his eyes focused on the small TV in the corner.

Simon followed the other man's eyes to the screen, surprised that there even was a television in the station, let alone that it worked.

A news broadcast was on the display, but the host was speaking in Romanian, making the subject matter indecipherable.

Momentarily overwhelmed with fatigue, Simon sat down heavily on a bench, happy to rest for a few minutes.

He and Christer were in Sinaia's small railway station, checking to see if Lou had passed through. There were trains to Bucharest and Brasov, so it was possible that she'd gone to one of those cities, but the employee behind the ticket counter didn't remember seeing anyone that fit her description either that day or the previous one.

Ian and Renee had met with similar success in their efforts to locate her.

It had now been a full day since they'd lost her, and they had asked after her in every open place in town, leaving no stone unturned. And still they had not found one trace of Lou anywhere.

That's when they'd come to the conclusion that she must have left Sinaia. But the bus station and the train station had been dead ends. No one had seen her.

Suddenly, something on the TV caught Simon's attention and he stood up, squinting.

No. He moved closer to the screen, convinced that he was imagining things.

But he wasn't.

A rough sketch of Lou was staring at him, the representation vague enough that it could be someone else, but not so vague that it couldn't be Lou. And Simon had a feeling that it was her.

Another picture filled the screen, a photograph of a gangly, dark-haired teenager, her wide mouth set in a camera-ready smile.

"Christer, what is he saying?" Simon looked sideways at Christer, keeping one eye on the screen.

The Swede was shaking his head slowly back and forth, his eyes wide. "It's Lou," he said, his voice barely above a whisper.

"Christer, what's going on?" Simon insisted. He would have given anything to be fluent in Romanian just then.

Finally, Christer tore his eyes away from the screen. "Simon, we missed the obvious answer. All four of us missed it."

"Missed what?!" He demanded, a note of exasperation creeping into his voice.

"Lou is gone from Sinaia, just as we thought. But she didn't leave on a bus or train. She's been hitchhiking."

"Hitchhiking," Simon echoed. Of course. *If only we'd thought of that sooner...*

Christer continued. "I think she might be in trouble, Simon." His voice cracked. "According to the news report, a man reported a hitchhiker yesterday to the police, saying that she had threatened his safety. He drew a sketch for the police and a few hours after it was released, someone reported seeing a woman who fit the description getting picked up in a van heading northbound on the E60.

"The van, the teenage girl who was driving, and the hitchhiker are now missing. They were last seen entering the outskirts of Brasov County." Christer's eyes traveled back to the television, but the news had segued into weather. "Simon, I just know it's her. I've got to call Renee."

Not waiting for a reply, he punched in her number on his blackberry and jammed the phone against his ear.

While he relayed the report to Renee, he failed to see the look of awful understanding that had settled on Simon's face.

An hour later the four of them were stuck in traffic on the E60, inching forward as if in slow motion. Walking would have been faster.

Ian squirmed in his seat, unable to stand the tension in the car. "Is this road always like this?"

"Almost always, yeah," Christer said. "It's one of the busiest roads in Romania."

Ian sighed. "Figures," he muttered.

Christer put the car in neutral and took his foot off the clutch, stretching his ankle. Bumper to bumper traffic was awful on any day, but it was absolute hell today. Things were bad enough without them losing valuable time stuck in the car.

For the first time since they'd gotten on the road, Simon spoke.

"Mihaela was right."

Everyone looked at him.

"This isn't something related to Lou's depression—it's not a breakdown like the one you shared with us earlier, Renee. Lou is possessed." He looked around the car at each of them, his voice taking on the lecture-like quality they all knew so well.

"Everything that she has done in the past week is proof of that. Her manner of speaking, the coldness about her, the poor quality of her photographs—it all shows that something about Lou as of late is fundamentally different.

"Whatever was in that mirror she took from Solovastru possessed her, just as it possessed Elena Korzha over half a century ago. Mihaela was right about what happened. Her stepmother changed until she wasn't recognizable—until whatever entity was possessing her gained control. Then she killed Mihaela's sisters and ran into the woods, ran to Solovastru Castle."

He paused, waiting for the information to sink in. "That's where Lou's going. She's not just headed to Brasov County. She's headed to Solovastru, just like Elena Korzha before her. Whatever has possessed her wants – or perhaps even needs – to go to the castle. It cannot just be a coincidence."

"Which means," he continued, "that Solovastru is our destination as well. I am certain that when we get there, we will find Lou. And then, my friends, we need to – we *must* – destroy that mirror."

Renee felt a chill come over her, one she couldn't shake off. "My sister is possessed," she whispered, her words barely audible. Her hands clenched and unclenched as if trying to grasp onto a sense of reality that was escaping like sand through a sieve.

Christer nodded slowly. "That's how she was able to talk to that child yesterday, the one who could only speak Romanian."

"And why she wasn't afraid to go out on her own the other night," Renee added. She felt hot tears stinging the corners of her eyes and she blinked them back. "Guys, be honest. Do you think we can get my sister back? Is there any chance?"

Never failing to be there when she needed him, Ian told her what she wanted to hear. "There's always a chance, Renee. I believe what Simon said is true: if we destroy that mirror, we can save Lou. Just hold on to that hope, okay?"

Renee nodded, her gaze shifting to the long line of taillights ahead of them.

For the first time in a long time, she found herself praying to God that Ian was right.

CHAPTER 26

Her hands were gripping the steering wheel as she pressed down on the accelerator, gunning the car along the winding road. Although the twinkle in her eyes was hidden behind the dead girl's sunglasses she now wore, her lips were curled upwards in a satisfied smile. It was an illusion, however, for her body was not her own, and the smug expression on her face was a reflection of someone else's emotions.

Inside, Lou was screaming. It was as if she were wearing a straitjacket, locked away in a padded room where no one could hear her. She was distant, a paralyzed victim of the person who now wore her skin.

Sabina.

Lou knew that was her possessor's name, as well as other things that made her skin crawl. When she'd first realized that she was no longer in control of her body, Lou had rebelled, battering herself mentally until her mind felt like an open sore. And it hadn't made a difference. Sabina retained a firm grip on her vessel, and no matter how hard Lou tried, she could not shake her off.

After a time, Lou had tried probing around Sabina's mind, looking for any information she might later be able to use against her. She'd found secrets more heinous than any she could have fathomed, crimes from the past filed away in gory detail. There was also a lot she didn't understand, fragments of Sabina's life: blood rituals and a woman named Xenia...

If Sabina knew that Lou was sifting through the mental diaries of her life, she gave no indication. Lou pushed out a little farther each time. It was exhausting, but Lou kept at it, determined. After discovering all the evil inside the woman possessing her, she couldn't give up.

Though Lou didn't often speak of it, the strength of her Hungarian grandparents had formed an innate sense of obligation within her to live up to their heritage and their story. Her grandparents had escaped communist Hungary many years before she was born, crossing the border into Austria in the middle of the night, under the constant threat of gunfire from patrolling border guards and indiscriminately placed land mines that could have ended their lives or that of their two small children. They had left all of their loved ones behind with unspoken goodbyes, and neither her grandmother nor her grandfather had ever seen their parents again. That sense of undying perseverance to survive had crossed the generations and Lou had vowed to be just as resilient as they had been. After discovering that Sabina was also of Hungarian descent, Lou felt it was her responsibility to act as the catalyst of Sabina's demise. She owed it to her blood to wipe Sabina from the world.

The murders of the man at the bar and now the motorist – whose body lay dumped unceremoniously in the backseat – had torn Lou apart. She had tried, in both instances, to stop Sabina, or to at least regain control of her body long enough to frighten her victims away. She had managed to regain her voice only once, but it hadn't been enough. She had failed, and it had cost both people their lives.

The teenage motorist had been Lou's tipping point. When Sabina cut her throat and Lou was forced to watch the girl jerk and sputter in her own arms, she had made a decision. If she could not oust Sabina, she would end her. Better that both of them perish than such evil survive.

Now was the moment Lou had been waiting for. Sabina was enjoying the sensation of driving, reveling in the speed of the car. Lou could sense how much she relished the newness of the experience, the enchantment she felt with automotive travel, something that had not existed in her own time. She was watching the sunrise on the horizon, one hand drawing lazy circles out of the open window as she sped down the road. She was completely distracted, her focus centered on the external world.

Lou mentally took a deep breath, preparing herself. She'd been practicing all night, making little motions with her fingers, subtle moves that Sabina failed to notice. She'd been able to do it with facile alacrity after a while, and now she was ready.

Her mind wandered briefly to her sister. *I love you, Renee*, she thought. *And please, please don't blame yourself.* That was what grieved Lou the most. If she succeeded, Renee would assume she had committed suicide and would hold herself accountable. The thought of her sister's anguish and guilt made Lou weep inwardly, but she also knew that stopping Sabina from fulfilling her plans was more imperative even than Renee's happiness.

Thinking back to that fateful day on the train – the day they had arrived in Romania – Lou now fully understood the old woman's trepidation at the Tarot cards she had chosen for her. Bella had foreseen the darkness that now controlled her physical body. Perhaps too, she had also seen what was to come next...

She drew in a mental breath and felt a moment of stasis, a surreal feeling of suspended animation that stretched before and behind her, a brief pause in time.

Now.

Lou screamed, a violent cry of determination that burst from her lips in a strident yell. Her hands, back in her control, grabbed the steering wheel and veered into the oncoming lane just as her foot floored the gas pedal. The engine made a squeal of protest as the van shot forward in its kamikaze mission. If there had been a car approaching, the collision would have been devastating.

Initially Lou felt no resistance from Sabina; she caught her entirely off guard and had a few blissful seconds of full control. But then her possessor was battling with her, grappling for control of Lou's body. Desperate, and not knowing how much time she had left, Lou twisted the wheel with sickening ferocity to the left, the van lurching off the side of the road, dangerously close to the guardrail which separated motorists from a steep embankment. Sabina reacted strongly, fighting viciously, and Lou felt a terrible seizing begin in her muscles. They spasmed painfully and she winced at the sting. It felt like her muscles were trying to perform two conflicting motions at once, being pulled violently in opposing directions, which of course they were. She and Sabina were battling to use the same body.

Lou felt a dribble of blood trickle from her nose at the inner strain, just as the side of the car made contact with the guardrail, the sickening screech of metal against metal filling her ears. For an instant, Lou allowed herself to go numb, willing the end to come. She was losing her strength; she needed to kill them before she was completely enervated.

But just at that moment, Lou felt her hands and feet jerk out of her grasp.

No! She cried, but the word did not make it to her lips.

She tried to regain control of her hands, but she was too broken. Sabina kicked her mentally, and Lou watched in agony as Sabina roughly turned the wheel, and jammed on the breaks, bringing the car to a temporary halt in the middle of the road.

No, please, no...

Lou felt herself fading, her thoughts now fragmented, as if she had been given a powerful drug. Frustrated over her inability to defeat her adversary and weakened by the immense struggle, Lou collapsed into unconsciousness, huddled deep within a corner of her own mind.

Sabina wiped the blood from her upper lip, enraged and appalled. How dare that girl try to kill them? How dare she?

She took a moment to compose herself. Her hands were shaking, and her body was utterly spent, a sheen of sweat coating every inch of skin. Never had she faced such rebellion from a host. *And never shall I again*, she vowed. She would have to tighten the bonds on Lou going forward; she could not risk another power play. Xenia would have been ashamed of how close she had come to being torn from her vessel, of how close she had come to being killed.

Once her breathing returned to normal and the tremors had subsided, she carefully put the van in gear and continued on along the highway, frowning at the mangled guardrail and black tire marks on the asphalt in her rear-view mirror that stood as testament to her near fatal loss of control. She picked up speed, and her mind calmed. Confident that Lou was completely absent now, she found her initial enjoyment returning. Driving was by far her favorite modern experience. She breathed in deeply as the cool morning air rushed in the open windows, swirling her long hair around her face and filling her nose with the sweet scent of dew.

I am close, she thought. *Close to home.*

The feeling was almost physical in nature, its potency almost tangible.

And close she was. Inexplicably she knew where to go, as if her whole being were a compass that could only point towards her singular destination.

Her reverie was broken by the foul, pungent odor emanating from the backseat. She glanced back, her smile waning.

The girl's body, bloodless and broken, was beginning to smell as dead as it looked. She would have to dispose of it soon. Sabina sighed in resignation. Killing was a thrill; cleaning up afterwards was a mundane chore.

This particular killing had been a necessity, nothing more. The girl had started to become suspicious and the chance that she might talk to somebody wasn't worth the risk of letting her live. Fewer witnesses meant less exposure, and that was what mattered.

One less teenage girl in the world was no great loss anyway.

A few miles in between exits, in a place where the road curved away into empty countryside, Sabina pulled over. It was still very early in the morning and not many cars were on the road, so no one noticed her as she dumped the body into a thicket just off the road and made her way back to the van. As she began driving yet again, the miles flew by, her mind elsewhere. Within a short time, she was precisely where she wanted to be. She parked the car while the sun was still low in the sky, most of the day yet before her.

Sabina felt the old spark of excitement stir as she stood in her woods. It was the same feeling she'd had when she'd journeyed back home wearing

Elena Korzha's skin: that Xenia was close and that everything she'd longed for would soon be hers.

She began walking away from the van but paused only a few steps later, looking over her shoulder. After a moment of indecision, she went back, taking out her knife. Its blade was crusted with dried blood; there had been no way for her to wash it earlier. Still, a clean blade wasn't necessary at the moment.

With strong thrusts, she slashed the tires, moving around the van until all four were cut and deflating.

She wouldn't be returning the same way, and the vehicle had served its purpose.

Now it would be useless to anyone who might happen upon it.

Satisfied, she made her way onto the overgrown path, her feet easily navigating the familiar territory.

As the forest grew denser, her heartbeat began to accelerate, and her breathing began to quicken. She could almost taste the sweetness of reunion now.

And then she was there, the clearing opening out in front of her, the castle standing like an oasis in its midst.

Looking up to the sky, she closed her eyes and sighed.

Home.

CHAPTER 27

A chill wind moved through the forest of firs, one with just enough presence to rustle a few leaves as it passed through on its otherwise silent journey. No animals were about; few often were. They avoided the densest areas of forest as if by instinct, their innate alarm senses warning them to stay out of the deep woods. Even the predators, the lynx and wolf, seldom passed through.

They knew that something fiercer than they lay in wait in the deepest, darkest places of forest, the places where the wind alone traveled, something that would turn even the deadliest among them into prey.

The only ones that resided in the depths of the woods were the feared ones themselves. They mostly kept to themselves, coming out only to hunt. On those days, every creature of the forest put as much distance between themselves and the hunters as possible. It was on those days that the entire mountain itself seemed dead.

Still and silent, it was indeed one of those days.

Shrouded by a thick canopy of trees, face turned up to meet the wind as it passed, stood one of the feared ones.

Surrounding the figure were seven others, all of them looking at the first. They were more motionless and rigid than the trees, their flat eyes unblinking as they waited.

Their leader turned when at last the breeze had gone, the motion almost disconcerting in its speed, but none of the others were startled. They simply retained their rigid stances, waiting.

Looking from face to face, the leader made sure that all were listening and watching, more out of habit than anything else.

Once, he had made an example out of a dissenter. A very graphic example. Since then, there had been no more problems. All of them prized their survival too much to try and cross him.

In a way, they feared him almost as much as they had respected *her*.

They would never dare to ignore him.

"It has begun again, my friends." His voice was low and quiet, hollow in a dead way. "But this time is different. This time, she has awakened and remained so." He paused for effect. "This time, we have the chance to regain what we once had—a chance that has not come along in a very, very long time." He moved among the others, weaving in and out as they followed him with their eyes.

One of them spoke, their voice cracking from disuse. "Do you think that she will return after all this time? Is it even possible?"

The leader spun around, eyeing the speaker. "Yes. It is very possible. She has survived all this time, holding on to a mere fraction of existence. Someone that powerful is *meant* to return." He pierced the seven with his eyes, taking up a stance in front of them again. "Remember the old times, my friends, because they are returning to us; they are within our grasp."

He turned to face north, his innate sense of direction better than any compass. "All we need now to bring her back is the missing piece, which has again returned." His face curled up into what could only be described as a lipless smile. "It is time we go retrieve it."

He crouched down, the others following suit. "We run."

Then he was gone, a blur of blinding speed disappearing into the night, the other seven close behind him.

Romania, 1430 A.D.

Sabina Solovastru stood in her bedchamber, erect, clothed in a deep purple gown that accentuated her pale face. She was as inert as the fixtures in the room, her carriage motionless and regal.

Beneath her facade of placidity, however, she was breaking, the very fiber of her being crumbling into dust. Even she, with all her practiced mannerisms and perfected composure, could not fully conceal her fear of dying.

And die she would. Her trial- though she thought of it more like a sentencing in itself than an actual trial- had been brief. She'd been found guilty of twenty-two murders and suspected of over eighty more, though all of the bodies had not yet been found. Her sentence was execution, though she was spared the axe. Because she carried a title- Istvan's title- that style of execution did not suit. Instead, it had been decided that she would be walled alive in her room, left to die a slow death in darkness and solitude.

Yes, her hour of death was very close indeed.

Moving only her eyes, she surveyed the surrounding men, the workers bricking up her chamber. They avoided contact with her, not even glancing at her, afraid that if they even looked upon her, they themselves might be tainted by the devil.

It suited her just fine; she did not wish to meet their gazes. All she would find in them would be hate and anger, expressions that she did not want locked in her grave with her. No, it was better to see through them than at them.

One worker made his way towards her, bent over, a tool in his hand. Sabina assumed he would step around her, for he too kept his gaze averted like the others, but instead he charged her at the last moment, knocking her down. Before his supervisor could stop him, he kicked Sabina hard in the ribs, eliciting a gasp of pain from her.

"Get away from her! There is no need for that. She's going to rot within these walls soon enough; you don't need to speed up the process. Come now, back away from her."

The worker responded to his superior, but not before he grinned down at Sabina, his expression full of malice.

Cursing under her breath, Sabina rose and brushed herself off, trying to regain her dignified bearing. She shouldn't have gasped; the last thing she wanted to give these worthless dogs was the pleasure of hearing her pain.

Wilted slightly but keeping her chin held high, she sat down gingerly on the edge of her bed, clasping her shaking hands in front of her.

Oh Xenia, how I wish I could but see you again. You who alone know me, who alone can calm me when I'm afraid...

She felt the sting of tears in her eyes and blinked them back. As much as she craved the comfort of her wise friend, she hoped Xenia was far from Solovastru Castle, safe from harm. If she came back now, it would be a death sentence for her; the townspeople were still thirsty for blood, their vengeance not yet sated. If Xenia wanted to escape with her life, she had to stay away. She would die alone.

At least I'll die knowing that she is alive somewhere, free of any chains, she thought.

An odd shuffling drew her attention and she looked up. An older man was working a few feet from her, his breathing ragged. She couldn't imagine why he'd been assigned to a task that involved manual labor; he appeared far too ill to do much of anything.

The feeble worker moved towards her, ever so slowly.

Sabina looked around for his supervisor, the one who had intervened before, but he was nowhere to be seen. She glanced back at the man coming towards her, her alarm bells ringing.

She forced herself to breathe. *He is weak.* The thought came unbidden into her head and her racing heartbeat instantly slowed. Instead of fear, she felt the tingle of power in her veins.

I could kill him, she thought. *Just because I'm able to. And no one would do anything about it. After all, I'm already condemned to die.* Her lips pulled up into a smile.

Then he reached her. He stood up, his face inches from hers, his limbs no longer shaking. His weak demeanor had only been an act: the person standing in front of her was no old man.

Sabina held her breath, shocked and unable to formulate a plan. She looked into the man's deep, green eyes, preparing herself for the hate...

It wasn't there. The green eyes were full of pity, full of sorrow, full of love.

She recognized the eyes. They were the same eyes that she'd looked to for love and help and counsel for countless days. Even in the faultless disguise, Sabina knew the eyes.

"Xenia," she breathed. "Oh, Xenia."

The green eyes swam with tears. Xenia reached out and grabbed Sabina's arm, her grip conveying all of the emotions that she couldn't express in words.

Sabina's voice choked in a sob. "Xenia," she whispered, "you...must leave. Now. Don't let them find you." She struggled to breathe. "My only consolation in dying is knowing that you will live. Please, for me. Go."

Xenia reached her free hand inside her worker's uniform and pulled out something small. Sabina looked down as Xenia pressed it towards her. It was a small vanity mirror, beautiful and ornate, encircled by intricate flowers cut of expensive ivory.

Not needing to be told, Sabina quickly concealed the mirror within her own clothing, tucking it away and out of view.

Again, she met Xenia's eyes, her own mirroring the sorrow they held. "How I wish we could have had more time together," Sabina murmured. She reached up and touched Xenia's cheek. "I love you."

Tears ran down Xenia's cheeks, but she ignored them. She leaned in close, putting her lips to Sabina's ear. "This will bring you back to me. This mirror... will help us be together again. And then we shall *never* be parted. I promise."

Then, before Sabina could respond, Xenia kissed her on the cheek and was gone, slipping silently from the chamber.

The workers continued going about their duties, ignorant of the interchange that had taken place.

Filled with a new sense of purpose and a hope that eclipsed her fear of death, Sabina lay back on her bed and closed her eyes.

A worker named Stefan Vulpes rose to wipe his brow, letting out a long puff of air. From the corner of his eye, he noticed an older worker near Sabina, bent close to her form.

Stefan did nothing. He was hoping that the man would hit the witch or cause her harm in some way.

Instead, the worker kissed her and left.

Stefan's jaw dropped, his eyes traveling after the fleeing worker in disbelief. Without saying a word to anyone, he pursued the man, grabbing a shovel as he left.

The worker made his way out onto the grounds, oblivious to Stefan.

Stefan was afraid that he'd lose the man; he was moving at a pace faster than believable and had reached the grounds ahead of him, moving away from the mouth of the castle.

Then, in a stroke of luck, the worker fell to his knees, his hands clutching the ground in front of him. "Sabina..."

The whisper drifted back to Stefan and he drew in a sharp breath.

The worker's voice belonged to a woman.

Suddenly all the pieces fit into place. He knew of the rumors regarding Sabina Solovastru's elusive accomplice. The witch that people talked of but had never seen. The woman who had helped Sabina murder all of those girls, including his own daughter.

His little Elisabeta. His precious child that would never see her tenth birthday.

Fueled by the unparalleled rage of a grieving father, Stefan charged the woman, shovel held high overhead.

At the last second, she turned, whipping around to face him with blinding speed. Her hands came up and reached for him, clawing at his face.

Stefan was already bringing the shovel down, however, and she'd delayed her attack a moment too long.

The blade of the shovel caught her on her temple, knocking her to the ground.

Though he'd swung with enough force to kill a woman of her size, she began to pick herself up, spitting drops of blood.

His fear did not slow his reaction. Again, he brought the shovel down on her head, cringing when he heard a splintering crack.

Fearing he'd killed her, he reached down and was about to feel for a pulse when he heard her draw in a ragged breath.

Acting quickly, Stefan put a foot on her back, pinning her, and dropped the shovel. Then he cupped his hands around his mouth and called for help, screaming until his voice grew hoarse.

Two days passed, filled with rain and snow. The ground around Solovastru Castle grew muddy and dark, and the bark of the trees in the forest were dyed black with water. All of nature was stark and bleak, and as the snow began to fall, the sky and ground blended into a gray wasteland, the line of the horizon waning into an indiscernible sameness with its surroundings, its distinction lost.

The only contrast to the grayness was a pillar of dark smoke rising from the center of town. Beneath the smoke, orange flames rose to the sky, hungry and brilliant, reaching to the heavens.

A crowd of spectators stood around the source of the fire, their eyes flickering in the reflection of the flames. Every gaze was fixed upon the lit stake, trying to make out the figure all but engulfed beneath.

The witch was burning. That was all they knew. Her name, where she had come from, why she had helped Sabina Solovastru kill her victims—all remained a mystery. Still, they knew enough from stories to relish her death and come as witnesses to watch her die.

She hadn't screamed when they'd lit the fire or when the tongues of fire had begun licking at her robes and the skin beneath. She'd remained immobile, her eyes gazing out over the crowd into some far-off place. While the townspeople had been hoping for more of a show, they were content enough to watch her die even a silent death. They were happy in the knowledge that she would cause no more pain.

Hidden in plain sight among the crowd were eight black-clad figures, their heads bent in unspoken grief. No one noticed them; they didn't stand out in any particular way and weren't doing anything to draw attention. Their faces were hooded, shielding their skin from the overcast light. Despite the risk, they had come out during the day to be with their Maker as she met her death.

They remained there even after the flames died out and the smoke thinned, its final tendrils blowing away into the gentle breeze; even after all of the other spectators had left, until they alone were all that remained in the square.

They remained, and the ashes of their Maker.

Without saying a word, they came together, moving like vultures towards a carcass.

Miksa moved ahead of the others and up to the remains of the fire. Bending down, he touched the ashes reverently, his hands caressing the charred mass.

Then, carefully, he reached into the mass, his hand swallowed temporarily. The others gathered around him, forming a tight semicircle.

Seconds passed, seconds as still and motionless as a calm, deep sea.

When Miksa's hand finally emerged, something was clutched in it. Something perfect and beautiful, untainted by the fire, a small keepsake no larger than his palm.

Xenia's heart.

With a gentle protectiveness, he wrapped it with cloth from his robes and tucked it away from the elements, sheltering it from the light.

Then they too were gone, disappearing like wraiths into the woods, leaving not even footsteps behind.

It was as if they had never been there at all.

CHAPTER 28

I an, look...just ahead. Stop!" Renee barked the words so loudly that Ian almost lost control of the wheel.

He'd noticed it just before Renee had shouted out- the abandoned vehicle partially obscured by the forest overgrowth. He felt a sinking feeling in the pit of his stomach. Neither he nor anyone else needed to verbalize the suspicion that had now become a certainty: that this was the missing vehicle driven by the teen that the authorities had been searching for.

Their assumption had been correct. Lou was heading back to Solovastru Castle just as Mihaela's stepmother had over a half a century ago. Ian was near sick with fear for Lou at the thought and one glance at Renee's face told him that she felt the same.

Ian slowed the car and pulled up behind the van. Everyone was out in a flash, circling it. A quick inspection confirmed that it was empty, no sign of Lou or the teen inside or out.

After taking in the four slashed tires and badly damaged passenger doors, Simon approached the driver's side window and peered in, his eyes picking up on the dark stains on the driver's seat and door.

Swallowing hard, he turned to the others. "There are bloodstains in the front seat." He lowered his head. "Something tragic happened to the young girl driving this car—I'm sure of it. And I think Lou was responsible."

"O God, no...no." Renee sobbed and sank her head into Ian's shoulder, leaning into him for support. "My sister would never do this. She just wouldn't. She isn't capable of harming another person."

Ian gently disengaged himself so that he could look in her eyes. "Renee, the person that did this is not Lou. I think we are all convinced that whatever entity is possessing your sister through that mirror is the thing responsible. Our job is to find Lou, destroy that mirror and get her back, if we can..." His voice trailed off.

"Ian, don't even think 'if'. We are going to get her back." Renee's now dry eyes were alight with a steely determination.

The sound of breaking branches halted conversation and the three turned to see Christer emerging from the dense trees that butted up to the road.

"I made a quick sweep of the forest just around the car just to see if I could find any trace of Lou or the driver, but I didn't find anything. Not a whisper."

"Let's not waste any more time here then, okay?" Renee spoke with renewed urgency. "The faster we get to Solovastru, the better."

"Agreed," Simon and Christer echoed in unison, and the foursome headed back to their car. It would have been wiser to walk, as they had the last time, but they didn't want to lose the chance of catching up to Lou.

Ignoring the discomfort of jolts endured on the rough, unpaved surface of the road, Ian took liberty with speed and had them at the castle within twenty minutes, almost half the time it had taken them on their first outing to the castle. They ran across the wide clearing, their feet pounding the earth. The wind had begun to pick up and clouds swirled overhead as if predicting an impending storm. Renee, shivering as she ran, whispered a silent prayer that they would be able to find Lou.

She wasn't outside of the castle, and in unspoken agreement the four headed for the walled room, certain that there, they would find Lou. Renee in the lead, they picked their way through the debris and into the chamber.

And there, sitting immobile on the floor, facing away from them, the mirror clutched in her hand as she swayed back and forth as if in a trance, was Lou.

"Lou!" Renee ran to her sister, dropping to her knees in front of her.

Her sister's eyes were fixed and staring wide, their color a crystalline blue.

"Lou?" She reached out and gently took hold of her sister's shoulders.

"Renee, wait! Don't touch her!" Ian shouted in warning a moment too late. Simon and Christer moved forward, but Renee held up a hand and they stopped, waiting.

She gently shook her sister's shoulders, and when that did nothing, shook them with more force. "Lou? Lou!"

Not receiving any response from her, Renee focused her frustration and rage squarely on the object that was the cause of the problem: the mirror.

Before any of the others could stop her, Renee reached out, grasped the mirror and pulled with all her strength, trying to dislodge it from her sister's unnaturally firm grip.

She should have heeded Ian's warning.

In a flash, like the spark of a match struck, Lou came alive, eyes blazing with fury. With supernatural strength she leapt to her feet, pulling Renee with her.

"*Naiba*!" Lou snarled the curse at her sister in Romanian, followed by a diatribe of indecipherable words.

Momentarily stunned by her sister's reaction and the venom communicated in the foreign words, Renee failed to react.

Lou didn't. She moved with lightning speed, shoving Renee hard and propelling her across the room and into the stone mantle.

Renee's head struck the mantle with a sickening thud and she collapsed in a heap, unmoving. Ian was beside her in a flash, cradling her head in his hands.

Lou blinked rapidly, as if trying to clear her head; her voice hitched as she saw her sister sprawled on the floor. "Renee...?" She took a step towards her sister.

Simon and Christer took advantage of the moment and charged her, Christer grabbing her from behind and locking his arms around her torso, Simon trying to grab hold of her arms. When her movements became more enraged and frantic as she tried to break free, Christer tackled her to the ground, pinning her to the floor.

Even pinned down, she shrieked, her eyes full of fiery malice.

As he looked into the eyes of the stranger beneath him, Christer's hope of ever seeing Lou again started to fade. He felt an ugly lurch in his chest, but he forced himself to push his emotions aside.

Lou thrashed and raged, continuing to shout and curse in Romanian.

"Hold her down!" Simon shouted at his friend as he worked to pry the mirror from Lou's hand.

Seeing Simon's purpose, Lou fought with renewed effort, screaming out in rage, her face distorted, a tendon on the side of her neck bulging with the strain.

Finally, he wrested it from her grasp, falling back from the force he'd exerted, the breath knocked out of him.

But he'd gotten the mirror. It was in his hands.

"*No!*" The word had never sounded more ugly or more desperate as Lou screamed it.

Simon stood up, his legs shaking slightly. Glancing quickly in Renee and Ian's direction, Simon breathed a sigh of relief as he saw Renee struggling to a sitting position.

He looked back at the mirror in his hands. It felt unnaturally warm.

"Simon, break the damn mirror! Now!" Christer's command propelled him into action.

Hesitating no longer, Simon brought the mirror down on the tiled floor with as much momentum as he could muster.

All five of them held their breath, watching as it made impact.

The mirror fractured and broke, the ancient glass shattering into a multitude of glimmering pieces, flying out in all directions.

In a moment all of the shards had settled to the floor.

A pregnant silence hovered over the room.

All eyes turned to Lou.

She looked unconscious, her arms and legs limp, her eyes closed.

Looking down at her, Christer realized that he was holding Lou's arms so tightly to the ground that bruises were beginning to form. He slowly relaxed his grip, flinching as he saw the imprints his fingers had left.

Just as he released his hold on her, Lou opened her eyes and sat up.

She ran her hands gently over her face and neck, ascertaining that there were no injuries. Then she looked around at the others, her gaze finally landing on Christer.

Her eyes were still blue.

In that instant, he realized with horror that they had been wrong. They had been so eager for their solution to work that they'd forgotten the possibility of failure.

And now it was staring him in the face.

The blue-eyed woman began to laugh, a maniacal sound that filled the chamber.

"*You've succeeded, my love,*" she said in a whisper, a cat-like smile curling her lips. Then she addressed them, her tone triumphant.

"Do you think that by destroying my mirror you can defeat the magic that has brought me back to the world of the living? *She* is more powerful than you can image, little men, and I share in her power! It lives in me!"

Before any of them had the chance to process what was happening, the physically agile woman spun away from the big Swede and bolted for the door.

Christer and Simon gave immediate chase, tearing out of the chamber after her.

By now, Renee had regained her equilibrium and was able to get to her feet with Ian's assistance. Blood trickled from the wound on her head where it had made contact with the stone mantle. Dizzy but otherwise unhurt, she and Ian followed their two friends in pursuit.

It was evident to both Simon and Christer that the entity possessing Lou knew its way about the castle. She moved ahead of the two men with ease, finding her way about the winding corridors, taking a twisting route that the others were not familiar with.

Simon grabbed Christer's arm. "We can't follow her this way. We could get lost or worse—we don't know which parts of the castle are safe. We have to go back."

Christer looked forwards and back, at war with himself. "Shit!" he cursed. He gave an exasperated sigh. "Fine. Let's double back."

Knowing that they'd lost precious time, they ran back the way they came and then headed in the direction of the exit, guessing that she'd be doing the same. Once outside, though, it was evident that the chances of catching her had significantly diminished. She seemed to have vanished into thin air. Rolling leaves and the wind in the tall trees were the only sounds that greeted them in the clearing.

In tacit agreement, they simultaneously split up, searching in opposite directions.

Deciding to search the area near the chapel, Simon headed for the dense trees that obscured the path. As he moved into the mouth of the woods, he though he heard the faint noise of footfalls on the leafy undergrowth. Encouraged, he picked up his pace.

Suddenly, the path ahead of him seemed oddly bright, as if illuminated by glowing embers. He stopped dead in his tracks.

The trees were still and the forest quiet- a strange quiet. Despite the sudden fear he felt, he couldn't look away from the unearthly glowing.

Then the light was gone and something else was in its place.

He blinked.

In front of him stood the little girl he had glimpsed once before, the same girl that had appeared to him the day he'd first come to Solovastru- the one he'd thought his subconscious had conjured up. Dressed in jeans and a flannel shirt, her long blonde hair secured in two braids, his sister looked exactly as he remembered.

"Gretchen," he breathed.

The little girl cocked her head as if listening and then looked at him with wide eyes, holding up her hands.

It was a clear indication that Simon should go no further.

Still, he took another step, intent on his task. Gretchen shook her head and continued to hold her hands out in warning. In her childlike eyes, Simon could read fear and warning.

He stopped. "What are you trying to warn me of, Gretchen?"

Gretchen lowered her hands to her sides and looked at him.

Then she changed. Her form morphed into something hideous, something veiny and grotesque, and Simon stumbled back in fear.

Then she was Gretchen again. Her form seemed to shimmer and loose clarity, fading away like a mist after a heavy rain, but not before Simon saw his sister raise a finger to her lips as if to signal quiet.

"Gretchen, wait..."

But she was already gone.

For a moment, Simon was paralyzed. Reaching up, he wiped a tear from his cheek. Then he turned and headed back to the clearing, heeding the warning of his phantom sister.

By this time, Christer had realized that the search was futile. The sky was darkening, and the woods of Solovastru were impenetrable enough during the day; searching at night could be dangerous. Not wanting to lose his way, he made his way back to the clearing where the other three now stood waiting.

In Renee's hands were the gathered pieces of the shattered mirror.

Christer reached them, shaking his head. "Nothing. I didn't find any trace of her." He turned to Simon, his expression already hopeless. "Anything?"

Simon shook his head. He didn't mention Gretchen, as he was still questioning the enormity of what had occurred. "We need to leave for now and figure out what to do next. And we should have a doctor take a look at you, Renee. You took quite a blow."

Renee waved away his concern. "I'll be fine, Brody. What we *need* to do is save my sister." She looked at them each in turn, her eyes teary. "I know she's still in there—I heard it in the way she said my name after I hit the ground. I know in my heart that we can still bring her back, that Lou's holding on somewhere deep down. We just have to help her." She shrugged her shoulders in defeat. "I just don't know what the hell to do now."

"I might have an idea," Ian offered. "When we were shooting at Peles I had a conversation with a woman there named Chalea. She's a Roma and she seemed pretty knowledgeable with regards to the magic, witchcraft, or whatever it is that they practice in the Roma. She might be able to help us, especially if we bring this mirror to her. Maybe she can explain the significance of it or lead us to someone who can."

"Sounds like a good place to start, I guess," Christer said hollowly.

The four began walking back to their car, their hope as waning as the sunlight leaving the clearing as night descended.

Romania, 1430 A.D.

Miksa tore through the woods, claws out and extended, gouging trees with merciless ferocity in his anger. Dust, debris, and flying bits of bark spun out in a woody whirlwind behind him, leaving a forest floor of ruin in his wake. He stopped only when the forest gave way to rockier terrain. With a wail of fury, he thrust his talons against a large boulder, leaving deep marks in its surface. Minutes passed in silence as the sounds of nature returned and hushed away all memory of his violent rampage. His body morphed then until he stood, shaking with rage, in his human form, his hands spread out in the craters his claws had made.

He had barely been able to maintain his tenuous façade of calm as he and the others had gathered Xenia's heart from the ashes that were once her earthly form. Now in solitude, he could give in to his true emotions.

Sinking to his knees, he carefully removed the heart from his robes. He laid it down gingerly and stood up, backing away from it. There was hatred and envy and anguish in his eyes as he stared down at it.

"Xenia!" He screamed, the word torn like a blister from his mouth. "You have ruined *everything*!" He cried. "All those years of planning, all of my preparations! Gone!" He began to pace back and forth in a manic fashion, his eyes wild. "Because how can I challenge you now, Xenia? How? I cannot claim victory over a heart with no vessel! I cannot become the next Maker without slaying *you*!"

He fell again to his knees, raking tense hands through his hair. "You took everything from me the day you turned me!" He said, the volume of his tirade diminishing as he spoke. "And now you have taken my last, rightful hope of revenge. I am and shall always be unfinished. All because of *you*." The rage left him like the flame of a candle being blown out, disappearing into smoke. All that was left was his misery. "What but my hatred for you has sustained me, Xenia? Nothing! My hatred and my plans for vengeance were all I had. And now they too are ashes, as you are." He gave a mirthless chuckle. "Even in death you have bested me." He fell silent.

He stayed kneeling like that for hours, immobile. The world moved on, but he remained, a lone figure waiting for nothing. Time passed and the sky grew dark. Stars appeared on the nighttime canvas of the sky and they were more alive than the man they shone down upon. They were fire; he was ice.

Finally, Miksa gathered himself up and scooped the heart into his hands, giving it a last lingering look before returning it to his robes. He sighed then, but it was not a sigh of weariness or defeat. It was only to steady him. He had been dealt crippling blows before and survived. While he had given into his anger temporarily, there was only steely determination in his eyes as he walked back through the forest.

He was patient and his time would come. No matter how long it took, he would find a way to move forward with his plans.

After all, he had all the time in the world.

CHAPTER 29

She shrank against the tree, holding her breath as she listened. She thought she'd heard footsteps a few minutes earlier, and the sound of someone breathing. Her hiding place wasn't very good, and she had feared discovery.

But then the footsteps had retreated, leaving her in blissful silence.

When she was sure she was alone, she slumped, sliding down the trunk of the tree until she was sitting at its roots.

She wasn't sure what to do next. Until now, her focus had simply been to escape.

Going back to the castle had been her main goal and she had thought it would lead her to Xenia.

But it hadn't.

Tears of frustration welled up, and she dug her fingers into the dirt, clawing the earth.

After countless years of waiting, she had finally found another opportunity to return, breaking through the veil of death to life anew. Each time before, her quest to reunite with Xenia had been thwarted and the host destroyed. This time would be different; she had come so far. She would not fail.

And yet she felt empty, abandoned.

Xenia, where are you?

She had imagined that Xenia would be waiting for her, ready to welcome her with open arms and a dangerous smile, and that hope had been her motivation for centuries. She had pictured their reunion a thousand times, each fantasy more dramatic and fulfilling than the last.

What she had never once pictured was being alone.

Like a spoiled child deprived of a favorite toy, frustration gave way to rage. Unable to contain her emotions any longer, she threw back her head and let out a scream, heedless of the need for concealment. Pounding her fists into the sodden earth of the forest, she felt hot tears coursing down her cheeks. *Xenia, why aren't you here?*

Possibilities rushed through her head, a stream of what ifs that made her heart sink.

After so many years, it was possible that Xenia had moved on, that she had found someone else to love. Maybe she had grown tired of waiting for her and was with someone else even now.

Or maybe something had happened to her.

That particular thought crushed her more than any of the others, but like flies to a carcass, she couldn't swat the idea away.

It had been so very long. How was she to know that something terrible hadn't befallen Xenia? A lot could happen in hundreds of years, and even though she had always held Xenia on an immortal pedestal, it was possible that even she had succumbed to a power greater than hers at some awful moment in time.

She could be dead.

Enraged with herself for even thinking it, she stood up abruptly, clawing at her head as if to cut out the traitorous thought.

Once she'd drawn blood, she forced herself to calm down. Hurting herself wouldn't solve anything; she needed to think.

Her breathing gradually returned to normal, and it was then that she felt an emotion stir within her, one that had been dormant for a very long time.

Fear.

While she had been lost in her own musings, she'd failed to notice something of great significance.

The forest was too quiet.

Immediately she dropped into a crouch, her eyes scanning the now-dark woods around her.

How could I have been so oblivious?

Her failure to be on guard galled her.

Her alarm system working overtime to make up for her negligence, she noticed at once when the figure materialized from the trees and stepped forward.

Seven others materialized behind him, detaching themselves from neighboring trees and fanning out behind the first like a Cimmerian entourage.

Innately sensing the danger of the figures before her, she prepared herself for a fight to the death.

The first figure walked towards her on silent footfalls.

When he was only an arm's length away, he stopped, cocking his head to the side and appraising her.

Then he smiled. "I mean you no harm, so please be civil and relax yourself."

Against her instincts, she did as he asked. There was something in his voice that made her accept that listening to him would keep her alive longer.

"I have waited a very long time to meet you, Sabina Solovastru."

"You know my name?"

He laughed, a hideous cackle. "I know much more than your name, child," he said. "We," he gestured behind him, "have been waiting for you to return for a long, long time."

She was momentarily speechless as she looked at them. Then she felt a stirring of memory, somewhere in the nether regions of her mind.

She forced her voice to be strong. "Do I know you?"

"You know of me, I would imagine. I am sure that Xenia mentioned her family at least once in the time you were together."

It clicked. "Miksa." She remembered Xenia talking about him, about how dangerous he was.

Never fear, though, my love. As long as I am here, you have nothing to fear from ones such as Miksa...

But how was that possible? Miksa had lived in *her* time, hundreds of years ago. Did he possess the same magic as Xenia...had he done something to her?

Sabina gaped at the dark man, able only to articulate a single word. "How?"

Miksa chuckled, a cold sound devoid of any mirth. "I commend your recall, Sabina. As for your question, simply know that I am the same Miksa that walked with Xenia. I will explain everything later, as well as fill in the gaps that Xenia has obviously left in your knowledge of us."

She looked into his eyes, forcing herself to hold his gaze. "Where is Xenia?" The question burned in her throat as she spoke it. "Tell me," she ordered, narrowing her eyes.

He looked her up and down before answering. "Hmm. Perhaps I do understand why she was so taken with you; there is fire in your spirit..." He reached out and stroked a finger down her cheek, then stilled. "Xenia is dead."

"No." Sabina hadn't been expecting that, and she fought to quell that tide of misery that threatened to drown her. "Xenia can't be dead."

"Ah, but she is, dear one." Miksa drew in a deep breath, once again letting a venomous smile play on his face. "But so were you, Sabina. And here you are."

"Yes, but that is because she brought me back!" She shouted at him. "With her power, her magic. It isn't like she can do the same for herself!"

Miksa held up his hands. "No, but you can." He paused to let the words sink in. "Xenia was executed mere days after you were walled up; she was caught on her way out of the castle. She was burned alive, a spectacle for the entire town to see."

Sabina shook her head, trying to awaken from the nightmare he was weaving.

"We were there at the end, though, and I saved the most precious part of her, the part that couldn't ever be destroyed by fire." He placed a hand over his chest. "Her heart."

Sabina looked at him, incredulous. "Her heart?" She echoed.

Miksa nodded. "Yes. Xenia was a Maker, and while I know that means little to you, try to understand. Makers cannot be killed as easily as others can. If she were truly dead, we would all be dead as well. But she isn't. Her heart is safe, and it has come alive since your return.

"I think there is a way to bring her back now that you are here, Sabina. Come with us and you might just get the one thing you want more than anything: Xenia."

The tide of despair was receding, replaced by a faint hope of what was to come.

"Take me with you, then," she said. "I will do anything for Xenia."

Miksa bowed slightly. "We are ever grateful, Sabina."

Then he reached out with surprising strength and grasped her arms, throwing her to the biggest of his companions as if she weighed nothing at all.

"Whatever you do, do not let go."

Then he was running, the others close behind him, wraiths sprinting away into the night.

CHAPTER 30

I t was a long night.

Renee spent most of it wrapped in Ian's arms on the sofa in the hotel room, trying to derive some measure of comfort to quell the ache in her heart. She was wearing an old t-shirt and Ian's sweatpants, and her hair was a mess, unwashed and unkempt. Usually, she would have taken much more care in her appearance, but at the moment she couldn't care less about how she looked. The reality of losing Lou at Solovastru had finally sunk in and the weight of it had brought Renee to her breaking point. There was only so much hurt a person could take.

Even though he lay as awake as Renee, Ian said nothing, for really, there was nothing to say. Words wouldn't bring Lou back. So instead, he just held her as tight as he could, willing himself to be strong for her.

Few words were exchanged as they packed the car in the dim light of the early dawn, but few were needed. Everyone shared a single thought, much like a squad preparing for battle: keep trying. Find Lou and help her. Bring her back.

By the time they arrived at Bran Castle, the first tour of the day was just wrapping up. Ian instructed the others to wait in the coffee shop while he tracked Chalea down. Finding the vivacious Roma was not difficult; Ian spotted her at the head of a tour group just setting out from the entryway.

He walked alongside the group until he caught her eye. When she saw him, Chalea excused herself briefly and made her way over to him.

"Hello again," Ian said.

Chalea looked surprised, her expression a mix of friendliness and puzzlement. "Ian. It's good to see you again, though I really can't say I was expecting it." Remembering their previous conversation, she recalled the young photographer's assignment and the fact that his group had been heading to Peles Castle next. "Did you come back to retake your pictures?"

"No."

She noticed the way his face fell and felt a stirring of worry in the pit of her stomach. Eyeing the tourists behind her, she stepped in closer. "Ian, is everything all right?"

"No, Chalea. Something... well, I really need to talk to you. It's very important."

Some of the tourists were starting to grumble impatiently. She wanted to abandon the tour and talk to Ian, but she wasn't one to break an obligation. Her brow furrowed. "Ian, I'm sorry, but I cannot talk with you now; I have a tour that is just about to start. Please wait, though. I'll be as quick as I can." After a pause she squeezed his arm, reconsidering. "If you can't wait, though, I can come now."

Ian shook his head. "It's okay; I'll be waiting with my friends in the coffee shop. I could use some caffeine anyway." He gave her an anemic smile.

She gave his arm another good squeeze before letting go. "I won't be more than an hour."

As Ian watched her depart with the group, he hoped that coming to talk to her wouldn't be a wasted effort. Troubled, he turned back towards the coffee shop, aware that the next hour would seem like an eternity.

And an eternity it was.

No one spoke; everyone simply stared off into different directions of the room. Only Christer occasionally moved, shifting the still untouched mug of coffee around on the table in front of him.

When Chalea finally appeared, she had no trouble finding them; they were the most dejected-looking group of people in the room.

Brief introductions were exchanged. Intuitive by nature, Chalea sensed immediately that the woman was the most upset of the four. She lingered a moment as she shook her hand, giving her a reassuring smile.

Renee felt warmed by the unspoken gesture and she felt herself relax slightly.

"So," Chalea said, addressing Ian, "tell me. What is wrong? And why do you need to talk to me?"

"Something terrible has happened to one of our team members. Renee's sister, Lou, is... gone." He held up a hand before she could interject. "Chalea, we think Lou has been possessed by something she found, something connected with Solovastru Castle."

At the mention of Solovastru, Chalea visibly stiffened, the color draining from her face.

Ian continued in spite of her stricken appearance. "We went to Solovastru after hearing about it by chance, and while we were there, Lou found this mirror. We didn't even know about it until much later, until after she'd started to change." He lowered his voice. "We're desperate. And we don't know where to turn for help. The last time we talked, you mentioned groups of Roma that practice magic and dark arts. I know this sounds crazy, but I think they may be the only ones able to help us."

Chalea leaned back, trying to process everything. "Okay. Tell me everything, from the beginning. Especially your connection to Solovastru." She whispered the name as if the word itself were a curse.

Ian quickly recounted their first visit to Solovastru, the changes in Lou, the discovery of the mirror, and the events leading up to the confrontation at the castle and Lou's escape.

Chalea sat passively as he spoke. She didn't say anything, but her demeanor became increasingly agitated as he told the story, knots of fear building inside her as she thought of the mess they had found themselves in and the fate of the poor, possessed girl.

When he was finished, she asked, "Do you have the broken mirror?"

Ian nodded.

"Please show it to me."

Renee reached into her bag and produced the small sack that held the broken pieces and handed it over. Chalea carefully laid out the pieces of the mirror on the table so all would have a view. For a moment, she remained silent; then she gingerly picked up the ornately carved handle and studied it carefully.

To Renee, the carvings looked like haphazard flourishes, juxtaposed between curious symbols.

Chalea exhaled slowly, squinting. "These markings...I'm assuming that you thought they were decorative?"

They all nodded.

"Well, they aren't; it's a script. Very, very old... ancient, in fact. Given time, I would be able to translate it for you. What I *can* tell you is that this style of writing almost predates my people's history and is related to the black arts and magic, to the casting of spells. These runes are indicative of the Roma I mentioned the day we met, Ian. They are descendants of an ancient cult that worshipped Kali, the Hindu goddess of destruction. They are in no way related to the modern-day Hindu religion, however."

"The goddess of destruction? So my little sister is being used by some ancient cult of devil worshippers? Why?" Renee asked, her face stricken. Her eyes pleaded with Chalea. "Where do we go from here?"

Chalea sat rooted in her seat, struck by the other woman's words. The image of her own sister's face appeared in her mind, and she knew in that moment that regardless of the risk, she had to help these strangers.

"I can help you," she said. The other four went silent, everyone's attention riveted on her. She could sense their hope, as fragile as it was, and she longed to tell them everything. Still, she had to be cautious; the safety and secrets of her people came first. "Before I begin, I must have your assurance that you will not speak of this conversation to anyone. What I am going to tell you is for your ears alone. I need your promise." She paused, fixing her intense gaze on each of them, listening as one by one they vowed not to breathe a word to anyone.

Satisfied, she leaned forward, lowering her voice. "Very well. As you know, I myself am a Roma. I come from a very reclusive tribe, and while I choose to interact in the modern world by working here at Bran, my people remain separate, living in accordance with traditions and beliefs that are millennia old. We too have knowledge of magic, but we are not slaves to the dark demons the Kali serve." She looked at Renee, wanting to comfort her in some small way. "I believe we are your best chance of getting your sister back."

She exhaled, imagining the lecture she would receive from Ferka for doing what she was about to do. "I will take you to my tribe." She spoke the words slowly, as if to convince herself she had actually said them. "We live several kilometers south of here, on the border between Brasov and Dâmbovita Counties, but you would not be able to find our camp without my help. After so many years, my people have mastered the art of hiding in plain sight." She paused. "A word of warning: my people will not be welcoming; we have strict rules regarding outsiders. I need you to be prepared to plead your case. I will help you, but it is up to you to convince the tribe leaders of your cause. Tell them everything and bring the mirror."

"Chalea." Renee reached across the table and took her hands into her own. "Thank you. I can imagine that by helping us you are risking the anger of your tribe."

Chalea exhaled slowly, her breath making an audible sigh. "That is true," she said. "But that is not your concern." She stood up, looking down at them. "For now, I must return to my duties. Take tonight to prepare for a day-long journey, part of which will be on foot. I will meet you here early tomorrow morning before the castle opens for the day and we will go."

They nodded their assent, and Christer promised to help them pack whatever provisions they might need.

Chalea watched them get into their car and drive away, her mind uneasy. She could almost taste it in the air—the mounting tension that came before the storm, the false calm that was a portent of impending danger.

First Irina, then our scouts, and now a foreigner... What does it all mean?

She whispered a silent prayer for them all, for in her heart she knew that their journey would only become more difficult and perilous as it progressed. They were mixed up with supernatural forces that they could not begin to understand, and she found herself struggling to believe that they would succeed if they found themselves face to face with the darkness. The more they sought the possessed girl, the more the dangers would increase. It would be a miracle if they returned unharmed.

It would be a miracle if they managed to survive at all.

CHAPTER 31

The pale, yellow sun waned overhead, a giant orb set against a cloudless sky. Now they were traveling on foot, following a trail that was barely recognizable as such. The journey to this point had taken most of the day, as Chalea had predicted. Meeting early in the morning at Bran as agreed, the party had set out, traveling by car for over two hours before leaving the rented vehicle parked near an obscure mile marker on state game lands used by hunters and hikers. From there, Chalea had taken them deep into the hill country at the base of the mountains. Their passage was dotted with the occasional hunting lodge and small camping sites at first, but the closer they came to the mountains, the less populated the area became until there were virtually no signs of civilization.

Even Christer admitted that he had never ventured so far into this mountain range.

Despite the circumstances leading them there, Renee couldn't help but marvel at the beauty of the untouched woods. The forest stretched on endlessly in every direction, quiet and peaceful. The tall trees let in dappled sunlight that added a shimmer to the dark dirt floor, and she could just make out the sound of a brook somewhere in the distance, its soothing currents a serene soundtrack to the Grimm-worthy scenery. A few times Chalea stopped to point out something, trying to educate the rest of them as to how she navigated the forest, though only Christer seemed to benefit from her knowledge.

The foliage growing ever denser as they progressed, combined with the canopy of tall firs overhead, obscured the late afternoon sun, diminishing what was left of the natural light. The deepening gloom was an ever-present reminder to the group that time was the enemy and the day's end was fast approaching, still with no sign of any people.

It wasn't a comforting thought.

By evening, the hike was becoming difficult for Renee. Conversation was sparse and being alone with her thoughts was proving disastrous; the last thing she needed was time to think. Every imagined scenario of her attempt to save her sister was worse than the one before. Renee was in a dismal mood, angry at her uncharacteristically defeatist train of thought.

Shifting her pack to her other shoulder, Renee tried to ease her weary muscles. Before leaving, Christer had insisted that they all carry a backpack and blanket since their chances of returning in one day were slim to none. Chalea agreed that it had been a wise decision.

Renee looked at the dynamic guide, her curiosity about the Roma woman and her clan renewed.

Why would they choose to isolate themselves this way?

It seemed strange. They were miles from anything that resembled civilization and the forested mountain trails were wilder than even the badly overgrown ones surrounding Solovastru Castle. The more they walked, the harder it was for Renee to make out any path at all.

If something ever went wrong, these people would be totally on their own. There would be no way to get help. Just like we wouldn't be able to get help if something should happen to us out here...

The thought chilled her.

Grateful that she was sandwiched between Ian and Brody on the trail, she tried to relax, wondering if the others were coping better than she.

"We are very close," Chalea suddenly announced, stopping at the top of a ridge. Sensing the weariness of her companions, she added, "let's rest a moment."

Ian stopped and shrugged off his backpack, letting it fall to the ground at his feet. "No offense to you, Christer," he joked, "But I'm glad that

Chalea was our guide today. There is no way in hell we would have found our way here otherwise."

Christer responded with feigned indignation. "What, no faith in the hired help?"

Renee chimed in, eager to join in the moment of levity. "Don't take it too hard, Christer. If we had to rely on Ian to navigate, we'd probably be in Bulgaria by now."

Her boyfriend clutched his chest, eyes wide in mock horror. "Ouch, right to the heart." He laughed. "Though probably true..."

Before anyone could say anything else, Chalea silenced them. "They have found us," she said.

Their playful banter died as they turned to see four men on horseback emerge from the path ahead of them and surround them. They had materialized so silently and suddenly that Renee would have thought them to be apparitions had Chalea not announced their arrival.

The men were of varying ages, but all of them looked hard and weather-beaten. Cold, appraising eyes stared out of leathery faces—eyes devoid of any softness. Renee took note that each carried a bow and sling of arrows, and three of the riders had long sabers secured to their belts with fringed sashes.

They had found Chalea's Roma tribe.

Or rather, the Roma had found them.

In a flash, Chalea positioned herself in front of the group and addressed the oldest rider, a muscled man with black wiry hair, speaking rapidly in Romanian.

Renee couldn't understand what they were saying, but she didn't need to. It was obvious that the leader of the group was extremely unhappy with Chalea. The Roma was gesturing emphatically, his voice rising in pitch. After a terse volley of conversation between the two, the man finally held up a hand and Chalea fell silent, waiting. Renee watched as he looked them over, worried by the acute disapproval she saw in his eyes.

After a pregnant pause he spoke, Christer translating for the rest of them. "Chalea has led you here without permission to do so. She says that your situation is dire and that you need our help, but it is not for Chalea to convince me that this is the truth. You are not welcome here until you can prove your need."

When Christer finished translating, Renee's anger and frustration boiled over and she pushed ahead of Ian, coming to Christer's side. "Christer, tell them that we are *not* leaving, that we wouldn't have come here unless we had nowhere else to go. They'll have to shoot me before I go back. If they can help us find Lou, I'll be damned if I give up now." She was shaking with emotion.

Christer put his hand on Renee's shoulder and urged her to stay quiet. "Trust me, okay? I'm not going to give up that easily."

The Roma leader was now looking at them disparagingly. In the male dominated culture of the Roma, Renee's intrusion was particularly unwelcome.

Chalea gestured for Christer to speak. "Choose your words carefully, and do not forget to show him the mirror."

Christer nodded, composing himself. "We are outsiders seeking aid," Christer began. "Chalea brought us to find you because she took pity on us. I pray that you will find it in your hearts to do the same. We have a problem that involves magic and we've journeyed very far in the hope that you can help us."

The leader gave him a withering look. "We do not help outsiders."

Christer turned to Renee, determined to win the Roma over. "Get the mirror out of your bag. Quickly, before they get impatient."

As soon as he grabbed the broken pieces from Renee, Christer quickly handed them to the old gypsy. Studying it briefly, the man turned to his companions and exchanged a hurried dialogue. The other men became agitated, gesturing and shaking their heads. Their expressions darkened.

Christer continued, "That mirror is from Solovastru castle. Our friend took it from that place and since then, terrible things have happened. She changed into someone unrecognizable. We fear that something unnatural is controlling her—that something is possessing her. She may have killed someone. We don't know what to do; we broke the mirror in the hopes of freeing her, but it didn't work. We came to know Chalea, who told us that there is dark magic at work and that you may be able to help us." Christer returned the stare of the oldest Roma with a stony one of his own. "If you have the power to help us, please do so, because if you don't, an innocent girl will be lost forever."

The Roma held his gaze for a long moment before turning to the other riders. As they debated, Renee tried to breathe evenly despite her racing heart. *If they don't help us, I will never see my sister again...*

Finally, the Roma men seemed to reach an agreement.

The matter resolved, the gypsy stuffed the pieces of the mirror into a pouch secured to his waist. Then he turned his horse around and issued a one-word command over his shoulder, directed at Christer. "Come." One of the others hoisted Chalea up on his horse. Once seated, she glanced back at them, nodding in unspoken encouragement.

Renee started forward, intent on regaining possession of the mirror, but Christer held her back, whispering that it would be unwise to challenge the Roma. She hesitated but then relented. A part of her wanted to keep the mirror close because she felt that it was a link to her sister, but she was just being foolish. Lou was long gone and having the mirror with her wouldn't change that. And Christer was right; it would be foolish to make demands of the Roma when their entire objective involved staying on their good side.

Exchanging looks amongst themselves but saying nothing, all four picked up their packs and followed after the riders on foot. As they began walking yet again, Ian reached out to hold Renee's hand, squeezing it tightly in his own.

They followed the trail as it wound its way upwards for another twenty minutes until they came to a large stretch of trees on flat terrain. Beyond the trees was a clearing, and there, nestled along the face of a mountain, were caves, tents, and other structures that resembled patched-together shacks.

They had arrived at the reclusive Roma camp.

CHAPTER 32

Conditions were extremely primitive. Communal cooking fires dotted the camp, and a few gaunt dogs roamed free. Women and children gathered near tents and watched the party as they approached, eyeing them warily. Whispers trailed after them, but no one would look them in the eye. As they passed by, most people went inside their tents, hiding themselves from the outsiders.

The riders led them to a large, thatched hut, their apparent destination. They dismounted, seemingly unperturbed by the overall silence in the camp.

The leader moved to the front of the structure and ushered them inside.

The circular hut had an open oculus in the roof that allowed for a fire pit in its center. The fire that burned there was a welcome sight. Nightfall had brought a deepening chill, and despite their uncertain situation, they were grateful for the warmth. All four gathered round the pit in an attempt to dispel the cold. Once there, they were instructed to wait and the men departed with Chalea, leaving them temporarily alone.

Ever observant Simon, who had been unusually quiet the whole day, was the first to speak. "It is so curious…"

Christer cocked a brow. "What is?"

"Everything—these people, this camp. They are an amazing anomaly in our modern world. Their seclusion and self-reliance are staggering; it's virtually like stepping back in time several hundred years." He adjusted his baseball cap, wiping off a bit of grime from his forehead. "The question is: why are they living like this, removed from other Roma? I've been to Roma camps before, and I would imagine you have too, Christer, and I can't recall another camp quite as archaic as this one. So, so curious..."

Before the others had time to hypothesize, a teenage girl entered the tent with refreshments in the form of dried fruit and ale. As she set the tray down, she said nothing and was careful to avoid eye contract with the men, though she did furtively meet Renee's gaze.

The girl seemed to be appraising her, but her expression wasn't hostile. She seemed fascinated with Renee's appearance and clothing, especially her short, cropped hair and denim jeans, the likes of which she had never seen before. While they were both women, the differences between them yawned like a chasm.

Renee tried to give her a small smile, but the gesture seemed to frighten the girl and she hurried outside.

Their respite was short. Almost as soon as the young serving girl left, they again had company.

The Roma entered the hut: the man who had led the party on horseback came first, followed by a younger man who bore striking resemblance to him, two sturdy-looking young men, and Chalea.

Chalea had changed her clothes and now wore the traditional long skirt of the Roma, an ornately beaded vest, and a white shirt with voluminous sleeves. Despite the coldness of the late fall night, she wore no shoes, though her ankles were adorned with rows of beaded bracelets. Her waterfall of dark curly hair was tied back with a silk scarf, the colors of which brought out the depth of her large green eyes. The transformation was nothing short of amazing.

Renee found herself staring, and she wasn't the only one. Ian, Simon and Christer also seemed unable to take their eyes off of her. Chalea had transformed from a modern tour guide into one of her own people, and in that moment, Renee thought Chalea was the most striking woman that she had ever seen.

While she was still gawking, the man from the trail introduced himself as the leader of the tribe, addressing his remarks to Christer.

His name was Ferka, and the man to his right was his son Gavril. He didn't offer the names of the other two men, but instead turned to Chalea and motioned for her to speak. Renee noticed that his anger seemed to have waned.

"First," she said, "I am happy to tell you that my people have agreed to help you find your friend. Now it is time you understand who we are." Chalea folded her hands in front of her. "You know who I am and yet you do not. I am not only a member of my tribe but a *chovihani,* as well as *drabardi* for my people. My role here is like that of a shaman—a person who has special knowledge passed down through generations. I have the gift of second sight, and I am well versed in the art of magic."

Seeing the looks of incredulity on their faces, she nodded as if to punctuate the veracity of her words.

"As I suspected, the mirror you carry with you was fashioned by someone we have been seeking for a very long time, a person with great knowledge of occult powers."

"Were you able to determine this based on the writing inscribed on its handle?" Simon asked.

"Yes," she replied. "The runes on the mirror summon the magic, magic that is of a powerful and ancient strain."

She tented her fingers in front of her. "My people were blessed with a special task many, many generations ago. It is a task that requires us to learn the ways of our ancestors, their magic and their history. Because of this, we act as we always have and always must, as protectors against the darkness that roams the lands. As you are outsiders, I know you have no knowledge of these things and may not even believe that they are possible, but I tell you that they are. For you to understand, I will tell you some of our history.

"Thousands of years ago, the goddess Kali walked the earth with human feet. Kali was darkness and death—all that is evil. She struggled against God; she was a demon who delighted in chaos and destruction and freedom from all fear. Like other demons, she had followers who chose to pit themselves against what is good and light and worship her. These people imitated Kali, spreading ruin and death wherever they went.

"This cult of followers was once very strong and plentiful. They killed countless innocents in the most gruesome of ways, and constantly sought darker and more unholy rituals to increase the destructive power that pleased their black goddess. Because they wanted to transcend fear, they would strive to make their victims more and more terrified before their deaths. The spilling of their victims' blood and the drinking of it was an integral part of their religion.

"Eventually, Kali herself was banished from the earth, but not before she chose her six. The six were her most special disciples, the vessels in which she chose to leave her essence and her powers. They became known as Makers; they are immortals, and their immortality comes at a price: everlasting blood lust. They are creatures of the night, evil without any chance of redemption."

"Like vampires?"

Renee interrupted before Chalea could answer Ian's question. "What does this have to do with the mirror?"

Chalea pointed to the runes on the handle. "These marks come from an ancient script used by followers of Kali; the figures here are identical to ones we've seen on other devices cursed with her brand of dark magic."

Simon pursed his lips. "You are insinuating that the owner of the mirror we found at Solovastru was one of these Kali disciples—a Maker?"

"Yes, I am." Chalea met Simon's disbelieving stare with grim seriousness. "We will answer all questions, I promise, but first, you must tell the elders everything you have told me so far...starting with your discovery of this object and everything that has happened since."

Simon deferred to Renee, who recounted their tale, embellishing with as many details as she could remember, no matter how insignificant they seemed. Now and again, Simon, Christer, or Ian would interject with a detail or observation, eager to impart as much as they could. Renee ended with the events at Solovastru, including her suspicion that Lou had murdered the motorist.

After hearing Renee's tale, the Roma conversed for some time. Finally, Ferka spoke, Christer translating as fast as he could.

"Your situation is most serious; we cannot lie to you. From what Chalea has deciphered, we know that the runes on the mirror were designed to allow one who is dead to possess a living person and walk again. We suspect that a Maker intended to bring someone dead back to life with this magic, for some purpose we do not know. Perhaps the person was important to the Maker in some way. But here is the truth: unless we hunt down the Maker and destroy it, you cannot hope to save your friend."

Christer faltered in translating the last sentence, a wave of grief making his voice shake. After a pause he managed to finish, his voice heavy.

At those words, Renee choked back a sob, her eyes turning to Ian in desperation, needing his strength.

Ian, holding her hand tightly in his own, turned to Chalea. "You said that these Makers are immortal. If that is true, how can we hope to destroy one and save Lou?"

"They are immortal and powerful, yes, but they are not omnipotent. We do have knowledge as to how to destroy them. We have hunted the six since their creation. In the old days, a few brave Roma gifted in the arts of war and magic banded together and formed a secretive group set apart from other Roma in the area. They are our ancestors and they made it their mission to destroy all of the Makers, a mission that has persisted throughout the generations. Four of them we have killed; two remain. For years now, the Kali have been hiding, but we know they are still out there. When there are unexplained deaths and disappearances, my people search."

She gave a rueful smile. "We too were once many in number, but to be a Kali hunter is an unforgiving life and many of us have died in our quest to destroy them."

"You said that your people have killed four of these Makers. How?" Christer's determination was palpable. If the creatures could be killed, not all hope was lost.

"The blood of one Maker is poison to another. Kali made it so that no Maker could kill another and assume their power; it prevented any one person from being as powerful as she. We use this knowledge to battle them. A Maker must be pierced through the heart with a weapon containing another Maker's blood, and the body must be burned until no trace remains. The Makers' progeny can be destroyed with wooden bullets; it is not necessary to burn them or stab their hearts."

"Progeny?"

"Makers have the ability to create ones like themselves, albeit beings that are less powerful and easier to kill. They are susceptible to a number of elements that do not affect Makers. Ironically, progeny can also kill their Makers, though I've only ever heard of it happening once. If a progeny challenges a Maker and wins, the Maker's heart and power are forfeit."

"Even if we were to succeed in killing these creatures in battle," Simon noted, "how would we ever find them?"

"I will lead you to them." Chalea took a deep breath. "It is just as important to us that we find your friend as it is to you. And I have my own reasons for wanting to find *them*..." She trailed off. "I and my people needed to be sure that the events surrounding Renee's sister were related to our own mission. Strange things happened in the time of Sabina Solovastru—things tied in some way to a Maker. At the time, my people thought they'd been mistaken, for Sabina's confidante was burned at the stake and they found no heart when they inspected the ashes. Perhaps they overlooked something, though alas, I do not know more.

"But we have pressing matters now, so that will have to wait. The group of Kali here in Romania has been inactive for some time, aside from the occasional kidnapping or disappearance. They have kept to the shadows and we have not been able to seek them out. In recent months, however, that has changed. They are making their presence known once more. I fear that Lou is a catalyst for something yet to come, though right now I cannot see clearly..."

Her eyes seemed to go vacant for a moment, but then she returned to the present. "If you provide me with something that belonged to Renee's sister, I will sense her presence in the body that the *mulo* now controls. I am sure that she is with the Kali. When we find her, we shall find them."

As Chalea's word sunk in, Renee's fragile resolve crumbled. She clung to Ian's hand like a ship to an anchor, hoping that he would be strong enough to keep her from drifting out to open water.

Saving Lou would endanger all of them. As much as she loved her sister, could she trade Ian's life for Lou's?

Looking around at the others, though, she realized it was no longer her choice to make. Come what may, the Roma were going to go after the creatures of the night, and she and her friends would be right there with them.

It was no longer only Lou who was in danger.

Renee watched as Chalea left the tent with Lou's necklace clutched in her hand. To aid the seer's search for her sister, Renee had given Chalea the cross pendant she had worn around her neck since they had set out to find the Roma tribe; it was a favorite of Lou's that she often wore, before the events of the last week. Now, Renee felt naked without it, like the last piece of Lou had been stripped from her.

She turned back to the fire slowly, sitting down heavily next to her boyfriend. Their somber foursome was again alone, but no one spoke. The reticence was as thick as the cloud cover that hid the stars outside.

Simon finally broke the silence, addressing Renee. "How are you holding up? He asked her. "I can't imagine what you must be feeling right now." She could hear the concern in his voice.

Terrible, she thought. *But not so terrible that I need you three to sacrifice yourselves to help me. I need to be strong on my own now.*

Drawing a deep breath, she met Simon's gaze, buoyed by their bond of friendship. "Finding Lou is going to be dangerous, more dangerous than anything any of us has ever done. *I* have to do this, but you don't need to put yourself at risk like this." She looked at each of them. "That goes for all of you," she added.

Both Christer and Simon motioned to speak in unison, but Renee raised her hand to quiet the spontaneous protestations she had anticipated. She continued, "I won't think less of any of you if you walk away now—even you, Ian," she said softly. "I love you too much to trade my sister's life for yours." She uttered the words with raw sincerity, knowing that it was entirely true.

Ian shook his head, sighing. Cupping her chin, he turned her face upwards to meet his and said gently, "Do you know how much I love you?"

Renee simply nodded, keeping her eyes locked on his.

"Good. I love what you love, babe. And I know how much you love Lou. I have always thought of her as my little sister too. She is a part of our lives and *we—*" he squeezed her hand to emphasize the word, "—are in this together. I would never let you do this alone."

To punctuate Ian's declaration, Simon and Christer nodded their agreement.

Simon uncharacteristically removed his baseball cap and studied it as if he were searching for the right words. Without looking up, he spoke quietly but with firm resolution. "I can't claim to have strong emotions for Lou, although I respect her as a friend and colleague. But I feel called to be a part of this." He finally looked up at Renee. "This may sound as if I've lost my mind, but I feel a sense of obligation in this. I don't know if you can understand – truth be told, I don't even know if *I* understand – and I know I am doing a poor job of articulating, but I feel that by helping find your sister, I can atone for my failure to save my own so many years ago." He turned the baseball cap over in his hands. "You have always been there for me, Renee. Please let me do the same for you."

Renee nodded a silent affirmation, too moved to speak.

Christer stood. "Count me in, too. I haven't had a true purpose to my life in a long time. Since I came to know Lou, I've realized that and made some effort to carve a new direction. I feel like I'm finding myself again." Looking at all of them, he added, with a crooked smile, "And besides: I've never been one to miss a good fight."

Simon and Ian concurred with the Swede, bolstered by his good spirits, but Renee found it hard to join in. She was incredibly touched by how invested they all were, by how much they all cared. And yet...

She looked up at them all, committing their faces to memory. *How did I get blessed with such good friends?* She felt butterflies of anxiety in her stomach. *And what will I do if something happens to them because of me?*

CHAPTER 33

The caves were cold and dark, their earthen walls illuminated only by the candle held in Miksa's hand.

Sabina Solovastru followed closely behind him, not wanting to lose her way in the twists and turns of the labyrinthine underground.

Despite her misgivings about Miksa, she couldn't help but admire him for choosing such a place to hide away.

They were high up in a remote region of densely forested mountains, ensconced in a network of caves that would protect against anything that might dare to intrude.

Not that anything would. Since their arrival, Sabina hadn't noticed even the slightest whisper of another creature anywhere nearby. Even the trees around the caves were still, their branches hanging immobile, casting fixed shadows on the forest floor. There was a heaviness to the silence that made the whole area seem dead.

It was an oasis of isolation, the perfect den for such an esoteric clan.

Miksa stopped in front of her and faced the wall to his left. Without speaking, he ran a finger down the side, tenderly, as if he were caressing a lover.

The wall moved.

Sabina jumped back in surprise and Miksa sneered over his shoulder at her, making her blush in anger.

Beyond the false wall was a room. As Miksa moved inside with the candle, Sabina drew in a breath. Whatever its purpose, it was no doubt a place of sacrosanct importance.

It was of medium size, shaped in a perfect circle. Runes and carvings were etched on the walls, figures full of intricate details and grand flourishes, the work of countless years and meticulous hands. It was also clean and spotless, from the ground to the high ceiling overhead. There was no debris or dust, no signs of wear or time.

It was beautiful.

Sabina was so entranced by the room itself that it took her a minute to notice where Miksa had gone.

He was standing on the far side of the room, his back to her, facing what Sabina assumed must be an altar.

She moved towards him, but then paused, looking down at her feet.

Snakes.

She stopped short of crying out, though she did jerk her feet back in fear.

He brought me here to kill me!

As soon as the thought entered her mind, however, she pushed it away.

The snakes were not real; they were drawn onto the floor, the product of such artistic talent that she had thought them to be moving, living creatures.

She let out a breath and studied them closer.

They were drawn all over the floor, black serpents with oily coils for bodies. They were all facing the same way, as if moving towards where Miksa was, towards where the altar stood.

Sabina moved with them, coming up beside Miksa.

He was staring down at the center of the altar, at a small, closed chest. It was made of gold and gleamed faintly in the soft candlelight. Like the walls, it too was covered in the elaborate etchings.

He addressed her without taking his eyes off of the chest. "This room is located at the precise center of the caves. It is the very core of the network. It is the reason that we chose it; there could not be a more suitable place for our inner sanctum. For this." He gestured to the chest.

"What is inside it?" Sabina motioned around the room. "This chamber is obviously constructed around this altar. Around that. Why?"

Miksa spread his hands out in front of him and stepped back. "Behold."

Sabina stood where Miksa had been standing and put her hands on either side of the chest. She frowned. It was tingling, almost as if it was a living thing, and it was warm to the touch.

Gingerly, she unfastened the latch and opened the lid.

"What?"

The word came out in a hiss. She clutched the altar to steady herself, her eyes wide in shocked disbelief.

It was impossible, and yet it was so very, very real.

Inside the chest, resting on a cushion of black velvet, was a heart.

And it was beating.

"I told you that I saved a part of Xenia that day, a part that could never be destroyed by fire. What I didn't tell you was that I meant that literally, not metaphorically; I saved her heart, the physical part of her that can *never* be destroyed by fire."

Sabina's spoke in a hoarse whisper. "Xenia's heart. This..." She held the chest in her hands as if it were made of glass. "Oh, my love," she breathed.

Miksa shook his head at the tenderness in her words, his heavy brows lifting in bemusement. "Human love is such an enslaving emotion. Even after all of this time, you are still bound by your feelings for her. I cannot understand it."

Sabina placed the chest back on the altar and managed to compose herself before turning to face him. "Her heart is beating, Miksa. How is that possible?"

"The answer is you, Sabina. Or rather, Xenia's love for you." He looked at her as if she were an enigma, a curious puzzle he couldn't decipher. "You see, Sabina, every time you've returned to this world, even when the tenacity of your existence was less tangible than a spider's web, her heart has started to beat. Every time you've departed it, her heart has grown still and cold. Now, this time, you have remained in this world, and Xenia has remained with you."

Sabina nodded slowly. "So, you think my return is linked to Xenia's in some way?"

"I think that Xenia was no fool; she must have suspected that she would die as a result of your dalliances and somehow bound the magic between the two of you. Whatever magic she used, though, remains to us a mystery. Even Csilla cannot distinguish its source; it is from a time more ancient than any of us and beyond our knowledge. But you are living proof that such magic exists."

"Still," Sabina said, "this is only her heart; it is not Xenia."

A twitch of a smile played on his lips. "Not yet, but it will be. While we may not know of the magic that binds you together, we are not ignorant of the magic required for reincarnation. Xenia will walk again." He placed his hand over hers, a disquieting gesture that made her blood cool.

"We have been preparing for centuries, and we have everything we need. Now that you are here, we have the blood of a loved one." He saw the expression on her face and smiled. "Just a drop or two, Sabina. Xenia wouldn't be very happy if she awoke to find that we had killed her beloved."

He removed his hand, one finger at a time. "And a host, of course. You may help us choose someone, if you wish."

"I wish it." Sabina looked down at the beating heart and felt the rate of her own increase. "I wish it," she repeated.

Soon, so very soon, they would be together again. And this time, nothing would come between them.

Not even death.

CHAPTER 34

The late morning sun blazed overhead, its brilliance enhanced by the crystalline blue sky. The day was warm for the season and a few birds chittered as they passed by, their sweet songs drifting to the ears of the riders below.

The eight travelers had been riding since the early hours of the day, covering mile after mile as they headed south in the direction of Târgoviste.

The city was not their destination, however. They were headed instead for the Leaota Mountains north of the city, the same mountains that other travelers avoided at all costs.

It was said that something fearsome and evil resided in the most secluded regions of the mountain forests, something that brought death to everything in its path. The stories inspired such fear that the region was almost always devoid of life, a vast and empty stretch of peaks left abandoned by the living.

The group of eight that had set out that morning from the isolated Roma camp was seeking the uninhabited stretch of those very mountains, seeking the harbingers of death that dwelled somewhere within.

They rode until the sun was waning in the sky and their horses were tired and breathing hard. Having reached the last stretch of flat land before they would have to journey up into the mountains, they dismounted and started setting up camp for the night.

By the time the moon had risen, all eight were sitting around a fire, eating some of the provisions they'd packed before they'd left.

Ferka's son Gavril and his friend Costin were having an animated conversation about hunting while the others ate quietly, too tired to talk.

To the group from *Itinera*, it seemed like weeks had passed since they'd first met the Roma, though in reality it had barely been twenty-four hours. The photo shoot, the job and the reason they had come to Romania seemed now like a distant memory.

Chalea had been trying to pinpoint a location on Lou ever since, and she had finally been successful late the previous night, announcing to all of them that they would set out early the next morning.

Now she sat without eating or speaking, staring into the fire.

Christer interrupted her reverie. "Chalea, could I ask you a few questions?"

The seer nodded.

"You said before that Makers have progeny. How are they created?"

In the light of the fire, her green eyes glowed like those of a cat, enhancing the aura of mysticism that Christer already sensed about her.

"On a full moon, the bite of a Maker will turn a human. Only on a full moon, however. On any other night, a Maker's bite will mean death; it is like a poison to humans."

The others leaned in closer, listening to what she had to say.

"A Maker's progeny is not as powerful as the Maker, but they do have abilities beyond that of mortals. I warn you all not to underestimate them. As Ferka and I have already explained to you, progeny can only be killed using wood; it is why we carry guns with wooden bullets, arrows made of wood, and knives with wood-infused blades.

"But there are other things you should know. They have the ability to read minds. You need to guard your thoughts, keep them hidden. If you leave your mind open, they will use it as a weapon against you. They are quick and strong – not like Makers – but stronger and faster than us. They also have the ability to summon creatures of the night. Sometimes, the stories of people being killed by animals are not accidents, but deliberate attacks from the Kali; we've found that it happens when people get too close to them."

Like Chalea's sister, Ian thought.

Chalea reached into her pack and pulled out a strange-looking orb. It was opaque, almost like a crystal ball, but smaller; it fit in the palm of her hand.

"This is a talisman that we have had for generations. It will make an encounter with the Kali a fairer fight." As she spoke, she squeezed it between her hands until it began to glow. "The more you focus your thoughts on it, the brighter it becomes. The light it emits is reminiscent of the sun."

"Do these things burn up in the sunlight?" Ian asked.

Chalea stopped moving her hands and after a minute the light began to dim. "No. Those are only stories with no basis in fact. Sunlight will not kill them. What it *will* do is weaken them, hurt them. You see, the light shows them as they truly are, as living, animalistic corpses. It is why they do their best to stay hidden during the day; any person that laid eyes upon them in the light would know them and their presence would be discovered, something they fear more than anything else.

"The light also diminishes their extra sensory abilities, which means that I will have an advantage over them. They will be less able to defend themselves against my magic. It will also hinder them from getting inside your minds.

"Sunlight has less of an effect on Makers, and orbs like this have no effect at all. Pure, unadulterated sun will expose their true form, but it will not diminish their abilities in any way and will only weaken them slightly. Killing the progeny will be infinitely easier than killing the Maker, believe me."

As she put the orb back in her pack, she brought out three more, which she passed around to the others. Simon, Christer, and Ian all took one. Chalea apologized to Renee for not having a fourth. "We only have five and Gavril has the last one," she said.

As Simon put the orb in his pocket, a question occurred to him. "Back at camp, you mentioned that Makers could only be destroyed by the blood of another Maker. How have you weaponized their blood?"

"It is a good question. We have special blades infused with the blood and sealed with magic. If a Maker's heart is pierced with one of these blades, they will die."

Simon nodded slowly, absorbing the information.

"What about my sister?" It was the first time Renee had spoken since they'd left camp that morning. "Is she...like them?" She ran a hand through her hair. "I mean, is the person that's possessed her one of the Kali?"

A troubled look came over Chalea and her eyes grew distant as she gazed into the fire. "I do not know. I've been trying to see, but to no avail..." She looked at Renee. "It troubles me greatly that I do not have an answer. I am positive that there is a connection between Solovastru Castle and what has happened to Lou, but it is unclear." She threw a rock into the fire. "Everything is unclear. It makes me uneasy."

They all sat in silence after that.

When he was sure the others were asleep, Christer walked over to where Ferka was keeping watch, crossing his arms over his chest to keep warm as he moved up beside the Roma man.

A question had been nagging at him for days, but it was one he had wanted to ask in private, away from the others. Especially away from Renee.

He was about to speak when Ferka beat him to it.

"You lost someone." Ferka's tone made it clear that it was a statement.

Christer was nonplussed; that had been the last thing he'd expected to hear. Either the Roma was extremely perceptive, or he was gifted with some ESP of his own.

"Yes, I did. My wife Annika. She died in an accident."

Ferka's voice was gentle, compassionate even, but it held a tone of authority. "Your loss is written in your eyes." He looked at Christer. "You must put it away and hide it. Chalea has told you that the Kali can see inside of you and it is true. Do not let them get to you through the one you keep in your heart."

Christer swallowed, working hard to choke down the emotion threatening to burst from his throat. Ferka was right—he knew that. Loss and grief hung heavy on him, their gravity like a dirge pulsing ceaselessly in his head. He was trying to keep the pain at bay, but it was a daily struggle. He had lost Annika and now he was losing Lou—if she was not already gone. He couldn't hold on to the people he cared about, no matter how hard he tried.

His train of thought led him back to his original question, and despite his fear of what the answer might be, he forced himself to speak it aloud.

"Ferka, tell me truthfully: if we succeed in finding the Kali and destroying the Maker, is there a way we can get our friend back? Is there a chance we can save her?"

The older man was still for many minutes, looking off into the darkness of the night. When he finally answered, his voice was so quiet that Christer had to strain to hear him.

"Life is so capricious, is it not? People are born and people die, sometimes before their time. But the world is full of mystery, and I believe in both accidents and miracles. Evil is strong but God is stronger still. Possession is never complete; the person inside is always there, no matter how far they are buried within. If we manage to conquer the evil, I believe that your friend will find her way back. You must have hope, Christer. If you hold on to anything, hold on to that."

An image of Lou, painting out on the balcony, came to Christer unbidden. He let out a breath. "Do you really think it helps?" He asked. "Having hope?"

Ferka looked at him. "Yes," he replied simply, firmly. "Hope has the power to give us the strength we need to keep fighting, even when all seems lost. Hope *is* strength."

Christer let a deep sigh escape his lips. *Gavril, you are lucky to have such a wise man for a father,* he thought. He nodded slowly and then grasped Ferka's arm. "Thank you. I think I've been needing to hear that for a very long time."

Ferka nodded. "Go sleep for a while, Christer. You will need your strength for what lies ahead."

Christer did as he was told, wrapping his blanket tightly around him as he lay down near the others. In mere minutes, he was drifting off to sleep.

Meanwhile, Ferka kept watch.

CHAPTER 35

Csilla entered the room like a whisper, her robes billowing around her as she turned the corner.

"Miksa, I need to speak with you."

He beckoned her forward. "Come in, Csilla. You can speak openly in front of Sabina; she will be one of us soon enough."

Csilla did as he requested, not even glancing at Sabina.

He could almost taste the tension emanating from the seer. "This has to do with your dream," he stated.

She nodded. "Yes. I was right, Miksa. Another seer has been seeking us and now she has found us." Csilla finally looked at Sabina, judgment flashing in her eyes. "This body you've acquired is causing the trouble. The girl's sister and her friends are with the seer, as well as a few others. They are searching, and with the help of the practicer, they are no longer blind."

Sabina held her chin up high. "You have no just cause to be angry at me; I did not have the pleasure of choosing the body I returned in." She narrowed her eyes. "Maybe you should have protected our location better with your magic."

Csilla's fists clenched at her sides and a dangerous edge crept into her voice. "Is that what you think?"

Miksa stepped between them. "Enough. Csilla, it is no problem. We will send the others out to do some hunting, with specific instructions to be careful around the seer." He stroked his chin. "Then again, perhaps we should all go. I haven't been on a hunt in much too long and I'm..." He glanced at Sabina. "In need of one."

Csilla laughed, a light bell-like tinkering. "Don't you mean hungry, Miksa? Or are you pretending for Sabina?"

His face darkened momentarily.

Before he could reply, Sabina spoke. "I'm well aware that you live on blood, Csilla. Do you think Xenia and I never drank of human life?" She licked her lips. "It is quite intoxicating."

A look of surprise registered on the seer's face. "No, I did not know. I only knew that you killed together, and what her intentions were for you..." Her voice trailed off before she turned her attention back to Miksa. "So, we will all go hunting, then?"

"Yes."

"Wait." Sabina held up a finger. "I have a better idea." She smiled. "We need a host for Xenia. Well, why go looking for one when the perfect host is coming to us?" She looked at both of them, excitement dancing in her blue eyes. "The girl's sister Renee. Don't you see? She is the perfect host for Xenia. If it as you suspected and Xenia is bound to me through magic so strong that it has survived centuries, shouldn't both of our hosts be connected in some way to heighten the strength of the magic? And what better connection could there be than a blood tie—the bond of a sister?"

The look of respect that Csilla directed at her made it clear that her suggestion had been a brilliant one. "How deliciously taboo," she murmured.

Miksa clasped his hands together and inclined his head towards her. "Sabina, I commend you; it is no wonder that Xenia thought you worthy of becoming one of us."

He turned to Csilla. "We will go hunting, but not yet. The plan I have is slightly more detailed than just a slaughter. Sabina's advice is wise, and we shall take it. For now, do all in your power to block our location and our plans from their seer. It is imperative that she not know what is waiting for her."

Csilla nodded. "Of course. I will start immediately."

"And now?" Sabina looked at him expectantly.

For the first time since she'd met him, Miksa gave her a wicked smile that didn't make her recoil in distrust. Instead, it aroused her excitement even further.

"Now we set a trap."

CHAPTER 36

The second day's travel tested their resolve. As the group climbed higher into the Leaota Mountains, the trails became increasingly steep and treacherous. At times, their progress was painstakingly slow, and the horses were often skittish, as if they sensed the nearing presence of something dark and malignant.

The Roma had taken up the lead and rear of the party, sandwiching the others like bookends as they rode single file for most of the ascent up into the mountains. Renee, Ian, and Simon rode close enough to one another so that they could exchange bits and pieces of conversation and encouragement when necessary.

Simon, who had never before spent much time on a horse, was having a rough time. He struggled to control his mount, which at times would rear in protest at his inexperience, causing him to lose footing and periodically send a shower of loose rock down the vertical incline.

Taking note of his distress and valiant effort to maintain a calm exterior, Renee was quick to cast him a reassuring smile now and again.

Christer had positioned himself at the lead with Ferka. The two had been conversing in Romanian for most of the morning, their conversation quiet but animated. Renee noted that the two men seemed to have developed a bond that crossed the boundaries of culture and age.

Strange friendships are born of strange circumstances, I guess. And it's not surprising; these circumstances are pretty much the textbook definition of the word, she thought wryly.

Stopping only briefly to rest and eat, they traveled well into the heart of the mountains by late afternoon. Gathering clouds blotted the sun and a creeping chill permeated the air. Exhausted and unaccustomed to travel by horseback, conversation among the friends waned.

Like a constricting web, the mountain forests became increasingly claustrophobic, the dense firs and shadows swallowing the trail ahead and behind.

Aside from the heavy breathing of the horses, the air was still and silent. Almost too silent—a realization that only increased their growing apprehension as the day wore on.

As night fell, the group reluctantly broke to make camp. Renee and Chalea gathered wood for a fire and the men set up tents and determined the sentry schedule so that everyone could steal a few precious hours of sleep. Ian, Simon, and Christer had all volunteered to take a shift, determined to stand shoulder to shoulder with the brave Roma who had chosen to help them find Lou. The Roma had appreciated the gesture and assignments were made to all of the men in the party in two hours shifts.

As they worked, Renee positioned herself next to Chalea, hoping to ask the gypsy woman a few questions, though she never managed to get the words out. When they had gathered enough wood to keep a fire going through the night, Chalea sat down, Renee joining her.

Passing her a canteen, Renee studied the seer, unsure of how to begin the conversation.

Sensing Renee's hesitancy, Chalea broke the ice. "You want to ask me about your sister, so please ask." She softened her tone. "You wish to know if I sense she is close?"

Renee let out a long exhale, watching her breath swirl in the nighttime air. "Yes," she said simply, the weight of her worry written plainly on her face.

"We are very close now, perhaps within a half-day's travel or so. By midday tomorrow, I believe that we will find your sister and the Kali she is with."

Renee nodded. Only two days ago, she had been unsure whether or not she would ever see Lou again. Now, after all that she had learned, she wasn't sure that she was ready to face Lou so soon. *But at least there's a chance I might get my sister back, that things might be as they were.*

Chalea would never get that chance.

Renee weighed her words before she spoke them. "Ian told me about your sister." She looked at the other woman, trying to read into her unfathomable eyes. A complicated eddy of emotions seemed to swirl there, pain prominent among them.

"Irina. She would have been eighteen now." Chalea picked up a stick by her foot, turning it over in her hands before casting it into the fire. They both watched as it crackled and burned.

"I'm so sorry, Chalea," Renee said. "I can't imagine what I would do if Lou..." She bit her lip. *No—I refuse to even think it.*

"Losing my sister was the hardest thing that has ever happened to me," the seer admitted. She sighed, a ghost of a smile playing on her features. "I remember so many little things now, about when Irina was younger. She had a passion for dancing. She had a passion for *life.*" Chalea laughed. "And she was always getting into some kind of trouble. Once, she decided to hide in a cupboard all day as a joke. The whole village was out searching for her and she just popped out at dinnertime, wondering what all the fuss was about and asking when supper would be ready. Our mother was furious."

Renee shook her head, bemused. "It must be something about little sisters. Lou had a complicated childhood, but during her happier times, she was like that too—always involved in mischief. She loved pranking people, me most of all. God, when I think of some of the crap she pulled..." The memories made her smile. "When she wasn't busy causing trouble, Lou was drawing. She still does; our apartment is filled with her pieces. She is an amazing artist, and I'm not just saying that because I'm her sister."

"I'm sure she is," Chalea said. "Just as I'm sure she looks up to you." She gave Renee a gentle smile.

Renee was touched. She felt a wave of empathy with the Roma woman, joined to her by the bond of being older sisters. Before, she had thought of Chalea as a different breed of person than her, too alien to relate to, but now she sensed that beneath it all Chalea might feel just as vulnerable as she did.

"Are you afraid of what might happen when we find my sister?" Renee steeled herself for the answer.

"I would be lying if I told you that I wasn't. I know enough of these beings to fear them." Chalea stretched her legs out in front of her. "I will tell you this, though: my people have hunted down the Kali for generations and we have survived. We have not lost our fight."

"Lou is a survivor too. I feel – I *know* – that she's resisting the thing that's taken hold of her. She is gentle and sweet, but she's also a fighter; she won't give up." Renee stood up. "She's also my best friend. If our roles were reversed, she would be here sitting with you, trying to get me back. I know it. Please tell me that counts for something."

"It does." Chalea stood too, so that she was eye level with Renee. "Love is a very strong emotion, and it can be used to bring about much good. The love you share with your sister is the kind of love that is miasma to the Kali. Let that be a source of strength for you in the battle to come."

Renee nodded. "I will. I believe both of us have the strength of sisterly love on our side." She looked at the Roma woman with sincerity. "I sense that love in you, too," she added.

Chalea nodded her affirmation. "I want to help you get your sister back more than anything," she said at length, "because in some way, it will be like I did right by Irina." Her green eyes flickered in the firelight, and Renee could see the tears brimming there. "And because now I feel like we are sisters in this fight, and I want to do right by you."

Moved by her words, Renee impulsively reached over and hugged Chalea tightly, her eyes wet with unshed tears. Chalea returned the embrace and then patted her back, encouraging the exhausted photographer to eat and seek sleep early.

Chalea watched her retire, a sense of unease growing within her. When she'd touched Renee, she'd sensed a flash of impending danger, an electrified jolt that coursed through her psyche. Not wishing to alarm the young woman, she had concealed her emotions and kept her thoughts to herself.

Perhaps it would have been wiser to warn her...

But no—she was already burdened enough with worry for her sister.

Chalea offered up a silent prayer to the heavens. *Please let us save Lou, and in turn save Renee from feeling the pain of the loss I bear. We are strong enough to beat the Kali.*

But were they? Truly?

She wished she didn't feel so unsettled.

Her heart heavy with trepidation, Chalea turned towards the fire. Gazing into the bright flames, she prepared herself to stay awake and keep watch, for she sensed the Kali were close.

Closer than the shadows of the night.

CHAPTER 37

Christer rubbed his hands together, trying in vain to regain some feeling in his numb extremities. By midnight, the temperature had dropped considerably and the small fire he had maintained at the perimeter of the camp did little to ward off the chill of the mountain air.

His was the third watch of the evening and the others were fast asleep. He glanced at his watch.

One o'clock. Only one more hour to go.

Throwing a few more twigs on the dying fire, he shifted his position and peered out into the darkness, scanning the dense forest for any movement.

Nothing.

The complete stillness of the night was a bit peculiar.

As a tour guide, Christer spent a lot of time camping in the woods, watching out for his hikers as they slept. On every occasion, even the deadest parts of the night still contained some audible activity; nature was never truly silent.

This was different. The ordinary sounds he expected to hear in the deep woods were strangely absent, as if the wildlife had scattered and left only emptiness behind. Put mildly, it was a little unnerving.

Trying not to dwell on the ominous silence, Christer stifled a yawn and turned his gaze upwards. For a brief moment, he was lost in the beauty of the onyx sky, its canvas sprinkled with stars that shone like diamonds. The clouds from earlier in the day had dissipated and the cool air had brought clear skies that literally showcased the celestial marvel. In the midst of it all, a nearly full moon cast a silvery glow on the trees and land below. It was a sight that could only be enjoyed far from the lights of civilization.

He chuckled to himself. *That's right, Christer. Enjoy the scenery; this might be the last time you get to gaze up at a sky like that.*

The fatalistic sentiment made him think of Annika.

Forgetting Chalea's warning against guarding his mind, Christer allowed himself to see her as he remembered: long blonde hair, crystal blue eyes full of intelligence, big dimples on her cheeks when she smiled at something he'd said.

Her image in his memory was as clear as if he'd seen her just yesterday. Christer remembered the last time he had kissed her lips, the last time they'd made love before the accident.

God, you have no idea how much I miss you, Annika. The familiar ache in his heart returned with a vengeance.

Suddenly, he was aware of movement just inside the line of trees to his left, barely a dozen meters away from the sleeping party. The noise was followed by a low sound.

Jumping to his feet, he grabbed his gun- its chamber loaded with wooden bullets- and moved in the direction of the sound. He was careful to walk silently as he neared the trees, moving as noiselessly as possible.

When he was nearly there, he heard the sound again.

Someone was calling his name.

Slowly, a figure emerged from between the trees. He couldn't make out what it was; its form was too undefined in the darkness.

Holding his breath, he stepped closer, raising his weapon.

Then he recognized the person in front of him.

He dropped his gun to the ground where it landed with a dull thud.

Impossible!

He knew every line and curve of that body, had worshipped every inch.

It was Annika. There, standing right in front of him, not aged a day from when he'd last seen her.

The rational part of his mind was trying to make him see reason. *Wake up, Christer. Annika is dead! This isn't possible; it isn't real! It's just a hallucination!*

Like a moth to flame, however, he was unable to stop himself as he began to move towards the figure that was now beckoning him with arms outstretched.

CHAPTER 38

"Simon, wake up."

"*Wake up now! Christer needs you!*"

The voice was so loud and insistent that it echoed in his mind, reverberating. Simon was jolted awake, the threads of sleep vanishing as quickly as a flash flood.

There was no mistaking his sister's voice. "Gretchen?" He whispered.

Glancing around, he almost expected to see her standing there in front of him, just as she had been in the woods of Solovastru.

But she wasn't. It had only been her voice in his head.

A voice that had said...

She had warned him before, and he wasn't about to ignore her now. Bolting to his feet, he shouted to the others and made for the sentry post where Christer had taken the last watch.

He wasn't there.

Spinning around, Simon took in the perimeter as quickly as he could, finally spotting Christer.

He was headed for the tree line, walking towards a beautiful blonde woman.

Simon felt a sinking feeling in his chest as he realized that Christer was headed right for the ridge with the drop off. The figure was drawing Christer to his death.

Bloody brilliant idea, making camp so close to a cliff...

"Christer!" His voice caught everyone's attention but the Swede's.

Realizing that Christer was either unable or unwilling to hear his cries to stop, Simon sprinted to his friend, running as fast as he could. He had to reach him before he walked off the cliff face.

He got there just in time, launching himself on the bigger man with as much force as he could muster.

Both men hit the ground hard, mere feet from the edge. The force of the tackle was enough to snap Christer out of the illusion and he looked up at Simon in confusion.

"Annika. I saw her. She was just there—"

"No, she wasn't, Christer. No one is there."

In a suspended moment of recall, Christer suddenly remembered the Roma girl at the bar back in Cluj. She had scared him, had said something crazy. *"It's not her..."*

She had been warning him.

He snapped up in a heartbeat, pulling Simon to his feet. "Oh my God, Simon, it must be the Kali."

Both men ran back to camp, stopping short when they saw Ferka and the others spread out in a circle, facing the trees with weapons at the ready.

In a moment, they knew why.

The moonlight showed them the truth: some of the trees had more than one shadow.

They weren't alone.

The Kali had found them.

In the span of a second, pandemonium replaced stasis and everything went crazy.

Counting at least four, Christer was immediately aware of how fast they moved. It was like someone had pressed the fast forward button; no matter which way he turned, he seemed to only glimpse them in his periphery, moving out of his line of sight.

"Tighten the circle!" Ferka's command was obeyed at once, and Christer and Simon raced to join them, stopping only to retrieve weapons from their packs while Gavril and Costin covered them.

"Simon, look out!" Christer swiveled and aimed his crossbow at the figure behind Simon, shooting just as Simon ducked. The arrow sailed into empty space, the Kali easily evading it.

Dropping back, Simon and Christer sought refuge behind a large outcropping of rock. Simon loaded his gun with shaking hands, his eyes darting back and forth, searching for their hunters.

They heard the sound of a gun fired nearby, towards where the others had been. The first shot was followed closely by two more, then silence.

Christer heard footfalls reach them just in time to take aim.

It was Gavril and Costin.

Christer took his finger off of the trigger just in time. "Jesus," he rasped.

Gavril put a finger to his lips. "There are two approaching from behind. We have to try and take them. Don't aim directly at them; they move too fast. We will be more likely to hit them if we aim a little to the right or left. We have to anticipate their movement."

Christer translated for Simon just as Gavril cried, "Now!"

They turned, launching arrow after arrow and bullet after bullet into the tree line. The dark figures seemed to sidestep their shots as if it were child's play, screeching in laughter as they darted out of the line of fire. It was a sound that made the hair on the back of Christer's neck stand up.

Costin screamed suddenly, looking up.

A Kali had climbed on top of the rock and was clawing at them with curved talons that seemed to sprout from its arms like tumescent thorns.

It swiped at Costin, drawing a nasty gash along his cheek.

"No!" Gavril drew a short blade from his belt and jumped up on the rock, tackling the Kali. In a mess of limbs, they fell off of the other side.

That propelled Christer into action. He barked at Simon, telling him to make sure Costin was okay, and then he was racing around to help Gavril.

He dropped his crossbow and took out his gun, loading it as he ran.

Instead of finding Gavril and the Kali, he came face to face with Ian.

Ian released his quivering finger from the trigger of the crossbow he was holding. "I was with Ferka...but I can't find him. He went after one of them."

Christer cursed. "They're picking us off, Ian. We need to think of something, quick."

A sound caught their attention and they looked up to see a Kali approaching from the trees in front of them.

"Over there, too." Ian motioned with his bow. Another Kali was closing off their retreat, approaching them from the rear.

They were trapped.

Chalea could no longer see any of the men, but she didn't move from her position. She had assured Ferka that she would defend the camp, and so she would. She had set up a perimeter with her magic around most of the camp, but she'd been rushed, and it was weak. It wouldn't keep the Kali out, but she would at least know if any of them got in.

Fumbling in her pack, she grabbed the orb just as she felt an intrusion on the perimeter.

A Kali was in the camp.

Wasting no time, she raced towards Renee's tent, her senses screaming at high alert. She knew without a doubt that Renee was in danger- she'd sensed it earlier. Whatever the Kali were planning, she had to stop them, even if it meant sacrificing her own life. Failure was not an option.

Rounding the Roma tents, Chalea found herself face to face with a nightmare.

The shrouded figure struck her hard, knocking her to the ground. Momentarily disoriented, Chalea fumbled for the orb, grasped it and held it high, commanding the light.

The orb blazed white-hot, and the Kali withdrew a few paces, shrieking. In the halo of light, Chalea had her first look at the Kali they sought.

The woman, who was barely recognizable as such, was hideous. Her eyes were a pupilless black and rows of razor-sharp fangs were exposed in a mouth too wide to be human. Dark grey veins streaked the thin, wrinkled skin of her face and long talons with wicked claws extended from her arms where her hands should have been.

She emanated pure hatred as she stared at Chalea.

Chalea noticed a smell coming from the Kali, the faint aroma of magic.

"You are the one that's been trying to block me," Chalea said. She searched her mind. "Your name is Csilla."

Csilla's eyes narrowed to slits and she rubbed the long talons of her hands together, the sound like nails on a chalkboard.

Chalea sensed the attack a moment before it came, dropping and rolling to the right to avoid being torn to bits by the Kali's claws. Summoning her strength, she began to chant the incantation to ward off a named demon. From her pack, she withdrew a crucifix.

Csilla snarled at her, feigning move after move, trying to get at Chalea without being hit by any of her magic.

For a second, Chalea lost sight of her opponent as she weaved with blinding speed around her.

A second was all it took.

Csilla came at her from behind, slashing a deep gash into her back and knocking the orb from her hand.

Chalea fell hard, gasping. She flipped over, summoning what little magic she could as she braced herself for another attack.

With the orb's light diminished, the Kali that stared down at her again looked human, her features those of a young woman.

The Kali gave a venomous smile as Chalea struggled to her feet. Chalea took her moment of gloating as an opportunity, unleashing the incantation she'd been chanting on the Kali.

Her injury thwarted her own attempt, slowing it enough so that the Kali reacted a millisecond before impact.

Csilla vanished in the blink of an eye, leaving Chalea alone.

Without a moment's hesitation, Chalea hobbled over to Renee's tent and pushed inside, hoping that she had not arrived too late, hoping that Renee wasn't dead.

The elder Bryant sister wasn't dead. She was gone.

The tent was empty.

"*No...*" Chalea withdrew and quickly scanned the area around the tent, calling for Renee. There was no reply. Panicked, Chalea bolted towards the tree line at the camp's perimeter, only to run into her own party.

Everyone was alive, though Costin and Ferka were injured, and everyone was confused, looking to her for answers.

"I don't get it," Christer said. "They just left. They had us cornered and then they just disappeared."

"They got what they came for." Chalea's voice was heavy with defeat.

It occurred to Ian at that moment that Chalea was alone. The awful realization knocked the wind out of him. "Renee?" His stricken question hung in the air.

Chalea simply shook her head.

Ian ran to the woman, grasping her by the shoulders. "Is she dead... is Renee dead?" He nearly choked on the words.

She winced at his grip. "No, Ian, Renee isn't dead. They took her. All of this—" she gestured around them, "—was a diversion to ensure the success of their real purpose: to take Renee."

"Fuck!" The word tore from Ian's lips as he looked back at the trees where the Kali had been moments before. "Why? What do they want with her?" His voice hovered on the edge of hysteria.

"I do not know, but it is nothing good. We must...pursue them." Chalea seemed to stumble over the end of her sentence, and then, to everyone's surprise, she crumpled at Ian's feet like a rag doll.

Ian dropped down beside her, cursing the fact that he hadn't reacted quickly enough to catch her. He cradled Chalea's prostrate form, finally seeing the torn and bloody state of her clothing. Ferka was immediately at her side too, ignoring his own injuries.

"How bad is it?" Christer asked from somewhere behind Ian.

"The lacerations are deep, but we will tend to her. She is strong—a healer. She will survive."

Gavril addressed Christer. "Gather up all of the weapons and talismans that we have. Prepare us for the journey ahead and be quick. We will leave as soon as Chalea is able to."

"Gavril, see to Costin."

Gavril nodded at his father's words, turning to his friend, while Ferka lifted the unresponsive Chalea into his arms and headed for her tent.

The others needed no further encouragement. Within the hour, they had broke camp, amassed their weapons, and saddled their horses.

By this time, Chalea had reappeared. She looked pale and worn but insisted that she was strong enough to ride.

As the first lights of dawn streaked the eastern sky, the group began the last leg of their journey, their determination reinforced by Renee's loss.

Soon it would all be over.

It just remained to be seen who the survivors would be.

CHAPTER 39

S top. Everyone, please stop." Chalea's words drew everyone's
attention, halting their progress.

Ferka turned his horse and faced the seer. "What is it? What do
you sense?"

Chalea breathed deeply, still not completely healed from the attack the
previous night. "Magic." She dismounted, stretching her legs. "I've
suspected as much for a while now..." She gestured at the woods around
them. "We have been traveling all day and still haven't found the ones we
seek. Why?"

Her rhetorical question was met with a protracted pause.

"The Kali are very near now, just as they were very near this morning.
We have been traveling around them, quite literally."

Gavril raked a hand through his hair, grimacing in frustration.

"The Kali are preventing us from locating them. Is that what you
mean?" Simon posed his question as he too dismounted, taking a
moment's relief for his aching limbs.

"Precisely. These woods have been spelled. To find the Kali, I must
break it." She sat down on the ground. "It is very thorough, a polished spell
that must have taken years to complete. It will take me a while to snap its
bond. Keep watch while I work."

With that, she closed her eyes and began breathing deeply and audibly,
as if she were practicing *ujjayi* breath.

The others dismounted and shared their remaining canteens of water, thirsty from the hours of riding.

No one spoke while Chalea worked, only the sound of her occasional chanting filling the silence.

Ian stood apart from the others, somber and weary. Out of all of them, he looked the worst for wear, even more so than the wounded Costin. The loss of Renee had taken something out of him and the determination that had spurred him on earlier in the day had diminished into despair. Both Simon and Christer tried talking to him, but neither could get a response out of him. In the end, they left him alone, not knowing what else to do.

After what seemed like an eternity, Chalea opened her eyes.

A slight wind blew through the trees around them, and for a moment, the ground seemed to vibrate beneath their feet.

Slowly, the seer stood. "It is done," she said. "The spell is broken. They cannot hide from me now. Let us ride."

The others commended her, hastily getting back on their horses.

Chalea followed suit, allowing herself a small smile of satisfaction. Csilla may have gotten the better of her before, but not this time. She had shattered the Kali's old spell in a fraction of the time it had taken her to create it.

They began riding again, Chalea in the lead. The sky overhead grew progressively darker, night stealing over the mountains.

After only a few minutes, Chalea suddenly stopped.

"Something's wrong," she breathed.

The others looked around, peering into the woods around them.

"What is it?" Christer asked.

His question was answered a second later.

A growl sounded from in front of them, low and menacing, followed by more on either side of them, growing in number.

"Wolves..." Ferka whispered. "Get your weapons out. Use the metal rounds for the guns, not the wooden ones."

The others complied mechanically. Instinct took over, and all seven of them had their weapons out and at the ready in seconds.

The first wolf appeared in front of Chalea, its teeth bared in a ferocious snarl.

The rest of the pack came from the sides, closing in on them slowly, all as menacing as the first, their hackles raised dangerously as they eyed the riders.

Christer felt the hair on the back of his neck stand on end when he saw them. There was something different about these wolves, something wrong. The pack seemed to look at them with a feral intelligence beyond that of normal wolves and in their eyes, Christer thought he could detect... *hatred.*

The pack leader turned his snout to the sky and howled, beginning an eerie chorus that the others picked up.

When he finished, he growled and charged, his fangs ripping into Chalea's horse before she could react.

The others tried to assist her, but the other wolves stopped them, charging them with teeth bared.

Chalea fell sideways off of her horse as the wolf tore out its throat, unsheathing a blade from her belt as she darted out of the way of the falling animal.

Done with the horse, the wolf came after her.

She jumped to the left at the last moment, narrowly avoiding its jaws. Then she lunged forward with her blade, slashing at its legs.

It snarled in rage and pain as she made contact, ripping one of the tendons in its hind leg.

The wound should have slowed it down, but the wolf kept coming. Its jaws clamped down on her arm, drawing blood, and Chalea screamed, bringing her saber down and slashing at its neck.

She stumbled back as it released her arm, watching as it whimpered in agony.

She expected it to collapse, but instead it pierced her with a gaze full of such malice that she felt a wave of panic shake her body.

Before it could charge her again, Costin was there. He rammed his spear straight through its head and the beast fell twitching in death throes to the ground.

Chalea spoke in a rush. "Costin, they're possessed. The Kali are using them. I have to sever the connection or else they'll keep attacking."

The burly man gave a terse nod, yanking his spear from the dead wolf, its tip smeared with blood and brain. "I will keep them at bay while you work." He understood what she needed and faced the onslaught, no fear in his eyes.

At the same time, the others were facing the rest of the pack. Christer and Ian had taken down a wolf, as had Ferka. Simon and Gavril were fighting back-to-back, covering each other as best they could, sweat drenching their clothes as they swung their blades wildly, trying to fend off their attackers.

All of the horses save for two were dead or dying; the wolves had made quick work of the helpless creatures.

"Ian, look out!" Christer shoved his friend as hard as he could, knocking him to the ground just as a wolf ripped at the space where his head had been a moment ago.

The large grey wolf landed on the ground with a thud and swiveled around with blinding speed, preparing for another attack.

Christer was faster. He shot it between the eyes, and the beast went down with a thud.

No later had Christer helped Ian to his feet than they heard Costin calling for help, his voice carrying over the growls of the wolves.

They sprinted to his aid, Christer shooting yet another wolf as they made their way to the young Roma.

The situation wasn't good.

Costin was battling off three wolves at once, his body and clothes a mess of cuts and bites. He had done his job well, though; Chalea knelt by his feet, her arms crossed over her chest as she murmured incantations, her person unharmed.

Christer shot the nearest wolf but missed its head, the bullet lodging in its shoulder.

It shot around, howling in rage, and charged Christer, knocking him to the ground and pinning him.

All he could see was teeth.

Gun forgotten, he shielded his face with one arm while trying to push the wolf away with his other.

It bit his forearm with gusto and Christer saw stars, the pain blinding him.

Driven on by Christer's screams, the wolf ripped into him again, harder than before.

His left arm bleeding profusely from the two bites, it fell uselessly against his chest and Christer again came face to face with teeth. He used his good arm to hold the wolf back by the neck, but he wasn't strong enough to hold it for long and the wolf's jaws were getting closer and closer to his face.

The wolf leaned in and aimed its teeth for his throat.

Christer closed his eyes, waiting for the end.

Instead, the wolf collapsed on top of him, dead.

It was a moment before he saw the knife in its back, lodged to the hilt between its shoulder blades.

Ian and Costin lifted the wolf off of him and Christer stood, cradling his wounded arm.

Chalea was standing now, her eyes shut tight in concentration. Her hands were shaking by her sides and her whole frame seemed to shudder.

The effort she was exerting was so great that her nose began to bleed, drops falling freely onto her shirt.

Christer realized then that he was watching her instead of the wolves and spun around, looking for their attackers.

He gawked in amazement as he took in the scene around them.

The six wolves that were left were no longer charging them; on the contrary, they seemed to have forgotten about their quarries altogether. All six were whimpering and shaking their heads from side to side, rubbing at their faces with their paws as if trying to ward off biting flies.

Chalea screamed, a high-pitched, blood-curling scream that made the men drop their weapons to the ground and cover their ears.

It was startling in its intensity and its effect was sudden and swift.

All six wolves howled to the sky as their heads exploded, their last cries echoing long after their bodies had fallen to the forest floor and the haze of blood rain had settled to the ground.

The men stood in shocked awe, gaping in turns at the dead wolves and the seer, rooted to the spot.

Chalea opened her eyes after a time. She wiped her nose, clearing the blood that remained on her face. When she looked down at the destruction around her, her expression was solemn rather than triumphant.

"I have done something awful." Her voice was rueful.

"You saved our lives," Ian said.

Chalea looked at him, her eyes clear and cold. "Yes. But this—" she brusquely pointed to the wolf closest to her, "—is awful. They were possessed, used by Csilla to do the Kali's bidding. They were meant to stop us, and they didn't have a choice. And I killed them. I couldn't save them."

Ferka laid a hand on her shoulder. "It was necessary, Chalea."

She stepped away from him. "I know." She looked again at the carnage around her- at the wolves, the horses and the bloodied men. When she spoke again, her voice was low and dangerous. "When we find the Kali – and find them we will – I *greatly* look forward to killing Csilla." She looked up to the dusky sky. "This is the last night she will walk upon this earth."

With that, she began retrieving weapons.

After a pause, the others did the same, all except for Costin, who was leaning against a tree, his eyes closed.

Gavril approached his friend, keeping his voice down. "Costin."

The other man looked at Gavril, meeting his gaze through partially closed lids.

"How badly are you hurt?"

Costin's breathing was erratic, and it took obvious effort to speak. "I did what I had to do, Gavril. You would have done the same. Chalea's more important than I am."

Gavril stepped closer. "Don't say that. You're like my brother, Costin; you're important to me." He swallowed hard. "I saw the wolf bite you there," he whispered, gesturing to Costin's torn side. The bite had been deep, and the wound was bleeding profusely, despite the makeshift tourniquet Costin had wrapped around his stomach.

"I'll be okay, Gavril. I'm always okay." He forced his mouth into a smile. "Let's go find our weapons so we can kill these demons and go home."

Soon they were armed with everything they'd been able to recover, and they all gathered around Chalea, who was facing west.

"Which way?" Ferka asked the seer.

She inclined her head, her mass of dark curls swinging. "Right ahead. The Kali are in the caves along the face of this ridge, not even one mile in front of us."

She started walking forward. "They can't hide any longer."

CHAPTER 40

Renee came to abruptly. For a moment, she was completely disoriented, like a swimmer caught in the pull of a riptide and unable to find the surface. The only thing she *was* immediately sure of was the pain.

Her head was throbbing as though her skull were about to split open at the seams, and she could feel hair matted to her face, plastered in place by a sickening amount of dried blood.

Reflexively, she reached to touch her head, the unnaturally heavy weight of her arms startling her. Confused, she attempted to bring her hands up again, only to realize that her wrists were bound and chained to a large circular ring affixed to the earthen floor. Glancing about, she could see that the only source of light in her perceived prison was the sliver of torchlight visible through the slats in a wooden door. The diluted light only allowed her to see the immediate space around her. The rest of the room remained in shadow. It was tomblike and dank, and it was impossible to know if it were day or night, how long she had been unconscious, or how much time had passed since she had been taken from the camp.

The attack.

It must have brought me here, that...that creature, Renee surmised.

She vividly recalled the woman that had appeared outside of her tent. She'd run back to get Ian's orb and the gun resting on her sleeping bag. Seconds later, she wasn't alone. A Kali was in the tent, staring at her. She'd quickly grabbed the orb and commanded the light as she'd watched Chalea do, but then she'd dropped it in fright. Nothing could have prepared her for seeing the Kali transform into the hideous, veiny beast that the light revealed.

The Kali had grabbed her wrists in a vise-like grip, angered by the orb's light. Despite its strength, Renee had struggled hard and at one point managed to retrieve her knife from her boot. She'd slashed at the Kali but missed. She remembered its maniacal laughter and then nothing. She never saw the blow that had knocked her out.

She had no way of knowing who'd won the confrontation.

She felt her pulse jump. *Oh God, what happened to the others?*

Bleakness settled in as she realized that there was a chance she might be the only survivor.

Alone and chained, Renee forced herself to resist the urge to give in to despair. The thought of losing her friends was almost too much to bear, and that, combined with the oppressive silence that buzzed in her ears like the pressure of a watery abyss, made not giving up more difficult than anything she'd ever done. Every breath was a small miracle.

All she did have were her thoughts, and they were less than pleasant to entertain. The one that kept coming back was *why*. Renee knew with certainty that the Kali wanted her alive for something; it would have been all too easy for her attacker to have killed her back in the tent.

But what could they possibly want with her? Had Lou had a hand in this?

Instinctively, Renee knew that she was in grave danger. Death might yet prove a preferable alternative to whatever the Kali had in store for her.

For the first time in her life, she knew the real meaning of fear.

After a time, her eyes adjusted to the dim light of the small chamber and she turned her thoughts to some means of escape as she surveyed her surroundings. The options were not good. The wooden door seemed to be the only way in or out, and it would no doubt be bolted shut. Then of course there was the more immediate problem: the shackles on her wrists.

Left without any other course of action, Renee decided that she had to first determine whether she was alone or if any of the others had been imprisoned with her.

She licked her chapped lips and swallowed in an effort to soothe her sore throat. Tentatively, she called out, "Ian, Brody, Christer...is anyone there? Can anyone hear me?"

There was no reply.

Renee called again and again, each time louder, but to no avail. Eventually overcome with desperation, Renee thrashed helplessly against her bonds, throwing herself away from the iron ring, endeavoring to dislodge it with the full weight of her body. But it was no use. Unable to budge the fixture and tired from the exertion, Renee dropped to the floor on her knees, all hope of escape deserting her.

I'm going to die here...

As if it were a confirmation of her thoughts, Renee heard of the sound of footsteps moving towards the chamber. She braced herself to face whatever was coming.

The door opened with a creak and a torch was thrust through, the sudden light making her squint in pain.

Blinking, her eyes focused on the nearest figure. It was Lou, accompanied by a tall, dark man whose face was partially shadowed by the large, hooded cloak he wore.

Renee felt a flood of emotions unleash as she faced her sister, a mixture of love and revulsion, pity and anger, hope and despair. Praying that Lou could still hear and see her, Renee found her voice and pleaded. "Lou, please—it's me, it's Renee. You need to help me. Please, Lou, remember who you are."

The woman who stared back at her had none of Lou's warmth. Icy blue eyes assessed her coldly. "I am Sabina Solovastru. Your sister is gone; her body has provided me with the vessel I needed to walk this earth again. Your pitiful begging will do you no good."

Renee flinched at her name and the words she'd spoken, and Sabina laughed, a sadistic glint glittering in her eyes.

"Miksa, shall we tell her what we have in store for her?" Sabina addressed her dark companion, glancing at him with undisguised excitement.

Miksa lowered the hood of his cloak and turned his gaze towards Renee as he answered. "Tell her if you wish to, Sabina. I know the thought of her transformation excites you, as it should, for we will all benefit from it."

"You bastard, what do you want with me? And what have you done to my friends?" Renee shouted. "And what do you mean, 'transformation'? I would rather die than let you use me like you've used my sister!"

Sabina approached her and took Renee's face in her hands, bringing it within inches of her own. Tracing her finger over Renee's lips, Sabina whispered, "You will die, foolish girl, just not yet. First you will provide your body for another who, like me, will walk again, one like no other. This one is powerful, immortal and *mine*." Renee's skin crawled at her sister's touch and the ominous implication in her prediction.

Maybe it is too late after all. Maybe Lou really is gone for good. There was no evidence of her sister's soul in the woman that stood before her. Only evil emanated from her.

Renee closed her eyes, refusing to meet Sabina's stare any longer. She would not give her the satisfaction.

Sabina let her go and wheeled about, facing Miksa.

"I am tired of waiting. We have a host; why must we wait to perform the ritual? We should bring Xenia back now!"

"Patience, Sabina. Our preparations are nearly complete. By dawn, you will have Xenia at your side. And with her return, we will be all-powerful; no one will be able to stop us. Then we will kill the others that are searching us out— an offering of blood to appease Kali and our own appetites."

"Oh, Miksa, I can hardly wait. My joy will be complete when I too can truly become one of you," Sabina cooed sensuously.

"With the rising of the full moon, our Maker will grant that wish very soon," Miksa answered her, his face expressionless.

With that, Sabina spun on her heels and left the chamber without a parting glance at their prisoner.

Renee had heard Miksa's ominous words, but instead centered her hope on the one thing he had revealed to her unwittingly: *the others are alive, and they are coming*. Hope blossomed within her, but she tried to keep her expression unreadable, unwilling to allow the Kali to sense her thoughts.

Miksa didn't leave with Sabina. Instead, he remained where he was, his eyes fixed on Renee.

She felt the hair on her neck rising. The way he was looking at her, like a cat would look at a mouse it had caught between its claws, was unnerving.

Slowly he approached her, his sheer size intimidating as he loomed before her. The man exuded darkness and danger.

Miksa leaned towards her, his fingers reaching to touch her face, and Renee recoiled at his touch. She retreated towards the wall, but Miksa continued forward until she had nowhere to go. He pressed her against the unforgiving surface and grasped her by the throat. Slowly, he ran his fingers down the length of her neck, a mockery of a lover's caress. Sweat beaded on Renee's brow and she trembled despite her valiant attempt to remain resolute and defiant.

The Kali leaned close and whispered in her ear, his lips so close that she could feel his breath on her skin. "You will have the unique privilege of dying twice, my dear. Your first death will be today, to bring Xenia back to us. And then, *then*, I will finally have what I have been waiting centuries for..."

He leaned back so that she could see his face and the cruel smile he wore. "I will rid myself of Xenia forever—she will die at my hands. I will drink her blood and take what should have been mine long ago. This time, her heart will remain silent." His expression altered slightly as he locked eyes with her. "It pains me to take the free will of another, but time has forced my hand. So find solace in this, human: the creature responsible for your sister's death and your own will soon meet the same fate. Her crimes will not go unpunished."

With that, he released her neck and Renee slumped to the floor, staring after the dark man as he retreated from the chamber and took the light with him.

Darkness and isolation closed over her once more, but this time she welcomed the silence.

CHAPTER 41

One mile proved to be an underestimation.

They walked for the better part of an hour, the sky above growing darker with each passing minute, the air colder as they climbed in altitude.

To Ian, the steady crunching of their feet on the now frost-covered ground created a monotonous rhythmic pulse that reminded him of a ticking clock—a clock ticking away what seconds Renee might have left. He shivered.

The two horses that had survived the slaughter during their encounter with the wolves now carried the majority of their supplies and everyone was forced to walk. The loss of their horses was keenly felt as it slowed their progress considerably. With Renee abducted and presumably in danger, time was indeed the enemy.

Ian felt the cold chill of the high mountain air through to his bones. He zipped his jacket as high as it would go, trying to keep out the cold.

He figured that the Roma were accustomed to the high altitude, Simon and Christer less so, yet neither of his friends had uttered a word of complaint. Barely a word had been exchanged among the party since the incident with the wolves. Chalea was lost in concentration, her mind engaged as she sought to discern darkness from danger, Ferka walking closely behind her.

Ian realized that they didn't stand a chance in hell of finding Renee without the gypsy woman. As she had demonstrated in a dramatic way not long ago, her psychic powers were real. He remembered with vivid clarity how Chalea had destroyed the possessed wolves with merely the force of her will. It was enough to convince even the biggest skeptic of her power.

He also found himself marveling at the normalcy with which he now seemed to reflect on all of the unbelievable phenomena: evil beings, possession, psychic powers, ancient cults...as if all of those things were ordinary events in one's everyday experience. The way he looked at the world had changed, and reality as he'd known it – home, city lights, take-out on Friday nights – seemed as if it existed in a parallel universe.

Home.

God, it seemed so far away. *Home with Renee, home with Bubba...*

In his mind, he could see his big Labrador, curled up on the floor next to him and Renee, trying to draw their attention from the movie on television, thumping his big tail on the floor.

Ian would have traded anything for that scene to be real—to have Renee at his side right now, far from this place and the events of the last few weeks.

He longed for her worrying, her perfectionism, hell—he even longed for her never-ending criticisms of his grossly casual wardrobe.

"Ian, you are not wearing that out to dinner! That shirt has more wrinkles than an elderly woman's backside. I mean, really..."

Yeah, he even missed *those* moments.

He'd always known that he loved Renee, but until now— until he faced the real possibility that he would never see her alive again— did he understand the depth of his love for her. If they survived this, he would never lose her again.

He thought of the engagement ring in his knapsack. It had now become almost a talisman, a promise of their future together, and he knew without any doubt that he would carry it to the ends of the earth if needed to make that future a reality.

Steeling himself with renewed resolve, Ian allowed a single thought to dominate all others, building in intensity until it reverberated throughout his entire being.

I will find you, Renee. I swear it.

From behind, Ian heard Gavril's voice calling out for a brief respite. Glancing back, he could see that the pause was not for Gavril's sake, but for his friend's. Costin had lost a significant amount of blood from the wounds he'd sustained in the wolf attack while defending Chalea. Although the Roma hadn't spoken a word of complaint during their trek in the dark, freezing woods, his face betrayed the extent of his injuries. Costin was pale and drawn, and despite the use of Gavril's arm as support, the beleaguered man just needed to rest.

Simon and Christer approached Ian and dropped their packs, taking advantage of the momentary pause. Christer, sensing Ian's disquiet, elbowed him lightly in the arm. "We're going to get them back you know— Renee and Lou. We've made it this far and we're all still alive."

Simon nodded his agreement.

"I know," Ian responded dully.

At his approach, Christer turned to Costin, his face etched with concern at his appearance. The young man didn't look like he would survive the hike, let alone the rest of the night.

In Romanian, Costin assured the Swede that his injuries were only slight and that he would be prepared for the fight ahead. Despite the steadiness of his speech, Christer felt that Costin was lying; he obviously didn't want to worry Gavril with the truth.

Glancing ahead, he noticed that Chalea stood rigidly still a few dozen meters ahead of them, at the edge of a small clearing. Her head was slightly cocked to the side, as if she were listening to a song that only she could hear, and her body was so still that she appeared inanimate; only the slight twitch in her fingers made it clear she was still breathing.

Suddenly, as if awakened from a trance, Chalea became energized, her eyes bright as she whipped around to face them.

"The Kali are here; I feel their presence." She spoke quickly as she walked back to join them. "We've found them. Their lair is beyond that clearing." She gave a sideways glance at Costin before continuing. "But they know we are near; I hear whispers in the trees ahead. I do not know by what means they will attack, but be assured, they will. Be on guard, all of you."

Ian caught her arm before she started away. "Can you sense Renee's presence too?"

"Yes." Chalea nodded, already turned in the direction of the clearing. "She is still alive, Ian. There is still time."

He let her go and retrieved his pack, a fresh sense of determination filling him.

Cautiously, the group moved forward. Everyone was on high alert, eyes scanning the trees in all directions. After their past encounter with the Kali, they'd all learned that the beings they sought moved with the speed of wraiths and the silence of wisps of smoke. They blended into their caliginous surroundings as if they were a part of the forest itself.

Ferka walked at Chalea's side, determined to protect the seer at any cost. It was his duty as leader of their clan; he would give his life to protect his family. It was the Roma way.

As they reached the far end of the clearing and again entered the dense woods, the air about them became increasingly oppressive. It was as if the night had taken on a weight of its own and was pressing down upon them. The eerie silence was almost cloying- it hung about them like a mist. It made all of them uneasy.

Simon was the first to notice the rustling. It seemed to be an echo of their footfalls. Looking around, he had the distinct sense that eyes were watching- watching from all sides.

The rustle came again, closer this time.

Convinced that the sounds were not a figment of his imagination, he began to scan the forest floor.

Almost immediately, he caught movement in the corner of his eye.

The ground was moving. Or rather, something *beneath* the ground was moving. Small and thin, it seemed to twist and curl beneath the surface like a snake.

He turned to Christer. "Did you see that?"

"See what?" Christer turned, scanning the trees around him.

Then the movement was right under them. "That!"

Christer jumped in surprise. "What the hell?" He exclaimed. The ground was...*shifting.*

Before he could think of a rational explanation, a vine-like tendril uncoiled directly beneath them, rising from the ground like the hand of an ancient crone, gnarled and knobby with decay.

With the speed of a Venus flytrap, the tendril clamped onto Christer's ankle, bringing the big man to the ground with a resounding thump. Before Christer could utter a cry of distress, the tendril began dragging him towards a large tree, its grip on him unshakable.

What the shit? "Help!" He cried. "The trees...it's the trees!"

Chalea cursed under her breath. Crying out to the others, she ordered, "Cut into the roots with the sabers and use the orbs! They will repel the vines!" She reached for her own orb, palming it. "And keep your eyes on the ground!"

Simon and Ian, who were within feet of Christer, flew into action. Both men hacked furiously at the roots that now entwined both of Christer's legs. As Ian drew his hand back to swing the saber, a long, whip-like root curled about his wrist, suspending his blade in mid-air. He cried out in frustration, too focused on Christer to realize his own peril. Desperate to recover his weapon, he tried to wrest it from the root.

Christer was almost entirely cocooned by roots, his cries cut off as a particularly thick root wrapped around his face.

Acting quickly, Simon reached into his pack and produced the orb.

And not a moment too soon. The vines were literally squeezing the life out of Christer, choking off his air.

With as much energy as he could muster, Simon called forth a stream of bright light from the orb, aiming it directly towards his two friends.

As if the roots had been seared by white-hot fire, they recoiled, releasing both men from their deadly grip.

Helping Christer up, all three retreated towards the Roma, who were viciously slicing at the earthy tentacles. With each passing second, more and more roots seemed to break free from the soil and emerge in a shower of dirt, until the entire ground around them was undulating like a sea of slithering snakes.

The mass of roots seemed to converge and move in Chalea's direction, as if they sensed that she was source of danger and they were determined to eliminate their most formidable adversary.

Ferka was doing everything he could to keep them at bay, blades in both hands working savagely as they struck down root after root. Still, he was becoming overwhelmed by the ferocity of the attack. The roots were like a sylvan Hydra; for each one he cut down, two more sprang up in its place. Tendrils clutched at his legs; he struck and parried.

More roots were reaching towards the seer as Ferka struggled. He used both blades to chop a massive one and managed to sever it completely, but one of his blades became lodged in the thick, sinewy bark. Before he could dislodge the weapon, other roots wrapped around his wrists and hands, disarming him. Chalea, seemingly unaware of what was transpiring about her, continued her battle in the supernatural realm, determined to win.

"Father, hold on, I'm coming!" Gavril shouted.

Costin nodded for him to go, and with a final glance at his friend, Gavril rushed to his father's aid, fighting like a man possessed, blade in each hand, slashing and cutting without regard to his own safety.

A strangled cry erupted from Costin. Weakened from the prior battle, the brave Roma was no match for the tree demons. Thick roots wrapped about his torso and the Roma was brought to his knees. Trying in vain with his bare hands to dislodge the tentacles of wood, his hands too were pinioned. Like a man in a straight-jacket unable to offer any resistance, the vines encased his entire body. Before any of the others could reach him, he was jerked away and down into the earth, his final screams choked off as he disappeared from sight.

The forest had swallowed him alive.

Chalea heard his screams and the cries of the others, but she didn't rush to their aid. She couldn't; to end the horror, she couldn't be distracted.

In her hand she held a glowing orb to the sky, her eyes closed in concentration. Her lips moved in ceaseless incantation as she tried to dispel the curse that had taken possession of the world around them.

A cackle disrupted her thoughts.

She opened her eyes, seeking its source.

Her eyes locked with the Kali's a moment later, her own narrowing in rage.

"*Csilla*," she hissed. "I should have known."

The Kali smiled.

In one smooth motion, Chalea unsheathed the saber at her waist and pointed its blade at her nemesis. "Time to die, demon."

She charged, running at Csilla with a burst of adrenaline-boosted speed.

The Kali stumbled back in surprise, bending back just as the blade whizzed by her ear.

Refusing to be bested by a human, Csilla rolled away and sprang to standing, calling forth her magic.

She shot it from her fingertips at the Roma woman, but Chalea was fast and had been expecting the attack. She brought her own magic to bear, shooting a bolt of searing light towards the Kali.

The light found its mark, hitting Csilla squarely in the chest.

Screaming, she went down, and Chalea was upon her before she knew what was happening.

Csilla's superior strength saved her. Using her hand like a knife, she chopped at Chalea's windpipe, making her stumble back and sputter to catch her breath.

In that moment, Csilla called forth another bout of magic, aiming it straight for Chalea's heart, screaming as she poured her fury into it.

The Roma went down without a sound, her eyes open and staring.

Breathing heavily, Csilla walked over to the still seer and bent over her cautiously, as if she were afraid the woman might jump up at any moment.

But Chalea didn't move.

A satisfied smile played on Csilla's lips as she stared down at her dead foe. "You never stood a chance, did you? Poor fool, what did you take me for, a novice? You could never have beaten *me*." She spoke the words simply to relish her own victory, loving the way they tasted on her tongue almost as much as she loved the kill.

She drew in a deep breath of pleasure, then jerked in shock.

The figure on the ground disappeared just as she felt the cold blade slice into her heart from behind.

Twisting the saber, Chalea leaned forward and whispered in her ear. "Then again, only a novice would fall for such an amateur trick." She pulled her blade free and stepped back. "Hell awaits, Csilla."

Eyes bulging in shock, the Kali fell forward, her form changing into the beast beneath her human skin. By the time she hit the ground, she was her true self, a heap of talons, grey veins, and flat black eyes.

In death, those eyes stared open and wide like the black gates of hell itself, and Chalea turned her back on them, carrying her bloody blade with her.

It was over in seconds following Csilla's death.

The roots fell to the ground, lifeless, and when the dirt and dust had settled, all that remained was a stretch of broken earth and mangled tree roots, torn and ripped from the trees to which they had given life. The survivors stood in the midst of a gnarled battlefield, covered in dirt, sweat, sap, and their own blood.

Gavril rushed over to the spot where Costin had disappeared and was down on his hands and knees, moving aside wood and earth, searching for any sign of his childhood friend. He stopped only when Ferka laid a hand on his shoulder. Fighting back tears, he stood, his eyes still fixed on the ground beneath his feet, waiting for Costin to return from below.

But the ground remained still.

Chalea wiped her blade on the side of her pant leg. "Csilla- the Kali's seer- is dead. Without her, we have a fighting chance." She sheathed her blade and looked at each of them, her green eyes aglow. "Costin's death will not be in vain. This ends now. We head for the caves."

Solemn but resolute, they all marched forward, going without pause until they stood at the mouth of a large cave.

They had finally reached their destination.

Dark and formidable, it exuded death. It was exactly the place creatures like the Kali would choose as their home.

With a finger to her lips to signal quiet, Chalea led them forward into the yawning mouth.

CHAPTER 42

Tendrils of vines hung over the cave entrance like a curtain, and as they passed through them, it felt as though they were entering another world.

The relatively small opening belied the vast size of the structure within. The vaulted ceiling of the main chamber rose upwards of fifty feet and giant stalactites hung like grand chandeliers throughout. Rocks and stalagmites studded the floor of the chamber and scattered pools of murky, stagnant water glistened in the semi-darkness, but the cave was otherwise devoid of any evidence of habitation by forest creatures. Even they, apparently, avoided the home of the Kali as if it were anathema.

They gawked at their surroundings, enamored with the otherworldly structure. It was minutes before the fear kicked back in and their focus returned.

The sense of openness and space that they felt in the main cave was short-lived. As they proceeded into the inner recesses, the ceiling and walls compressed to the point where they were forced to walk single file, crouching at times to avoid the calcium carbonate formations that hung from above. Now in pitch black, they resorted to using their flashlights to guide the way. Their lights cast long shadows along the sides of the walls as they moved forward, illuminating strange symbols and runes that looked as if they had been burned into the limestone.

Chalea and Ferka, who had taken the lead, signaled for the others to stop.

They had come to a fork in the road. A single cave now branched off in two separate directions, each looking dark and foreboding.

Ferka turned to the seer. "Do you know which way?"

Chalea pursed her lips, frustrated. She shook her head. "I cannot be certain. I sense them all about us, but I can't pinpoint their exact location. I think there are at least five Kali, maybe more." She shined her flashlight right and left, following its beam with her eyes. "We have to split up; each party will have to take a separate route from here. I have a feeling that these passages will rejoin at some point, but if one of them proves to be a dead end, we can't all be trapped there. We will be easy prey if that happens."

Nodding, Ferka quickly took charge and divided them into two groups: his own party consisted of Chalea, Ian and himself; the second, Simon, Christer and his son. Exchanging brief exhortations of caution, the two groups parted ways.

Simon, Christer, and Gavril quickly discovered that their route was a winding labyrinth of dead-end tunnels and interconnected branches that separated only to rejoin several meters later. Their senses on high alert, each man continuously scanned the darkness in each direction as they moved forward, conscious of the fact that their attackers could come at them from any angle.

Their flashlights heightened the feeling of being in utter darkness, for they provided only minimal light. Each time the beam moved, the section it left was plunged back into blackness. It was like trying to drive in an impenetrable fog with only one headlight working.

Worse than the darkness, though, was the pervasive sense that they were being watched- the sense that the Kali were toying with them, already one step ahead, and that when the attack came, as it surely would, they would be unable to respond with the speed necessary to stop it.

They had not spoken a word since they'd split up from the others for fear of alerting the Kali to their presence, so the only sound in the womb-like tunnel was the sound of their own labored breathing.

Until now. Barely discernible, the soft sound of moans reached their ears.

Simon and Christer exchanged a perplexed look, the same thought resonating in both of their minds. "Renee?" They mouthed in unison.

Gavril extended a hand in restraint. "It could be a trap."

Nodding that they understood, the men moved towards the sound of the voice, its source slightly distorted as it bounced back to them through the winding tunnels. As they drew closer and passed around another bend, they could just discern the figure of a woman lying prostrate and bound in a large cache hewn into the rock.

"It's Renee!" Simon blurted in an excited whisper. Determined, he quickened his pace, eager to rush to her side. He'd moved only a few feet when his advance was cut short.

The air directly in front of him began to scintillate and shift, as if the fabric of space there was malleable. Diaphanous particles of light vibrated with quickening intensity until they took shape—the shape of a petite little girl with blonde braids.

Gretchen.

Before, she had appeared tangible, *real*, but now, she was as transparent as a gossamer thread. She stood before Simon, her translucent braids swinging as she shook her head emphatically from side to side.

Gavril and Christer looked on in utter amazement as Simon acknowledged the apparition by name without any degree of shock or amazement.

As he glanced over his shoulder at his friends, the ghostly figure suddenly pointed behind them, her mouth open in a silent scream. Then she vanished as suddenly as she had appeared.

Whirling around, Simon zigzagged his flashlight beam into the darkness behind them. "It's a trap! Look behind you!"

No sooner had he uttered the words than the attack came. From behind them rose a hideous snarl. Gavril spun around, bringing his saber up in defense as he did so.

His quick action saved his life.

The thing that faced him had slashed downward with razor sharp talons. Gavril's blade had met the deadly arc of its swing, severing the monstrous appendage. The Kali screamed in pain and rage, its black eyes bulging in fury.

Christer and Gavril pursued the monster as it attempted to escape down another passageway, moving as fast as they could risk in the dark, their flashlights bobbing ahead of them. As they ran, Christer shouted to Gavril to draw his bow. They stopped once the tunnel dead-ended, weapons at the ready.

Now cornered, the Kali resorted to other tactics. Throwing its head back, the creature emitted a high-pitched keening sound, its grey veins throbbing wildly.

The eerie sound reverberated in the narrow space and moments later a thick cloud of bats spilled into the tunnel, attacking the two men viciously.

Satisfied that it now had the upper hand, the Kali advanced on Gavril, whose attention was directed towards his aerial attackers. Seeing its intention, Christer ignored the bats ripping at his face and neck and reached instead for his gun. Charging ahead, the Swede threw himself between Gavril and the demon, firing the pistol point blank against the creature's chest.

The bats scattered at the sound, their inhuman shrieks receding with them as they retreated.

The shot poorly prepared, the recoil knocked Christer back a pace just as black blood exploded from the wound, splattering his face and clothes. The smell of decay impregnated the air, choking the men with its foulness. The hideous corpse in front of them darkened before their eyes, its skin becoming deep grey, its veins protruding like old tracks etched into a riverbed. When at last the reverberations of the shot died away, silence again crept up around them.

Gavril extended his hand to Christer and pulled him to his feet, his eyes conveying unspoken gratitude for his act of bravery.

Without further hesitation, he drew his sword and severed the Kali's head from its body. "Just to be sure," he muttered.

It was only then that they realized Simon wasn't with them.

"Simon's back there with that thing pretending to be Renee. He's by himself. We have to hurry!" Christer shouted at the Roma. They wheeled around, racing back the way they had come.

CHAPTER 43

When the attack began, Simon kept his attention on Renee's doppelgänger, trying to protect Gavril and Christer as they faced the other Kali.

As soon as it realized that its ruse was foiled, the impostor rose to its feet, its appearance altering until the illusion was completely dispelled.

Now in its true Kali form, the demon advanced towards Simon, snarling, its sharp fangs extending out from a lipless mouth, its pupil-less eyes black and flat.

Simon reached for the orb in his pocket and extended it, calling forth its bright blue light. The Kali hissed and shielded its face from the penetrating ray, retreating into a hidden passageway. Simon proceeded after the wraith with the orb held high. Not taking his eyes from the path in front of him, he reached for his gun, determined to hunt the demon down now before it had another chance to sneak up on them. Wary of hidden traps, Simon moved slowly and quietly, staying close to the wall, his heart knocking around furiously in his chest.

Where the hell did it go?

There was nothing but empty tunnels in every direction. With no other ideas, Simon pressed his hands along the length of the flowstone as he moved forward, searching for any evidence of a mechanism that could disguise a hidden door or passageway.

Just as he was about to abandon his current route, his fingers lodged in a curved nook along the otherwise smooth stone. Exploring the niche, Simon found what he was looking for. "Gotcha," he whispered.

Wrapping his fingers around the protruding rock and exerting downward pressure, the latch moved, and the wall to his right fell back, revealing a concealed passage. He moved forward into the new tunnel. As he crossed the threshold the stone sealed behind him so seamlessly that it gave no evidence of a door.

No going back now. Swallowing his fear, Simon moved on. The short tunnel emptied into a chamber with a single exit opposite where he stood. As he moved towards it, Simon realized his folly and his footsteps slowed until he stopped completely.

The Kali had anticipated his pursuit and now it materialized out of the dark in front of him, moving towards him with undisguised triumph, its fangs and talons glistening in the light of the orb. Simon raised his gun and took aim, but it sidestepped out of the orb's illumination and vanished.

Moving with dizzying speed, it reappeared to his left. Simon's reaction time was boosted by adrenaline as he again took aim. He fired a round, aiming for its heart.

His bullet ricocheted off the stone wall of the chamber, sailing through nothing but empty space.

With a sinking feeling, Simon realized that he wasn't going to win this game of reflexes; the Kali was simply too fast for him.

He set the orb on the ground and slowly turned around, forcing his breathing under control. He scanned the entire cave but found nothing.

Where is it?

In one dreadful moment, the answer dawned on Simon and he looked up.

The Kali was above him, hanging from the ceiling of the chamber like a giant spider. As Simon met its eyes, it dropped directly in front of him, talons extended for the death blow. Unable to react in time, Simon managed a strangled cry before the talons wrapped around his neck, cutting off any further sound. The thing squeezed him hard as it brought rows of razor-sharp teeth towards his jugular, its intentions clear.

"Mmm, fear always makes a kill taste better." The Kali's snake-like whisper curled around him as tightly as the talons choking his neck. "Watching the life drain from your eyes will give me such satisfaction."

Simon could smell its fetid breath as he struggled to breathe. He knew there was no escape now; he whispered a silent prayer, recalling a childhood invocation he hadn't spoken in years.

St. Michael the Archangel, defend me in battle. Be my defense against the wickedness and snares of the devil...

He closed his eyes as the Kali opened its jaws wide.

A loud crack sounded in the chamber and the Kali's grip relaxed.

Dazed and shaking, Simon freed himself from its grasp and the beast slid to the floor in a heap. Looking up, Simon met the gaze of a bloodied but smiling Christer, an equally wounded Gavril at his side.

Christer twirled his gun like a cowboy in an old western and winked at him. "Bet you're glad to see me, eh, partner?" He drawled. Tucking the gun into his pants, he reached out with both arms and steadied Simon as he rose to his feet.

When he regained use of his motor skills, Simon stepped towards his friend and gripped the big Swede by the arms. "Words will never express my gratitude," he assured him. "Now let's go find the others."

CHAPTER 44

The maze of tunnels led Ferka's party to another antechamber, this one larger than the first. The calcite formations were so old that floor and ceiling had grown to meet in the middle, forming columns that gave the chamber a caged appearance. Crystalline formations twinkled from all around, sparkling in multicolor winks as their flashlights moved across the breadth of the cavern.

Senses on high alert, the men had drawn their guns and Chalea held her saber at the ready, her grip so tight that the muscles of her arm resembled chiseled marble.

They moved through the naturally formed bars of the cave, careful not to make any sounds.

The silence was so deep that the voice that cut through the stillness made them jump.

"So. You have killed Csilla."

It was low and mellifluous, but strangely lacking inflection. It was the voice of a cultured patience, one that had become disquietingly emotionless with the passing of time.

"And now you have come for your friend," it continued.

Chalea brought out her orb, casting its light into the dim areas of the cave. "Show yourself, Kali," she said.

Mocking laughter came as her reply.

Ian and Ferka tried to discern its source, but it was impossible to tell from which direction the voice was coming. The acoustics within the cave caused the sound to reverberate so that it seemed to fill the whole space.

Ian had the eerie feeling that he was in a fun house, surrounded by mirrors that obscured reality and morphed it into unrecognizable shapes. He swallowed hard.

Chalea began to chant then, her eyelids fluttering, her mind searching for a weakness in the dark man's magic.

The laughter turned to a growl. "Very well, seer. You wish to test your skills against mine? I shall acquiesce your request."

Chalea opened her eyes and spun around, crouched over in a battle stance. Ian and Ferka copied her, aiming into the darkness.

A man stepped forward, dark and tall. He exuded danger and power as he assessed them with unblinking eyes. His tall frame was clothed completely in black, accentuating his imposing stature. After a moment he moved closer towards them, a small smile curling his lips. He fixed his stare on Chalea, eyeing her with a mixture of admiration and loathing.

"The mouth can only stay open for so long." He spoke the words slowly, his eyes never leaving Chalea's. "And alas for you, I think it is time for the jaws to shut."

Her green eyes widened in understanding and she sheathed her saber. With more strength than they would have expected, she grabbed Ian and Ferka and propelled them towards the nearest tunnel.

Ian realized why a second later.

The man had disappeared, but two other Kali had appeared in his place at either end of the cave. With Herculean strength, they began kicking down the columns, making the whole cave shake. When they had destroyed enough of them, the remaining supports seemed to buckle under the weight and the floor began to vibrate in warning.

Chalea, Ferka, and Ian reached the tunnel just before the rocks started falling.

Chalea put her hands on her thighs, bending over to catch her breath.

"Won't they die in there?" Ian asked.

She shook her head. "No, they're too quick and strong for that to happen. That was meant to crush us, not them."

She stood up and Ferka grabbed her arm, gesturing to their left. "I hear them; they're coming towards us."

"We have to go. This way!" She darted off towards the right, Ian and Ferka following closely behind her, their pursuers close behind them.

They ran as fast as they could, their legs cramping with exertion and their eyes working overtime to adjust to the oppressive darkness all around them. They ran, twisting and winding deeper into the underground maze, choosing their direction based on the movement of shadows and snatches of echoes, but relying mostly on Chalea's psychic connection to the Kali.

As Ian was about to turn another corner, Chalea grabbed him by the shirt, jerking him back. "They're coming that way—and from behind as well," she said, panting. "We're trapped."

Their fear building, all three of them looked around, desperately searching the walls for signs of another passage, for something they had missed.

Ian looked at Chalea, his eyes desperate. "They're almost on us; we need to take defensive positions, now!"

"Wait," the seer rasped, her eyes drawn to the stone wall opposite them. Lunging forward, she ran her hand up and down its smooth surface. Responding to her touch, the wall moved, sliding to the side. They rushed through, watching in baffled fascination as it closed behind them.

"Holy shit, that was close!" Ian panted. "I think you just saved our lives, Chalea. How the hell did you know that was there?"

The seer didn't answer him. She was staring at the floor, which was covered in the most life-like snakes Ian had ever seen. When she at last looked up, her expression was one of defeat. "They wanted us to come here, Ian. They were herding us like cattle. *This* was the trap."

Ian shook his head in incomprehension. She was talking nonsense. "But why would they do that?"

"Look around; we're standing in their inner sanctum."

He looked, and everything he saw confirmed what she was telling him. The chamber was pristine, and runes filled its walls like a kaleidoscope of ornate decoration. The snakes on the floor were facing an altar, a stone giant draped in black cloth.

"What should we do?" He tried to keep the panic out of his voice, but his mind was abuzz with it.

Did they sacrifice Renee here? Are they going to do the same to us?

Chalea was already taking action, sprinkling a white powdery substance onto the floor around them. Without taking her eyes off of her work, she murmured, "Get in the circle and be quiet. I am doing what I can."

When she finished, she placed the orb in the center of the circle and chanted something incoherent at it, her hands hovering above its surface. The ground around the orb began to glow, and the light began seeping outward from it, its reach extending until it filled the circle of powder.

Which was precisely when the door slid open and four Kali entered, the dangerous man at the forefront. Only he retained his human form; the others were the veiny beasts they were now all too familiar with, their shark-like eyes assessing them, their wicked fangs protruding from lipless mouths.

He signaled for the Kali nearest him to attack and in obedience, the creature flung itself towards the circle, talons outstretched.

Instinctively, Ian took a step back, but Chalea grabbed his arm, motioning for him to remain still.

The Kali raised its arms and curved its talons downwards, aiming for Chalea's head. A moment before it would have sliced her open, a flare of light filled the air around them, making even the humans inside the circle cringe at the brightness.

The creature fell to the floor, writhing in agony and cradling its right arm. One of its massive talons had literally been burned away, as if it had been melted down by lava. The flesh around the useless stump was smoking.

The man looked without pity at his comrade on the floor, then eyed the circle. "I assumed as much, but I had to be sure you were not merely bluffing." He motioned to another Kali to help the first. "I am Miksa."

"Are you the Maker here?" Chalea asked, watching Miksa as he walked slowly around the circle, standing just outside of its protective boundaries.

"No. My Maker has been sleeping." He faced the altar. "But tonight, she will awaken. That is where your friend comes in."

He barked a command at one of the Kali and they left through the same door they had entered by—the only way in or out of the chamber.

"You must realize that we have won; you are trapped, and you will die. Stay inside your circle for now if you wish, but eventually you will have to emerge. And I will be waiting." He stood so that he was only inches away from Chalea. "Of course, if *you* come out, I may let your friends go. You see, now that you've killed my seer, we are in need of a new one."

Chalea spat at him. "I don't make deals with the dead," she hissed, her green eyes narrowing in hatred.

He stepped away, brushing his cheek. "So be it."

Then everything broke into chaos.

The Kali that had stepped out returned, holding a bound and gagged Renee in its claws. She looked awful. Dried blood was caked on her head and around her wrists where the bindings had chafed her skin, and her shirt was torn and stained, various holes showing off the bruised skin beneath. She wasn't moving.

Ian screamed her name and before Chalea or Ferka could stop him, he rushed out of the circle, gun drawn, shooting at the Kali's head.

Miksa moved with silent speed and backhanded him across the face, sending him sprawling, the gun spiraling across the floor and hitting the far wall.

Ian staggered up, hands fumbling for his dagger. He slashed as Miksa moved towards him again, but Miksa was quicker. The Kali evaded the blade and simultaneously hit Ian in the face with his right elbow and snapped his wrist with his left hand.

Screaming in pain, Ian fell to his knees.

The sound roused Renee, who looked on with horror, screaming through the gag in her mouth as she watched her boyfriend hit the ground.

The two Kali not holding Renee crowded around him like vultures intent on the kill, their eyes gleaming with bloodlust. Before they could strike, however, Miksa held up a hand.

"Restrain him, but do not kill him. Xenia will be hungry when she awakens." The larger Kali drew Ian up roughly and held him by the neck, his firm grip restricting Ian's airflow.

Miksa looked into his eyes. "You have saved me the trouble of hunting. For that, I am grateful."

Ian struggled against the restraining arm, wanting nothing more than to plunge a dagger into Miksa's heart. It was futile, though, and he eventually gave up, meeting Renee's eyes in despair. "Let her go, you bastard," he mumbled, spitting blood.

"Let her go?" Miksa cocked an eyebrow. "Your Renee is going to be the host for my dear Maker. And don't you find it fitting? After all, her sister is already serving one of us."

For the first time, Ian noticed Lou standing by the altar. Dressed in black like Miksa, she watched the others without saying anything, her eyes cold and pitiless.

Chalea had noticed her before, as well as the ornate chest she held in her hands. Without turning to Ferka, she crossed the fingers of her left hand over her right, silently communicating. Ferka nodded, his hand coming to rest lightly on the saber at his belt. The Kali didn't notice the interchange.

"Now we begin," Miksa said.

He moved over to the altar. "Bring the host."

The Kali holding Renee shoved her roughly forward until she was standing in front of Miksa. She eyed him with more hatred than she'd ever felt before.

Her loathing did nothing to shake him. "Place her on the altar and secure her," he commanded. Then he turned to Sabina, holding out his hand.

Gently, reverently, she opened the chest and scooped out a heart.

A beating heart.

"*That* is fucking gross."

Everyone whipped around, the Kali seething in anger.

Christer, Simon, and Gavril stood in the doorway, bloody but alive. It was Christer that had spoken, and now he stepped forward, his eyes lingering only briefly on Sabina. "So, which of you uglies should I kill first?" He smiled wryly.

Miksa's eyes darkened but his voice remained calm. "Kill them. All of them."

All of the Kali with the exception of the one holding Ian charged. The three men turned and ran, drawing them out of the inner sanctum. Ferka, shouting a battle cry and drawing his saber, chased after his son, giving a terse nod to Chalea as he left.

It was then that she made her move.

While the commotion had been going on, she had unsheathed the small dagger at her belt, the one infused with the blood of the Maker.

Running out of the circle, she lunged towards Sabina, the knife held high above her head, arcing down towards the heart in her hands.

Sabina, stunned, stood rooted to the spot, Xenia's heart held out in front of her like a pagan offering. She couldn't find the energy to move as the knife closed in; she couldn't even whimper in protest. She simply didn't move.

But Miksa did.

With a menacing growl he changed form and attacked, spearing Chalea with his long talons before she even had a chance to react.

Ian and Renee screamed as he pierced her, their anguished cries filling the small chamber.

Chalea hung, suspended on three of his claws, mere inches from her target. She cried out in frustration, blood bubbling on her lips. She had only needed two more seconds. Two more seconds and it all would have been over...

Miksa brutally withdrew his talons and Chalea fell, the dagger clattering to the floor by Sabina's feet.

His flat black eyes looked at her wounded body with voracious hunger. "It's a pity, really," he hissed. "You were their only chance, and now you have failed." He slowly morphed back into a man, the talons receding into hands, his fingers covered in her blood, which he couldn't resist tasting. The prominent grey veins and fangs receded too, until all that was left was his human form. "Hopefully you will live long enough to see my plan come to fruition, since yours has not."

He turned to Sabina. "I have Csilla's spell, so we can proceed." He pointed to the blade at her feet. "Pick up the knife. Such a blade shouldn't be wasted. We shall use it on the girl."

Sabina did as she was bidden, picking up Chalea's dagger.

Renee squirmed on the altar, thrashing against the chains holding her down, her eyes swimming with helpless tears as she looked at Sabina, trying to find her sister somewhere in the woman's icy eyes.

Ian screamed too, grappling with the Kali behind him. Not knowing what else to do, he bit down hard on the creature's arm, drawing a scream from it.

Enraged, the Kali shoved him to the ground and kicked him hard in the head.

Ian lay without moving, his wounds bleeding into the mouths of the snakes on the floor as if satiating them.

With no more resistance, Miksa began to read the incantation Csilla had composed. As he read the words aloud, he took the beating heart and placed it in the hollow of Renee's throat.

Renee jerked at the touch of the pulsating flesh against her skin, reflexively trying to dislodge the offensive organ. Her sudden movement was enough to loosen the bonds that had been tied so hurriedly, and she felt them slacken ever so slightly. *Thank God,* she thought, as she began frantically working to free herself.

Miksa's voice grew louder and louder, booming as it filled the whole chamber in escalating volume and pitch.

Whispering a silent prayer that the Kali leader would remain focused on his ministrations, she pulled her right arm free of the restraints, all the while careful to keep her body still. She didn't want Miksa to notice what she was doing. The heart at the hollow of her throat started to beat faster, matching her own racing pulse.

"Her body has been prepared." Miksa announced triumphantly as he lifted Xenia's heart and placed it beside Renee on the altar. "Pierce the woman's heart with the dagger, Sabina. Once it has stopped beating, Xenia's will replace it and she will be reincarnated, a revenant in the flesh."

Her eyes bright with desire, Sabina held the knife high above her head, swallowing as she steadied her grip.

After all this time, Xenia, we shall be together again...

Time stopped as she held the knife aloft, a stasis filled only by the sound of the beating heart. *Blissful reunion is ours, my love...*

Renee felt suspended in the moment, a quiet eeriness seeping over her. She'd gotten one arm free, but it wasn't enough. She'd run out of time, and now she was going to die. It was the first time her fate had felt like a certainty.

As she accepted this, Renee looked up, meeting Sabina's cold blue eyes. *Are you still there, Lou?* She wondered. A wave of pity moved her to speak.

"Lou," she said gently. "Lou, I love you, and I don't blame you for this." She smiled as tears filled her eyes, genuine love for her sister overshadowing everything else in the chamber, even her fear of death. "I forgive you, little sister."

An entire lifetime of love resounded through her words.

Sabina stood motionless, rooted to the spot. A wash of conflicting emotions played across her face, her features softening minutely as her brows knitted together in confusion.

Could it be...?

Emboldened, Renee willed herself to reach out to her sister one last time. "Lou, I believe in you!" She cried. "I believe in your goodness and strength! I believe in your love for me. *Fight her!* I know you can!"

Her battle cry echoed throughout the chamber.

Sabina Solovastru blinked, hesitating. Strangeness flooded her consciousness, memories not her own...

Her eyes widened.

No! This cannot be!

Frozen in the moment, she glanced down at Renee. No," she breathed, but it was too late. She felt herself fading, blackness creeping over her, obscuring her vision. She screamed then, but it went unvoiced, weakly echoing in her own mind as she was brutally ousted from her body.

"Sabina?" Miksa spoke sharply, a hint of concern lacing his voice for the first time.

Warm brown eyes met his gaze.

"Not anymore," Lou answered. Then she raised the dagger again, her intention clear.

Realizing that Sabina had lost control of her host's body, Miksa snarled with unbridled rage and frustration. "You worthless *human*," he spat as his countenance twisted with pent-up hatred, "you will not steal my victory from me now." Extending his talons, he lunged for Lou.

Miksa was lightning fast, but Renee was faster. Coming so close to death had sharpened her focus, honed her awareness, and as soon as she'd seen Lou regain control, she'd begun to work on her remaining restraint, anticipating that Miksa would take swift action against her. So, when the Kali lunged for her sister, Renee broke free of the remaining, loosened restraint and jumped—throwing herself between Lou and the enraged Kali. The razor-sharp talons intended for Lou sunk deep into her chest instead, and Renee went limp as blood began to pour from the gaping wounds.

"*Nooooo!*" Lou screamed, a wail of pain and anguish at the realization of what had just happened. Shaking with fury, she gripped the dagger in both hands and brought it down, plunging it into Xenia's feverishly beating heart.

Miksa's howl of rage filled the room like the wail of the damned. It was joined by another cry, an unearthly keening coming straight from the pierced heart, Xenia's final scream as she met death eternal.

The heart exploded, blood spattering all over the sanctum like a macabre firework, drops running down the runes on the walls and the snakes on the floor. It mixed with Ian's blood and Chalea's, rivulets converging to form a crimson stream. The knife was lodged deeply into the altar, the heart gone for good.

But the horror continued.

Miksa began to shake uncontrollably, spasms wracking his body as he changed involuntarily into his true form.

Once he was fully transformed, his pulsing veins began to bleed, as did his eyes, blood running down his hideous face and covering his skin. Shrieking in pain, he slashed at Lou, grazing her midsection with one of his talons. Lou retreated around the altar but with no real means of escape, she was hopelessly cornered. Miksa moved in for the kill, his fangs now dripping blood too. As he reached up to rip her throat out in a final act of violence, a loud crack reverberated through the chamber.

Ian, back on his feet, had stopped him with a bullet to the heart. Walking closer to where Miksa now lay on the ground, he raised his weapon and fired again.

"Go to hell," he said through gritted teeth.

Miksa convulsed, his body twisting in one final death spasm. And then he lay still.Ian had done Miksa a favor by killing him.

The other remaining Kali wasn't so fortunate. He screamed in agonizing torment as his veins burst and blood began seeping from every orifice. His ashen gray skin withered, revealing the skeletal form beneath. Like chaff blown in the wind, the beast shriveled, transforming into nothing more than a dried-out husk.

Then he, Miksa, and the others that had once served Xenia were nothing more than dust.

CHAPTER 45

The momentary silence was shattered by the sound of Lou's sobs as she cradled her sister in her arms. She turned to Ian, her face ashen and crumpled with grief. "She's dead, Ian. Renee's dead. She sacrificed herself for me. Oh God, she's gone. She's really gone." Lou rocked back and forth, moaning inconsolably.

The gun dropped from Ian's hand as he stumbled towards them, his strength evaporating with each wobbly step, pain etched onto his face. He fell to his knees at his girlfriend's side, staring at her torn, ruined chest. "Maybe we can do something, help her somehow..." The words stuck in his throat. He knew just from looking at her that nothing in the world could save her; she was already dead.

"Ian..."

He heard his name and turned his head, forcing his gaze away from Renee. Chalea was dragging herself towards them, her wounded body mostly useless to her. She could barely inch forward. Ian had forgotten completely about the seer, and now he stared blankly at her, unable to process what he was seeing in his shock-addled brain.

"Ian," the Roma woman rasped. "Please. Help me over to her—while there's still time." It took her an incredible amount of effort to get the words out.

Moving with mechanical numbness, Ian hobbled towards her, putting an arm around her and helping her limp back towards Lou and Renee.

Once there, he helped her down and she collapsed heavily on the ground, heaving.

Lou didn't even register her presence. She just kept stroking her sister's face, crying freely.

"Ian, I need to be closer to her. Bring her to me," Chalea requested, her voice wavering.

Ian didn't understand what she was asking. "What?"

Chalea coughed. "I need to be face to face with Renee, but I am too weak to move. Please hold her up."

He reached for his girlfriend, but Lou tightened her grip defensively. "What are you—" she began.

Chalea interrupted. "Lou, please let go of your sister. Only for a moment."

She relented, and Ian scooped his dead girlfriend into his arms, holding her head high on his shoulder, near to Chalea.

Using every last ounce of strength in her, Chalea moved forward and pressed her forehead to Renee's. She brought her hands up, placing them against Renee's still heart. Ian mumbled a question, but Chalea was concentrating too hard to hear him.

From a great distance, she heard Ferka and the others enter the chamber, heard Ferka calling her name, but she didn't move. The world around her was falling away, the darkness of the Kali's lair receding. All that was left was the binding spell she had formed between herself and Renee. It was something her grandmother had taught her long ago, though she had never imagined she would have occasion to put it into practice.

How surprising life could be.

Renee, this is the last thing I can give you. Her breathing became shallow, and she could feel her heartbeat slow. *It is time I go to my sister, and you to yours. Find peace, and return knowing that I am content.* Her heartbeat slowed even more and then stopped, leaving only quietness in its wake. She saw the edge of the horizon, far off and yet drawing so near, and she moved towards it, gliding effortlessly.

I'm on my way, Irina...

Renee opened her eyes, gasping.

"Renee!" Ian hugged her close, tears of joyous relief stinging his eyes. "You came back to us. You came back." When he finally pulled away, Renee smiled at him, reaching up to touch his face. "I love you," she whispered.

"Love you more," he said, kissing her forehead.

Suddenly, she frowned, staring down at her ruined shirt and the amount of blood staining it. "How...?" The question halted, reformed. "I was dead," she stated. "Gone." With shaking hands, she moved aside the tatters of her shirt to see the skin beneath. There were marks, almost scar-like, but no wounds. "How am I here...?" She breathed. Then she saw Chalea's still form at her feet. "Oh," she gasped. Her heart broke and she felt fresh tears in her eyes. "I...I thought she'd be okay. She was so strong."

Ferka spoke then, his voice grave. "She died for you," he said in English before switching to his native tongue. Christer translated the rest of what the Roma man said. "He says Chalea did a transference spell—it bonded her and Renee together. It's something that's only been done once before." He paused, in awe of what he was hearing. "Renee, she traded her life for yours."

Renee sat immobile in Ian's arms, stunned. *Oh Chalea, how can I ever repay this debt? I owe you my life.* Somewhere in her mind, though, she felt a sense of peace. It was inexplicable, and yet she felt sure that it was a vestige of Chalea's feelings, lingering because of the bond that had united them. *She is with her sister again*, Renee thought. *Just as...* She sat up suddenly, her eyes finding Lou.

Her sister was staring back at her, her warm brown eyes full of tears. For a brief moment they simply looked at each other, unable to act. Then the two sisters were in each other's arms, both too overcome by emotion to speak. "I never thought I'd see you again," Renee said at last, her voice shaking.

"Neither did I," Lou replied softly.

After a few moments, Renee held her sister at arms' length, worry creasing her brow as she saw the blood staining her sister's abdomen. "God, Lou, you're bleeding!"

Lou shook her head. "I'm okay. Miksa only grazed me; the wound isn't deep." She held her sister's hands in her own. "But it would have been fatal if you hadn't jumped between us. Renee, you saved my life."

"Of course I did. You're my baby sister, Lou."

"But you died. If it hadn't been for—" Lou looked down at the Roma woman's still form.

"Chalea. Her name was Chalea." Renee's eyes turned glassy with tears.

They were all silent for a moment, a gesture of respect for their fallen comrade.

Ferka bent to pick her up, holding her close to his chest as if he were about to sing her to sleep, and Gavril traced the sign of the cross on her forehead and closed her eyes. He wiped away a tear as he did so.

The two Roma lifted her reverently, understanding the depth of her sacrifice.

As the Roma stepped aside, Simon and Christer made their way over to their companions. They were hurt, sweat and blood staining their clothing, their faces badly scratched. Even Simon's baseball cap had smears of blood and grime on its surface. As they neared, though, all of their wounds were forgotten. The five embraced, holding onto one another with the fierceness of those who had seen the heights of battle and pulled through. It seemed miraculous that they had all survived despite everything that had happened, and after a minute they were all smiling and crying, just happy to be alive and together.

When they at last released each other, they surveyed the aftermath, their eyes sweeping the chamber.

The floor now appeared black, the ash from the crumbling bodies of the Kali mixing with the pooled blood. The ornately carved floor seemed to have lost its lifelike quality, no longer imbued with vitality by the creatures that had walked the earth long past their natural lifetimes. Now the chamber was a graveyard.

It was time to leave. They belonged in the world of the living, the world of daylight.

In unspoken agreement, the weary party turned to make their way out of the caves. The air seemed to clear with every step as they wound their way upward, and as they made their final ascent, the soft light of the rising sun was there to greet them.

The seven departed the cursed lair that the Kali had called home for years, and as they crossed the threshold that separated the world of the living from the realm of the dead, they greeted a new day, never once looking back.

CHAPTER 46

The leaves were changing colors, summer green turning to vivid red and bright yellow, their hues a harbinger of the cold weather that would soon follow. The late October afternoon indeed held a chill in the air, and Renee Bryant zipped up her leather moto jacket as she walked down the sidewalk, a spring in her step. She loved autumn, but she enjoyed the season most when she was home in Philadelphia. The colorful trees set against the backdrop of cobblestone streets and colonial buildings held a special charm for her.

She hurried up the stairs when she reached her apartment building. Inside, she threw her jacket on a chair in the kitchen and put the newest issue of *Itinera* down on the table. It was the prototype; the finished issue wouldn't hit newsstands for another month. "Lou?" She called out.

"Up here!" The reply came from the second floor.

Renee started up the stairs, taking them two at a time, eager to talk to her sister.

Lou was in her room, dressed in coveralls and standing amid a retinue of cardboard boxes.

"How goes packing?" Renee asked.

Lou gave her a tired smile. "Good. I'm just about finished, actually."

A familiar pang shot through Renee as she eyed the packed contents of her sister's room. She'd known this day was coming for a while, but she'd kept putting it off in her mind, kept pretending like it was just an idea instead of an impending reality.

"Hey." Lou had walked over and was standing directly in front of her. "You know I'm going to visit you guys incessantly, right?" She said, perceptive as ever. "Nothing is going to change all that much."

But it was, Renee knew. It was. "Yeah," she said. She tugged on the end of Lou's messy ponytail. "I just...I'm gonna miss you, Sis. We've lived together pretty much our whole lives. Bryant clan forever, you know? I can't imagine you not being here all the time. I...I'm just going to miss you so much," she repeated. It felt important enough to say twice.

Lou's eyes softened. "And you're still worried."

"I'll always be worried," Renee answered. "It's my job. But if this feels right to you, then I'll respect that."

"It does. After everything that happened, I just...I need a fresh start. A new place, a new focus." She smiled. "A new address."

Renee nodded. She gave Lou's ponytail one last tug and released it. "You want help finishing up in here?" She asked.

"No, I'm okay. I'm almost done."

"All right. I'll be downstairs," Renee said, and then she left Lou to her own devices.

Downstairs, she poured herself a glass of lemonade and sat down at the kitchen table. She looked down at the magazine she'd brought home and finally opened it, flipping to the page where their Romanian spread started. She read through Simon's article, impressed by his work just as she always was.

Brody. When she'd said goodbye to him in Romania the previous month, he'd seemed better than she'd ever seen him, and he'd been able to talk about his sister openly. He had been at ease for the first time in a long time, and Renee had a feeling his nightmares wouldn't be returning to haunt him any longer.

The featured castle pictures had turned out marvelously, each more impressive than the last. *We do make a good team*, she thought with pride. A bittersweet pang went through her when she reached the end, however, her eyes lingering on the dedication.

For our dear Roma friends to whom we owe so much. Thank you for everything.

She traced her finger over the words, her mind wandering.

After the final confrontation with the Kali, the *Itinera* team had accompanied Ferka and Gavril back to the Roma camp, staying for a day so that they could grieve the loss of Costin and Chalea with the Roma tribe and attend their funerals. By doing so, they were able to show in a small way the depth of their gratitude. They would all be forever in their debt. *Especially you, Chalea,* she reminisced sadly. Renee often thought about the seer. Even though she'd only known her a short time, she genuinely missed her.

"You okay, Sis?" Lou was leaning against the door, her head cocked to the side.

"Yeah, just thinking." Renee had been so lost in her own thoughts she hadn't even noticed Lou coming down the stairs. "Here, take a seat. I brought the magazine home with me."

Lou looked through the issue, her eyes intently scanning each page of the spread. Once she'd seen everything, she glanced up at Renee. "It's...great," she said. She sounded uncertain.

"But?" Renee prompted.

"Well, it's just... it seems like it's missing something without the real story of Solovastru, don't you think?"

Renee nodded. "Of course." She turned to the only printed evidence of their brush with the forces of evil, a two-page blow-up of Solovastru Castle. On the left was a picture of the exterior castle, on the right, a picture of the inner chamber and the bones they had found within. The caption read simply: the lost castle.

The lost castle.

Three little words that conveyed nothing of their terrible, harrowing experience.

"You know why we couldn't include it," Renee said finally. "Ferka specifically asked us not to." She sighed. "Besides, who would have believed it? The only person who needed to know our story was Mihaela Bochinsky, and Simon and Christer visited her before they left Romania. For everyone else, these two pictures of a mystery castle are as close as they can ever get to the truth."

"I know." Lou leaned back in her chair. "It's just…God, we almost *died* in those caves, Renee. You *did* die down there! And I never thought I'd break free from Sabina."

Renee looked into the familiar brown eyes she had missed so desperately in Romania. "Before the end, I didn't either," she admitted quietly. "When I was lying on that altar, I really thought I'd lost you…"

Lou's face took on a slightly haunted mien. "You did, Renee," she said at length. "The only reason I was able to come back was because of you. If it hadn't been for your love, I don't think I would have been strong enough to fight for control of my own body. Sabina was so powerful, and so evil. She would have won; I couldn't have done it on my own." Lou bit her lip. "She did such terrible things, Renee. I'll never be able to forget what happened while she was in control. I still see their faces—the man from the bar and the motorist. I still feel like I have their blood on my hands."

"Lou, we've talked about this; you were not the perpetrator of those acts and you cannot walk around with the weight of Sabina's sins on your shoulders."

"I know that. But it doesn't make it any easier." Her voice was heavy. "The guilt of it…it still feels like mine. I feel responsible for Sabina's actions."

"You're not, though. Not at all."

Lou made no reply.

Renee watched her for a moment, and then she mustered up the courage to talk about the elephant in the room. "Lou, can I ask you something?"

"You know you can."

"Dealing with all of this, going through this…how has your depression been? I know you don't like to talk about it, but I worry. I know how it's affected you in the past, and you've endured more than anyone's fair share of suffering since we got to Romania."

When Lou met her gaze, Renee could see the weariness in her eyes, but also a spark of something beneath that—the fire of resilience. "It's been hard," Lou admitted, "but I've felt more able to cope with it, more able to fight it." She paused. "Battling with Sabina made me want to survive. It made me aware of all the good things in my life, the things I'd taken for granted." Her voice dropped in pitch, and Renee sensed she was miles away. "When I was...trapped...inside...not in control, I'd recite things to myself," she murmured. "I'd say the names of people I loved, talk through my happiest memories, hum my favorite songs. I needed to do something to keep myself from... from *fading*." She swallowed, and then she seemed to return to the present, her voice regaining its strength. "Now, when I'm having a difficult day, I do the same thing. I remind myself of all the reasons I'm lucky. It's become a kind of tic, I guess, this repetitive thing that I do, but it's—it's helped me. A lot. I feel more secure in my own skin than I ever have before."

Renee's heart went out to her little sister, and she felt her eyes fill with tears. "I'm so proud of you, Lou," she said, the words thick with emotion. "And so sorry you've suffered so much." Lou would never be the same person that she'd been before going to Romania; a part of her had changed forever, and she'd lost an innocence that could never be restored. She was older and broken, a soul that had experienced things that others only saw in their nightmares.

But Renee would always be there to banish the nightmares away. "You know I'm still here, though, right? That having your newfound strength doesn't mean you have to lose mine?"

Lou's chin wobbled as she nodded. "I know," she replied, blinking back her own tears. "You've got my back. And I've got yours."

"Always," Renee answered fervently. Then she took a breath and wiped at her eyes. "Wow," she said. "Look at us: we're a big, blubbering mess." She closed the copy of *Itinera* and stood up. "Let's go out tonight," she announced, lightening the mood. "Ian said he owes us drinks and I think a little bit of fun will do us good."

Lou smiled, standing up herself. "It can't hurt," she agreed. "I'm going to go grab a shower."

Renee watched her leave the room. She sat down again, fiddling with the engagement ring she now wore on her finger, smiling as she watched it sparkle in the light. Ian had gotten down on one knee before they'd even left Romania, and she'd given him her yes without any hesitation.

Love was stronger than death; she knew that for sure now. And sometimes good did conquer evil.

She heard the shower turn on, and the faint chirp of birds outside. She leaned back in her chair, enjoying a moment of genuine happiness.

As long as they had each other, all would be well in the end.

EPILOGUE

He looked out over the balcony, taking in the glittering vista of the nighttime city.

Everywhere he looked he saw motion and movement, the mass of humanity abuzz with life.

He could hear cars whizzing by on the street and the sound of horns blaring in a cacophony of impatience, their drivers eager to get home and leave the troubles of the day behind them.

He could also hear people laughing, groups of young adults hungry for the weekend to begin and for its freeing pleasures.

He inhaled deeply, loving the taste and texture of the air as it filled his nose and lungs. City life was intoxicating, and he enjoyed every second of it.

Cities didn't just exist, weren't just a conglomerate of buildings and offices. They *thrived.* They had a vibrancy, a *joie de vivre* that never stopped. Even the darkest hours of the night were active, filled with excitement and an air of liberation that made people forget their lives and enjoy all the mischievous diversions available to them. All in all, cities never slept.

With a final parting glance at the twinkling vignette below, he stepped away from the balcony and turned, walking back into his hotel room.

He was staying in the penthouse, the best that money could buy. The furnishings were all new, the rooms immaculate.

It fit his personality perfectly.

A slight swagger in his step, he walked over to the complimentary refrigerator and took out the only bottle left on the shelf.

Twisting the cap off, he took a slow sip, enjoying the burst of sensation on his taste buds. Then he downed the rest of the bottle, tilting it high so as not to waste a drop.

When the bottle was at last drained, he set it down on the counter, an almost rueful look in his eyes.

You tasted so sweet, Carrie. Such a pity that I've finished you so quickly...

Carrie.

He chuckled. She had been a pretty girl, and a decent hooker.

She had been so eager to please him, so enchanted by his money and air of sophistication. He had enjoyed looking into her big doe eyes, eyes that had dominated her cherubic face, eyes that had been even more expressive as they widened in horror when she realized that being with him had been a mistake- a terrible, fatal mistake. Torturing her had been *oh so sweet*, and watching her last, terror-stricken moments of life had been euphoric. To say the least, he'd definitely gotten his money's worth with her.

He'd drained her slowly, filling bottle after bottle with her O+ blood. Then he'd disposed of the body, carefully and methodically. As always, no investigation would ever come to fruition; she would remain a designated missing person long after her bones turned to dust. Her fate was the same as that of all his victims.

After so many centuries, he had honed his meticulous nature past every precept of perfection, had learned every trick of the trade and then improvised his own. He had never, and would never, be caught.

Unlike the others...

Sighing, he turned on the sink and washed out the bottle.

Even after a year, he found it hard to believe he was the last one left.

The other five were gone. Dead.

It wasn't that he missed them; he didn't. Still, ever since Xenia had been destroyed, he'd felt...different, incomplete.

It was the hollow emptiness of being the last of a dying breed.

Once, they had been strong—undefeated and indomitable. But over the years, each of them had succumbed to the vestiges of their human natures and paid the ultimate price. Love, fame, and ambition had wormed their way in and brought them each to ruin.

He had predicted most of their demises, though Xenia's had taken him by surprise.

For centuries, she had been like him—detached and lethal. She had survived as the others perished. But then she had fallen in love with a human, and she and her entire clan had paid with their lives.

He dropped the freshly cleaned bottle into the recycle bin, listening as it hit the bottom with a dull thud.

Unlike the others, he hadn't turned anyone. He was a Maker without any progeny. And yet he didn't care. Being alone suited him, as did all the benefits that came with it. He never had to compromise, never had to watch out for anyone but himself, never had to face a challenger.

Instead, he enjoyed every ounce of pleasure that his immortal life had to offer and then some. His was a blissful existence.

Shrugging into a black leather jacket, he grabbed his room card and headed for the door, stopping only to admire his appearance in the mirror.

Piercing eyes stared back at him from strong, rugged features, a shock of tousled blonde hair and stubble softening the look just enough to make him look approachable.

Satisfied with what he saw, he strode out of the room, already humming with energy.

The elevator stopped five floors down and a beautiful redhead walked in, her stilettos clacking on the tile.

She eyed him up, obviously liking what she saw, and he returned her appraisal, cocking an eyebrow at her.

Like a mouse that doesn't recognize a cat...

He watched the seductive sway of her hips as she walked ahead of him out through the door and into the night.

It would have been fun to toy with her, but the night was young, and he was patient. His fun was only just beginning.

Idly humming a tune under his breath, he started walking left towards the center of the city and the myriad of lights.

His hunting grounds waited.

ABOUT THE AUTHOR

Anne Marie and Gina are a mother-daughter writing team that draws inspiration from their travels and enjoys exploring the darker side of their collaborative imaginations. Gina grew up listening to Anne Marie tell stories, a hobby that eventually evolved into the duo writing their own tales.

Their deep bond inspires their creation of strong female characters, and their love of thrillers fuels them to write stories that will keep readers turning pages.

Writing together has helped them remain close even when separated by distance. This is their first published novel together.

NOTE FROM THE AUTHOR

Word-of-mouth is crucial for any author to succeed. If you enjoyed *Revenant*, please leave a review online—anywhere you are able. Even if it's just a sentence or two. It would make all the difference and would be very much appreciated.

Thanks!
Gina and Anne Marie DiCarlo

We hope you enjoyed reading this title from:

BLACK ❀ ROSE
writing™

www.blackrosewriting.com

Subscribe to our mailing list – *The Rosevine* – and receive **FREE** books, daily deals, and stay current with news about upcoming releases and our hottest authors.
Scan the QR code below to sign up.

Already a subscriber? Please accept a sincere thank you for being a fan of Black Rose Writing authors.

View other Black Rose Writing titles at
www.blackrosewriting.com/books and use promo code
PRINT to receive a **20% discount** when purchasing.

Made in United States
North Haven, CT
08 March 2022

16927029R00198